Prai
Back to

"Top-notch fun."

—Steve Berry

"Like visiting with old friends, *Back to Brooklyn* captures the fun and spontaneity of every lawyer's favorite legal comedy, *My Cousin Vinny.*"

—William Landay

"Lawrence Kelter is an exciting new novelist, who reminds me of an early Robert Ludlum."

—Nelson DeMille

"This is the kind of book you will want to read again and again. I loved it!"

—J. Carson Black

"The characters of *Back to Brooklyn* have not only arrived back into my life like long-lost friends, but the novel has got me down on the floor laughing my tail off."

—Vincent Zandri

"...a murder mystery set in Brooklyn that is full of local flavor, twists and turns, and is just plain funny as hell. I loved it!"

—Scott Pratt

"I dare you not to laugh."

—Diane Capri

BACK TO BROOKLYN

STAY "Yout"-Ful!

Enjoy!

ALSO BY LAWRENCE KELTER

Stephanie Chalice Thrillers

First Kill
Second Chance
Third Victim
Don't Close Your Eyes
Ransom Beach

The Brain Vault
Our Honored Dead
Baby Girl Doe
Compromised

Chloe Mather Thrillers

Secrets of the Kill
Rules of the Kill

Legends of the Kill

Other Novels

Counterblow
Kiss of the Devil's Breath
Palindrome
Saving Cervantes

Season of Faith
Out of the Ashes
The Last Collar (with Frank Zafiro)
Back to Brooklyn

LAWRENCE KELTER

BACK TO BROOKLYN

Based on characters created by Dale Launer
from the screenplay *My Cousin Vinny*

Down and Out Books, LLC
3959 Van Dyke Rd, Ste. 265
Lutz, FL 33558
www.DownAndOutBooks.com

Edited by Chris Rhatigan
Cover design by James Tuck

ISBN: 1-943402-83-3
ISBN-13: 978-1-943402-83-0

*For Tessa, Isaiah,
and Azalia, our new additions*

FOREWORD

In the world of satire it is so incredibly rare that voices are created with such endearing charm and personality that they resonate with us still, decades later. Yet Dale Launer has done just that with the film *My Cousin Vinny*.

The film was released on March 13, 1992 and has become an iconic comedy classic, a tale about two wrongly accused young men who are defended in an Alabama murder trial by Vincent Gambini, an inexperienced, wildly inappropriate lawyer unaccustomed to southern rules and manners.

Mention the film by name or parrot any of the classic lines and you'll find that practically everyone within earshot is immediately on the same page, going tit for tat with smiles plastered on their faces. "Am I sure? I'm *pos-i-tive.*"

It's rated the #2 all-time greatest legal thriller by IMDB, the Internet Movie Data Base, second only to John Grisham's masterpiece *A Time To Kill*. To this day, the film is still used by professors in law schools as reference material in the instruction of courtroom procedure.

Today, fans of the comedy are still tickled by the film's wry sense of humor and sight gags. Personally speaking, I still get sucked in every time the film pops up on TV, and laugh just as hard as I did the first time I saw it. It just never gets old.

By the way, it may have taken Vinny and Lisa twenty-five years to drive from Alabama to Brooklyn but somewhere along that dusty stretch of state road they time-jumped from 1992 to 2017 and haven't aged a day. Well, maybe a day—but I'm sure you know what I mean.

Dale and I foresee a bright future for our sidesplitting couple, with Lisa investigating and Vinny litigating, much like Dashiell Hammett's Nick and Nora Charles.

I hope that you share my appreciation for this unique comedy. I look forward to continuing its legacy.

Enjoy!
Larry Kelter

"Men at some time are masters of their fates:
The fault, dear Brutus, is not in our stars,
But in ourselves, that we are underlings."
—Cassius from *Julius Caesar*, Act I, Scene II
by William Shakespeare

CHAPTER ONE
Leaving Alabama

Jimmy Willis was dead, gone in the blink of an eye, rocketed to heaven on the wings of a .357 magnum slug.

He took with him the dream of one day owning the Sack-O-Suds convenience store where he'd worked for many years. He'd saved every last dime and was a little shy of the down payment he needed to make the store his own. Old man Scruggs, the founder, hadn't been out of bed in years, but the store he'd built with his own two hands and operated for decades was supposed to live on through young Jimmy.

Supposed to.

The convenience store had been closed since the day of the shooting and would probably never reopen. Anything that had been fresh at the time of the shooting had rotted before the police finished with the crime scene. Vandals had looted all the canned goods and the gasoline tanks had been pumped dry. Old man Scruggs didn't have enough fight left in him to put the store back on its feet, and as such, a senseless act of violence had not only taken a life but reduced a thriving community business to little more than a rotting sarcophagus with grime-covered windows and a leaky roof—a hideaway for hormone-charged teens to use for their pleasure.

Down the road from the Sack-O-Suds, Ernie Crane sat high atop his old John Deere lawn tractor cutting lazy eights in the grass. He'd skipped the last day of the murder trial because he'd been called upon to testify and wasn't a fan of

1

the crafty defense attorney from New York.

A flask of moonshine slipped from his grasp as his eyelids grew heavy from the caress of the strong Alabama sun. He didn't see that New York lawyer and his girlfriend whizzing by, driving their car as if it were stolen, leaving a trail of dried Alabama mud in their wake.

Farm fencing disappeared a few miles north where fields of tall wheat bordered the road. Lanky blades of grass bent in the draft of a majestic red Cadillac convertible as it streaked by. Vince Gill's velvety voice poured through the speakers while Lisa piloted the big Caddy on the long journey home.

Across the cavernous front seat, Vinny's mind was some-where else, probably ten miles back in the Beechum County courtroom. He was still pumped from his first courtroom victory after successfully defending his cousin, Billy, and Billy's friend, Stan, against false murder charges. Sheriff Farley had arrested and railroaded the boys—making them the lead suspects in Jimmy's murder case.

Vinny, nothing more than a fledgling personal injury attorney, had somehow snookered the highly respected judge, convincing him that he had the credentials necessary to repre-sent the two boys in their murder trial. His heart thumped with a pang of guilt as he realized how very close he'd come to losing the trial and with it, the boy's lives.

He was staring at the countryside absentmindedly when his thoughts turned to his fiancée. His throat tightened for a mo-ment while he thought about all the love and encouragement Lisa had given him during the lengthy courtroom ordeal. Judge Haller did not suffer fools gladly. He had chastised Vinny at every turn and held him in contempt three separate times. But the tension and sleepless nights they'd both en-dured were now behind them, vanishing like the sun setting on the horizon. He recalled the county prosecutor's trial-ending words with great satisfaction, "We'd like to dismiss all charges."

Lawrence Kelter

His eyes were soft as he drank Lisa in. She was his every dream come true: young, beautiful, capable, nurturing, and as free-spirited as a wild colt. They'd been together more than a decade. With each sunset, he wondered what she saw in him and why she'd waited for him so long, why a woman of such beauty had chosen him. She could touch his heart or infuriate him with a simple glance or a single word, and he loved her all the more for it, that crazy cat and mouse game they played that drove him insane and more deeply in love with each exchange.

In his heart, he knew that her insights and testimony, her guile and savvy, played a significant part in winning the case. It wasn't his legal acumen alone that prevented a kangaroo court from sending two innocent boys to the electric chair. He gazed up at the blue sky and silently thanked God for her. She'd waited patiently for him to complete law school, pass the bar, and now finally win his first court case. They'd made a promise to each other many years back, and now it was time to make good on that sacred obligation. He had a sly expression on his face as he said, "I won my first case. You know what that means?"

She sassed him. "*Yeah*. You think I'm gonna marry you."

"What, now you're not gonna to marry me?"

"*No way*. You can't even win a case by yourself, you're fuckin' useless."

He considered for a moment. "I thought we'd get married this weekend."

"You don't get it, do you? That is not romantic. I want a wedding in church with bridesmaids and flowers."

"Whoa. Whoa. Whoa. How many times did you say that spontaneous is romantic?"

"*Hey*, a burp is spontaneous. A burp is not romantic."

He told her that he wasn't in the mood to quarrel but that wasn't the case, not even close. It was that old cat and mouse game beginning anew.

3

It was why Vinny would one day be a great trial lawyer.
It was why Lisa had been and always would be his match.
It was the very air they breathed.

CHAPTER TWO
Still Leaving Alabama

Lisa had developed a small fondness for country twang from hearing it day after day for almost two months. The wind was in her hair as "Wicked Game" played on the radio. The sorrowful, conflicted tone of Chris Isaak's voice turned her insides to jelly. As her mind wandered, she glanced over at Vinny and saw that he was dozing. She couldn't help but smile because she loved the infant-like face he made when he slept. She envisioned her wedding reception—dancing with Vinny as the band played *their* song, "Linger." For a few brief seconds, that dirt-swept stretch of Alabama roadway became heaven on earth.

She reveled in the moment and let her mind go. She thought about the life they would make together and a family of their own, a boy and a girl—they'd have the girl first... naturally.

And then...

She jammed on the brakes and swerved as a large raccoon darted from the shadow of a dense patch of brush, racing across the road just as the tires of the big Caddy threatened to pulverize it.

Vinny's eyes shot open and he clutched his chest. "*Whoa*! What the hell, Lisa? You asleep at the wheel or something?"

"Me asleep? *No*, I'm not asleep."

He took a deep breath and exhaled. "Lisa, you gotta be more careful. You scared the ever loving shit out of me."

5

"That's because *you* were asleep. Some copilot you are. I could've been driving down a backwoods road where some good ol' boys were waiting to go all *Deliverance* on your ass."

"Me asleep? Don't be ridiculous. I was just resting my eyes."

"Well while you were *resting your eyes* a rat the size of a leopard shot across the road like Secretariat coming down the home stretch and almost took out the front bumper. What did you want me to do? Hit the fuckin' thing?"

He rubbed the sleep from his eyes. "For the love of God, Lisa, look at the way you're holding the wheel."

"*What*? You don't like the way I'm holding the wheel?"

"No. No, I don't."

"What's wrong with it?"

"You got your hands at the bottom. Ten and two, Lisa," he instructed. "Ten and two."

"Listen, Vinny, I've got five times more experience behind the wheel of this car than you do. My hands are just fine where they are, thank you."

"Oh yeah? Then why do they instruct new drivers to keep their hands at ten and two when they take the test for their driver's license at the Department of Motor Vehicles?"

"They teach that, do they? What did you take your road test in? An Edsel? Or was it a horse and buggy?"

"Why? Are you saying something's changed?"

"Yeah, it did. Something did. That's right."

"Well I drive just fine and I didn't hear nothin' about it."

"That's because you've been in law school and taking the bar exam for the last ten years. Ain't ya ever heard of *air bags*?"

"What's that got to do with anything?"

"Because. During a collision, an air bag will explode out of the steering wheel hub at more than a hundred miles per hour. It's ignited by a detonator, just like the ones used to detonate bombs. As you know, it's designed to protect the driver's head and chest from slamming into the windshield, but with your hands at ten and two *or higher*, the driver's arms can be thrown back at very high velocity and you can get severely hurt." She nodded emphatically. "Keeping your hands lower down on the wheel prevents that. I routinely keep my hands at eight and four."

"I find that very hard to believe."

"Yeah? Well picture this. It's a beautiful sunny day. You got the top down and the sun is shining in your face. You're driving on a nice twisty road back to New York when out of nowhere the guy in the oncoming lane loses control, swerves, coming right at you, and *bam*! The next thing you know an explosion rips your arms out of their sockets and they're pointing backwards, dangling in the breeze like the scarecrow's after the flying monkeys had their way with him in *The Wizard of Oz*."

"Oh," he said. "So I guess you could say that eight and four is the new ten and two."

"*That's* a very good analogy."

"Just like when people say that sixty is the new forty."

"Also a good analogy. Only in your case, forty is the new eighty because you're using driving techniques that went out of practice with the stagecoach. And don't you dare wait until you hit the new sixty before you make a change in your driving habits."

"Oh, yeah. And why is that?"

"Because..." She glanced at him over the top of her sunglasses. "You'll be *dead*."

Lisa's father and brothers had all worked as automobile mechanics. Even though Vinny sometimes helped out in the garage, she had worked as a mechanic extensively and knew considerably more about cars than he did. She was a veritable compendium of automobile knowledge and had bested him yet again. He smiled nonetheless—he had a card up his sleeve and was dying to play his hand. He shook his head and grinned, slid closer to her and stroked her cheek affectionately. "You're pretty full of yourself, aren't you?"

She smiled happily. "Yeah, maybe I am. I mean it's been a very, very good day for me. I watched my fiancé save two innocent young men from going to the electric chair, and I received a proposal of marriage. Don't get me wrong—you proposed like a real dope. Still, things could be worse."

"So where do you want to get married? Back home in Brooklyn or right here in *Ala-fuckin'-bama*?"

"That's a *very silly* question."

"No it's not."

She looked at him as if he were crazy. "What do you mean? Didn't you hear what I said about being romantic? How could you ask me a question like that after what I told you?"

"It's not a silly question," he insisted.

"*Yes*. It is."

"*No*. It's not!"

"Why isn't it?" she asked, already sure from the confidence he displayed that he had her.

He pointed at the instrument cluster and tapped the fuel gauge. "Because, genius...we're about to run out of gas."

CHAPTER THREE
Stuck in Ala-Fuckin'-Bama

"What luck," Vinny boomed as he pointed up the road. "Look over there past the clearing in the trees. It's a gas station sign. Pull in over there."

Land was cheap in Beechum County. As they drew closer, they saw that the service station sat on acre upon acre of unimproved land, a Shangri La for rusted pickups and tractors. Weeds grew tall between the disintegrating car frames, taller than the cabin of one of the backhoes. A sapling had grown into a thick tree within a rusted car chassis and was now imprisoned by it. A scruffy white and gray mutt dashed out and howled at Vinny as he got out of the car. "Easy, boy," he said as the dog sniffed his pointy western boots.

Lisa glanced at the dog. "How do you know it's a boy?"

"What?"

"You said, 'Easy, boy.' How do you know it's a boy?"

He rolled his eyes. "Lisa, are you for real? I didn't literally mean the dog was a boy. Did you see me get down on my hands and knees and do an anatomical inspection of the dog's under parts? It's a figure of speech."

"Oh, yeah," she said. "I get it. It's a figure of speech, like when I say you're a pain in the ass it doesn't actually mean that my butt hurts."

The dog cautiously backed away only to dash after the next car coming down the road. Vinny threw his hands in the air and walked to the pump. He tried to lift the nozzle out of the slot but the pump was locked. "Shit!" He glanced in through the open doorway and saw someone behind the counter. "The pump's locked," he said wearily. "I'll be right back."

An obese man sat behind the counter. His T-shirt-covered belly billowed over his belt like suds over the top of an overfilled glass of beer. He had a full gray beard and wore a hunting cap. Before him, a slab of meat swam in a plate of brown gravy. He looked up at his new customer, covered his mouth, and belched before taking a bite of heavily buttered corn bread. He picked up a plastic knife and fork and used the disposable utensils to saw through his steak. "*Kin* I *hep* ya?" The morsel he stuffed in his mouth was large enough to feed an entire migrant family for three solid days.

Vinny's eyes grew large at the spectacle. "That's quite a lunch you've got there. You always eat like that?"

"Nope, I'm cutting back," he answered with a full mouth as he pulverized the meat between his molars. "But I had a big breakfast and my wife is bellyaching that I'm *gittin'* too fat." He focused on his steak, slicing the boneless cut into large chunks. He belched, this time without covering his mouth, just as a gray-haired woman in a housecoat emerged from the back room carrying a hefty plate of meatloaf also swimming in gravy.

"That's all I got left, Buck," she said. "That'll have to hold you 'til dinner." She smiled at Vinny politely.

"You gonna eat that too?" Vinny asked.

"Figure I am." He covered his mouth and made a sour face before narrowing his eyes at her. "Damn GERD. Jozelle, how many times do I have to tell you? Don't cook with so many onions."

"It don't taste like nothin' without the onions, Buck. How many times you tell me not to cook insipid? 'Sides, Oren's coming home for a visit tomorrow and you know how he'll holler if my cooking got no taste." She turned to Vinny beaming with pride. "Oren's our son. He's in his third year of medical school at Johns Hopkins Medical School. My boy is gonna be a pediatric surgeon one day."

"I'm impressed. A pediatric surgeon? He must be one hell of a smart kid."

"Smart? Hell, he was number one in his class at Northwestern. Didn't cost me a cent all four years he went to college." Buck looked up and drew a deep, fortifying breath. "He keeps warning me about my weight—I think startin' tomorrow I'm gonna go on some kind of diet."

"Hell, Buck, we goin' to dinner with Oren and the grand-kids at the Chomp-N-Chicken tomorrow," she reminded him. "Maybe you ought to start the day after."

The gas station mutt poked his head in the door, barking and howling loudly.

"Damn mutt," Buck groused. "Throw that damn dog one of them hush puppies and keep it from yapping, will ya, Jozelle?"

She reached into the pocket of her housecoat and hauled out a smoked pig's ear the size of a dinner plate. Cocking her arm, she flung it Frisbee-style and it went whizzing past the dog, which yelped excitedly and took off running.

Buck covered his ears. "I swear I'm gonna shoot that dog one of these days." He grimaced and put a hand on his chest. "I think I need a gas pill. I swear, if I thought my insurance would cover it, I'd get one of those lap band things."

Vinny was growing impatient. "I'm glad you're trying to take better care of yourself, *Buck*, but I'm kind of in a hurry and I noticed the gas pumps are locked. *So...how come?*"

Buck was still grimacing as he answered. "How come? I guess you ain't from around these parts, are ya?"

"Me? No, I ain't from around here."

"You from up north?" Jozelle asked.

"Why?" he laughed. "Don't I sound like a good ol' boy?"

She looked at Buck and shrugged.

11

Vinny continued, "Yeah, you guessed it. I ain't from around here. I'm from New York. Why do you ask?"

"That explains it," Buck said. "You probably ain't heard about the atrocious murder over at the Sack-O-Suds convenience store. I'm fixin' to install me one of them closed circuit TV systems. Two Yankee boys done shot young Jimmy Willis in cold blood."

Vinny thought about keeping his mouth shut, but he just couldn't. "Um...I don't think you got your facts straight, *Buck*. Those two *Yankee boys* were exonerated."

Jozelle became alarmed. "What? They fried them boys already?"

Vinny laughed. "No, dear," he explained. "I said *ex-on-er-ate-ed*, not *elec-tro-cute-ed*. They were acquitted," he said with a robust smile. "Found innocent of all charges."

"That so? Well then who shot Jimmy Willis?" Buck asked.

"Two other guys were arrested in Jasper County, Georgia, a couple of days ago. They found the gun they used and everything."

"That sounds like horseshit to me," Buck said. "They found another pair of boys with the same gun?"

"Not the same gun, *Buck*. The first set of kids...well they didn't have a gun...only a can of tuna fish."

"Where was those guilty boys from?" Buck asked.

"Sorry, I really don't know."

"Huh. What did I tell you, Jozelle? I heard them Yankee boys had some kind of slick, hot shot attorney. That's how them New York ambulance chasers work. They probably found two local boys to use as scapegoats." He reached under the counter and withdrew a Smith & Wesson 9mm. "I tell you what—I don't know much about any fancy legal mumbo jumbo, but this here sidearm is the only kind of justice *I* need. I'm surprised Jimmy wasn't carrying over at the Sack-O-Suds. For my money, I think everyone ought to carry a gun."

Vinny recoiled at the comment. "Really? You really think that?"

"As the Lord is my witness."

"*Whoa.* Ain't you ever heard of gun control?"

"Gun control, my *ass*," Buck said. He turned the gun around and offered it to Vinny. "You hold this gun in your hand and tell me it don't make you feel like a better man."

"Ah, that's all right. I think I'll just get some gas and go. Thanks anyway."

"Nonsense," he bellowed. "I ain't unlocking the pump 'til you hold this here gun in your hand. Careful, though—it's loaded."

"Uh, that's okay. Really...no. No, thanks."

"You want gas or don't ya? Take it. Go on. Take it I say. It'll change your life."

Vinny thought about the Caddy's empty gas tank and the prospect of getting stranded in the middle of nowhere. "All right...but just for a minute." He reluctantly accepted the weapon and considered the substantial piece of ordnance as he weighed it in his hand.

"How's that feel?" Buck asked with a grin. "Tell me that ain't a better solution than a room full of slippery-tongued lawyers."

"Still, you really think *everyone* should have a gun?"

"Damn right. Gun control ain't nothin' more than political horseshit. You show me a shootin' and I'll show you a criminal with a stolen gun. It ain't the law-abiding types that are killin' folks."

Buck's backwoods way of thinking was getting Vinny riled up. He considered keeping quiet, but once again, he just couldn't. "*Wait* a minute. What about all those poor innocent kids that got killed at the elementary school shooting? Are you trying to tell me that's not a valid argument for gun control?"

"Look stranger." He seemed to be growing hot as he

stuffed another chunk of steak into his mouth. A loud burp came out that made him grimace. "I don't mind you being from up north and all, but no one's gonna walk into my place of business and tell me who can and *who can't*—" His eyes bulged and his cheeks ballooned.

Jozelle panicked—she rushed to Buck's side as he keeled over face-first into his plate of chicken-fried steak and gravy. "*Buck!* Oh my God. Oh my God."

"*Shit.* Call nine-one-one!" Vinny hollered, still holding Buck's gun in his hand.

Just then the sound of a gun being cocked registered in his ears and a hostile southern voice shouted, "*Freeze!*"

Vinny felt his legs being swept out from under him. He barely had time to process what was going on when he slammed face-down onto the floor with a knee embedded dead center in his back. "Excuse me," Vinny said, "there's been a mis-understanding. You see, I'm a lawyer and—" He felt hand-cuffs ratcheting over his wrists. "Hey! What did I just—"

"Shut your trap, mister." Squawk from a handheld radio filled the air. "This is Deputy Ty Bembrey over at Buck's fillin' station. Better send an ambulance quick."

Jozelle blurted. "Buck ain't shot. He's choking."

"He's what?" Ty asked.

"He's choking, Ty. Can't you do the Heineken or somethin'?"

The deputy raced around the counter. Standing behind Buck he extended his arms as far as they would go, somehow managing to lock his fingers just below Buck's diaphragm. He grunted and his face turned red as he administered the Heimlich, repeatedly jerking him upward with all his strength.

Jozelle burst into tears. "The dern fool—I always tell him he don't chew his food."

Vinny managed to lift his torso off the floor and attempted

to crane his neck to see what was going on. His eye level had risen just enough for him to see a slab of steak come flying out of Buck's mouth. He tried to dodge it but it smacked him squarely in the face.

CHAPTER FOUR
Still Stuck in Ala-Fuckin'-Bama

By the time Vinny and Lisa were back in the car, the sun was little more than a sliver of orange on the horizon. The deputy had saved Buck's life, and Jozelle had explained that Vinny was nothing more than an innocent bystander. She asked Vinny and Lisa to stay for dinner but they thought better of the invitation. They were given a tankful of premium gas, a gift they gratefully accepted.

Lisa couldn't stop laughing. "When I walked in and saw you lying on the floor with steak on your face...what a sight you were, Vinny. Thank God my camera goes everywhere I do."

"You wouldn't dare show that to anyone."

"Oh yeah? You think I wouldn't? You got another guess coming, Steak Face. I'm gonna hold onto it for just the right moment, and one day when you piss me off real good..."

He shook his head. "Unbelievable."

"How in the world does crap like this happen to you anyway?" she said as they drove off. She'd walked in on the chaotic scene at the moment the deputy had forced Vinny face down on the floor. "And what in God's name were you doing holding a loaded gun?"

"I already told you. Buck and I were having a philosophical discussion."

"A philosophical discussion? With the guy choking on chicken-fried steak?"

"Yeah. Him."

"You have got to be kidding."

"I wish I was."

"So, what was this very important conversation about anyway?"

"It was about gun control and Buck wanted to make a point about gun ownership. It was just a simple misunderstanding."

"Simple is the operative word," she sniped. "Are you out of your mind? An officer of the law walked in on you while you were holding a 9mm on the cracker from *Duck Dynasty*. You're lucky that good ol' boy didn't shoot first and ask questions later or there would have been a second murder in Beechum County this year. Do you have any idea how lucky you are to be sitting here alive?"

"Stop exaggerating, Lisa," he said as he brushed dust off his jacket. "No harm no foul."

A large yellow banner adorned the roadside high above the opening of a giant tent. "Look. Fireworks," he said. "Let's bring some back with us to Brooklyn."

"*No way.* You're kidding, right?"

"No?"

"*No.*" She had a way of making even that simple word sound flirty.

"Why not? I'll hold them until the Fourth of July. The neighborhood kids will love 'em."

"I don't think so."

"Think about the kids."

"You mean the one I'm sitting next to?"

"Very funny. Come on, Lisa. You know you can't get this kind of stuff in New York. Stop being like that."

"Like what?"

"Like a Catholic school nun. When did you turn into Mother Theresa?"

"*Vinny.* I've been sleeping next door to a stockyard for

weeks. I've been awakened by freight trains and ear-shattering sawmill whistles in the middle of the night. I even spent a night sleeping in the car out in the middle of nowhere. I just want to get home, Vinny. I want to take a hot bath and sleep in my own bed. I want to sit down to a dish of homemade pasta and wrap my lips around a fresh cannoli. Do you know how badly I ache for a delicious piece of pastry and a decent cup of espresso? All they had in the local restaurant was that awful Bundt cake that smelled as if it was made with lard instead of vegetable oil. Do you think we can get home without you getting us into any more trouble? Is that too much to ask?"

"I guess not."

"You guess not?"

"Yeah, I guess not."

"*Thank you,*" she said before pressing down on the gas. "That's all I wanted to hear."

CHAPTER FIVE
I'm Outta Here

Sullivan Correctional Facility, Sullivan County, New York

Clang. The gate abruptly opened, permitting Sammy "Tool Man" Cipriani to walk from the prison yard to freedom for the first time in seven years. The rural countryside was covered with snow, the roads white from heavy salting. He'd never gotten used to the bitter cold and flipped up the collar on his beat up Knicks basketball jacket as a harsh wind whipped by stinging his cheeks. Just yards away, the passenger door of a jet-black BMW sedan swung open. The stunning vision now standing before him thawed him clear down to the bone.

Theresa had waited so long for this moment and began to cry the moment her arms closed around him. She'd only seen him in the prison visitor's room, under unnatural fluorescent lighting and he now looked especially pale and tired as she studied his face in the light of day for the first time in years. But it didn't dampen her spirit. The eyes she saw were still his eyes. The lips she longed for were still his. She put her mouth on his, trying desperately to wipe away years of emptiness and separation with one magical kiss. For a moment, all the pain and hurt faded away. No past, only a future. She had always been the strong one and tightened her grip around him so he could melt into her arms. They lingered, treasuring each other's embrace until a hearty voice broke their spell.

Anthony Cipriani bounded toward his kid brother and

wrapped him up in his massive arms. He choked out a solitary word, "Christ," then buried his head on his brother's shoulder. His chest heaved as he choked back tears. "You crazy son of a bitch. It's been so friggin' long." He looked him over. "When did you get so bald? I mean you've been losing your hair little by little, but…"

"There wasn't much left up there. I shave it," Sammy said.

Anthony ran his hand over his brother's smooth head. "You look like Mr. Clean. No one in the old neighborhood will recognize you for God's sake."

"Maybe that's a good thing," Sammy said.

"Hey! You okay?" Anthony asked. "You just got sprung. This is no time to get bummed out on me."

Sammy shrugged. "I'm a jailbird, Tone. We're all the same when we're on the inside, but now that I'm out…everyone's gonna look at me like, *What's this piece of shit doing back in the neighborhood?*"

"Screw them," Anthony said. "You paid your debt to society. If that's not good enough for your cranky neighbors, it's too goddamn bad."

"I don't know. I'll just have to take it a day at a time."

Theresa nuzzled his neck. "I'll bet *I* can make you forget all about it," she said with a naughty gleam in her eyes. "Anyway, that's enough out of the two of you and your screw-the-neighbors shit. Home, James," she ordered. "I'm freezing my firm young ass off out here."

Sammy slapped her on the butt prompting an impish giggle.

"Want to stop for a bite?" Anthony asked. "You must be dying to eat some real food. We passed a nice-looking steak-house on the way up."

"No way," Sammy replied. "I want to go straight home to Brooklyn. I'm gonna christen my mouth with a plateful of Mom's veal parmigiana. I've been thinking about her cooking since forever. For the last seven years, every time I bit into a piece of mystery meat I tried to imagine it was one of Mom's veal cutlets."

"Excuse me!" she protested. "What? I can't cook?"

He kissed her hand. "Of course you can, babe." He winked at her. "It's just that I need you to save your energy for certain other activities."

"Good save, brother of mine." Anthony watched her throw her arms around him as they piled into the back seat. She kissed him deeply as his hands found her for the first time in years. "Too bad I can't raise the divider and give you two a little privacy. Had I known how horny you both were I'd have rented a limo."

Sammy laughed. He took a hand off Theresa and ran it over the BMW's leather upholstery. "My big, important brother's got one sweet ride here, but I thought the leather would've been softer in an expensive car like this."

"I know what you mean," he replied. "The damn hides are too damn stiff. I think the Germans must be feeding their cattle Viagra."

She kissed Sammy's hand and pressed it to her cheek. "How do *I* feel?"

Anthony smiled as they went at it again. "Easy you two. You'll wear out the upholstery."

Theresa gave Sammy another long kiss before reluctantly pulling away. "Yeah. Who knows who the big shot deputy mayor has had back here." She had a small bottle of hand sanitizer clipped to her bag and offered it to Sammy. "Here, babe, maybe you ought to disinfect."

"You know what? You're right. Seven years in that shithouse and I never worried about what I touched, but who knows how many skanks big brother has had back here." He leaned forward and slapped his brother on the shoulder. "Still a hound dog, Tone?"

Anthony smirked. "Can *I* help it if the ladies still find me irresistible? We Cipriani men," he jested, "it's a curse. But I do my best to cope with it."

As they traveled down the road, Sammy noticed Woodbourne Correctional Facility, which, too, had served as his alma mater. It was where he learned to use burglar's tools and where he picked up the nickname "Tool Man". If medium-security Woodbourne was community college, maximum-security Sullivan was an Ivy League school and he had graduated from both. He'd majored in third-degree robbery, a class D felony offense, but had gotten a sweetheart deal because of his brother's clout with the district attorney. The plea bargain saved the New York County DA a long trial and Cipriani ten additional years of incarceration. He'd been away almost seven full years and would've done less time, but it was his third trip to the big house. Still, he was only twenty-eight and was supposed to have the rest of his life to look forward to.

Supposed to.

CHAPTER SIX
Home Sweet Home?

Bensonhurst, Brooklyn, three days later

Vinny sat on the commode reading the *Daily News* for the first time in almost two months. He'd spent most of the months of January and February unable to find any newspaper other than the *Beechum Daily Mountain Eagle* and had become accustomed to reading about raided stills and livestock robberies. He found it refreshing to catch up on neighborhood news stories like domestic violence, drug busts, and stolen tractor-trailers of top-shelf liquor. He tugged on the toilet paper roll and became unsettled when the last square came away leaving no cardboard roll behind. "What the hell?" He checked all around to see if it had somehow fallen silently to the floor. Needless to say, the unexpected irregularity left him feeling uneasy.

Lisa was lying on the sofa, provocatively posed in a sexy teddy, sending out a clear signal no healthy red-blooded male could misinterpret. She was fanning her hands and blowing on her fingernails to hasten the drying of her nail polish when she glanced up and saw Vinny hustling down the stairs.

"Hey, Lisa," he called out. "Doing your nails?"

"Yeah, I'm doing my nails. Yeah. Why? What's it look like I'm doing? Relining brake pads? What's up?"

"What am I holding?"

She stared at his hand and saw that there was absolutely

nothing in his grasp. She shrugged. "I don't know. Your teensy weensy brain?"

"Very funny. Maybe you ought to go into standup. Try again."

"You want me to go for two out of three? Okay...nothing. I see exactly nothin'."

"Correct. That's because the cardboard tube that's supposed to be in the center of the toilet paper roll is missing. Care to explain what the hell happened to it?"

"Oh yeah," she recalled. "Ma took me shopping at Walmart just before we drove to Alabama for Billy's trial and I figured I'd do a little something to help the environment. Good idea, right?"

"No, not right. My entire life there's always been a cardboard tube in the center of the toilet paper roll and now there's nothing."

"That's a game changer for you, is it?"

"Come on, Lisa, don't fool around with me like that. You know I'm a creature of habit."

"Oh my God. This is terrible. Are you going to have to be toilet trained all over again? I'm so sorry. I'll run out and get you some adult diapers in case you have an accident. I wonder if they make Huggies in a size commensurate with your precious rear end."

"I'm not laughing. Frankly, Lisa, I find the whole thing is a little disconcerting."

"Yeah. You look shook," she said with a laugh. "Maybe you ought to lie down for a while. I'll get you a cool washcloth to put on your forehead."

"Is everything a joke to you?"

"No. Is the planet a joke to you? Haven't you seen all the ads on TV? Every year Americans throw away enough toilet paper tubes to fill the Empire State Building two times over. Do you have any idea how many trees have to die so that Vincent LaGuardia Gambini has his little cardboard toilet paper tube? That's seventeen billion tubes each year. What are they supposed to do with all that stuff?"

"I don't know. Maybe they use them to fix some of the country's land erosion problems. I mean they're biodegradable, right? Anyways, who cares? They got enough room for seventeen billion tubes—one more ain't gonna make a difference. I only use a couple pieces at a time."

"Maybe you can get away with a couple of squares but I gotta wrap my hand like a friggin' mummy before I go down there. What do you need it for anyway? You planning on cornering the market on cardboard or something? Oh, I know. Maybe you can build yourself a little cardboard boat and sail it around the bathtub."

"Ha, ha, ha. Lisa, I'm not amused."

"And I think you ate too much deep-fried everything while you were in Alabama," she said as she continued to push his buttons. "Maybe your carotid artery is all gummed up with cholesterol and grits and you can't think straight no more."

He seemed befuddled. "Lisa. I mean why are you being like this? Did I say something?"

"What did you say? You big dope, it's what you didn't say. You didn't say a single word about the fresh flowers I bought or the fact that I got up early, did my hair, my nails, *and* my makeup to look pretty for you, and that I'm lying here in a lacy peignoir posed like Mae West. What do I have to do, Vinny? Pour gravy on myself and ring a dinner bell? None of that mattered to you, but the absence of a stupid toilet paper tube has you bouncing off the walls."

His shoulders slumped. "You're right. I am a real dope. I guess I just got a lot on my mind. I didn't purposely overlook all of your romantic efforts. I guess I'm just some kind of a non-romantic clod."

"Well why don't you come over here and take advantage of me?" she asked in a come-hither tone. "My nail polish is still wet. I'm completely defenseless."

Vinny grinned as he helped her up and slid his hands along her supple skin. He had time to give her just one kiss before the phone rang. "Who the hell could that be?" he snapped as he turned away and reached for the phone.

She moaned, grabbed his hand, and positioned it on her butt. "It can wait," she insisted in a sultry voice and kissed him again. "Maybe we ought to continue this in the bedroom."

His eyebrows peaked. "Yeah. May-be."

The phone continued to ring while they kissed. "It finally stopped."

"I hope that wasn't a business call. I could use a good paying case."

She pushed him away. "No shit! Why don't you go over your profit and loss statement while you're at it? Maybe you ought to check your D&B rating."

"Hey, what happened?"

"Did you have to start talking about money and ruin the mood? I'm in pumps and sexy lingerie, and we haven't done it in weeks on account you were too worried about Billy's case to *perform*. You think you can carve ten minutes out of your busy schedule to make me feel like a woman? I mean is that such a chore?" She stomped her foot. "Is it?"

"Look, Lisa, I ain't got two nickels to rub together. I didn't exactly make a king's ransom defending my cousin Bill in Alabama. All the gas, food, and hotels came out of my pocket. Not to mention bail money for all the trips I took to the pokey. You think *maybe* you can lay off me long enough for me to become solvent again?"

The phone rang once more.

"No, you didn't make a fortune on your cousin's case but think about all the good it will do for your career." She glanced at the phone with disdain. "Well, you're so worried about money—answer the stupid thing already."

He shook his head before reaching for the phone.

"Tonight, okay. I promise. We'll have a nice romantic evening. We'll crack open a bottle of wine and I'll put on a fresh pair of silk boxers."

"Yeah, yeah, yeah. Never mind. I'll get it." She bristled past him and snatched the phone out of his hand. "Hello? Oh, hi. How are you? Yeah. We just got back. Yeah. Last week... yeah. It was very exciting. Vinny won his first big case...yeah. He couldn't be happier." She had a telling expression on her face as she said, "Oh?" then turned away from Vinny.

Vinny waited patiently for Lisa to tell him who was on the phone but she continued to chat and ignore him.

"Who is it?" he asked.

"Just a minute." She covered the receiver and said, "Can I have a little privacy, please?"

"What's the big deal? Just tell me who it is."

"Take a walk, would you? It's for me," she said and once again turned away.

"Ah!" he swore and waved his hand dismissively before storming off.

Lisa watched until he vanished into the upstairs bedroom. "I'm back...yeah. He was standing right next to me." She glanced toward the bedroom to make sure he was still out of earshot. "That's great, really great. I can't wait." She picked up a pad and pencil and made a few notes.

Vinny was showered and in his briefs, standing in front of the bathroom mirror putting the final touches on his wet hair. "*You* were on the phone a long time."

"Yeah, I know. That was my Aunt Angie. She needs a favor."

"Angie from New Jersey?"

"No, Angie from Beverly Hills, Santa Monica, and Redondo Beach. What other aunt named Angie do I have?"

"What kind of favor is she looking for?" he asked somewhat distracted by a tuft of uncooperative hair he was trying to slick down. "Hey, Lisa, you think I need a haircut?"

She drew closer to him and ran her hand through his hair, combing it with her fingers out and away from his head, assessing the length. "Yeah, you're getting a little shaggy. Want me to even it out for you?"

"Nah, maybe later. Thanks." He finally got his cowlick under control. No sooner had he placed his comb on the sink ledge than his hair stood up like a springboard again.

Lisa whispered in his ear. "Let me take care of that for my big strong man." She massaged his scalp, seducing him with her fingertips. "How's that feel?"

"Jesus, that's amazing." He closed his eyes, savoring her touch as his head melted into her hands. Her technique was so relaxing that he didn't know she was giving him a trim until a clump of hair fell on his shoulder.

She blew softly, tantalizing the skin on his shoulder and neck with her warm breath. She kissed his earlobe and whispered, "All done." Several moments ticked by before he could will his eyelids to open. "Still feel like talking about my aunt?"

"No...I mean sure. I guess. So what's this favor Angie needs?"

"A favor from you, Mr. Very Impressive Personal Injury Attorney. Someone ran over her foot and she's thinking of suing the guy."

He perked up. "Yeah? What kind of car? She get a name? A license plate number? I'll call her right back."

"Yeah. Some blowhard driving one of those Mercedes storm trooper trucks. He's probably got plenty of dough."

"That's great, Lisa," he said. "This is just what the doctor ordered. What's her number?"

She leaned into him and fussed with the hair on his chest while kissing him lightly on the neck and cheeks.

"Lisa, please. What's the number?"

She ignored him and continued kissing him, noticing that he was getting worked up in spite of himself. "She kind of asked if we could pay them a visit. We ain't seen them in ages, Vinny, and seeing as she's gonna throw this big personal injury case your way…"

"Lisa, I can't think while you're kissing me like that."

"You want me to stop?" she teased.

"No." He closed his eyes. His head became heavy and rolled backward as he presented the length of his neck for her to tease with her lips. "Don't stop."

"Did you say, 'Don't! Stop!'"

"Stop fooling around, will ya? I said, 'Don't stop.'"

"Oh, I must've misheard you." Her fingers became legs and walked down the length of his torso where they slipped into his boxers. "Someone's happy. You been sneaking the little blue pill?"

"No, I'm just excited. That's all. It's been a really long time." He peeked into his shorts. His eyes gleamed. "I'm doing pretty good, huh?"

"I think if it stood up any straighter I'd have to get a set of horseshoes and play ring toss." She tugged on the waistband of his shorts. "Now come here, you. You're presiding in *my* court this morning. So get your fiancée-pleasing butt over here and approach the bench."

"But I'm already in your chambers."

"Yeah? Well, I'm a crooked official so if you want to win this case, you'd better grease my palm."

"I'll grease more than that."

"That's some mighty big talk. Are you sure you're up to it?"

"Am I sure? Yeah, I'm optimistic about my chances."

She threw her arms around him. "Then what the hell are you waiting for?"

CHAPTER SEVEN
Home Is Where the Heartburn Is

Lisa opened the door of the Caddy and slipped into the passenger seat. She was wearing a waist-length faux fur jacket, but her stocking-clad legs were all he saw as she rubbed her hands over them. "Christ it's goddamn cold outside. I only walked twenty feet from the house to the car and I got goose bumps already. Turn up the heat, would you?"

"It's twenty-six degrees outside, Lisa. It takes time to warm up a half-century old convertible. The hot air rises and passes right through the cloth headliner."

"Vinny, this car has a three-hundred-and-ninety-cubic-inch engine. The temperature at the exhaust manifold gets hot enough to melt the anchor on an aircraft carrier. I think it can throw off enough heat to warm the inside of the passenger compartment to a comfortable eighty degrees."

Realizing he was out-gunned, Vinny reached for the heater control and turned it up all the way. "Better?"

"Thank you."

"You know...you could've worn a pair of pants."

"You had to get the last word in, didn't you? You couldn't have just raised the heat and left well enough alone?"

"I'm just saying."

"*Why?*" she asked. "You saying you don't like my legs?"

"No, Lisa. I ain't saying nothing like that. You got beautiful legs. *Gorgeous* legs. They go on for miles and miles. I can't hardly take my eyes off them. It's just that a short skirt ain't the most practical thing to wear when it freezing cold outside."

"Screw practical. What's the sense of having pretty legs if you can't show them off? Maybe I should wear baggy, knit polyester pants like your ninety-year-old Aunt Rosalie. We're on our way to a—" She caught herself.

"To a what?"

"I mean we're on our way to visit relatives. You want them to say, 'What the hell happened to Lisa? She started dressing like a frumpy old hag?'"

"Never mind, Lisa. You look great. Who cares if Victor drops his napkin on the floor all night long just so he can look up your skirt." He adjusted the rearview mirror and pulled away from the curb.

"Angie's husband? He *does* not."

"No? I think he's got it tied to a rubber band around his shoe or something and as soon as he loosens his grip... Anyway, what am I complaining about? Thank God we're meeting in Staten Island and I ain't got to drive all the way to southern New Jersey."

"I don't know why you hate going there so much. It's like what...two, two and a half hours tops?"

"I'd rather drive back to *Ala-fuckin'-bama.*"

"Why? What's so wrong with New Jersey?"

"What's wrong with New Jersey? I'll tell you what's wrong with New Jersey. It ain't New York!"

"Yeah. Like Staten Island is a lot better," she said. "It's filled with everyone they threw out of Brooklyn. It's like Brooklyn had a baby, a redheaded stepchild that no one wanted and they named it Staten Island."

"Yeah? Well if Staten Island is the baby, Tom's River, New Jersey, is the fuckin' afterbirth." He blew out a big sigh as he approached the corner. "Anyway. Thanks for getting them to meet us halfway."

"Don't mention it." She checked her watch. "I just hope

your brother is dressed and ready to go."

"Yeah, *right.* Joe has never been less than two hours late for anything in his whole life. You could roast a twenty-pound turkey in the time it takes him to get ready to go out. I still don't know why he's got to come along. It's bad enough I got to pay for Angie and Victor because they're prospective clients."

"Well you ain't seen him in months. So what's a couple of bucks? Don't you miss him? You only got one brother."

"I know he's my only brother, Lisa. Of course I miss him."

"Angie said she hasn't seen him in ages either. It'll be good to bring him along."

Vinny's brother Joe emerged from the bathroom, shaved, showered, and groomed, his skin ruddy from the warmth of his prolonged stay in the steamy bathroom.

The house was all he had, an inheritance he and Vinny had somehow managed to hold onto despite Joe's long bouts of unemployment and his devastating losses at the track. He was in arrears on the property taxes and owed money to everyone he knew. But that didn't mean he had to look as if he were broke when he left the house. He'd pressed his shirt and slacks and shined his only pair of dressy shoes. He went straight from the bathroom to his upstairs bedroom with a towel wrapped around his waist. The clothes dryer had been broken over a year and his freshly laundered shorts and undershirts hung on a clothesline that extended from the window to a tall lamp pole in the backyard. He opened the window and felt the icy air sting his skin. He tugged on the line but it was caught. "Shit!" He tugged harder with no success, and again, and still again. He slammed the window shut and huffed before searching his dresser drawers for some clean undergarb but came up empty.

He went back to the window and searched for the spot

where the laundry line was jammed. It was affixed to the tall pole, but the line was caught on a bough of the old dogwood tree. He studied the clothesline and figured he could free it with the use of the six-foot stepladder he stored against the wall in the laundry room. He raced downstairs and stepped into his snow boots while peering through the glass panel in the door at the limb he needed to reach. He unlocked the back door, grabbed the ladder, and raced out into the freezing cold.

He was quick to set the ladder in place and scrambled up the rungs, but even standing on the very top of the ladder, the clothesline was just beyond the reach of his outstretched hand.

Vinny and Lisa hurried up the steps to Joe's front door and rang the bell while they shuffled in place to stay warm. A long moment elapsed before Vinny rang the bell again. "Son of a bitch. What did I tell you? He's probably still in the bathroom making himself gorgeous."

"So he takes pride in his appearance," she said looking him over head-to-toe, her gaze settling on the leather jacket he wore like a second skin and the black cowboy boots she had fallen out of love with years before. "You know you could stand a little makeover yourself. You're a big time attorney now. You should get a more professional wardrobe."

"Lisa, I ain't exactly a big time attorney yet. I only won one case."

"So? You never heard no one say 'dress for success,' or 'dress for the job you want—not the one you got?' Vinny, you want to be successful, you got to dress successful. You gotta stop dressing like a *chooch*."

"A *chooch*? *I* dress like a *chooch*?"

"Don't get insulted." She studied him again. "Maybe not that bad—maybe more like a *cidrule* than a *chooch*."

He shook his head in disbelief, and jammed his hands into

his pockets. "Lisa, you think that maybe we could discuss what kind of zhlub I most resemble some time later when I'm not freezing my balls off?"

She shrugged. "Maybe the doorbell is broken." She tried the doorknob and walked in.

"Joe?" Vinny hollered. "Hey, Joe, you ready yet?" He slapped his sides in frustration. "I told you. Did I tell you or what? He ain't never ever been on time for anything in his entire life. It'll be rush hour by the time we hit the Verrazano. We'll never get to the restaurant on time."

"Easy, Vinny. Don't get your shorts in a bunch. Maybe he's on the can."

He rolled his eyes. "I'll go upstairs and look for him."

"I'll check in the basement."

They parted ways, Vinny hurrying up the stairs while Lisa searched for Joe on her way past the laundry room to the staircase leading to the basement. Vinny came back downstairs a minute later. She was still in the laundry room, alone and staring out through the storm door. Vinny had just come up alongside of her. "Holy Christ!" she shouted. Joe was on the very top of a six-foot ladder, on tiptoes, reaching for the clothesline. But when he reached up on one leg to snare it, his bath towel dropped to the ground.

Lisa shrugged and cracked her gum. "Now there's something you don't see every day." She pulled out her little pink camera and laughed as she clicked off a couple of winners. "This one's going in the hall of fame collection along with your steak-face portrait."

"I may have just been scarred for life. Stop taking pictures, would ya? Joe's hairy ass is the last thing I ever want to see again." Vinny turned up the collar on his jacket and hurried outside to give his brother a badly needed hand.

CHAPTER EIGHT
Staten-Fuckin'-Island

Lisa looked in the vanity mirror and reapplied her lipstick as Vinny piloted the Caddy along the Brooklyn-Queens Expressway toward Staten Island. She turned back and looked at Joe in the rear seat, who didn't seem to be the least bit embarrassed about having been caught naked atop a ladder in his backyard. "So, Joe," she snickered, "you planning on going on any more nature walks?"

"Piss off, Lisa. I was out of clean shorts. What was I supposed to do?"

"Maybe they should make it a national event. You know, like Groundhog Day."

Joe gave her the finger.

"No, I'm serious. They can forecast the end of the winter by whether Joe sees his shriveling pecker or not."

"Lisa, leave him alone," Vinny said. "His clothes dryer is broke."

"So maybe he should get the stupid thing fixed instead of scarring the minds of every innocent child in a ten-block radius. I know *I'd* need some therapy if I were the kid who saw *that* spectacle."

"Lisa!" Vinny warned.

"Okay. Okay."

"Look at that asshole," Vinny said as a Benz cut him off without signaling, forcing him to jam on the brakes.

"He may be an asshole but he's an asshole with money,"

Lisa said. "That's a CLS Class 6.3 liter Mercedes AMG."

"Do you know what AMG means in English?" Joe asked. "It means you just got took because you paid the Germans three times too much for your car. Back in the day you could upgrade from a small V-8 to a big block for under a grand. Now they take you for an arm, a leg, and your left nut if you want a more powerful motor."

Vinny slammed on the gas. "Fuck this guy. I'll show him." The engine revved loudly as Vinny took off in pursuit of the Benz that had zigzagged around him and was now growing smaller and smaller in the distance.

Lisa laughed. "Good luck catching that guy—a twelve-cylinder six-hundred-horsepower biturbo? He'll blow your doors off, Vinny. You don't stand a chance."

"Yeah? Watch me," Vinny said. "No one but no one out-drives a Gambini." He floored the gas pedal and propelled the powerful old behemoth forward.

"Don't do this," Lisa said. "The car's fifty-five years old. You'll throw a rod. Trust me."

"Catch that twerp," Joe said. "Show him who the boss is, Vinny."

"*No!* Don't catch the twerp." Lisa scowled at Joe and wiggled her pinkie. "Listen, Short Shaft, don't egg him on."

"*Hey,*" Joe protested. "It was cold out there."

"Yeah, of course." Lisa giggled. "Because you're normally hung like a horse. Ain't you ever heard about the theory of mass conservation?"

"The hell does that mean?"

"Mass can neither be created or destroyed. Are you trying to tell me that your penis defies the principle laws of science?"

Joe flipped her the bird once again and then rested his arms on the seatback. The old Caddy was rumbling down the road like a runaway freight train closing in on the Benz. He slapped Vinny on the shoulder. "Nail that son of a bitch!"

The Benz was doing eighty when Vinny pulled up alongside and lowered his window. He leaned out and honked the horn but the Benz's driver was on the phone and not paying attention. Vinny continued to lean on the horn, ultimately getting the driver's attention. He flipped him off and yelled, "Fuck you, you road hog. Learn how to—"

The Benz took off like a shot, leaving Vinny in the dust, angry and frustrated. "Shit."

"Slow down, Vinny," Lisa said. "This car is older than dirt. It can't take this kind of—"

The sound of a mechanical drumroll banged from under the hood. Vinny came off the gas but it was too late. The clatter slowed in time with the decelerating engine but never disappeared.

"Shit," Lisa said. "What did I tell you, Vinny? You threw a rod—I hope the block ain't cracked."

"Yeah. Sorry." He turned to Lisa. "No sweat. I can replace a set of push rods in my sleep."

"Yeah. And I can do it in half that time but that's if the engine block's not damaged. If a pushrod broke or bent, who knows what could've gotten fucked up."

Vinny shrugged. "It don't sound too bad. Hey, Joe, that sound bad to you?"

"The hell do I know, Vinny? I'm tone deaf."

Lisa crossed her arms and remained silent as they crossed over the Verrazano Bridge. She didn't say another word until they were well into Staten Island, cruising down Hyland Boulevard. "*Ah.* Damn it." She grimaced and clutched her stomach.

Vinny turned his head. "What's wrong? You okay, Lisa?"

"No, I think I'm getting my friend."

Joe furrowed his brow. "You're getting your friend? What do you mean?"

Lisa glanced at Vinny and rolled her eyes.

"Joe, *her friend.* Don't you know nothing? Her friend... You know. Little Red Riding Hood."

Joe put his fingertips together and shook his hand. "Vinny, what the hell are you talking about?"

"Her friend. Her friend," Vinny said. "You know. Scarlett Johansson."

Joe grinned. "*Marone.* I'd like to tap that."

"Yeah. I'm sure she's pining away for you too, Joe." She grimaced. "Vinny, pull over. I got to use the rest room *right now.*"

"Right here? We're just a few minutes from the restaurant. You can't wait until we—"

"Right *now*, Vinny!" she snapped and pointed to a catering hall just up the block. "The Great Kills Chateau. A place like that has got to have a clean restroom."

Vinny cut the wheel and pulled into the circular drive. Lisa opened the door and bolted from the car with urgency.

CHAPTER NINE
Vinny to the Rescue

Joe glanced at his watch. "Jesus Christ, Vinny, she's in the can like fifteen minutes. What the hell's she doing in there?"

"She's got her period, dimwit. You didn't get that?"

"Oh. So that's what all that Red Riding Hood horseshit was about?"

"That's right, genius. Ain't you never heard a woman refer to her period as her friend before?"

"Never."

Vinny shook his head in disbelief.

"I'm going in there to get her. Angie will have a baby if we don't get to the restaurant soon."

Vinny laughed. "At her age? Trust me, Angie ain't popping out another kid anytime soon."

"I'm still going in to get her."

"No you're not." Vinny checked his watch. "Yeah. Shit. It is getting pretty late. Stay here. I'll get her."

He jumped out of the car, hustled up the stone stairway and through the revolving doors into the reception hall. He looked around the opulent foyer, which was constructed with a tumbled marble floor and decorated with a massive ornate chandelier. "Lisa?"

The door to the ladies' room swung open and Lisa hobbled out, bent over, still clutching her stomach.

"Lisa, you okay? What the hell is wrong? You look terrible."

She took a few steps and sat down in a chair. "I'll be all right. I just need a few minutes."

"Are you sure? Maybe we should go home. You look awful."

"No, I took something for the cramps. I just need a little time. Maybe a cold drink would help."

Vinny spotted the maître d' and flagged him down. "Yes?"

"My fiancée ain't feeling so good. You think maybe she could have some cold water?"

"I'm so sorry to hear that." He looked at Lisa with concern. "Of course. Right this way."

"Stay here, Lisa. I'll be right back. You're not gonna pass out are you?"

"No, I'll be okay. Just get me some water." She pushed him away. "Hurry, okay?"

The maître d' motioned for Vinny to follow him down a long corridor and through a set of double doors. He held the door open for Vinny to walk through.

CHAPTER TEN
Homecoming Is Such a Scene

"Surprise!"

Vinny clutched his chest and reeled backward as a thunderous greeting bombarded his ears and camera flashes dazzled his eyes. It took a moment for him to realize what was going on. The first face he recognized was Lisa's, who'd somehow managed to enter the banquet room through another entrance and stood in front of him fully recovered, snapping pictures with her hot pink camera. She rushed to his side and planted a huge smooch on his cheek. "Are you surprised?"

"Am I surprised?" he gasped. "Are you fuckin' kidding? I almost had a heart attack." He glanced at the faces in front of him. "Holy shit. My cousin Billy. His friend Stan. Angie. Her dirtbag husband Victor. My late-as-shit brother Joe. Holy shit!" He smacked his cheek in disbelief. "Judge Molloy? Your mom and dad?" He grabbed Lisa, wrapped her up in his arms, and kissed her passionately.

"I did good, right?" she asked, glowing with pride.

"Yeah, you sure did. That's a lot of people."

"Billy and Stan wanted to show their appreciation for all you did for them. We invited everyone you know."

"You're fuckin' kidding."

"No, I'm fuckin' not."

He scolded her playfully, "So you really didn't get your period, did you?"

"No. I didn't. Are you fuckin' mad?"

"No fuckin' way!"

In the next instant Vinny was mobbed by his friends and family. Billy was the first to come forward throwing his arms around him. He kissed him on the cheek. "Fuckin' Vinny Bag O' Donuts. I fuckin' love you."

"Whoa. Whoa. Whoa. I love you too but what's with the language? You're a college man. You can't be running around swearing like some *gavone* from the back streets."

"Vin, *really?*"

"Nah, I'm just fuckin' with you. When'd you get back?"

"You kidding, Vin? Stan and I got the hell out of Alabama the second the trial was over. We crawled up I-95 so we didn't run any speed traps and didn't even stop for food or gas until we were north of the Mason-Dixon line.

"Not taking any chances, huh? That was smart…a notorious criminal like you." He slapped him on the arm. "You okay with school? I mean not showing up on account you murdered a store clerk?"

"Yeah, Vin. Stan and I are enrolled for next semester. They felt bad for us because of the bullshit arrest and applied our tuition fees so that we didn't lose any money."

Angie approached with her arms open wide. Vinny looked her over and saw she was indeed wearing a cast on her foot. He glanced up at heaven with clasped palms. *Thank God.* "I'll catch up with you in a little while. Okay, Billy?"

"Sure, Vin." Billy hugged him again and moved off.

"Vincent! Lisa, you look gorgeous," Angie said as they kissed hello. She gave her a light pat on the butt. "And look at that ass…*Marone*, Lisa, you've got an ass like a ten-year-old-boy. I used to have an ass like that. Now my butt looks like a bag of cannoli cream. You're a lucky son of a bitch, Vinny. She's a real beauty, your fiancée."

Lisa blushed.

"Yeah, I think I'll keep her," he said with a laugh. "So. I kind of overheard you on the phone with Lisa and I'm

42

guessing that you had something to do with setting up this here little shindig. Is that correct?"

"Billy and me couldn't have done it without her," Lisa said. "She put the whole thing together."

"I cobbled it together the best I could," Angie said.

Lisa looked impressed. "You're one *hell of a* cobbler."

"Yeah." Angie cackled. "The caterer is an old friend of mine. I blew him so he'd give us a good price. He wanted a hundred bucks a head. So I said, 'Fuck that! Give me a hundred bucks and I'll give *you* some head.'" She patted the back of her head à la Mae West. "He was very appreciative—threw in the Viennese table for nothing."

Vinny snorted and studied Angie's foot. "That looks pretty painful. You get run over by a steamroller or something?"

"No, it was one of those Nazi trucks, the ones that look like the rolling gas chambers from World War II. I was out walking The Pope and was bent over cleaning up after him when this ghetto-looking Mercedes truck rolled right over my foot."

"Ghetto-looking?" he asked.

"You know, the one's they shrink-wrap in that dull-looking acrylic shit. It looked like something straight out of *Mad Max Fury Road.* I was screaming bloody murder and the no good arrogant son of a bitch starts yelling at me because *I* was in the street. The prick almost killed my Shih Tzu. I think we should sue this guy's ass off. You want to take my case, Vinny?"

"I would *love* to take your case. I'd consider it an honor to ream this guy."

"Great." She winced. "I'm gonna sit down and rest my foot." She spotted her husband. "Victor. *Victor,*" she hollered. "Make me a plate, you lazy son of a bitch. My fuckin' foot is killing me." She patted Vinny on the cheek. "Good job defending your cousin Billy. I heard those rednecks were ready to send the poor kid to the chair." She began to limp away. "We'll talk later. Have fun, you two."

He smiled at Lisa. "You think you're pretty sly, don't you?"

"Yeah, I do," she said.

"Joe knew all about it, didn't he?"

"Of course he knew all about it. We rehearsed that bit about me having my friend for over an hour."

"He actually understood what we meant by Little Red Riding Hood?"

"Yeah. And Scarlett Johansson too. Although he was telling the truth when he said that he'd like to bone her...I mean what guy wouldn't."

"I hope he lets the poor girl get on top."

"Be nice, Vinny. It's not cool to make fun of other people's weight problems, especially Joe's. He's got enough shit going on in his life already."

"I guess you're right. Sorry." He spotted a tall gray-haired man standing alone, sipping a glass of red wine. "Um...why don't you say hello to our guests, Lisa. I want to thank Judge Molloy for all his help."

"Good idea, Vinny. That man saved your ass in Alabama attesting to your credentials the way he did."

Vinny grabbed a seven and seven at the bar and approached his dear friend and mentor. "Judge Molloy," he began, "I'm so happy you could make it."

"Ah. The conquering hero returns."

"Thank you, Judge, but I think you know that I would've been dead meat down there in Alabama if you hadn't verified my—"

He put his pointer finger to his lips, "Shhh." He gestured as a magician might to indicate he would make something disappear. "We need never speak of this again. Do you understand what I'm saying?"

Vinny nodded. "I do, Judge, but thanks, thanks all the same."

"I would love to get a copy of that courtroom transcript. From what Lisa told me the chips were stacked against you, and that Judge Haller sounded like a god-awful pain in the ass."

"Yeah. He was, but he just wanted things done right. When push came to shove, he wasn't such a bad guy after all."

Molloy grinned. "I'm happy to see you've acquired an appreciation for those of us seated on the bench." He patted him on the shoulder. "I'm proud of you, Vinny. When I met you, you were going nowhere, but when I saw the way you put that pompous highway patrolman in his place...well, I just knew you had what it takes to become an officer of the court. You've got a promising career ahead of you. Is there anything I can do to help?"

He shrugged. "Um...can you lend me a twenty?"

Molloy's eyes grew large. "Don't tell me you're broke?"

"As you know I did my cousin's case pro bono. I lived out of pocket almost two months while I defended him in Alabama."

Molloy rubbed his chin for a moment while he thought about Vinny's predicament. "Hmmm. I'm guessing that you haven't done any assigned counsel work before?"

"Assigned counsel work? No, Judge Molloy. What's that?"

"Well it's hardly what I call quality justice, and you'll have to hustle your ass off, but it'll put some quick money in your pocket, and you should still have time to pursue your career in personal injury law."

"Hustling is fine, Judge. I'll do anything that'll put food on the table."

"You'll have to qualify as a panel attorney first, but I'm pretty close with Mike Saperstein who oversees the 18B Central Screening Panel. You successfully defended two young men against homicide charges in a kangaroo court. I don't think he'll find any issues with you."

"Thank you, Judge Molloy. I can't tell you how much I appreciate this."

"Don't mention it."

"So, what are the nuts and bolts of this here assigned counsel thing?"

"As I mentioned, it's hardly what I think of as quality justice, but it's a necessary part of the legal process. The court system provides private attorneys to the indigent in cases where a conflict or multiple defendants prevent a legal aid attorney from accepting the case. The pay isn't much. Sixty dollars per hour for a misdemeanor case and a paltry seventy-five for felony work, but I know a couple of hardworking attorneys who pull down four to five thousand a month doing it. It helps them to make their ends meet."

"Four to five thousand? That would be great."

Molloy flashed his hand like a stop sign. "Now hold on. The attorneys I mentioned are highly experienced at the assigned counsel game. Even if you work like a dog, you'll be lucky to make half that at the beginning."

"Half's better than nothing, Judge, which is exactly what I'm making now."

"That's fine—as long as you're going into this with a reasonable level of expectation. In the meantime, I'll keep my ears open for any casework that might reward you more handsomely. Do you have any business cards with you?"

Vinny jammed his hand into his suit pocket. "All you want, Judge Molloy." He handed him a stack an inch thick.

Molloy's eyes opened wide. "That's a bit more than I was thinking, but I'll hold onto them and try to put them to good use." He split the pile in two and slipped the two stacks into his pockets. His eyes lit up when he saw Lisa approach. He took her hand and kissed her on the cheek. "You're a feast for the eyes, Ms. Vito." He turned to Vinny. "You know I was happily married for over thirty years and I loved my wife dearly, but God rest her soul Mrs. Molloy was a plain-looking gal." He grinned as he patted Vinny on the shoulder. "I don't know how you do it, my friend. You've got one hell of a gift."

CHAPTER ELEVEN
Scream a Little Scream for Me

Sammy was there beside Theresa when she woke up. She turned on her side so that she could study him as he slept. He looked different without hair but his sleep face hadn't changed. He was still her Sammy, rugged and handsome, the cleft in his chin darkened with stubble.

A couple of moments passed as she tried to be patient but couldn't wait any longer. She kissed his lips, bringing him to life. His eyes were still closed as he kissed her back, his arms encircling her, pulling her closer. She'd missed him so much and had ached for this kind of closeness, to be in his arms, warm and secure. She was about to say, "I love you," when somewhere off in the distance a shrill noise pierced her consciousness and interrupted the moment. It grew louder and louder and so insistent that it couldn't be ignored. She finally recognized the sound as the wail of a siren.

Bam! Bam! Bam!

The loud noise snatched her from the rapture of sleep. She shrieked as she shot up in bed, clutching her chest, her eyes snapping open. The space beside her in bed was empty. "Sam?" A moment passed before she realized that she had been dreaming.

Bam! Bam! Bam!

"Sam is that you?" She threw back the covers and scrambled out of bed, wrapping a robe around her as she hurried to the door. "Sam?" She rose on her toes to see through the peephole—on the other side was a face she didn't recognize. Her heart pounded. *Where are you, Sammy?* "Yes?" she asked as she grew nervous.

"NYPD," the stranger announced as he held up his gold detective's shield so that it could be viewed through the peephole. "Ms. Cototi? Ms. Theresa Cototi?"

She glanced around the apartment, hoping Sam might be in the bathroom and would come running to her side. Her voice trembled, "Yes?"

"May I come in, ma'am?"

"Why?"

"I'd rather not yell through the door."

She'd only had Sam back for a few short days. His return still felt so tenuous, as if he could be ripped away from her at any moment. "Is it about—" The words died in her mouth and were swallowed by dread.

"Can I come in, ma'am? It's very important that I speak with you."

She was more afraid of the news she suspected the police officer carried than of letting a stranger into her home. She began to shiver and felt lightheaded, then faint. She slid down to the floor with her back pressed against the door, lost in fear.

Bam! Bam! Bam!

The door continued to shake beneath the force of the policeman's blows. "Ma'am," he persisted. "*Please...*open the door."

CHAPTER TWELVE
He Said, She Said...No

The Caddy sat on the street all the next day because Vinny and Lisa were both terribly hungover, too impaired to drive after Vinny's surprise party. God only knows how they made it home afterward.

Lisa's father Augie grimaced when he heard the noise coming from under the hood of the big red Caddy as it rolled into the repair bay the following day. "Lisa, you threw a rod?" he asked with disappointment in his voice.

Lisa and Vinny hopped out of the car. "Me? I didn't throw nothin'. It was Captain Lead Foot over here." She smirked. "He thought he could go up against a Mercedes AMG."

Augie frowned. "Vinny, for real? Before or after you got loaded at the party?"

"Before," she snitched.

"Benedict Arnold. When did you become such a tattle-tale?"

"Face the music, Mario Andretti."

"Ah, I didn't push her so hard. Maybe the oil pressure was low or something."

"Oil pressure, my ass," she said. "Listen, Vinny, I change the oil every two thousand miles and check the oil pressure while I'm at it. It's always around thirty-two PSI, which is well within tolerance for this motor."

"She's right," Augie said. "Thirty-two is right on the money." He felt under the hood for the release latch and popped the massive hood. "We may be lucky," he said and pointed to the left valve cover, which had a prominent bump on the top surface. "The rod broke while the piston was on the way up. We'll pull the valve cover and see what's going on."

"You're a lucky fuck, Vinny," she said. "If the rod broke while the piston was on the way down, it probably would've cracked the block and then we could've thrown the whole engine in the garbage."

Vinny was gazing at the concrete floor as he pulled off his leather jacket. "Augie, you got a set of coveralls I could use?"

"No way!" Lisa said. "We're just a few blocks from the house. You put on a suit and go to work. *I'll* fix the valve train."

As usual, she was elegantly attired in pumps and a skirt.

Vinny's eyebrows peeked. "Dressed like that?"

"No, ya dope. I'll walk back with you and change into *my* coveralls."

"You two go ahead," Augie insisted. "I'll remove the bolts and we'll talk about the repair when you get back." He kissed Lisa on the forehead. "Besides, you know how much I like having my little girl around the shop."

"Thanks, Pops." Lisa blushed and pushed Vinny toward the door.

Vinny unlocked the front door and pushed it open.

"So, what's your plan for today?" Lisa asked.

"I'm gonna go see Judge Molloy's friend to file my application for that assigned attorney thing. Then I'm gonna call Angie and start working on her case."

"What about taking some office space like we talked about? You know, so you got a place to talk to your clients."

"Yeah. I'll look into that too...if I got the time."

He was starting for the staircase when the phone rang. The

voice on the end of the line sounded foreign. "Hello. This is Detective Parikh."

"What? Did you say, 'Detective *Prick*?'"

"Yes."

"Fuck you!" He slammed the phone onto the cradle. "The nerve of that guy."

"Who the hell was that?" Lisa asked.

"Some asshole wasting my time with a prank call. I can't believe the son of a bitch called just to break my balls." The phone rang again. "Ah shit. Do you believe this guy?" He answered the call in a hostile voice. "Listen up, wiseass. This ain't funny."

The caller interrupted. "Is this Vincent Gambini?"

"Yeah. Who wants to know?"

"Detective Parikh."

"Detective *Prick*?"

"Yes."

"Get a life and stop wasting my time, you sick bastard."

"Mr. Gambini, this is Detective Nirmal Parikh of the New York City Police Department."

"Normal prick? Yeah, well, *Normal* Prick, I'm a big prick and I'm gonna kick the ever-loving shit out of you if you don't hang up and stop calling this number."

"Hey!" Lisa said. "What's with all the foul language? You don't know who that is."

He covered the receiver. "Friggin' asshole. I'll teach him not to screw around with a Gambini. Watch *this*."

"Vinny, are you sure about this?" she asked. "Maybe you just oughta hang up."

"A guy like this? Forget about it. He'll never stop calling. Give a guy like this an inch and he'll take a whole mile." He uncovered the receiver. "Hey, Normal Prick, why don't you hang up and call back when you grow up and become a full-size prick."

"Mr. Gambini," the caller asserted. "This is Detective

Nirmal Parikh with the New York City Police Department. I'm calling on official police business."

"Yeah, right. Who is this? Hey, is that you, Giacomo, you sick bastard? I know it's you, you crazy son of a bitch. You still hung over from my party the other night?"

"No," the caller insisted, "I already explained, sir, this is Detective Parikh."

"Now listen, *Prick*, I've got lots of friends in high places and if I ever find out who this is, I'll kick your teeth in." He disconnected again. "*There*. I showed him."

The phone rang again. Lisa stepped in front of him and answered the call. "Can I help you?" She listened for a few moments and then turned to Vinny with a look of abject horror on her face. "Oh my God. Yeah? I see." She remained quiet while she listened to what the caller had to say. "Sure. Yeah. I understand. I'll put him right on. Hold on." She covered the receiver and turned to Vinny with a look of utter disbelief. "Yeah. You showed him all right. The man's name isn't *Prick*. It's pronounced *Par-eek*. It's an Indian name, ya dope."

"How was I supposed to know with that thick accent of his? I couldn't understand a fuckin' word he said."

She shook her head. "Forget all that. It's important. He wants to talk to you about some woman named Theresa, Theresa Cototi."

"Theresa Cototi? Who the hell is that?"

"Like *I know*." She shoved the phone into his hand. "Would ya just talk to the man already."

"Yeah, yeah, sure." He put the phone to his ear and began to pace the room. "Uh...Detective...sorry about that."

CHAPTER THIRTEEN
Son of Zeus

It took Vinny about an hour to shower, dress, and get down to the police precinct. He shoved the doors open and charged into the vestibule. He hurried to the counter and presented his business card. "Vincent Gambini. I'm here to see Detective Parikh."

The desk officer scrutinized his business card, then examined Vinny's face. "Wait right here," he said as he turned and walked through the door to the inner office.

Vinny drummed his fingers on the counter while he waited for the officer to return.

He didn't have to wait very long. "Detective Parikh is on the phone," the desk officer said and pointed to a row of chairs lining the wall. "Have a seat."

"Have a seat?" he asked.

"That's what I said. *Have* a seat."

Vinny reluctantly found a chair and sat down in the only available spot, between an oversized woman and a man in a tracksuit wearing a cervical collar.

Scarcely a minute had passed before the man with the neck brace made his acquaintance. "Hey, man, you look like a lawyer. You a lawyer?"

"Yeah," Vinny replied without looking. "I'm a lawyer. I'm here to meet with a client." He turned his head, noticed the neck brace, and offered his hand. "Vincent Gambini, Attorney at Law. I specialize in personal injury cases. And who might

54

you be, my seriously maimed friend?"

"Hercules Lopez. I'm here because a detective is questioning one of my employees. I hope she don't get booked."

"Hercules, huh? That's an interesting name."

"I got a brother named Apollo and a sister named Aphrodite, too. My father's from Puerto Rico but my mother's from Athens."

"Oh. I see. Your neck looks pretty bad, Hercules. What the hell happened?"

"Some woman was chasing me down Eighty-sixth Street under the elevated train tracks when I slipped and did a number on my neck."

"I see. And now I suppose you'd like to sue this broad who was chasing you?"

"Not exactly. You see, man, I want to sue JPMorgan Chase."

"The bank?"

Lopez nodded, his movement greatly restricted by the brace. "Right. The bank."

"And how is it you feel the bank is responsible for your injury?"

"Well you know, I blacked out from the fall, but when I came to, the first thing I saw was the great big electric Chase sign in front of me and I swore, 'JPMorgan Chase, those no good sons of bitches.'"

"You'll have to excuse me, Hercules, but I fail to see what the bank had to do with your slip and fall."

"Mr. Gambini, is it?" "

"Uh-huh."

"I fell in front of the bank and there was some slippery shit on the sidewalk, some grease or something. You're a lawyer. Can't you prove that the bank was negligent? I mean it's their responsibility to keep the street in front of the bank clean, isn't it?"

"Negligent of what?"

"Like I said—the slippery goddamn grease that made me fall."

"Do you know for a fact that JPMorgan Chase was responsible for the slippery grease being there? Did you take a sample of this slippery grease or do you possess some other evidence that I could use to prove your claim in a court of law?"

"Shit, man, it's a big goddamn bank. Even a settlement has got to be good for six figures. Shouldn't it? I hate those bastards anyway. They turned me down for a mortgage."

"Oh, *I* see. You're unhappy with the bank because of a credit decision you disagreed with and now you figure you'll screw them on some trumped up personal injury case? Is that about the size of it?"

"What they did to me wasn't right. I'm a businessman. I've got cash. Those bastards discriminated against me."

"And how exactly did they do that?"

"Some mumbo jumbo about something called debt ratios."

"That's not all that unusual, Hercules. Banks have these *things* they need before they'll agree to lend you money."

"I've got things. What kind of things do they want?"

"Things like assets, provable documented income, acceptable credit, collateral...*things*. Anyway, I thought you said you were in some kind of business. How is it you had such an issue with your debt ratios?"

"I *am* in business, and I'm making a killing."

"I guess I should ask what kind of business you're in."

"I'm in the package business." He reached into his pocket and handed Vinny a business card that simply read: "Delivering the goods, Manhattan to Montauk." It had a phone number and website address.

"So, you're in the freight business, like UPS or FedEx, correct?"

"Not exactly." He edged closer. "Packages, man. Packages." He paused for a moment. "Picture this, Mr. Gambini.

The wife is out of town and you're feeling lonely. You call me and I deliver a hot little package."

"What's in this...package? Something to put a smile on my face like freshly baked muffins or a tin of Moose Munch?"

"No."

"I don't get it. What's in these packages?"

"Come on," Lopez said. "You know, man."

"No, I *don't* know. Anyway, how much do you charge to deliver one of these packages?"

"From two hundred anywhere up to five hundred... depending."

"Depending on *what*?"

"Depending on what kind of package you want."

Vinny grew weary of the conversation. "Okay, Hercules. Humor me for a minute. Hypothetically speaking, let's pretend that I need a package. So, I call you up and I say, 'Hercules, I'm all alone and I've got absolutely nothing to do. Send me over a package.' And you say..."

"What kind of package would you like, Mr. Gambini?"

"What kind of packages do you got, Hercules?"

"Bronze, silver, and gold."

"And I say, 'Let's go for broke. Send me over one of your top-of-the-line special gold packages.' How long does it take for said gold package to arrive? A day or two? Does it come overnight or by standard delivery?"

"Super priority rush."

"What's that mean?"

"About an hour—door to door."

"*Whoa.* That's pretty fast. All right, let's say an hour passes. There's a knock on the door. I open the door and the package gets delivered. *What* did I get?"

"Morena, a six-foot tall Boricua with an ass that moves up and down like it's on ball bearings, bleach blonde hair extensions, big-ass titties, a whip, and a quart of Astroglide."

"*Oh.*" Vinny said. "*Now* I get it. You're a *pimp.*"

Lopez nodded.

"I see. And the reason Chase wouldn't give you a mortgage loan is because you're in a cash business and couldn't document your income."

Lopez winked. "Now you've got it."

"And that young woman who was chasing you down Eighty-sixth Street when you slipped on that slippery grease and fell in front of the bank—that wasn't by chance Morena, the ravishing six-foot tall Puerto Rican hoe with giant, massive silicone-augmented breasts, was it? And could it have been the lube from her quart-size bottle of Astroglide that you slipped on?"

"No way, Mr. Gambini."

"Meaning?"

"The girl chasing me was Sophie, a fifty-year-old Polish woman with a hip replacement and a lazy eye. She's strictly bronze package, and she don't come with no free bottle of lube."

Vinny froze. The conversation was interrupted when someone called his name. He looked up and saw a slight, dark-complexioned man beckoning for him to come forward.

He carefully enunciated, "Detective *Par-eek?*"

The detective nodded.

"I'll be right with you, Detective." He reached into his pocket and handed Lopez his business card. "I think we should talk."

CHAPTER FOURTEEN
A Parikh by Any Other Name

"*Sit down*," Parikh said. "Do you always answer the phone like that? You're lucky I maintained my cool."

"No, Detective. I'm sorry about that. No offense intended. I just came back from a long trip and I'm kind of sleep deprived."

Parikh gave Vinny a hostile stare and sat down.

"How is it you called me on this matter?"

"Ms. Cototi is pretty shaken up. I asked if she had a friend or a family member that could help her and the only person she could think of couldn't be reached. She placed another call and then asked if I could get in touch with you."

"I see," Vinny said. "So why is it this Ms. Cototi is so distressed?"

"Her boyfriend committed suicide late last night—took a leap from the roof of the eight-floor apartment house she lives in."

Vinny winced. "Jesus. That's *awful*."

"You don't know the half of it—landed right in front of an oncoming car that ran over him—turned his head into a street pizza."

Vinny shuddered. "I suppose you found a note?"

"No note. Not yet anyway."

"But you *are* ruling it a suicide?"

"For the time being...pending further investigation. They don't always leave notes."

"They?"

"The suicide victims. It doesn't happen often, but sometimes they don't even have the will to jot down their last few words."

"Anyone see it take place?"

"No. The body was just taken to the morgue. The crime scene investigators are still collecting evidence. We're still canvassing the neighborhood and looking for possible witnesses."

"I see. And there was no one else she could call?"

"I just told you that. As I mentioned, she tried reaching out for a friend, the deceased's brother, but he was inaccessible."

Vinny removed a legal pad from his briefcase and began scribbling notes.

"You're a lefty?" Parikh asked in a critical tone.

"Yeah, I'm a lefty. There something wrong with that?"

"I don't know," he replied with matching sarcasm. "Do you have a problem with cops?"

Vinny grinned, covered his mouth, and said in a muffled voice, "Fuck you."

Parikh's jaw dropped. "What did you say?"

Vinny shrugged. "Say? I didn't say nothing. I belched. I'm a no-good, sleep-deprived, left-handed lawyer with indigestion." He looked down at his pad. "Cototi—one *t* or two?"

"One," Parikh grumbled, his eyes shooting daggers. "Well, two actually, but not together."

"What was the deceased's name and what was his brother's name, the one you couldn't reach?"

Parikh read from his notes, "The victim was Samuel Cipriani. His brother is Anthony Cipriani, the deputy mayor."

"The deputy mayor, huh? No shit? And he didn't come down here when he heard his brother was dead?"

"He's out of town, Mr. Gambini. He's been notified and is flying back from California on the redeye this evening. He lands tomorrow morning."

"California, huh? That's a long ways away. Vacation I guess?"

"I suppose. Would you like to see Ms. Cototi now or are you planning to irritate me further?"

"Anything else I should know before I meet Ms. Cototi?"

"Yes," Parikh said. "Samuel Cipriani was just released from Sullivan County Correctional. He did seven years for armed robbery. It was his third offense."

"You thinking maybe this guy Sam screwed someone over while he was on the inside and the shove off the rooftop was some kind of payback?"

"That occurred to me. But it's way too soon to make any assumptions."

Another detective approached Parikh's desk and handed him a white bag that was printed with red words: The Curry Club. It bore a picture of Buddha. He glanced at Vinny. "Who's this guy?"

Vinny jumped up eager to make the detective's acquaintance and extend his sphere of influence. He extended his hand. "Vincent LaGuardia Gambini, Attorney at Law."

"Mulholland," he replied as his nostrils flared. "Jesus, another lawyer? I swear, there are more of you lawyers than cockroaches and you're even harder to get rid of." He turned away.

"Wait. How much?" Parikh asked.

"Ten even," Mulholland replied.

Parikh handed him a bill. "Thanks."

"You bet," Mulholland said as he walked off.

"That smells great. Lunch?" Vinny asked.

Parikh took a sealed aluminum dish out of the bag and sniffed it. "Kolhapuri chicken curry. Just like my mother used to make. I get it over on Eighty-sixth Street. There's a family-owned takeout place right next to the bank."

Vinny's eyes lit up. "The Chase Bank under the el?"

"That's right. You know the place?"

"Nah. But I have a client who slipped on some grease in front of the bank. That's why I'm familiar with the area."

"Train grease?" Parikh asked.

"*Train* grease," he repeated. "Why didn't I think of that?"

"Happens all the time," Parikh said. "Works its way out of the wheel hubs and falls off the axles." He pushed his lunch aside. "Like I said, Ms. Cototi is pretty shaken. She's in Interview One. Would you like to see her now?"

"Oh, yeah. Of course." He shook his head as if to clear cobwebs. "I think I need a good night's sleep. Thanks. And thanks for overlooking my little faux pas on the phone this morning."

Parikh pushed his business card across the desk. "One get-out-of-jail-free card, Mr. Gambini. Make sure it never happens again."

CHAPTER FIFTEEN
Hottie Cototi

From a distance, Theresa Cototi looked like a kid sitting in an adult chair at the conference table, her legs too short to reach the floor. She jumped out of the chair when Vinny was shown into the room. Her petite figure was formidable in tight jeans and a cropped rib top, making it obvious that although she was young, she was no child. She wasn't wearing makeup and her long brown hair was disheveled. "You're Mr. Gambini?" she asked. Her nose was red and her eyes glassy.

The interrogation room looked drab and was painted in shades of green that had darkened from years of accumulated grime. Vinny smiled warmly to put her at ease and to take her mind off the dreary surroundings. "Yeah, I'm Vincent Gambini. Sorry to hear about your loss." He placed his briefcase on the table and shook her hand. They both stood in silence for a moment before Vinny suggested they sit down. "I guess you didn't get much sleep last night. Your boyfriend takes a header off the roof..." He whistled, his eyes wide.

She shook her head and wiped her nose while tears popped out and drizzled own her cheeks.

"You know that you really don't need an attorney at this juncture. You're not a suspect or nothin'."

"I know."

He could see the muscles in her throat tighten. A half-filled cup of water was on the table. Vinny slid it toward her.

She took a sip. "Thanks."

"So how come you asked for an attorney?"

She began to sob. "I guess it was because I was so upset and I don't really have any family in the area...A friend of mine told me about you. He said that you were a very skilled and persistent attorney...someone I could trust. So, I figured I'd ask you for your help."

"A *friend?* Which friend?"

"Is that important?"

"No, I'm sure plenty of people could've mentioned my name. It just would've been nice to know."

"My friend." She averted her eyes. "He's kind of private. I don't think he'd want me to mention his name."

"Oh, yeah? Okay. You do realize that I don't do this for free."

She nodded then shrugged. "I've got some money."

Vinny was thinking about how much to charge when the figures Judge Molloy mentioned at the party popped into his head. He was going back and forth between seventy-five and a hundred dollars an hour, wanting to ask for a hundred but afraid she'd balk.

"What do you get? Like three hundred an hour?" the trusting young woman asked. "I've heard that's what most attorneys charge—some get more. You don't charge more than that, do you?"

"No...not for an initial consultation, which is all this is at the moment. Can you afford that much?"

She nodded and reached for her bag on the floor. She opened her wallet and handed him three one-hundred-dollar bills.

"That's not necessary. I can send you a bill."

"Take it. A few years ago another attorney told me the same thing when I was trying to buy an apartment, then he turned around and dicked me—the whole deal went south."

"Figuratively speaking I hope?"

Confused, she chose to remain silent.

"Well, you don't have to worry about me, Ms. Cototi, I never dicked nobody. Do you mind if I ask what you do? I mean for a living?"

"I dance," she said.

"You dance? You mean like Swan Lake? Like you're a ballerina or something?"

"No," she said. "I dance in a G-string with a brass pole between my legs, and to answer your next question…no, I'm not a hooker. But I make good tips and I can pay you if that's what you're worried about."

He looked her squarely in the eye. "Do I *look* like I'm worried about getting paid?"

"No. Not really."

"Good. Because I think we're getting a little off topic. You feel up to discussing your boyfriend's death?"

He could see that she was having difficulty swallowing and shifted in her chair before speaking. "I guess we should."

Vinny pulled out his legal pad. "I understand that your boyfriend, Samuel Cipriani, just got out of jail where he was incarcerated for seven years. How long have you known him?"

"I met Sammy about a year before he went away."

"Did you know he had gone to jail before?"

"Yes."

"But you dated him anyway."

She nodded. "Uh-huh."

Vinny tapped his pencil on the pad. "His being a convicted felon didn't bother you none?"

"At first—yeah. But he didn't act like someone who had been to jail. He was confident and very generous and he didn't disappear into the night like most guys do after the first time you sleep with them."

"And at that time you had no idea he was planning another caper? Um…I mean another crime?"

"No."

"But he always had money in his pocket?"

"No. Not really. Not all the time. He seemed to be up and down with the money thing. Sometimes, when he was broke, I paid for the things we did."

Vinny pushed out his lips and scribbled something down. "Okay. So you didn't know he was planning a heist, but he did. He was arrested, tried, convicted, and went to jail, and you waited for him for seven *long* years."

"We were in love."

"I hope to Christ you were. He was a very lucky man having such a beautiful young woman wait for him all that time."

Her face contorted, making her look sad and pitiful.

"Hey. Take it easy," he offered, consoling her. "Take another drink of water if you need to. This won't take long. You okay to continue?"

She nodded.

"Okay. So he got out of jail. Then what happened?"

"We picked him up and drove home."

"We? Who's we?"

"Me and his brother Anthony."

"Anthony?" It took a second for Vinny to make the connection. "Right, the deputy mayor?"

"Yes."

"This must've been right before he went to California."

She began to fidget. "I didn't know he was going away. He drove us home. We had a nice dinner together with his parents, and then he left."

"And when was that?"

"Monday."

"Monday. Today's Thursday, so that was three days ago." He leaned forward with his hands tented. "And what happened in those three days, dear?"

She shrugged and averted her eyes. "We stayed in."

"Stayed *in*? Where?"

"My apartment."

"For *three* entire days and nights?"

"Mostly."

"I guess you were *very* glad to see him."

She cast an angry glance. "He was away seven years, Mr. Gambini. Do you really think three days is such a long time?"

Vinny cleared his throat and looked away momentarily. "And in those three *wonderful* days and nights, did he say or do anything to lead you to believe that he might commit suicide?"

"I don't think so."

"What? You don't think so or you know so?"

"He was a little gloomy about his future. You know, 'I'm a con. I'll never get a good job. People think I'm a lowlife. Blah, blah, blah.' That kind of thing, like he was feeling sorry for himself…but I never thought he was so upset that he'd kill himself."

"So why would he do it?"

"I don't know, Mr. Gambini," she said once again on the brink of tears. "I just don't know. I figured we were going to spend the rest of our lives together and now, once again…I've been dicked."

"Uh-huh. I see." Vinny stood and paced. "Can you take me through it, dear?"

"Take you through it?"

"Yeah. The night Sammy died. What happened? Step by step."

Her shoulders rose, then settled in a heap. "I don't know. I was asleep until…"

"Until what, dear?"

"Until the police came pounding on my door."

"You slept through the whole thing?" he asked, his eyes wide.

She covered her mouth. "I didn't even know he'd gotten out of bed. How could that be, Mr. Gambini? How could I not have known any of it happened? He got out of bed, left the apartment, and went up to the roof. I remembered hearing sirens in my sleep, afterward, but..." She became hysterical crying. It took some time before she could continue.

"You're one hell of a deep sleeper, Theresa. Do you use any sleep aids?"

"No. Nothing."

"Never?"

"Never."

"Not even Sominex or one of them other over-the-counter sleep aids?"

"No."

"Were you drinking before you went to bed?"

"Just wine."

"How much wine?"

"A couple of glasses. We opened a bottled and drank it together."

"And he gave no indication whatsoever that he was about to end his life?"

She shook her head.

"I see. So, the next thing you knew, the police were knocking on your door. Was that when you met Detective Parikh?"

"Yes."

"And he explained what happened?"

"Yes."

"That must've been one hell of a shock."

She clutched her chest and took several deep breaths finding it difficult to calm down.

"What's the matter, dear?"

"My heart is racing."

"All right, just try to settle down. I know it's not easy, but..." He patted her hand, smiling sympathetically, but not knowing how to comfort her. "There, there, Theresa, everything is gonna be all right."

"Are you sure, Mr. Gambini?" she asked, sniffling, desperate for assurance.

"No doubt," he postured. "We got this."

CHAPTER SIXTEEN
Good Karma Ain't Bad

Lisa stood in front of the stove with a vacant expression as she stirred a pot of sauce. She looked up when Vinny came through the door at the end of the day.

He had a big grin on his face as he bounded toward her and planted a huge smooch on her cheek.

"Someone had a good day," she said. "You get nominated to the Supreme Court or something?"

"Very funny, Lisa. But actually I had a *great* day."

"Yeah? You get hired by that woman the Indian police detective phoned you about?"

He took the wooden spoon out of her hand and tasted the sauce. "Needs more sugar."

"More sugar?"

"Yeah. More sugar."

"Okay." She took a pinch out of the sugar bowl and cast it into the pot.

"Lisa, that ain't enough."

"Vinny, it's marinara sauce. It's supposed to have a little bite to it. Anyway, it's got plenty of sugar in it already."

"You know I like it sweet."

"Oh, you like it sweet?" She picked up the sugar bowl and dumped all of it into the sauce. "*There.* That sweet enough for you?"

"What's the matter with you? Give me that," he insisted, once again grabbing the wooden spoon and quickly removing as much of it as he could before it dissolved into the sauce. He blended in the remaining sugar and tasted it before kissing his fingertips. "There. Now it's perfect."

"*Yeah*, now it's perfect," she mimed.

"Lisa, what's wrong with you?"

"What's wrong with me? You should know."

"What do you mean I should know? I ain't got a clue as to what you're talking about."

"Oh no?"

"No."

"Well then I'll tell you what's wrong. Ten long years I'm eating sauce sweet enough to gag a maggot. That's what's wrong. Did you ever stop to think that maybe I don't like it so sweet?"

"No. You never said nothin' before."

"That's because *you should know*. And I shouldn't have to say nothing. That's your problem, Vinny. You're friggin' oblivious sometimes. It's like you leave cracker crumbs on the table when you're done or you start eating your meal before I have a chance to sit down."

"Lisa, you getting your friend for real this time?"

"No, I ain't getting my friend. I threw you a lavish party the other night. I spent an entire day fixing the engine you effed up, and now I'm cooking you a nice dinner with…" She stomped her foot twice in time with each word, "*Sweet sauce.* The least you could do is bring me a nice bouquet of flowers. Is that too much to ask?"

"Lisa, you want flowers? I'll get you some."

"No," she said with disappointment. "I don't want them no more."

"Lisa, would you please make up your mind? Do you want flowers or don't you?"

"No." She turned her head, craning her neck as far as it would go, making it obvious that she didn't want to look at him.

"Lisa, look at me."

Even in the midst of hostility, she sounded cute to him. "*No.*"

"Please."

"*No.*"

"Lisa, I'm not a friggin' mind reader. How am I supposed to know what you want unless you tell me?"

"You should know!"

"I should know what?"

"We're together ten freakin' years, Vinny. You should *just* know."

"I should just know?"

"Yeah."

"Okay. Starting tomorrow *I'll know.* Now would you please look at me?"

"No."

"But why?"

"Because you won't know nothin' tomorrow either."

He blew out an exasperated sigh. "Lisa, I came home chocked full of good news that I couldn't wait to share with *you*, Mona Lisa Vito, the love of my life. Don't that count for nothin'?"

"I suppose," she answered, clearly warming. She turned her head slightly in his direction.

"Tell you what—why don't you watch some TV. I'll finish getting dinner ready and I'll call you when it's on the table."

"Oh *yeah?*" she asked with surprise.

"Yeah. Go watch *Jeopardy* or something. I got this."

Lisa had a subtle smile on her face as she untied her apron and walked from the kitchen.

There were no flowers, nor cards, nor chocolates, but Vinny had set the table with a tablecloth, opened a bottle of red wine, and poured a glass for each of them. He waited for Lisa to sit down and pushed in her chair for her.

"This is *nice*," she said.

He sprinkled her pasta with Romano cheese. "Bon appétit."

She twisted the spaghetti onto her fork and very reluctantly tasted it. Her expression brightened. "What did you do, Vinny? It's not disgusting."

He beamed proudly. "I added another can of crushed tomatoes to the sauce to cut the sweetness."

She smiled as she wound more spaghetti around her fork. In truth, the sauce was far from delicious but it was the effort he made that mattered. "Thank you so much for this wonderful meal. *So,* how was your day?"

"It was fuckin' great. I met with that woman at the police station and she hired me on the spot." He reached into his pocket and spread three one-hundred-dollar bills across the table. "Paid in cash for the hour we spent together."

She appeared to be overwhelmed. "You must've really impressed her. What did she do?"

"Nothin'."

"Nothin'? So why did she hire you?"

"She needed someone to commiserate with on account her boyfriend jumped to his death and got run over by a car."

"Wait. He jumped to his death *and* got hit by a car?"

"That's right. The police brought her in to talk. She was kind of worked up and needed someone to talk things through with."

"You must be one hell of a talker. But there's no case against her so it was just a one-shot deal, right?"

"Probably. I don't know. But I met this guy while I was waiting there and I think I've got a solid slip-and-fall case to work on."

"You see, Vinny, it's all about karma. You do good for someone and it comes back to you in spades. Like you helped

Billy and Stan and now you're getting a return on your generosity. The Caddy's fixed too. I did a complete rebuild of the valve train assembly on both sides and Dad picked up a replacement valve cover for chump change. She's purring like a kitten again."

Vinny kissed both of her hands. "Thank you *very, very* much."

"Any news on that appointed attorney thing?"

"Molloy's friend said I could start tomorrow."

"*Tomorrow?*" She sounded surprised. "That's terrific. You'll be a partner at a big prestigious law firm in no time."

"Whoa. Let's not count our chickens before they hatch."

"Well, you got to admit it's all positive news."

"Uh-huh." He picked at his food. "I have to confess, I'm a little worried about this appointed attorney thing. Being that Judge Molloy went out on a limb for me the way he did..." He shrugged. "I don't want to screw it up."

"Vinny, ain't you got no confidence after winning that big case?"

"I don't know," he sulked. "Maybe that was just a fluke. What if I can't cut it in a New York courtroom—I mean with the fast pace and all the high-powered attorneys I'll have to go up against."

She reached across the table and rested her hand on his arm. "You worried about it because you're dyslexic?"

"Yeah." His shoulders slumped. "You know I can't read too fast and these New York judges...they can be impatient."

"You know what I think?"

He shook his head.

"I think you should drink some more of this wine. We'll get into bed early. You get a good night's sleep and go into that court tomorrow ready to kick some ass."

"Oh yeah? You think so?"

"I know so. Now pass me a chicken cutlet already. I'm friggin' starving."

CHAPTER SEVENTEEN
Jitters

Lisa offered to accompany Vinny to court the next morning and he was quick to accept her support. He'd struggled with dyslexia his entire life—it slowed him down and his inability to keep pace with others often wreaked havoc on his confidence, rendering him helpless as a strategic thinker.

He wrung his hands as they stood outside the courthouse, the Brooklyn Central Court Building, its commanding influence projecting outward, proclaiming that *here is where the law is laid down*. It was an intimidating edifice to be sure, one that might easily overwhelm a fledgling lawyer with a confidence issue.

A few lawyers hurrying to court made quick stops at the coffee cart before entering the building. "You know that looks like a good idea. I think I'm gonna get a cup of coffee."

"Vinny, stop wasting time. We been standing out here a full ten minutes and I'm freezing my butt off. Caffeine ain't gonna make you any less nervous."

"I'm cold, Lisa. My teeth are chattering."

"It's *a hell* of a lot warmer inside. Besides, you're just anxious. You'll get over it once you're in action."

"You really think so?"

"Of course I do. Now come on. You can do this. You think there's anyone inside this building that's tougher than Judge Haller? I don't think so. Besides, I'll be with you every step of the way."

He patted her arm. Exactly who he was reassuring was unclear. "Okay. Okay. Let's go."

They walked arm in arm once they passed through security. Lisa was overwhelmed by the grandeur of the renaissance revival/beaux arts classical structure and snapped pictures as they explored the interior. "Where are we supposed to go?" she asked.

"Mike told me to wait in the attorney's room."

"Who's Mike?"

"Mike Saperstein. Judge Molloy's friend. He said he'd come and find me if he had a case for me."

"Then what?"

"Then I read the defendant's file and meet him in the courtroom for the arraignment."

"That seems pretty quick. How much time do they give you to read the file?"

"Not much. But actually...I'm not sure."

She looked around. "This is a big place. You see a directory?"

He glanced around. "Actually...no."

"Maybe we should ask someone where this attorney's room might be found."

"Forget about that. You want me to look like I'm wet behind the ears? We'll find it on our own."

"Yeah. Of course we will," she said sarcastically. "Get that chip off your shoulder." She flagged down the first man in a suit that passed by. He was tall and athletically built—prematurely balding. "Excuse me...sir. Could you please direct us to the attorney's room."

He stopped and smiled at the pretty brunette. "Why, are you an attorney?"

"No, I'm fuckin' Judge Judy," she sniped. "What's the difference?"

Vinny scowled at him for good measure.

He flashed his palms defensively. "Take it easy now. I just

asked." He pointed in the general direction of the attorneys' room and headed off with a scowl on his face.

"What a creep!" Lisa said.

"Yeah. Friggin' creep," Vinny said. "What's *his* problem?"

The attorney's room was hot and stuffy, crammed with lawyers talking to their clients on cell phones. Two hours passed. Lisa looked so bored she could scream. She was tugging on the collar of her sweater and squirming in her seat when she suddenly smacked him on the arm.

"Ouch! That hurt."

"Sorry."

He rubbed his arm. "What was that for?"

"I don't know...I guess you were handy."

"That's *it*? I was handy?"

"Yeah. You were *handy*. What can I tell you, Vinny? I can't stand it no more—I'm literally jumping out of my skin. How long do they expect you to sit around here?"

"Lisa, that's what lawyers do, except that after they get enough cases they don't have to do this no more."

"Yeah? Well if something doesn't give soon I'm gonna assault somebody and then you can defend me."

Vinny grinned at her dysfunctional remedy just as someone called his name.

"Mr. Gambini?"

He looked up and saw Mike Saperstein making his way toward him. "Mr. Saperstein." He offered his hand but settled for a quick pat on the shoulder. "I been waiting here like you said."

Saperstein dropped a pile of folders on an empty chair and began flipping through them. "They just brought over a big group of defendants from Central Booking and they want to process all of them before lunch." He selected a file. "Here's the complaint, arrest record, and the CJA report. Give this a quick read on your way downstairs. Judge Finch runs the arraignment courtroom like a well-oiled machine. You'll have three, four minutes at most once the case is called. I'll use this case as a barometer of your skills. If it goes well...It's a Class-B misdemeanor. Introduce yourself to the client, waive the public reading, enter a plea, and if applicable, negotiate a low bail amount in thirty seconds or less. You good with that?"

Vinny agreed mechanically.

"Good luck." Saperstein turned and hollered, "Kalish? Where are you, Ben?"

Lisa rushed to his side. "You got a case. That's *great.*"

"Yeah. It's great. I got to read this on my way downstairs, meet my client, and enter a plea all in the time it usually takes me to tie my shoes."

She was quick to point out, "You wear western boots."

"Yeah...that's exactly my point."

CHAPTER EIGHTEEN
Semantics

Vinny approached the holding area, observed the other attorneys as they called out their client's names, and did likewise. "Aidan Boydetto?"

Boydetto was short and narrow across the shoulders with dark curly hair and a good bit of dark stubble, thirtyish. He rose slowly and approached, nodding as he said, "That's me."

With Lisa's help, Vinny had just enough time to read his assigned client's complaint and arrest record before arriving in the courtroom. His memory was sharp and he recalled the short list of details he'd just learned.

It took Vinny a moment to fight through his nervousness. He found Lisa, who was watching him from a seat in the back of the courtroom, smiled gratefully, and dove in. "Hello, Mr. Boydetto, I'm Vincent Gambini, your assigned counsel. I'm here to represent you at arraignment." He glanced over his shoulder to observe Judge Temperance Finch and her handling of defendants, moving them in and out of court with the precision of an assembly line robot. "As you can see, Judge Finch ain't wasting no time up there. In fact, she might call your case at any second."

His mind was flooded with a memory. He was back in the Beechum County courtroom and Judge Haller was berating him for being unfamiliar with courtroom procedure, a lesson he learned at great expense.

"Now I see from your file that this is your first offense, so let me tell you how this works. They're gonna call your docket number and the clerk is going to very briefly read the charges against you. Then the judge is gonna ask me how you plead. I'm guessing you want to plead 'not guilty.'"

"Don't you want to know if I'm guilty or not?" Boydetto asked.

Vinny glanced at the judge again. She seemed to have found another gear and was dispatching cases at breakneck speed. "Actually...no. Like I said, we might get called at any second, so this is all we have time for."

"But I didn't do it."

Vinny rolled his eyes. "Of course not. But you see, the judge don't care about that right now. All she's gonna want to know is how you plead, determine if bail is to be set, and if so, how much? You got that?"

Boydetto nodded. "But I'm not guilty."

Vinny's eyes grew large. "Didn't you hear me? All she wants to hear is 'guilty' or 'not guilty.' We've got—" He was cut short when his client's docket and case number were called. "See what I mean? That's us."

The court officer approached and took Boydetto by the arm.

"Now remember what I said," Vinny reminded him. "I'll say 'not guilty' and you keep your mouth shut."

He watched as his client was escorted before the judge. He glanced over at Lisa, who raised her eyebrows and shooed him in the same direction.

Vinny hustled toward the bench and stood alongside his client. He studied the judge for a moment, then turned to face the ADA. He hadn't recognized him from the back of the courtroom but now realized that he was the gentleman Lisa had rudely rebuffed when they were looking for the attorneys' room earlier that morning. He nervously straightened his necktie and cleared his nostrils.

The ADA gave Vinny a thumbs up that meant *fuck you!*

Judge Temperance Finch was an attractive lady of color with a no-nonsense expression chiseled so deeply that Botox wouldn't have been able to remove the deep creases in her face. She glanced over the top of her glasses at Vinny. "I don't believe I've had the pleasure," she said in a welcoming tone.

"Thank you, Your Honor," he said with a happy lilt in his voice. "The pleasure's all mine."

Her expression changed. It now seemed more amused than businesslike. "That's very gallant, Counselor, but I was hoping you'd introduce yourself to the court."

"Oh. Yeah. Yeah. Right. My name is Vincent Gambini, Your Honor."

She raised an eyebrow. "And you're listed with the bar?"

"Yes, Your Honor, and I was just approved by the Central Screening Committee for 18B work."

She glanced up looking through the courtroom. "Is that correct, Mr. Saperstein?"

He nodded.

"Well then, welcome to my courtroom, Mr. Gambini," she said. "Now without wasting any more time…" She adjusted her glasses and turned to the court clerk. "Please read the charges."

The court clerk read the complaint. "The defendant is charged with issuing a bad check at Speedy Check Cashers at ten-twenty-five Eighteenth Avenue, Brooklyn." He handed the complaint to the judge. "Breach affidavit is signed." He glanced at Vinny. "Waiver of rights not be read, counsel?"

It took Vinny a moment to respond. The ADA turned to him asking, "Yes or no, *rookie?*"

The judge scowled at him.

"Sorry, Your Honor," the ADA said.

The wheels in Vinny's head began to turn. "Yes."

The judge turned to Vinny. "Counselor, this is a Class-B misdemeanor. How does your client plead?"

Vinny opened his mouth to answer but Boydetto beat him to the punch, "I didn't do it?"

Vinny turned to Boydetto, partially covered his mouth, and whispered in a harsh tone, "What did I tell you?"

The judge removed her glasses, her expression turning angry. "Mr. Gambini, have you instructed your client as to plea options at this time and that you will be answering in his behalf?"

"Yes, Your Honor…absolutely. I did."

"Then is it fair to assume that he won't be wasting any more of my time?"

"That's correct, Your Honor."

"Good." She shook her head. "Once again, Mr. Gambini, how does your client plead?"

Boydetto once again blurted, "But I didn't do it." His lips turned down at the corners and his head dropped.

Vinny elbowed Boydetto and grumbled, "Dummy, you want to get held in contempt?"

She huffed and turned toward Vinny, with shooting daggers.

Vinny panicked, remembering the three trips he'd made to an Alabama jail. He made the quick assumption that in New York, bail would be a far more expensive proposition than the paltry two hundred dollars Haller had assessed him for each count of contempt. He quickly cried, "My client pleads 'not guilty,' Your Honor."

"Well hallelujah." She turned to the ADA. "Mr. Doucette, you have any thoughts on bail?"

Doucette quickly studied his notes and then looked up. "Yes, Your Honor. We request the defendant be remanded." He turned to Vinny and winked.

Vinny whispered aside to Boydetto, "You got any money for bail?"

He shook his head, his eyes large, pleading, *No! Please don't let this happen.*

The judge took a moment while she studied the recommen-
dation of the Criminal Justice Agency, facts about the defendant's life, a curriculum vitae of sorts. She spoke without
looking up, "Mr. Gambini, do you have anything to add
before I set bail?"

Vinny had been formulating his argument from the second
the ADA had winked at him and rattled it out in one continu-
ous stream of conscious thought. "Your Honor, as you will
note from the documents prepared by the Criminal Justice
Agency, my client has virtually no savings and doesn't even
have a driver's license. In fact, he's lived in the same apartment for the last eleven years and has worked in the same
slumarea since—"

"Excuse me," she interjected, "did you say, 'slum area?'"

Vinny grinned. "That's correct, Your Honor..." He
glanced at his documents. "Since 2006."

"In a *slum* area?"

"That's correct."

"A slum area?"

"Uh-huh."

"I'm confused, Counselor. Are you saying that the defendant works in a heavily populated urban area characterized
by substandard housing and squalor?"

Vinny finally realized that he was being misunderstood.
"Oh. *I'm* sorry, Your Honor. What I meant to say was *sal-u-
mer-i-a*...a *pork* store," he explained most matter-of-factly.

"Oh my dear Lord." She turned her head and mumbled,
"And they say black people can't be understood." She
gestured to him. "Are you finished, Mr. Gambini?"

"No, Your Honor. The defendant lacks the resources to be
a flee risk. The stable nature of his living arrangement and his
long tenure working in a *sal-u-mer-i-a* show his strong ties to
the community." He raised a finger as he closed. "*This*
coupled with the fact that this is my client's first offense and
that this is an extremely minor infraction should be more than

sufficient proof that Mr. Boydetto can be released on his own recognizance."

Lisa was so impressed with Vinny's argument that she jumped out of her seat and yelped. The judge cast a wary eye in her direction. Lisa sat down but was unable to suppress her immense smile. She pointed to Vinny for the benefit of the woman sitting next to her and boasted, "That's my fiancé."

The judge turned to Vinny. "Mr. Gambini, you may be a little rough around the edges but I like your gumption. And regardless of your recent arrival in my court you're certainly no *rookie*." She turned toward Doucette, the ADA, with a disparaging expression. "The defendant is hereby released on his own recognizance. Preliminary hearing is scheduled for Monday morning at nine a.m." She winked at Vinny and instructed the clerk to call the next case.

Vinny grinned ear-to-ear as the clerk called out, "Docket number KN089986...Joseph Gambini."

CHAPTER NINETEEN
Quid Pro Schmo

Vinny's jaw dropped as the next defendant was led before the bench. "Joe?"

"You know him?" Doucette asked.

He was still bewildered as he answered the ADA. "Um...yeah. He's my brother."

"Two Gambinis in court on the same day? How lucky can a guy get?" Doucette grabbed his case file, flipped it open, and noted the offense. He snickered. "Public lewdness? I can't believe he was actually booked on a two forty-five. This is too funny to be true. It states that your brother mooned a customer at Tiffany's Luncheonette."

Vinny covered his mouth and mumbled, "Fuckin' idiot," before saying to Doucette, "Yeah. He works there. He's a part-time short-order cook."

Doucette thought for a moment, then presented his hand. "I think we got off on the wrong foot. Peter Doucette. Assistant District Attorney for Kings County."

Vinny slowly reached out and took his hand. "Yeah. I'm sorry about that too. We were having a rough morning."

"No hard feelings?" Doucette asked.

"No. None. And thanks for being such a standup guy."

"Sorry I called you a rookie. I guess I was just sore from our encounter downstairs." He whispered in Vinny's ear. "I think the Borough of Brooklyn can survive one quick peek at your brother's rear end, don't you?" He placed his hand on

Vinny's shoulder. "This one's on me." He moved toward his table. "See you around, Counselor."

Vinny grimaced, confused about what he'd just been told.

Lisa looked worried. "What the hell is going on?"

Vinny shrugged. He looked Joe in the eye as he walked past him to Lisa, shaking his head in disbelief.

"What was that all about?" Lisa asked the moment he sat down.

"I'm not sure."

"That bald ADA bustin' your balls?"

He shushed her. "I don't know, Lisa. He said, 'This one's on me.'"

"'This one's on me?' What the hell does that mean?"

"I think he's gonna kick the case."

"But why would he do that?"

"I don't know. Maybe he ain't the bald-headed prick you thought he was."

Vinny could do nothing more than sit and watch as his brother's charges were summarily read. Joe's attorney, a young woman plead, "Not guilty," on Joe's behalf.

Judge Finch turned to the ADA. "Mr. Doucette, are you asking for remand?"

Doucette studied his notes before speaking, "Although not entirely a victimless crime, the incident was not recorded on video. It's a he-said-she-said matter and I see absolutely no need to waste the taxpayer's money on this charge, Your Honor. If the plaintiff wishes to pursue a civil remedy, that's entirely up to her. We move to dismiss."

Lisa's jaw dropped. "Holy crap, Vinny. You were right."

"Don't get too excited. Nothing comes for free. This is a quid pro quo situation."

"Meaning?"

"He did me a favor. Now he expects one in return."

"Oh. Is that so bad?"

"It depends on the favor he's looking for."

The judge dismissed the case.

Joe turned, found them in the courtroom, and projected a euphoric smile.

Vinny shook his head in disbelief. "Even though he got off, Joe's still a fuckin' idiot."

Lisa nodded. "You got that right."

CHAPTER TWENTY
The Quintessential Joe

Vinny tried to get in behind the wheel but Lisa yanked him out of the way. "I'll drive," she said. "Before you put another rod through the hood."

He scowled at her good-humoredly before walking around to the passenger door and getting into the Caddy. He turned to his brother in the backseat. "What the hell, Joe? You dropped your drawers at the luncheonette?"

"Some uppity broad was busting my balls."

Lisa looked at him in the rearview mirror. "Why didn't you just spit in her food like you usually do?"

Joe shrugged. "It was like eleven o'clock. Everyone was on their lunch break and I was there alone. I had to cook *and* serve this pain-in-the-ass woman all at the same time."

"*So?*" Lisa asked.

"So, she complained about everything: her fork was dirty, the chicken was dry, her coffee was cold...yada, yada, yada. She had me bouncing back and forth between her table and the griddle like a goddamn pinball. The nasty old broad was driving me nuts."

"So maybe she was right," Lisa said. "That don't mean you yank down your pants and stick your fat ass in her face."

"She started yelling at me. Then she walked up to the counter and wouldn't stop. She told me that she used to be a tribal princess before she moved here from her native country. She said I should be honored to wait on her."

"Well maybe she was a princess," Lisa said. "That ain't cause to moon her. Is it, Vinny?"

Vinny seemed a little flustered. "I don't know, Lisa. The woman does sound like a real pain in the ass."

"She was so difficult to handle that Joe was within his rights to moon her?"

"I don't know. How do you honor a tribal princess anyway?" Vinny asked. "Was Joe supposed to slaughter *an ox* and present it to her as a sacrificial offering?"

"Stop taking his side."

"Was he supposed to wrestle a camel into submission? Flog a llama? Oh. Oh. I got it. Maybe he was supposed to subdue a wildebeest." He folded his arms and turned his head away.

"Fuck you," she snapped and turned her attention to the road. She drove in silence until they were back in the neighborhood, just down the block from where Augie had his garage. "My dad said he was going to be shorthanded this afternoon on account my brother Dino is off with one of his girlfriends again. I'm gonna see if he needs my help." She put the gear selector in park and opened the door. "See ya later. You can drive Jiggle Butt Joe back to work, Vinny—that is, if he still has a job."

He turned back to see Joe shaking his head.

Lisa paused at the office door and peered into the shop. Augie was alone, standing in front of a 1972 Buick Riviera with a new four-barrel carburetor in his hands. She could see that the old one had already been removed and that the manifold had been prepared for the installation of the new carburetor. She watched in silence while her father stood transfixed, not so much lost in thought, but just lost. He stared at the prepped manifold with a blank expression. Carbureted engines had become rare. Still, Augie had been swapping carburetors since he was eleven years old and could install one in his sleep if he had to.

Her lip twisted as she watched him. She'd seen him like this more and more lately, confused and disoriented. She'd suggested that he go to the doctor a few times but he'd always refused. This time she'd insist, make the appointment, and take him there herself if need be.

"So what's your problem?" she asked as she took the carburetor out of his hands. The fenders and front end were covered with mechanic's blankets. She leaned into the engine bay and positioned the carburetor atop the gasket, aligning the bolt holes in the gasket with those in the body of the carburetor. "What's going on, Pops? You look like you just lost your best friend."

"I skipped lunch." He leaned over and gave her a kiss on the cheek. "My blood sugar must be low." He saw the new carburetor sitting in place just waiting for the installation to be completed. "Put on some coveralls before you get your good clothes dirty." He turned and walked into the office.

Lisa followed him and saw him sitting behind the counter with his arms hanging at his sides. "You're going to the doctor. I'm making you an appointment this week."

"There's nothing wrong with me," he said looking at her as if she were crazy. "All I need is a cup of coffee."

"Bullshit, Dad. You look me in the eye and tell me there's nothing wrong."

"Lisa, you've become a bigger ballbreaker than your mother. What do you want from me?"

"I want you to see a doctor. Let them run a few tests. You've got insurance."

"Bah! Doctors are bullshit—unless you break a bone or something. They don't know what's wrong. They just guess, like anyone else."

"Oh yeah?" She stood in front of him tapping her foot. "Let me ask you something. Say someone drives in with an old Pontiac Firebird and the car makes a sound like a chicken is getting strangled every time the steering wheel is turned. You ain't checked it out yet but you got a pretty good hunch that the steering box was manufactured on a Detroit assembly line at four-thirty on a Friday afternoon and ain't worth a shit, now don't ya?"

"Yeah. So?"

"So what's your guess?"

"About what, Lisa?"

"About what's going on with you?"

"For Christ's sake, Lisa...I told you. I'm fine." He attempted to stand but she put her hand on his shoulder and forced him back into the chair.

"Well *I* got a guess. I'm guessing that smoking since the age of ten has hardened the arteries in your head. That's my guess. You've seen people with severe Alzheimer's. Is that what you want? You want to look at your own daughter one day and not know who she is? You want to lose your dignity?" Her throat tightened and a tear ran down her cheek. She wiped it away. "No. *Screw that.* I'm taking you for a checkup."

He got out of his chair and put his arms around her. He looked into her eyes and for the first time truly understood what she feared. "Okay, baby girl. You don't have to cry...I won't fight you no more...I'll go."

CHAPTER TWENTY-ONE
A Job with Great Benefits

Vinny changed out of his suit and hung it on a proper wooden suit hanger. He pushed aside his leather jacket and made room for it next to the ridiculous burgundy tailcoat he'd been forced to wear before Judge Haller when his only business suit had fallen into the mud and his only option was to shop in a secondhand store. Lisa had since taken it to the drycleaner—it was now fresh and wrapped in plastic. He held it up, gazing at the loud half-inch satin trim on the wide peaked lapels and vest. It would be a keepsake, a reminder of the murder case that had changed his life, the case he desperately worried he might lose.

Hercules Lopez's business card sat atop his dresser. He was feeling invigorated from the arraignment and hurried downstairs to call the prospective client.

The phone rang several times. When the call was finally answered, no one spoke. He heard soft moaning and the sound of a man building to a crescendo. The wailing sounds grew louder and louder and more frequent. "Holy shit," Vinny mumbled. "Do you believe this crap?"

He heard a woman's voice a few moments later. "Hello?"

"Sorry that I *disturbed* you. This is Vincent Gambini calling."

"What you want, *papi?*"

"I *want* to speak to Mr. Lopez. Is he there?"

He heard her say, "Hey, Hercules, it's for you."

Lopez complained in the background. "Shit! Right now?" He came to the phone nonetheless. "Who this?"

"Mr. Lopez, this is Vincent Gambini. We met at the police station the other day." He snickered. "I *hope* this ain't a bad time."

"Oh, Mr. Gambini," he said, his attitude changing immediately. "Sorry, huh? You want to take my case and sue those bastard bankers?"

"Very possibly but I think we should meet to discuss it first. I have some information that might change the way we proceed."

"Wow. You're working on my case already? Sure. You want to come here?" he asked.

Vinny pictured a small apartment filled with lingerie-clad prostitutes lounging about on worn sofas, the carpet sticky to the touch. "Maybe my office would be a better choice."

"Okay. Where's that, Mr. Gambini?"

Vinny checked his notes for the address of the Rent-N-Office space he'd called a few days earlier and gave the address to Lopez. "Will you remember that?"

"Stop that," the woman complained. "Don't use my lipstick to write on my ass."

Vinny smirked.

"Yeah, I got it Mr. Gambini. You know, Giselda doesn't have a client until late tonight. You want me to send you over a package? On the house."

"Is she silver, gold, or bronze?"

"Gold, man...twenty-four karat."

"Thanks, Hercules. But as much as the prospect of tearing into one of your gold packages sends shivers up and down my spine, I'm afraid that I'm a little busy right now. Maybe some other time. No offense, okay?"

"It's cool, Mr. Gambini. I get it."

"Good. So how about we meet tomorrow morning? How's ten o'clock work for you?"

"Ten is good, Mr. Gambini. I'll catch you tomorrow."

Vinny heard him say, "Damn, Giselda. The towel's *cold*." Then the line went dead.

Vinny was feeling encouraged when he hung up. The receiver was still in his hand as the phone rang once more. He assumed that Lopez had forgotten to mention something and was calling right back. "Hello?"

The woman's voice on the end of the line was trembling. "Mr. Gambini?"

"Yes," he said. "Who's this?"

"It's Theresa Cototi, Mr. Gambini...I thought you said I had nothing to worry about?"

"Yeah. I did say that. Why? Is something wrong?"

"Uh-huh." She sniffled. "That detective hauled me back into the police station."

"You're kidding. Don't get worried. I'll come right down."

"Hurry, Mr. Gambini, I think I'm gonna be arrested."

CHAPTER TWENTY-TWO
It's Your Funeral

Vinny got back into his suit and hustled down to the precinct he'd visited a few days before. Winter sunset came early as he drove the short distance to the police station. The sky wasn't quite dark but evening was no more than minutes away. He'd phoned Augie's shop and asked Lisa to get a ride home with her dad, explaining why he couldn't pick her up when the shop closed for the day.

At the station, he asked the desk officer to see his client and was once again told to wait. "I don't need to remind you that once an arrestee has asked for their attorney the police are no longer allowed to question them, do I?"

The desk officer gave him a steely cold stare and turned away. This time all the seats in the waiting area were empty. Nonetheless, Vinny was a creature of habit and took the same seat he'd taken the first time.

The time passed slowly without Hercules Lopez there to regale him with colorful tales of sex workers and lawsuits against national banking institutions.

Still expressionless, the desk officer summoned him with a flick of his hand toward a closed door. He walked through and found Parikh waiting for him on the other side.

"So, Detective *Par-eek*...how's it going?"

Parikh moved off without answering.

Vinny followed him to his desk. "I'd like to see my client."

"You'll want to hear what I have to say first." Parikh sat down at his desk.

Vinny continued to stand, looking down at the seated detective. "Why has my client been brought back for questioning? I thought this was a suicide."

Parikh kicked back in his chair. "Now I'm thinking I might've been wrong. We found a witness who states that your client was on the roof just seconds after the victim fell to his death."

"And did this witness say that my client pushed the victim off the roof?"

"No, but that doesn't mean she didn't do it."

Vinny dismissed the allegation with a wave of his hand. "That don't mean shit. I've discredited plenty of witnesses who thought they saw something they didn't. I'm sure you had a better reason for bringing her in than that."

"Blood."

"Whose blood?"

"The victim's," Parikh said with his eyebrows raised.

"What? That's it? I refuse to believe that the DA believes he can bring a homicide case with evidence as circumstantial as that."

"The crime scene team found random blood smears on the roof."

"How come you never mentioned this before?"

"Someone must've cleaned up the blood because it wasn't visible to the eye but it showed up when we used Luminol. The blood was checked in the lab and the DNA is a thirteen-point match with the victim's."

"Everything you just said is bullshit and don't mean nothin'."

"We've got her footprints on the roof as well."

"I'm still not worried. Now can I see my client or are we gonna keep playing Trivial Pursuit?"

"You must be a very confident lawyer, Mr. Gambini."

"Confident?" Vinny mulled over Parikh's observation. "Only when I know my client's innocent."

"Maybe you're a little overconfident. I'm pretty sure this girl is not as innocent as she seems."

"Are you ready to charge her?" he asked.

"I'm waiting to hear from the DA's office."

"Well then show me to my client."

"It's your funeral," Parikh said. "Follow me, Gambini. I'm just getting warmed up."

CHAPTER TWENTY-THREE
They Got Nothin'

Vinny hurried into the interview room and set his briefcase down on the table.

She stood by the window with her back to him, peering between the holes in the security grating. "Is this what it's like?" she asked, demoralized.

"Is this what *what's* like?"

"Being in prison? Being locked away? Stealing glimpses of the outside from behind prison walls?" She slowly turned so that they were facing one another.

Vinny approached her and placed a hand on each of her shoulders. "Now don't go getting all down on yourself. You ain't been charged with nothin'."

"Not yet."

"Don't go thinking the worst. Did you tell this guy anything, this Detective Parikh?"

She shook her head.

"Anyone else try to question you?"

"No, but Parikh said they have evidence and witnesses. That's when I said I wanted to call you."

"You did the right thing." Vinny was quiet for a moment. "Why don't we sit down?" He directed her to the table. "How long have you been here? Has this clown offered you anything to drink or the use of the restroom?"

"I'm only here a couple of hours, Mr. Gambini. I'm okay."

"You need anything?"

"No, thanks." She dragged the chair away from the table and sat on it, her back slumped and her knees wide apart. "So what do we do now?"

"Now don't worry. The police question people all the time. That doesn't mean they're gonna make an arrest. In most cases, the police discuss what they've got with the district attorney, and he's the one who decides whether the evidence is strong enough to make a case. They say they got a witness that saw you on the roof seconds after Sam fell but the annals of court history are full of witnesses who think they saw something."

"But I told you already—I was never on the roof," she said with panic in her voice. "How could they say that I was?"

"It don't mean shit, Theresa. And the fact that they found some of your boyfriend's blood..." Vinny cracked his neck and then leaned his chin on thatched fingers. "That don't mean that you were involved."

"So you don't think I'll be arrested?"

"I would hope not."

"I was asleep when they say the accident took place. I didn't even know that Sammy had gotten out of bed."

"Yeah. I remember that." He drummed his fingers on the table.

"What's bothering you?"

"What's bothering me is that the victim's brother is a deputy mayor and very high up in the city's administration. So the DA ain't just gonna bury his head in the sand because, sure as shit, he don't want to damage his relationship with the mayor, or hurt his chances for reelection. And the deputy mayor's brother was a recent ex-con, so a lot of negative publicity is the last thing anyone in City Hall is gonna want."

She began to tear up. "They're going to make me a scape-goat, aren't they?"

"Nonsense, why would you even say that?"

"Because, it's fast and easy. Think about it. I'm a stripper dating an ex-con. I watch TV. I know how they'll paint me. They'll make me look like some kind of lowlife slut."

"There, there." Vinny patted her hand. "I can see why you'd be worried but don't go jumping to no conclusions. You're forgetting one very important thing."

"And what's that?"

"Motive. Why would you do it?"

"I wouldn't. I loved Sammy. I waited seven years for him to get out of prison." She'd convinced herself that he was right and smiled weakly. "You really think so? You really think I'll be okay?"

"Of course, dear. All of their evidence is circumstantial. They ain't got a thing. I mean except for the witness. But I ain't too worried about that. They say they found your footprints on the roof." He picked at a tooth. "You sure you ain't been up there recently?"

"It's crazy cold outside. Why would I go up there?"

"That's what I thought."

"That bothers you though, doesn't it?"

"From a trial perspective...no, but from an evidentiary perspective...a little bit. Yeah. I don't like it. It's looking more and more like Sammy was killed and not so much like he took his own life, so someone's going to trial. I just hope it ain't you. Can you think of anyone who might want to kill Sammy?"

The blood drained from her face. "Do you really believe that Sammy was murdered?"

He weighed the premise, moving his head side to side. "That's what I think...*yeah*. So, if we can produce a person of interest, someone who might've wanted Sammy dead..." He was being brave for her sake, but was worried that it was only a matter of time before she was arrested. "Think, Theresa. Who might've wanted to have Sammy killed?"

"I have no idea. He was in jail so long. I just don't know."

He patted her knee. "Don't worry, dear. We'll figure it

out." But he sighed a troubled sigh.

"I can see it on your face. This isn't going away, is it?"

"The more I think about it...I don't think so...no. It ain't going away. I need to think of a strategy so that—"

He heard the door opened behind him, and was surprised to see Theresa smile with relief.

"Tony," she blurted as she stood up tall, her expression suddenly optimistic. "Thank God."

She moved toward him, her arms wide to throw around the man who'd helped her get through the long ordeal of Sammy's incarceration.

But as Vinny turned around, he saw Parikh move in front of the deputy mayor and reach for his cuffs.

Her eyes went wide with terror when she saw the cuffs in Parikh's hand. "Tony. Tony. What's going on? Can't you stop this?" But the man she expected to come to her rescue was silent, his eyes cold and harsh.

Parikh reached for her arm to cuff her. "Ms. Theresa Cototi," he said, "you are under arrest."

CHAPTER TWENTY-FOUR
War Hats?

Theresa was taken to her arraignment trial, but not before midnight had come and gone. She'd been read her rights and rushed down to central bookings.

Vinny didn't have much experience with New York arrest protocol, but it occurred to him that his client's file had been processed with lightning speed and whisked through a process he believed normally took most of a day, several hours at minimum. The deputy mayor was likely working behind the scenes to see his brother's killer punished with the greatest possible speed. The file had been red flagged and was getting top priority.

His adrenaline was spent. He felt absolutely exhausted as Theresa was brought before the judge. The time on the large wall clock read 3:45 a.m. He'd had several cups of coffee but the caffeine wasn't helping. He felt clammy and nauseous from a combination of nerves and fatigue.

Ever dutiful, Lisa had gotten a ride downtown from Augie and looked like a mob wife sitting in the back of the courtroom wearing a kerchief over her head and dark sunglasses to mask her bloodshot eyes.

Theresa's rapid processing allowed Vinny little time to confer with her on the case or decide on a strategy.

The court clerk looked as if he wanted to be anywhere else but where he was and frowned when Vinny refused to waive the lengthy reading of the complaint. He already knew what was going to be read but wanted to hear it objectively, thinking that the words coming from someone else's mouth might jar free an idea that would ignite his thought process.

It didn't.

And when the clerk read, "Murder in the first degree," Vinny was shaken to the point that he had trouble stringing his thoughts together and coming up with an argument for bail.

Peter Doucette was the assigned ADA. He shook his head when Vinny looked over and mouthed, "Not this time."

Anthony Cipriani sat behind Doucette, staring at Theresa with loathing. He mouthed, "You conniving little bitch!"

Vinny ran his finger inside his shirt collar to loosen it because he felt as if a noose were tightening around his neck. *Think. Think.*

The honorable Larsen Whorhatz pressed the back of his head against his chair forcing the folds of his bloated neck to push forward and engulf his chin. Deeply cut lines that delineated his jowls framed his mouth. His eyes were dark and recessed. Vinny thought he felt the judge's eyes on him, but when he looked up, Whorhatz was studying the complaint.

He turned to Vinny, studying him as if he were under a microscope. "It's an arraignment not a firing squad, Mr. Gambini. How does your client plead?"

"'Not guilty,' Your Honor."

Whorhatz turned to the ADA. "I imagine you're going to ask for remand, Mr. Doucette?"

"We are, Your Honor." Doucette pried off his glasses and made direct eye contact with Whorhatz. "Judge, Ms. Cototi is accused of first-degree murder. She is accused of savagely pushing the victim off the roof of an eight-story building in an act of premeditated murder."

Whorhatz pressed the pads of his fingers together. "You have a witness to substantiate this allegation?"

"We do, Your Honor. This is an open-and-shut case of

premeditated murder. The defendant hails from Ohio and has few ties to the community. The defendant is a stripper, Your Honor and—"

Vinny shouted hotly, "I object, Your Honor."

Whorhatz seemed to find the outburst amusing. He tilted his head, appearing inquisitive. "You have...an objection?"

"Yes, Your Honor. The assistant DA has belittled my client with his callous reference to her occupation, and has violated the federal rule of selective or vindictive prosecution." He concluded his statement by poking the air with his finger.

Lisa ripped off her sunglasses and blurted, "Holy shit! That was great."

Whorhatz scoured the courtroom. Finding Lisa, he said, "I take it you're impressed with the defense attorney's objection, Miss...?"

Lisa stood. "Vito, Your Honor. Mona Lisa Vito."

"Well Ms. Vito, is this your first time in a court of law?"

"Oh no, Your Honor. I've been to court many times."

"And despite all your accumulated courtroom experience, you were sufficiently moved by this objection to make an outburst?"

"Sorry about that, Your Honor. But yeah, I thought what the defendant's attorney said was really great."

He pursed his lips. His stoic countenance resolved into a small grin. "So did I...but in the future, please try to express your enthusiasm quietly. Can you do that?" he asked politely.

Lisa nodded eagerly before turning to Vinny with a beaming smile.

"Mr. Gambini, the ADA has every right to express his thoughts regarding remand and bail without objections during arraignment. However..." He turned to the court reporter. "Please strike the word 'stripper' from the record and replace it with 'exotic dancer.'" He grinned at Vinny before turning to Doucette. "Please continue."

Doucette nodded. "Thank you, Your Honor. As I was saying, Ms. Cototi is an...exotic dancer." He turned, seeking Vinny's approval. "As a rule of thumb, these women generally earn lots of cash tips, and despite her claimed meager net worth, she likely has access to a great deal of non-memorialized savings—in other words, mattress money. It also stands to reason that in her line of work, she likely has access to many reprobate individuals who could assist her in leaving the state. We believe this makes the defendant a flight risk and we ask for remand without bail."

Whorhatz nodded to indicate he'd noted the ADA's points before turning to Vinny. "Mr. Gambini, I've known you all of about five minutes but I have the sense that you're going to disagree."

"That's right, Your Honor. Everything the ADA said was..." He was aching to say "bullshit" but remembered just how well that had gone over with Judge Haller. "Contrived."

"Care to elaborate?" Whorhatz asked.

"Yes, Your Honor, I would. The prosecutor has done nothing but cast aspersions as to Ms. Cototi's character. He's painted her as a call girl who consorts with criminals and hides her income from the Internal Revenue Service, when in fact, Ms. Cototi is a hardworking single individual with a stable job history."

"Stable for a stripper," Doucette wisecracked.

Whorhatz cut him down with a stare. "Take it like a man, Mr. Doucette...Continue, Mr. Gambini."

"As I said, Ms. Cototi has a stable job history and we can document her reported income. She pined away for *seven long years*, waiting for Samuel Cipriani to get out of jail and paid him frequent visits while he was incarcerated." He'd been on a roll but realized that he'd run out of ammunition. "I think that more than proves her dedication and devotion to the victim, and ask that a reasonable bail amount be set...that's it."

Whorhatz scribbled a note. "Thank you, Mr. Gambini. I'm looking forward to seeing more of you in my courtroom." He leaned back in his chair. "While I agree with the defense attorney that the defendant is not a scamp nor a tax cheat and that she remained devout to Mr. Cipriani while he was incarcerated, this is a capital murder offense. Bail is set at five million dollars."

Vinny was aghast by what he considered to be an excessive bail amount. His mouth fell practically to his knees. "Five million dollars?" he muttered. "Why didn't you just make it a billion?"

Whorhatz narrowed his eyes. "Did you say something, Mr. Gambini?"

Panicked, he replied, "Um...I'm famished, Your Honor, and I was thinking about what I should get to eat once I'm done with court...and I said to myself, *huh*, how about *Brazilian*? I mean I ain't had a good Brazilian meal in a seriously long time."

"Is that right?" Whorhatz asked skeptically. He banged his gavel. "I'll hear preliminary arguments this coming Monday at nine-thirty a.m. Next case!"

CHAPTER TWENTY-FIVE
Ma?

The sun was rising as they trudged up the stairs to the house. Vinny's legs were so tired and rubbery they could barely carry him. Lisa stood alongside him with her eyes closed as he slipped the key into the lock and turned it. They heard the clatter of pots and pans as the door opened.

Vinny shrugged. "Ma?"

Lisa's reaction was identical. "Ma?"

"Finally. I thought maybe they threw the two of you in the hoosegow along with Vinny's client," Ma said as she unpacked one of several grocery bags.

"That's not funny, Ma," Lisa said as she dragged her weary body into the kitchen and planted a kiss on her cheek.

"Well, after all the trips he made to the state jail when he was in Alabama...I figured maybe he learned to like it."

Vinny sneered at her comically before favoring her with a kiss of his own. He glanced around at the shopping bags. "So what are you doing with all this here *stuff*?"

She playfully bonked him on the forehead with the heel of her hand. "What does it look like I'm doing. I figured you'd both be hungry and tired. I bought a few things so that I could make you breakfast."

"A few things?" he asked. "Did you say a few things?"

"What do you want from me?" she asked dryly. "They had a big sale."

"A big sale?" Lisa asked. "You got enough stuff here to

feed all the homeless people in Bensonhurst. Who else is coming for breakfast?"

"Lay off me, would ya, Lisa. Where's it written that a mother can't give her daughter a little help once in a while. You kids have been away for months. Your poor fiancé, he's been living off grits and ham hocks so long he'd probably squeal if I poked him. When's the last time he had a good dish of spaghetti?"

"A couple of nights ago, Ma." Lisa folded her arms waiting for a snappy comeback.

She seemed surprised. "Really? My daughter the grease monkey pulled her head out from under a car chassis long enough to make a nice home-cooked meal?" She pinched Lisa's cheek. "That's my girl. Why don't the two of you go wash up? I'll whip up some bacon and eggs and have it ready for you by the time you come back."

"I don't even have the strength to lift the fork to my mouth," Vinny said. "I just want to go upstairs and get in bed. I have to meet a client at ten then head over to Rikers Island to talk to the woman that was arraigned last night. I got barely enough time to grab a catnap and get showered, shaved, and dressed." He rested his weary head on hers. "Next time, okay?" he asked before turning and ambling off.

"What about French toast?" she shouted. "I stopped at the kosher bakery and got a fresh challah."

Vinny waved bye without looking and headed up the stairs.

"What about you?" Ma turned to Lisa. "Want some of your mother's special French toast?"

"You want to make French toast? That's good with me. I'll help."

"Nonsense." She shooed Lisa away. "I made fresh coffee. Pour yourself a cup and talk to me while I beat the eggs."

Lisa yawned and trudged over to the coffee pot, peeking into the grocery bags along the way. "Thanks for buying all these groceries, Ma. I've picked up a few things since we got back but I haven't had time to do a big shopping."

"But you had time to rebuild the valve train on the Caddy."

"What? You saying I ain't gonna make Vinny a good wife or something? Vinny was gonna fix the Caddy himself but I told him to go get some cases. We spent almost everything we had when we were in Alabama. We ain't got five cents between us."

"I understand. Trust me, honey. I know that you can't live without money. I'm just saying..."

"*What?* Saying *what?*"

"Well when your father and I got married, I used to get up at six in the morning on Sunday to make him fresh sauce with meatballs, sausage, and braciole. We'd have the whole family over and I mean aunts, uncles, and cousins...even the ones I didn't care for like pain-in-the-ass Aunt Mathilda. We'd eat from three o'clock in the afternoon until ten, and I'd bake Italian cookies and cheesecake for dessert."

"Oh yeah? How are you at rebuilding an engine?"

Ma showed the back of her hand. "Don't get wise. Vinny's job is to make a good living for the two of you and your job is to keep him happy."

"Oh really? That's a very enlightened perspective you have. Times have changed, Ma. How about if we both make money and we both keep each other happy?"

"*Bah,* that only works in theory. For crying out loud—why do you think so many couples are getting divorced these days? The man goes out to work and the woman stays home with the kids. That's the way it's supposed to be."

"So what you're saying is it's a woman's job to cook, shop, clean the house, do the laundry, raise the kids, and fuck her husband senseless."

"Whoa! Language." She sprinkled cinnamon into the beaten eggs and added a splash of cream. "You can't argue with success, Lisa. You know what they say about the way to a man's heart being through his stomach."

"Believe me," Lisa began in a cynical tone. "Anyone who believes that the way to a man's heart is through his stomach has a shitty sense of direction. Besides, Ma, we ain't even married yet and the way things are going..." She frowned.

Her mother dropped the whisk and hurried over to her. "Oh no. What's wrong, Lisa? Is he seeing other women? While I'll—"

"Vinny?" She smirked and her eyes went wide. "Ma. No. Please. Vinny doesn't know other women exist. It's just that..."

Ma covered her mouth. "Don't tell me he's got a wet noodle."

Lisa hacked out a laugh. "Now you're embarrassing *me.*"

"*What* then?"

Lisa looked into her mother's eyes and then off into the distance. "Vinny's not romantic. I mean I know he loves me and all but he's got no idea of how to show it."

She thought for a moment. "Maybe you need to try new things. You know...in the bedroom."

"Ma! There's a difference between sex and romance. Vinny doesn't have any performance issues. It's just that he treats me like..."

Ma seemed confused. "Like what?"

"Well, like one of the guys. He don't bring me flowers or say sweet things. It's not that he don't care for me, he just doesn't understand what he's supposed to do. The man is fuckin' clueless."

"This got anything to do with his dyslexia?"

"No, Ma. He's just not sentimental. He doesn't get the reason for candlelit dinners and walks along the beach. It just ain't in him."

"So what are you going to do about it? You can't wait until he gets set in his ways."

Lisa blew out a sigh. "I don't know. And right now he's so worried about his career and making a living...well it just ain't a good time."

"I thought the two of you were going to get married right after Vinny won his first case."

"That was the plan. Yeah. He proposed to me you know. We were driving back and he said, 'I thought we'd get married this weekend.'"

"And what did you say?" she asked excitedly.

"I told him I wanted a real wedding. You know, a church wedding."

She sighed. "You've got some soul searching to do, Lisa. A man is either romantic or he's not. If you love Vinny, you have to decide if he's good enough for you just the way he is."

"Or what's the alternative?" she asked.

"Or you move on."

"Move *on*? *I* love him. I don't want to *move on*."

Ma shrugged. "Then I think you just answered your own question."

Lisa looked unsettled. "Yeah, I don't know. Like you said, I have to do some soul searching." She took a sip of coffee. "By the way..." She took a deep breath. "Not to change the subject but I think Dad is getting worse."

She pressed a thick slice of challah bread into the egg batter until it was fully saturated, then dropped it in the skillet. There was a tear in her eye when she looked up. "He's been fighting me, tooth and nail, Lisa. Did you tell him he's got to go to the doctor?"

"Oh I told him all right. I told him I was going to make an appointment for him if he didn't do it on his own."

"Do you think he'll go? You know how strong willed he is."

She took another sip of coffee. "He'll go, even if I have to drag him there by the scruff of his neck." She placed her coffee mug firmly on the counter. "Speaking of which...where did I put the phonebook? I'm gonna make him an appointment right now."

CHAPTER TWENTY-SIX
You Want to Ask Me Some Questions?

Vinny was groggy as he lumbered into the rented office he'd secured for his meeting with Hercules Lopez. He was functioning on two hours of sleep and three cups of coffee. Unfortunately, multiple doses of the stimulant had given him the runs. He'd just come back from the men's room when he heard Vanessa, the office receptionist, talking with Lopez as she escorted him down the hallway.

She was a curvy girl wearing a sweater dress and pumps. Lopez followed her, taking full advantage of the view from the rear.

"*Aye, mami,* you do this full time?" Lopez asked, his eyes all over her.

"The name is Vanessa."

"Yeah, yeah, sorry. Vanessa, you're a pretty girl. You want to make some extra cash?"

She turned up her nose. "I don't think so."

"Don't say 'no' so fast. It's a great opportunity."

"Doing what?"

"Delivering packages. It's part time work and it pays great."

"Packages? Do I look like a goddamn UPS man to you?"

"No, no, *mami.* You got it all wrong." He attempted to hand her his card. "Call me. I got a good opportunity for you. You can make up to sixty percent of the total invoice."

She stopped in her tracks, took the card, and grinned at

him mockingly. "I go to law school in the evening but I'm sure your opportunity has that waste of time beat cold. Are you trying to tell me that all I have to do is deliver your packages and I get sixty percent of the total?"

"That's right."

"I don't get it."

"Well, that's because you're going to have some expenses."

"Yeah? Like what?"

"Wear and tear on your car. You drive, don't you?"

"Uh-huh. I've got a car. What else?"

"Clothes."

"I've got clothes."

"Specific clothes."

"You mean like a uniform?"

"More or less...*mostly less*," he said under his breath.

"Does that cover all of my overhead?"

"You'll need a doctor's exam."

"Why? To prove I'm fit for work?"

"Exactly. Actually all you need is a blood test."

"A blood test? Why?"

"Just to make sure you don't give nothing to nobody."

"I don't get it. How can I not 'give nothing to nobody' if it's my job to deliver packages? That's redundant isn't it?"

"Don't worry, *mami*. You'll figure it out."

"Anything else?"

"No. That covers it, Vanessa. I supply everything else. Call me. I'll hook you up. You'll make enough cash to put yourself through law school. Honest."

Vinny met them at the door and smiled when he saw that Lopez was still wearing a cervical collar. He offered his hand. "Hercules, thanks for coming in. Come right over here and have a seat."

They shook hands. "You've got a very sweet girl working for you, Mr. Gambini. She's gold package material." He turned to Vanessa with a big smile, put his thumb to his ear

114

and his pinkie near his lips. "Call me, *mami.* I'll show you the ropes." He walked past Vinny and sat down at the desk.

Vinny escorted her to the door.

"Hey, is this legit?" Vanessa asked in a hushed whisper.

Vinny had heard the entire pitch. His eyes went wide and he pointed his fingertips toward his throat, waving them back and forth in a desperate effort to convey his message. He mouthed, "Ixnay. Ixnay. Not a chance," and shooed her away.

She noted his cue and dashed off.

Vinny drew a deep breath before closing the door and turning toward Lopez.

"Your receptionist is one sweet little treat," Lopez said. "You don't mind if I help her out, do you?"

Vinny walked around the desk and sat down. "You know I don't think she's gonna work out, Hercules."

"How come?"

"She goes to the ENT all the time?"

"The ENT?"

"Yeah, the ear, nose, and throat doctor. She's got a terrible gag reflex. Can't even eat one of them baby carrots without tossing her cookies. I'm sorry."

Lopez seemed dubious. "For real?"

Vinny nodded.

"Man, that's too bad. A big-boned girl like her...guys pay extra for that. She'd clean up."

"Yeah. Well...*sorry.* Anyway, I see you're still wearing your collar. How are you feeling?"

He grinned. "I'm feeling like you're going to make me a rich man." He reached into his jacket pocket for a folded piece of paper. "So, Mr. Gambini, if you don't mind. Some of the girls thought I should ask you some questions before I hire you. That okay?"

Vinny was taken aback. "Let me get this straight. Your *employees* think that you should *voir dire* me to ascertain if

I'm qualified to handle your case? Is that right?"

Lopez wrinkled his nose. "*Voir* what? Is that like being a voyeur? Because I ain't calling you no peeping Tom."

"No, it don't mean *voyeur*. It means that you want to question me to check out my qualifications." Vinny leaned forward in his chair. "I mean that makes perfect sense—coming from your gold package call girls and all. I mean they must get *voir dired* all the time." Vinny paused, then grinned. "Let's see if I can guess what the girls get asked most often." He rubbed his chin as if deep in thought. "Oh, here's one. Do you have crabs and *if so*, do I have to buy a full dozen? Is half-and-half on the menu and is it ultra-pasteurized? Or my personal favorite—If I go around the world with you, how many mileage points do I get and which airlines accept them?" Vinny folded his arms and gazed at Lopez defiantly. "How'd I do? Did I nail it? I wonder if Letterman ever did a top ten list of questions hookers gets asked before they put out."

"Gee, easy, man," he showed his palms and apologized. "I didn't know you'd take it personally. I just wanted to know if you've had any experience with this kind of case before and how it went?"

"You want to know what kind of experience *I've* had? Not a problem, but before I answer you, maybe we should talk about who we're actually going to sue."

Lopez turned his head askew. "I don't get you."

"I've done some research and I'm not sure we have a case against the bank."

"We don't?" Lopez asked, sounding confused. "Then what am I doing here?"

"Our case, my hoe-peddling friend, is against the MTA, the New York subway system."

"Where'd you get that from?"

"You see, Hercules, the grease you slipped on most likely came from a passing train on the el. The grease works its way out of the wheel hubs and falls to the ground below. Now, the law has been written in such a way as to protect the MTA from incidents just like this, *but...*" He raised a finger. "If we can prove that it was in fact grease from a passing train you slipped on, and that the routine maintenance on said subway cars was overdue, *then* we have cause to file a complaint on the basis of negligence, and *that* is a case I think we can win."

Lopez smiled. "That's great. I friggin' love you, Mr. Gambini. How do we prove it was train grease I slipped on?"

He glanced at Lopez with a sly expression. "Do you still have the shoes you were wearing when you took that nasty spill?"

"Yeah. Made a mess out of a new pair of Jordans."

"And by Jordans, do you mean basketball shoes?"

"Yeah, why?"

"And do these basketball shoes have grooved soles to assist with traction? Grooves in which some of that grease might still reside?"

Lopez nodded happily.

"Then all we have to do is have a sample of the grease analyzed to see if it matches the grease used on the wheel hubs on the subway cars, and if it does..."

"We nail the SOBs?" He jumped out of his chair. "I knew there was something I liked about you, Mr. Gambini." He scratched his groin. "I think my spider sense is tingling."

Vinny glanced at his crotch and grimaced. "Uh...you sure that you ain't got crabs?"

Lopez laughed. "No, man, my girls are clean. So you think we can make some money on this?"

"Maybe. Hopefully. But it'll take quite a bit of work. We have to prove that the MTA was negligent with its maintenance, and we have to do this all within ninety days of the accident so that we can file a timely notice of claim. After that, you can expect the suit to take from eighteen to twenty-four months from start to finish." Vinny wore a confident expression. "Now, about those questions you wanted to ask me…"

CHAPTER TWENTY-SEVEN
Mea Culpa

Vinny was jotting down notes when he heard someone clearing their throat. He looked up and saw Vanessa standing in the doorway of his office.

"You've got another visitor, Mr. Gambini. This one doesn't look like a total douchebag."

"Yeah...sorry about the last guy. I mean he's all right but I don't think you want to get to know him any better than you already do."

"Is he a crook?"

"A crook? No, he ain't no crook. I wouldn't represent anyone like that. He's just very intense about his business. I don't think the two of you would work well together. Anyway, I ain't expecting no one else. Who's here?"

She looked down at her secretary's pad. "A distinguished looking man. Henry Molloy?"

Vinny's eyes grew wide. "Judge Molloy? Here? Send him right in. He's a good friend of mine." He hurried out into the hallway. "Judge Molloy, what are you doing here?"

He patted Vinny on the back. "Can't I stop in to see my old friend?"

"Of course. It's just that I wasn't expecting you. How'd you find me?"

"I spoke to your lovely fiancée on the phone. She gave you up in a heartbeat."

"Sit down. Sit down. They got coffee here. Can I get you a cup?"

"No need to fuss, Vinny. I just wanted a few minutes of your time."

"Sure, Judge Molloy. What's up? Is there something you wanna say to me?"

"Yes." Molloy paused. "There's something I have to tell you. I wanted to tell you sooner but I didn't want to dissuade you from taking Ms. Cototi's case on you own."

"I don't get it. How'd you even know about that?"

"Did you ever wonder why Ms. Cototi called you?"

"Yeah. I mean, I asked her and she said a friend told her to call me. She didn't want to give me a name or nothing and well...I guess I forgot about it."

"She got your name from me."

"*You*, Judge Molloy? *You* told her to call me?"

"That's right." He seemed to grow sad. "Her parents, Ray and Lydia...Nice people—they didn't get the time they deserved on this earth. Ray was an old friend from law school. He graduated, married Lydia, and moved to Ohio where Theresa was from originally." He paused and swallowed with great difficulty. "Lydia lost her battle with cancer when Theresa was just fourteen, and Ray...he was never the same afterwards. Walked out into traffic one day and...I don't know what to say, Vinny—I'm her godfather. Been keeping tabs on her since Ray passed on...I know she's a stripper, but that doesn't make her a bad person. I think things would've turned out differently if she'd had her folks around a while longer. I...well, I kind of feel responsible for her."

"I gotta say, Judge, I'm glad you had enough faith in me to give me the case. I'm sure you know a lot of seriously accomplished lawyers at gigantic law firms who could do the job, but you sent Theresa to me anyway. That means a lot to me, Judge. I won't never forget it."

"I know a ton of good lawyers, Vinny, but none that I

thought would put their heart and soul into her defense the way I know you will. There's just one question I have to ask."

Vinny seemed concerned. "What's that, Judge?'

"You're going up against a deputy mayor, not directly of course but you'd be foolish to think he's not going to exert his influence on the DA. So tell me straight up, Vinny, can you handle that kind of pressure or are you going to let the man scare the smarts right out of you?"

"Me? Scared? I think you know better than that. Judge Molloy, I boxed some of the biggest bastards you ever seen, guys who could drive nails into a two-by-four with their bare hands. There were a few times I got my head handed to me so bad I didn't know where I was. You think a couple of guys in suits is gonna intimidate me?" He rolled his eyes. "I don't *think* so."

CHAPTER TWENTY-EIGHT
A Parikh by Any Other Name

Lopez had signed a letter of engagement naming Vinny as his legal representative. It resided in Vinny's briefcase along with the other cases in his starter collection, the one signed by Boydetto, the bad check passer, and most importantly, the one signed by Theresa Cototi. As he and Lisa approached Rikers Island in the Caddy, the notion of having a swelling caseload made him smile.

He checked in at the security gate and was directed to a parking space.

"You know what I think?" Lisa said in an exuberant tone. "I think you're really on your way. You've got cases coming in and you're developing a real daily routine. You're an honest to God lawyer, Vinny." She threw her arms around him and kissed him on the cheek several times. She looked deeply into his eyes. "You know what?" she began in an impish tone. "I'm really proud of you." She nuzzled his neck. "We ain't never done it in a prison parking lot," she said and caressed his chest with her fingertips.

"Lisa! Lisa! Get a grip," he said. "Are you out of your mind? They got guards and security cameras everywhere. The last thing I need is a video of my fat ass surfacing somewhere I don't want it seen."

"I can't help it," she purred. "You've got me all turned on. I love it when you're all freewheeling and in charge like you are now. And here, next to the prison...I'm a bad girl. Punish me, Counselor. Threaten me with writs of habeas corpus or something...*anything.*"

"What? Do you even know what that means?"

"No."

"It means to produce a body."

She began to unbutton her shirt. "You want a body, Counselor? Here you *go*. My heart's pumping, my hormones are surging, and I'm ready to be treated like a hostile witness." Her blood pressure rose and her cheeks grew flush. "God forgive me, I want to do you right here and now."

"Lisa, have you lost it? An innocent woman is in prison on murder charges. I got to have a clear head when I meet with her."

"Really? Not even a quickie?"

"Lisa, I'm functioning on two hours of sleep. I got more cases than I've ever had before, and a client who's accused of killing the deputy mayor's brother."

She slid her hand down his shirt but he grabbed it before it arrived at its intended destination. "Stop it. Just stop it." He exhaled through his nostrils. "I tell you what. When we get finished here we'll go have dinner, then we'll go home early, and...well you know."

She began to fan her face, playacting, halfheartedly attempting to cool down. "This is terribly disappointing. I ain't never had prison yard sex before."

"Yeah? Well if they catch us screwing in the parking lot you're gonna get all the prison yard sex you can handle and then some. Can't you at least wait until I'm done with my work?"

"If I have to *and* you promise we'll have a nice romantic evening. Okay? You promise?"

"Of course I promise."

"Where do you want to go?"

"For dinner?"

"Uh-huh."

"Do I have to think about that right now? I'm trying to focus on the meeting with my client."

"Okay. Forget it." She said, somewhat upset.

"Lisa, don't do that to me. We'll go to a nice place. I promise."

"I just thought that maybe you had an idea about where you wanted to go. That's all."

"If I pick a place will you get off my back?"

She nodded.

"How about that new place on Benson Avenue?"

"The place that's always empty?"

"I doubt it's always empty. People are talking about it all the time."

"That's right. They are. Except you never took the time to listen to what they were actually saying, did you?"

His forehead wrinkled. "Why? Just what the hell are they saying?"

"That the place sucks. It's always fuckin' empty!"

CHAPTER TWENTY-NINE
Pocket Change

Once inside Rikers, they checked in with security. Vinny presented his bar card and driver's license photo ID.

The female guard glanced at Lisa, who looked smoking hot in a flame red minidress and heels. As always, her gorgeous mile-long legs preceded her. "Is she a lawyer, too?" the guard asked.

"Uh, no," Vinny said. "This is Ms. Vito, my legal assistant."

The guard seemed perturbed. "She plan on going inside wearing that?"

Lisa scrutinized her outfit, not understanding the guard's question. "Yeah. Why? What's wrong with it?"

"You can't go in there showing all that skin. You'll incite a riot."

"I know I look good, but a riot?"

"Ain't this an all-women's facility?" Vinny asked.

"That's right. It is," the guard said with assurance in her voice. "And it's one hundred percent lesbian free. Lady, you go in there like that and you'll have more hands up your skirt than a bride at a seamstresses' convention. You got something to change into? Like a pair of pants maybe?"

"Pants? You think I've got a pair of pants in my bag? No, I ain't got a pair of pants."

The guard reached under the counter and handed Lisa a pair of black cotton drawstring pants. "Now you do. That's ten dollars for the rental. You can drop them off on the way out."

Lisa examined the worn, stained, and lint-covered garb dispassionately. "I ain't wearing that hideous thing. It's absolutely disgusting."

"It's up to you, ma'am, but you're not getting in the way you are," the guard said.

Lisa grimaced. "Holy shit. Vinny, can't you do nothing?"

"What do you want me to do? Just slip them on so we can get in."

Lisa was seething. "Yeah? Well don't come crying to me when I give you the crabs." She gritted her teeth and reluctantly yanked the pants off the counter.

"How about your bra?" the guard asked.

"What about my bra?" Lisa asked indignantly.

"Underwire?"

"Yeah. What's wrong with that?"

"The metal detector is sensitive. It'll set it off."

"This is getting ridiculous. Now I got to take off my fuckin' bra?"

The guard nodded.

"Fine," she huffed.

"And your hair."

"*What?*"

"Your hair."

"What's wrong with my hair?"

"It's big, ma'am."

"*Big?*"

"Yeah, it's big. You've got it teased up with tons of hairspray. You could be hiding almost anything up in there."

Lisa lost it. "My hair? My fuckin' hair? What the hell do you want me to do? Shave my goddamn head? I ain't got nothing in my hair. You think I'm smuggling the prisoner a Colt automatic up there?"

"Large hair pins, sharp objects..." the guard rattled off a

list. "Anything you could pass to a prisoner that could be used to cause harm." She pulled a pair of blue nitrile gloves out of a box and snapped them on.

Lisa laughed. "If you think you're gonna touch my hair you've got another guess coming. I worked an hour on my hair this morning."

The guard stood and leaned over the reception counter. "You want to get in or not?"

Lisa stared at Vinny, her gaze slicing flesh from the bone. "*Fuck you, Vinny.* You had no idea this was gonna happen?"

"You think I had any idea about this? What do you want me to say? I'm sorry. Anyway, she's got gloves on."

"All right. But she better not make a mess out of it," she warned.

"Yes, your majesty."

Lisa grimaced while the guard pressed on her hair, feeling for foreign objects and doing her best to make a mess of her carefully coiffed hair.

"My God," the guard said. "You'd think I was performing a cavity search."

Lisa scowled. "Don't you even think about it."

The guard finished and turned to Vinny as Lisa pulled out her compact and frantically checked her appearance. "What about you, handsome? You got anything that'll set off the metal detector? Keys, cell phone, a metallic pen...a gun or a knife?" she bantered as she noticed that he was wearing several gold rings, a gold chain, and a gold bracelet. "All that bling got to go, Kanye."

"Uh, yeah, I got all those things. Um...except for the knife and gun of course. What do you want me to do with them?"

"Lockers are opposite the visitor restrooms. You can leave them in there. Twenty-five cents."

He checked his pockets. "Hey, Lisa...you got a quarter?"

She huffed with exasperation, arched her neck, and shook her head in disbelief.

* * *

"I look ridiculous," Lisa complained as they walked back to the prison after she'd changed in the car and they had stashed anything they thought might set off the metal detector. The drawstring pants were tremendous on her—the cuffs on the absurdly baggy pants scraped the ground as she walked across the parking lot. "I'm braless and wearing a pair of inmate pants under my skirt over platform pumps. This is some kind of God-awful joke. If my friends ever saw me like this they'd laugh their friggin' asses off."

He laughed. "Yeah, maybe we ought to take a picture and add it to your collection along with my steak face photo and the one of Joe's naked behind on the ladder. Lisa. I'm truly sorry, but you know how much I value your opinion. I want you there when I interview my client...for your insights. I mean now that I know Judge Molloy handpicked me to represent Theresa...I don't want to miss a trick."

"You want an insight?" she snapped. "Here it is. I look like a freakin' clown. Didn't you know that you have to be all covered up to visit someone in prison? How about a heads up, Vinny?"

"I swear I didn't know. It's like I said. There's a lot of on-the-job training."

"I'm really beginning to hate it when you say that."

"What? On the job training?"

"Yeah. That. I don't want to hear it no more...ever!"

Theresa was a tiny little thing, not more than five feet tall, and without her heels, her prison coveralls hung on her like adult clothing on a child. She looked down at the floor as she entered the room under the watchful eye of a prison guard, then looked up and saw Lisa standing next to Vinny wearing the baggy pants under her dress. "Jesus. And I thought I looked bad."

"Yeah?" Lisa said aside to Vinny. "At least I get to take this crap off when I leave."

"Ms. Cototi, this is my legal assistant and fiancée, Ms. Vito. She's here to help me with your case."

"Just as long as she's not here to help me with fashion pointers. Jesus Christ. What *the hell* are you wearing? You look like the poster child for a K-Mart blue light special."

"They made me put on these ridiculous pants. They said I was showing too much skin. It's a good thing the fashion police aren't here or I'd be your cellmate."

"That's no joke," Theresa said. "I've only been here overnight and I've already been propositioned three times. You ever get catcalls from another woman?"

After a moment's thought, "Actually, yes." She extended her hand. "You poor thing. Call me Lisa." She glanced around, taking in the somber meeting room. "The place could use a coat of fresh paint...maybe a plant or two."

"Call me Theresa, okay? I don't have a lot of friends."

"Sure," Lisa said as she cracked her gum. "I love your hair."

"Thanks, Lisa."

"Ms. Cototi is from Ohio. She ain't got no family around," Vinny explained and then gestured toward the table. "Why don't we all sit down?" Once seated, he pulled out a pad and pencil and placed them on the table in front of him.

"So, I'm in a lot of trouble, huh?" Theresa asked with a worried expression.

"I won't lie," Vinny began, "This is a serious charge but the only thing that really worries me is the victim's brother."

"Do you think I could talk to him?" Theresa asked. "I don't know what's gotten into him. He was looking at me like he wanted to kill me. He's known me for such a long time. He has to know that I didn't kill Sammy. I loved Sammy. I waited seven years for him to get out of prison, and I didn't even have one date while he was away. Doesn't that mean anything to him?"

"He may be too grief stricken to think straight," Vinny said. "Hopefully he'll calm down and come to his senses. A guy with that kind of juice...he could be our worst nightmare."

"So how do we get him to calm down?" Lisa asked.

"I don't know, Lisa. I hope he'll start to see things more clearly once the case gets underway."

"You think we'll definitely go to trial?" Theresa asked.

"I'm afraid so, dear, unless the DA offers to plea bargain. Doucette is asking for murder in the first degree and that carries a life sentence."

Theresa's eyes opened wide and her mouth dropped. "*Life?* He wants to send me away for life? But I didn't do it, Mr. Gambini. I would never...You believe I'm innocent, *don't you?*"

Lisa put her hand on top of hers. "You bet your ass I do. You didn't wait for this guy seven years just to push him off the roof. It don't make no sense at all."

"That's what we have to prove in court," Vinny said. He picked up his pencil. "So, tell me absolutely everything you can think of, Theresa. *Everything.*"

CHAPTER THIRTY
What the Hell Am I Eating?

"So, what do you think?" Vinny asked. They had just gotten off the expressway after leaving the prison and were cruising down the avenue on their way home.

"You mean, do I think she did it?"

"Yeah. That."

"No fuckin' way. She's being set up."

"Who? Who's setting her up?"

"How should I know, Vinny? I just know she didn't do it. I can see it in her eyes. She's hurt and she's grieving. That's a hell of a thank you for being loyal to a convicted felon for so long. If you ask me, the woman is as good as gold. What possible reason could she have for killing him? Like I said, it don't make sense."

"Yeah, that's what I'm thinking. Only the prosecutor has got to have something big up his sleeve, something we've got no idea about. It has to be, because otherwise his case is too weak."

"What could he know?"

"I don't know yet. Parikh said they got the victim's blood at the scene, Theresa's footprints on the roof, and a witness. That ain't a hell of a lot."

They stopped for a traffic light. "Hey, Lisa, you ever notice that place over there before?"

"The Chinese restaurant on the corner?"

"Yeah. The one with the piano in the window?"

"Uh-huh. Yeah. I've seen it."

"I wonder what kind of music they play."

They turned to each other, shrugging for a moment before both arriving at the same conclusion, "Chopsticks?"

Lisa looked around from just inside the entrance, marveling at the glittering gold statues of Buddha and the other traditional forms of Chinese art. "This place is really pretty."

"Forget the décor," he said sniffing the air. "It smells great in here and I'm so hungry I could eat a horse."

"Oh look," she said pointing at rows of steam tables. "It's a buffet—all you can eat. You okay with that?"

"Lisa, I just spent two months eating broasted chicken, hog jowls, and chicken-fried everything. If eating all that *stuff* didn't kill me, one simple little buffet dinner certainly ain't gonna put me in my grave."

"You're not worried that you'll eat too much? You won't be able to fit into that nice new suit you bought."

"Lisa, I'm hungry. Can I eat a good meal *now* and worry about fitting into my new suit in the morning? Okay? Can we do that?"

"Whatever. It's your waistline." She pulled out her pink camera and snapped a few pictures of the décor. "I hope the food is good. My girlfriends would love it here."

"Who?" he jibed. "Your friends Dopey, Doc, and Bash-ful?"

"Hey! That ain't nice. They don't call you no insulting names."

"I'm just having some fun. Lighten up."

As they waited, an immensely oversized man sat down at the piano and began to sing, "On the Street Where You Live."

He'd barely begun when Vinny commented on his per-formance. "Listen to him, Lisa, he sounds just like friggin' Vic Damone."

"Oh yeah? He looks more like the guy who ate Vic Damone."

"Very nice," he bantered. "Making fun of someone because of his weight."

"I ain't making fun of him. I'd weigh that much too if I worked at an all-you-can-eat buffet." She patted his tummy. "You'll be halfway there by the time you finish loading up on appetizers."

Vinny scowled at her.

"Two?" The hostess asked.

Vinny looked around. "You see anyone here besides us?"

"Right this way," the hostess said with a forced smile. But as she turned and walked away she mumbled, "*Asshole.*"

Vinny studied some of the items on his plate, pointing to one of them. "You think this is real crab?"

"Real crab? No. At nine dollars and ninety-nine cents for an entire dinner? Don't be ridiculous. It's one of those surimi fish sticks."

"I don't want to sound like a know it all or nothin' but don't you mean sashimi?"

She scolded him lightheartedly. "Don't *you* know nothing? Sashimi is a sliver of expertly sliced raw fish and it's very expensive. Surimi is manmade. They take little bits of fish, blend them together into a giant fish milkshake, remove the liquid, and mold the fish paste into sticks. It costs about a dollar ninety-nine a pound at the supermarket."

He wrinkled his nose. "So what I'm eating here is some kind of fish milkshake?"

"Uh-huh. That's right."

"That sounds disgusting. What kind of fish do they use?"

"Mostly pollock, whiting, and cod—the kind of stuff they can catch by the ton. They throw out a giant net and what-ever gets caught goes into the milkshake."

"What about the shrimp in the shrimp and lobster sauce?"

"I think I saw a few real shrimp in there but most of it is imitation, also made from surimi."

He pushed his plate away. "What the hell are the noodles made of?"

She laughed. "Noodles, you dope. Not everything here is made of surimi. The chicken is real chicken, and the chewy beef is real chewy beef. It's just the expensive seafood they screw around with to cut costs."

"I guess you must be some kind of fish expert."

"No, Vinny, I don't have to be. I can tell what's real and what's not just by biting into it. Real food has a unique consistency that can *never* be duplicated in a factory. You can just tell it was once a real living thing. It's not a uniform blob like the phony crab sticks on your plate. It's got integrity."

"Hey, you think Nunzio uses this fish paste in his shrimp parm? I mean it's covered with sauce and gobs and gobs of cheese. How would anyone know?"

"Believe me, if Nunzio ever used fake shrimp in his restaurant he'd have to shut the doors so fast it would make his head spin. Are you kidding?" She snickered. "With the clientele in our neighborhood...the wise guys would run him out of town on a rail. They'd dump him in the river next to Luca Brasi. Forget about cooking the fish—he'd be sleeping with 'em."

Vinny seemed pensive. "So, what you're saying is that there's something about all living things that make them different from imitation. They've got integrity."

"*Correct*. You can't just take things at surface value. You've got to look deeper."

"What about my client, the one who's on trial for murder? She got any integrity?"

"Theresa? Yeah, she's got tons of it."

"You really think so, huh?"

"Vinny this girl is *all* alone. Okay, she dances naked for a living so she ain't exactly a nun, *but* she says she doesn't turn tricks and I believe her. Think about it, a hot little number like that? She could walk into a strip joint in any state in the country and get a job in two seconds flat, but she didn't. She stayed put, alone, and with no family to support her in New York because she was devoted to her man. He was a three-time loser and probably didn't deserve her but that didn't matter. She dug her heels in and stayed. And I respect that."

"You know, that was a very convincing argument you just made. Maybe you ought to think about going to law school."

She wrinkled her forehead. "*What?* And become an attorney? Screw that. I hate those sons of bitches. Present company excluded, of course."

Vinny stared at his plate disapprovingly. "Maybe we should've gone to The Great World. At least there, the fish is real fish."

"Ain't that the place you and Joe used to go with your folks when you were kids?"

"Yeah."

"But your mom doesn't eat Chinese food no more. Did she have a bad experience there or something?"

"Yeah. Only it had nothing to do with the food." He continued to eye his dinner plate suspiciously without commenting further about his mother."

"Well?" she asked. "What already?"

"*Oh*, I get it. You want to know what ended my mother's Chinese food-eating career."

"No, I'm Sherlock-friggin'-Holmes and I want to figure it out on my own."

Vinny used his hands to add flair to his telling of the story. "Well, when I was...about nine or ten I think, this new kid shows up at school. What do they call it? Oh yeah, a transfer student. Anyway, this kid...Eddie, he was kind of wise in the ways of the world so to speak and he kind of...he sort of took me under his wing if you know what I mean?"

She shook her head. "No, I don't know what you mean."

"Come on, Lisa. Use your imagination. What do all young boys talk about? What do they think about all day long?"

"I don't know. Baseball cards? Peashooters? Picking their nose? I was never a little boy. Clue me in."

"Sex, Lisa. What else is there? You weren't a kid once?"

"Yeah. I was a kid. I just didn't have a penis."

He laughed before continuing. "Now most of my friends, we were pretty naïve—I mean we didn't know nothing about girls. But this kid Eddie, he was seriously knowledgeable, and well, one day he takes me aside and tells me every freakin' thing there was to know about girls and sex."

"What's that got to do with Chinese food?"

"Just hold on and I'll tell you. Eddie taught me so much *stuff* in just one afternoon that my head was literally exploding with sex terms, names of anatomical parts and reproductive functions. I mean he told me so much I couldn't keep any of it straight."

"So what'd you do?"

"What any young kid in my situation would do. I asked my big brother."

"*Joe?*" she snickered. "You asked Joe?"

"Yeah, Joe. Let me finish. I tried to explain all this new stuff to Joe and he had absolutely no idea what I was talking about. And then, well, my parents decided it was time for our monthly trip to The Great World for dinner."

Lisa blew the hair out of her eyes. "Vinny, my food is gettin' cold. We anywhere close to the end of this?"

"Yeah. Well back in the day, Chinese was the only kind of restaurant my folks could afford to take the whole family to dinner. Back then a family of four could eat like kings for maybe twelve bucks and still take home leftovers."

"I don't get it. It sounds to me like your mother was still eating Chinese food."

"Yeah. She was, but like he always does, my father ordered all kinds of stuff because it's so cheap. I mean he ordered chicken chow mein, shrimps in lobster sauce, spare ribs, eggrolls, wonton soup. There was so much food left over at the end of the meal that we needed a gigantic doggie bag to fit it all into, only I had all that sex stuff floating around in my head, right? So when the waiter asked if we was finished I said, 'Yeah, we'll take the rest of it to go. Put it all in a scumbag.'"

Lisa burst out laughing. She laughed so loudly that the waitresses and nearby customers all turned around to stare at her.

"Funny, right?" Vinny asked. "My mother was so mortified she never went back to The Great World or any other Chinese restaurant ever again...ever! It's like she was permanently traumatized."

Lisa was still doubled-over with laughter, clutching her gut, barely able to breath.

"Take it easy. I know it was funny but you're turning red."

She laughed even harder.

"Lisa, stop it already. Everyone in here is looking at us."

"*Ah. Ha, ha, ha.*" She was gasping for air, doubling over.

"Lisa," he demanded. "That's enough. Stop it already. Stop!"

"I can't," she said laughing so hard she could barely get the words out.

"What already? What is so fuckin' funny?"

"You," she snorted.

"Me? I'm funny?"

"Yeah," she howled. "I can't believe it."

"You can't believe what?"

"I can't believe that everything you know about sex, you learned from a ten-year-old boy and your dumb shit halfwit brother Joe."

CHAPTER THIRTY-ONE
Fashion Police

It was a mild Saturday morning, one that hinted spring was around the corner. The sun was intense and warmed Lisa's face through the window. "What do you feel like doing today?" she asked.

"I didn't sleep so good," Vinny said with a sour expression on his face.

"Heartburn?"

"Yeah, heartburn," he said as he clutched his stomach.

"Well what did you expect? Just because it's an all-you-can-eat buffet doesn't mean you have to eat until you're ready to burst. You were popping eggrolls like they were M&Ms."

He sat down at the kitchen table in a short robe, still wearing his black Banlon socks from the day before. His wife beater peeked through where his belly pushed the robe apart.

"*Oh*, you are a sight this morning," she teased and fanned her face with her hand. "I'm getting so hot and bothered. I don't know how I can keep from tearing your clothes off."

"Quit it, would ya? I get it. We were supposed to have a romantic night. I'm sorry, Lisa. What do you want me to say?"

"You should know."

"Here we go again. I should know? What is it I should know?"

"Are you completely clueless about these things?"

"What things?"

"Man and woman things."

"Is this is all because we didn't do it last night? I'm sorry if I didn't feel like getting passionate in between trips to the bathroom."

She dismissed his reply with a disapproving wave of her hand. "Ah, Vinny, that ain't the half of it. When are you gonna learn your role in this relationship?"

"I don't know my role? I think *I do*. I'm supposed to be putting food on the table. Ain't that the man's job?"

"*Yeah*," she said. "*That's your role.*"

"So if you agree with me, why are you still looking at me like you want to punch me in the face?"

"You know what? Just forget it. It's a beautiful day. Let's take advantage of it and do something nice. It'll probably be freezing cold again tomorrow."

"I hate to burst your bubble but I was thinking about going back to the prison."

"But it's Saturday," she said, disappointed. "I was thinking maybe we could go for a nice ride somewhere."

"I'm sorry, but I've got preliminary arguments coming up on Monday morning and I got to get prepared."

Lisa seemed disheartened as she pulled out a chair and sat down at the table. "Whatcha thinking?"

"I wanna ask Theresa if Sammy ever spoke about any of the other inmates. Maybe one of them had it in for him and you know...either they got out of the joint already or reached out to someone on the outside who could've iced Sammy."

"Yeah, that sounds like a good thought. You ought to follow up on it."

"Come with me. I won't be there more than an hour or so. We can jump on the parkway afterwards and head upstate a ways. That sound good to you?"

"*Yeah.*"

"And you won't be mad at me no more?"

"No." She stood and began to pace the kitchen. "Except

now I have to figure out how to look halfway attractive in a pair of stretch pants and a fuckin' training bra. There's no way in hell I'm gonna wear those prison cootie pants again." She scratched her thigh. "I'm still skeeved out from having to wear those filthy things. I took a long hot shower and threw away a brand-new pair of pantyhose."

Vinny stood and put his arms around her, providing the smallest glimmer of hope that he wasn't completely brain-dead when it came to romance. "Lisa, you are the most beautiful woman I ever laid my eyes on and it don't matter to me whatsoever what you wear. You'd look good in a burlap bag for Christ's sake. So stop agonizing about your wardrobe selection. Oh by the way, we got any TUMS?"

She was caught off guard by the request and gave her head a brain-rattling shake. "What is wrong with you? TUMS? Are you freakin' kidding? You're telling me how pretty I am and that I look good in everything and then in the same breath, you ask me for TUMS?"

"Yeah, the heartburn is coming back. I think the pork buns must've been reheated."

"Get 'em yourself," she huffed and bolted out of the kitchen.

Vinny shrugged as he watched her disappear. "Now what did I say?"

CHAPTER THIRTY-TWO
The Big House

They were on their way to visit Theresa when Vinny decided to comment on the smooth powerful ride of the Caddy. "I've got to hand it to you, Lisa. You did some job on that valve train. She's purring like a kitten again.

"The old lifters were all gummed up, so I replaced them with high performance hydraulic valve lifters when I swapped the push rods. When GM originally built the engine in 1960, they were pretty lax on their build tolerances. *I* adjusted all the components to basically a zero tolerance using a Matco valve adjustment tool with a pivoting handle and an inspecting window so that I could see the adjustment screws while I tightened them."

"Well, it shows. I can't hardly remember the old Caddy having so much pep."

"While I was in there I also threw in new springs, rocker arms, stud mounts, and roller tips."

"I never heard the car run so smooth. You're the friggin' Michelangelo of the engine bay."

Lisa blushed at the compliments—coming from Vinny, it was like being told she was gorgeous. They drove into Queens taking the BQE to Astoria Boulevard and over the Rikers Island Bridge that ran parallel to LaGuardia Airport. Lisa snapped pictures of a plane as it raced down the runway and lifted into the air. "I wonder where that one's going," she said.

Vinny had a look of intense concentration on his face. He was focused on his upcoming meeting and knew she'd said something but missed it. "Sorry, what was that?"

"Wasn't important. So you think Theresa's case is going to trial?"

"There's no doubt about it. The deputy mayor's brother was killed. Someone's going to do time and right now the only one they got is Theresa. The preliminary hearing ain't gonna be nothing more than a formality."

"Poor little innocent Theresa. The only thing she's guilty of is standing by her man and look what she's getting for it. It's like they say, 'no good deed goes unpunished.'" Another jet took off and the wash of the jet engines nudged the Caddy out of its lane. "Did you feel that?" she asked. "Almost two-and-a-half tons of steel and the jet engines pushed us around like we was a feather. I'd love to do a tear down on one of those jet engines one day. That would be freakin' awesome." Her enthusiasm was lost on him as they rolled up to the prison complex entrance gate. "You look terrible, Vinny. Don't worry. You'll figure it out."

"I hope so. I'm kind of worried that I just got lucky with Bill and Stan. I got that ache in my gut again and I don't think it was the sesame chicken from last night."

"Don't let it get to you. Think about how much more you know about how to handle a murder case than you did before. You won the case in Alabama and you didn't even know what the hell you were doing. You ain't gonna make the same mistakes again."

He turned to her and smiled. "You really think so?"

"*Yeah*," she said. "Once you're out there doing your thing...you're a Gambini, and no one pulls the wool over the eyes of a Gambini. You ain't never been suckered. It ain't humanly possible. Now get a grip and wipe that gloomy expression off your face. You look like a pregnant basset hound overdue to deliver her litter. You want to scare Theresa with that sad sack puss of yours? You look so bad the poor kid will end up taking her own life before she even goes to trial."

The same guard was waiting for them when they arrived at the check-in area and seemed eager to bust their balls again. But they'd learned their lesson. Vinny flashed his naked fingers. Lisa lifted her untethered breasts and blew the guard an insolent kiss, flipping her off as she walked by just for good measure.

"I didn't think I'd see you today," Theresa said. "So you even work weekends?"

Vinny was dressed casually in a sweater and slacks. "I got to do whatever's necessary to win the case."

Theresa turned to Lisa and managed a weak smile. "I love your boots. Are those Tory Burch?"

"Thanks. Yeah, I got them at DSW. A Christmas present from Vinny." She covered her mouth, mumbling, "That I picked out for myself."

"I've been picking out my own Christmas and birthday presents from Sammy for the last seven years, and now..." Her chin quivered and she began to sob.

Vinny offered his handkerchief but the guard stopped him, shouting, "Don't hand anything to the prisoner."

"But she's friggin' crying," Lisa snapped. "How about a tissue? You think she's gonna fashion a shiv from a flimsy little tissue?" She fixed the guard with a cutting stare and the guard relented with a gesture. "Easy now," Lisa said as she handed her the tissue. "You gotta take it one lousy day at a time...it'll get better."

Vinny's legal pad and pencil were once again out on the table. "I know I already asked this question but are you *one hundred percent sure* you don't know anyone who might have wanted to kill Sammy? Think hard, okay? Because it's really important."

Theresa was still drying her tears. She took a deep breath and settled into thought. "I don't know, Mr. Gambini. I just don't know. Sammy would've never told me anything like that. Even if there was someone after him—he wouldn't have wanted me to worry."

He seemed disappointed. "Yeah, I suppose."

"Hey, how about this?" Lisa said. "Is there anyone we could talk to, a friend of his perhaps, who might be closer to the situation? A cellmate maybe? Think, Theresa. There had to be at least one person that Sammy was close with." She turned to Vinny, her expression soliciting, "That's a good idea, right?"

"Yes," Theresa said, her eyes flickering with encouragement. "Bald Louie. I actually met him once, during a visit. Sammy said he was a real crazy son of a bitch but they got along. I think it was because they were both originally from the same neighborhood in Brooklyn."

Vinny wrote down the name. "Bald Louie, huh? You wouldn't possibly know this Bald Louie's last name, would ya?"

"No," she said. "He only mentioned him the one time, when he was in the visitor's room. Sammy said, 'That's my friend, Bald Louie,' and Louie said, 'Hey, Tool.' They waved to each other and that was pretty much it."

"Tool, huh? That's what they called him?" Vinny asked.

"'Tool Man' was Sam's nickname in the joint because he had a reputation for being good with burglar's tools." She paused. "Wait. What I said wasn't true. There was this one other time...Sammy told me that Louie had just been released."

"That's okay." Vinny circled the name and looked up. "We'll give this information to our investigator and see if he can dig up any information on this Bald Louie guy."

Lisa's expression was classic. *Investigator? What the hell are you talking about?*

"You think that'll help?" Theresa asked.

Lisa shrugged. "It couldn't hurt."

"You happen to know this neighborhood that both Sammy and Bald Louie came from?" Vinny asked.

"I know where Sammy used to live," she replied.

"And where was that, dear?"

"Seventy-Third Street, off the corner of Eighteenth Avenue."

"That ain't far from where I grew up," Vinny said.

"That's where the Café Napoli is," Lisa said. "I know that place. That's where all the guidos hang out."

"A guido?" Theresa asked. "You mean...?"

"A *jabone*," Vinny said. "It's a guy who sounds like he just got off the boat from Italy except that he's been living in New York most of his life. They talk in Italian because they feel English is beneath them. They wear brightly colored shirts with the word 'Italia' monogramed on them in gold letters."

Lisa laughed. "Just so no one's confused about where they came from. They're Italian men, who just can't let go of the old country...guidos."

CHAPTER THIRTY-THREE
A Man with a Plan

"What the hell was that all about?" Lisa asked as they walked past the security guard on their way out. They had turned the corner and were out of the guard's line of sight when Lisa leaned back, extended her arm, and one again gave the guard the finger.

"You shouldn't do that, Lisa. I know she busted your balls and all but I got to keep coming back here and I don't need her making it tougher and tougher for me to get in."

"Yeah. Sorry. It's just that she was such an ass yesterday, making me put on those cockroach pants on over my tights. Anyway, who the hell is this mystery investigator you mentioned before?"

"You."

"*Me?* What the hell are you talking about? I ain't no investigator."

"Who's better than you? You're always taking pictures of everything. It was your pictures that helped us figure out that there were two different but almost identical cars at the Sack-O-Suds, wasn't it? Theresa said that Bald Louie is from the old neighborhood. All you got to do is ask some questions." He schmoozed her, "I doubt that someone with your investigative skills will have any difficulty ascertaining the identity of this Bald Louie guy."

"Yeah? Wait a minute. Taking a few pictures is one thing

and I am most certainly not a wuss, but you want me to rub elbows with criminal types?"

"The guidos ain't criminals. They're just a bunch of Italian-speaking tools. Anyway, take Joe with you. He's got nothing to do. Trust me, no one's gonna give you a hard time with Joe around. I know he looks a little dumpy these days but he threw plenty of beatings when he was in his prime. My big brother didn't take any shit and everyone knows it."

"So what do you want me to do, Vinny? It ain't like I went to the police academy or nothing."

"Just take Joe with you to the café. Tomorrow being Sunday, the place will be packed wall to wall with guidos watching the soccer matches. Buy a cup of espresso and some biscotti and ask a few questions. I would go with you but I got to spend the day preparing for court on Monday. You think you can handle that?"

"I suppose I can. You think Joe will come with me?"

"You're kidding, right? When was the last time my *gavone* of a brother passed up free anything?"

CHAPTER THIRTY-FOUR
Mighty Joe and the Guidos

Joe approached the café's display case and looked into it while grabbing his waistband and yanking up his pants. He pointed at some of the pastry. "Lisa, look at the friggin' size of the *sfogliatelle.*" He ran his tongue over his lips like a starving hound. "And the *cassata* cake—holy shit that looks good."

The café was packed with men in brightly colored warm-up suits monogrammed with words like Italia, Ferrari, and Cinzano. The cafés decorating cues had come straight out of a Roman palazzo. The walls were finished in handcrafter wood and the floors were pure white marble. There was enough glass on display to bottle all the Coke and Pepsi produced for the next ten years. Lisa had her pink camera out and was snapping pictures when she noticed that her legs were drawing unwanted attention from some of the regulars. She tugged down the hem of her skirt. "Listen, Joe, I'm gonna sit down before one of these guys makes a move on me." She handed him a twenty. "Get whatever you want and meet me at the table in the corner."

"Can I get two things," he asked.

"Yes, Joe. Get two things. Just hurry up."

"What do you want?"

"Just coffee."

"What kind of coffee? Espresso? Cappuccino?"

"Just coffee."

"You sure?"

"Yeah, I'm sure." She sat down and began sizing up the crowd. She was looking for the right guy to talk to when one of the men watching soccer looked under the table at her legs and winked at her.

"F-off," she said rejecting him with a scowl.

Joe whistled happily as he made his way over and put a tray down on the table upon which rested a foot-long cannoli cream-stuffed lobster tail and a mammoth piece of cake.

"You gonna eat that all by yourself or did you invite the Green Bay Packers?"

"I figured we'd share," he said as he squeezed his substantial rump into the dainty little chair. He picked up his petite cup of espresso and sipped with his pinkie extended. "Try something. It all looks amazing." He picked up his fork and shoved a huge piece of cake into his mouth.

There were four men at the next table. One of them had a dense mop of dark hair. It looked as if it had been groomed with axle grease. He watched as Joe went to town on the dessert. "*Gavone*," he contemptuously announced to his friends as he nodded in Joe's direction.

Joe noticed Lisa shooting the man daggers. "Whatsa matter? That guy bothering you?"

"The scrawny goomba over there called you a gavone," she said. "He don't like to see other people enjoy their food."

Joe glanced over. "Who? That guy?"

"Yeah. Him."

Joe put down his fork and turned around. "Hey, Helmet Head, you got a fuckin' problem?"

He said something to his friends in Italian before turning to Joe. "Me? No. Enjoy your cake." He whispered, "*Maiale*," the Italian word for pig too low for Joe to hear.

"Ask them," Lisa whispered. "Ask them if they know Bald Louie."

Joe wiped his mouth and turned toward their table. "Say, where you guys from?"

They snickered over the absurdity of the question. One of them pointed to the word *Italia* emblazoned on his warm-up jacket.

"Yeah, of course," Lisa said in a snide manner. "Just in case you were afraid someone might mistake you for someone from Norway."

One of the other men replied sarcastically in a heavy Italian accent. "We're from Milwaukee. Where the hell do you think we're from?"

"Oh yeah?" Lisa said. "Four wops from Milwaukee? You must be in fuckin' witness protection."

"You're funny," the man with the long, over-gelled hair said with a laugh. "I might need witness protection after I spent the night with you."

Lisa snorted. "Me go out with a greaseball like you? That's ridiculous. I'd rather get bamboo shoved under my fingernails."

He reached over and laid his hand on her arm. "How you know you wouldn't like me?"

She stared at his hand with contempt. "Take your fuckin' paw off me before I—"

Joe grabbed his fingers and crushed them in his huge hand. He rose to his full six feet of stature, looking like three hundred pounds of trouble, as tall and wide as a double-door refrigerator.

The man grimaced.

Joe still had the man's fingers in his hand as the other three men got to their feet. "Sit the fuck down," Joe ordered. "Before I make your friend's fingers look like cooked linguini—permanently!"

They looked from one to the other before backing down.

Joe towered over the seated man, staring into his eyes with a cold and menacing expression. "Now before I twist your fingers so they stick out your ear the next time you go to pick your nose—I want to know one thing. Where the hell do I find Bald Louie?"

CHAPTER THIRTY-FIVE
Masters and My Johnson

"Joe was *fuckin'* great!" Lisa bragged as she dropped her coat and rushed toward the kitchen table where Vinny was preparing for court—books and notes covered every inch of the table. "You should've seen him, Vinny. You were right."

His mind was on his work. He looked up at her, confused. "Right about what?"

"Your brother. One of the mooks over at the café was giving me a hard time and Joe cut him down like he was dry twig."

"He hit someone?"

"No, he just squeezed the jerk's fingers but that was all it took. The guy said that Bald Louie got out of jail about six months ago."

"That's great," he said with a glimmer of enthusiasm. "I mean we kind of already knew that. You get a last name and address for this guy?"

She shook her head. "They thought he was still in the neighborhood but they didn't know where he lived. They said he comes into the café once in a while but not often. That was all they knew."

"Well at least we confirmed that he's out of jail where we can reach out for him. Getting approval to meet with him in prison would've been a big hassle. We just got to find him and see if he can think of anyone who might've wanted Sammy dead."

"You come up with anything powerful to say in court, Mr. Bigtime Lawyer?"

His expression shouted failure. "No, not much. I've been reading and studying all afternoon so that I'm prepared for anything they might throw at us during Theresa's preliminary hearing. My brain feels like roadkill."

"Like roadkill? Your brain feels like a dead raccoon lying in the gutter?"

"Yeah, like that."

"I think you're too tense." Her eyes blazed. "I've got just the solution." She grabbed him by the shoulders and straddled him. "You look so studious sitting here with your books and legal pad." She fussed with hair. "I can't hardly keep my hands off you."

"Lisa, *what* are you doing? I'm hopelessly buried in courtroom procedure, in motions and inculpatory evidence. I ain't even begun to write my brief yet."

"*Well*, as your *official* legal assistant I would be remiss if I didn't point out the therapeutic benefits of blowing off a little steam. I've read that there's a long list of benefits to having sex, including glowing skin and a healthy prostate." She continued to pontificate. "Top industry experts have now determined that by teaching your mind to focus solely on pleasurable stimuli during sex—and let's face it, *why wouldn't you?* You aggressively train your brain to zero in on and focus better while studying."

"I'll be damned," he said. "When did you become friggin' Masters and Johnson?"

Lisa pulled her dress off over her head and tossed it aside. "I don't know nothing about those two nerds but smart money says I can master *your* johnson any day of the week." She put her mouth on his and kissed him. "I'd like a sidebar, Counselor. How 'bout you take me upstairs and I check your briefs?"

"Oh yeah? What will you be looking for?"

"Large, shocking allegations. Swelling concerns. Probing questions. Dangling participles." She kissed his neck. "Am I getting warm?"

" *Yeah*, you're getting warm."

"Good," she said, swooning. "Then get your ass upstairs and drill me on wrongful tarts."

"Don't you mean *torts*? Wrongful torts?"

"Stop teasing me, ya big dope, or I'll have grounds for justifiable homicide."

"You gonna help me study after this?" he halfheartedly asked before lifting her and carrying her up the stairs.

She'd had enough of the sexual innuendo and wanted only to be taken. "Sure, Vinny," she answered. "Anything you want—provided you bang me unconscious."

CHAPTER THIRTY-SIX
Too Many Balls in the Air

Vinny never got back to the books. His eyes opened to the sight of his gorgeous fiancée sleeping soundly next to him. He drank her in, the gentle sweep of her nose and her long delicate eyelashes, the hollow of her neck that he had kissed over and over again, the contour of her waist and the round-ness of her hips. He fell in love with her again every time he saw her. Time seemed to stand still while he basked in her beauty. But along with that rapture the same nagging question always arose: *What is someone so beautiful doing with a big lug like me?*

The alarm clock blared, fracturing the moment as if a pane of glass had shattered. "Oh shit! Court!" he blurted and scrambled out of bed, leaving Lisa struggling to awaken. "Get up," he hollered," as he stepped into the shower. "We slept the whole night. I ain't prepared."

Lisa hit the clock and rolled over, feeling supremely rested and satisfied. "It was worth it," she said, her response practi-cally incoherent, her brain saturated with endorphins.

"Help me get ready," he said calling over the torrent of water cascading upon him in the shower.

"Yeah, yeah, yeah," she responded, grousing about having to leave Eden behind. "Keep your pants on. I'm coming."

* * *

155

"Turn right here," Vinny directed from the passenger seat as they closed in on the courthouse.

"Where? Right here?" Lisa asked, already braking, her hands poised to turn the wheel.

Vinny had his books open on his lap, studying precedents and points of law as they drove. "Yeah. Atlantic Avenue. Right here."

Lisa turned as if she were taking a hairpin turn on the race-course at Le Mans. Vinny's books went flying.

"Are you nuts?"

"Yeah, I'm nuts? You're the one who's in such a damn hurry to get to court."

"I told you I need time to prepare on account we passed out after having sex last night and didn't wake up until this morning."

"Yeah? You got a complaint about last night?" She took her hands off the wheel and held them out as if she were ready to be handcuffed. "Oh my God. I wanted to make love to my fiancé. Lock me up and throw away the friggin' key."

"Lisa, just stop it and put your hands back on the wheel. I already explained that I wanted to get to court early so that I didn't feel rushed."

"And it's my fault the BQE was bumper-to-bumper? I told you we should've taken the subway. Relax. Would ya? I can see the court building from here. I'll pull up in front. You can get out while I go park the car."

He stuffed his books into his briefcase and had a leg out the door as they pulled up to the building. "I'll see you inside. Go park the car."

She grabbed him by the shoulder and yanked him toward her before he could get out, planting a big kiss on his cheek before letting go. "Break a leg. Don't worry. You'll be great!"

* * *

156

Vinny was at his table completely set up and ready before the ADA arrived. Spectators had just begun to file into the courtroom when he heard, "Psst."

Lisa was standing in the public section with a look of urgency on her face trying desperately to get his attention.

He slapped the sides of his legs with exasperation and mumbled, "Now what?" He hurried over to her. "What, Lisa? Can't you see that I'm—"

She handed him a sticky note. "This must've fallen out of your briefcase when I turned and everything went on the floor. I think it's important."

"Oh shit!" He knew what it was without reading it. He'd written the note before leaving the arraignment for Aidan Boydetto. "Crap!"

"What is it?"

"Damn. I was so worried about Theresa's court date that I completely forgot about the other one."

"Which other one?"

"The one for the guy who wrote the bad check."

"So? When is it?"

He checked his watch. "It started five minutes ago in the courtroom upstairs."

"You got the file with you?"

"I think so, yeah. It should be in my briefcase."

"Then hurry your ass and get up there. You got twenty-five minutes to get upstairs, handle the other preliminary hearing, and get back down here before Theresa's case is called."

He started toward the table where his briefcase rested when Lisa yelled. "I'll get the fuckin' file. You get the fuck upstairs."

Vinny arrived in the upstairs courtroom panting and out of breath.

Judge Finch cut him down with a scorching gaze as he hurried down the aisle to the table where Boydetto was already waiting.

Doucette looked at Vinny, tapped his watch, and shrugged.

Vinny slapped his client on the shoulder. "How you doing? All right?"

Finch drummed her fingers on the bench. "Nice of you to grace this courtroom with your presence, Mr. Gambini. I hope we're not taking you away from anything important."

Vinny lowered his head, groveling. "My apologies, Your Honor. I left in time to get here early but the BQE was bumper to bumper. I'm very sorry, Judge."

"Are you prepared to begin immediately?" she asked.

Vinny nodded.

"Fantastic," she said sarcastically. "Mr. Doucette," she began as she turned toward the ADA. "We're ready...*finally.*"

Doucette was a busy man with a completely unmanageable caseload. It was apparent as he read from his notes that he considered Boydetto's case a nuisance and wasn't going to spend one minute more of his precious time on it than necessary. He read in a dead-flat disinterested monotone. "Your Honor, the accused is charged with passing a bad check at Speedy Check Cashers at ten-twenty-five Eighteenth Avenue in the borough of Brooklyn. The cashier became alarmed when the accused refused to furnish photo ID. The cashier subsequently called a security guard. The entire event was captured on videotape. The people..."

"Psst! Psst!"

Vinny turned to see Lisa waving at him furiously with a file in her hand just as the judge howled, "Oh dear God. Her again." She refocused on Vinny. "*Mr. Gambini,*" she barked.

He responded meekly, "Yes, Judge?"

Her eyes were wide with rage. "Who the hell is that, and why is she waving at you like a long lost sibling you were separated from at birth?"

"That's my legal assistant, Ms. Vito, Your Honor. You see, in my haste to get here on time—"

She interjected, "Which you *didn't accomplish.*"

"Yeah. Like I said, I'm sorry, because in my haste I left my case file in my car. As you can see, Ms. Vito retrieved it for me and has it with her now. Do you mind if I go...get it?"

"Sure. Why not," Finch said. "We're already behind. Take all the time you need, Mr. Gambini. Have a cocktail while you're at it."

Several people in the audience laughed at her remark.

Vinny bowed slightly before hurrying off to Lisa. She extended the file toward him, which was open, and pointed to two areas she had circled in red. He nodded, grabbed the file, and walked back to his table, studying Lisa's notations along the way.

"Are you finally ready, Mr. Gambini?"

He was so captivated by what he read that he missed the judge's question.

She banged the gavel twice. "Mr. Gambini, may we proceed?"

He looked up while using his finger to keep place on the file. "Yes, Your Honor. Go ahead."

His eyes were back on the file and missed the judge's infuriated expression. She turned to Doucette. "Continue."

Vinny was lost in thought while the ADA finished his argument, not hearing a single word he said. He didn't stop reading until he detected that the courtroom was silent and felt the judge's eyes searing a hole right through him.

"Let me catch you up," she said scolding him. "Because this infraction concerns a very small amount of money, Mr. Doucette has opted not to call any witnesses which would only waste the court's time and the taxpayers' money. I'll hear from you now," she continued with a raised eyebrow. "That is if you have time for us."

"Your Honor, my client is not guilty by reason of the fact

that he has a long and documented history of dissociative personality disorder."

Finch leaned forward and thatched her fingers. "Dissociative *what?*"

"Let me explain," he said. "Dissociative personality disorder is the new term psychology professionals use for multiple personality disorder."

"I *know* that," she said.

"Oh, you do? That's good."

"Of course I do—you just caught me off guard. Are you serious about proceeding with an insanity defense on a token misdemeanor charge?"

"Yes, Your Honor."

"Why am I not surprised," she muttered. "Proceed."

"Thank you. As I mentioned the defendant has more than one personality. So when Mr. Boydetto said, 'he didn't do it,' he actually...*didn't.*"

The judge's eyes became large. She glanced over at Doucette before stating, "Gentlemen, this is a one hundred and seventy-five dollar infraction. In the interest of not sending the defendant for costly psychological evaluation, I suggest the two of you work something out...and quickly."

Doucette jumped aboard. "Your Honor, the people are more than happy to—"

Vinny cut him off. "Excuse me, Mr. ADA...Judge. There's one particular piece of evidence that should settle this matter once and for all."

"Of course there is," the judge wisecracked. "And what is that, Mr. Gambini?"

"May we approach, Your Honor?"

She waved the attorneys forward. "What do you have, Mr. Gambini?"

"If you look carefully at the signature on the check you will clearly see that it wasn't signed by Aidan Boydetto at all, but in fact by his alter ego." He folded the file open and

160

placed it before the judge so that she and Doucette could both see it. The note in the comments section read: For sexual favors. The signature circled on the photocopy read: Lindsay Lohan.

Doucette snorted.

The judge bit her lip and then turned to the ADA with a probing glance.

Doucette read between the lines and nodded in agreement.

She banged her gavel. "Case dismissed."

CHAPTER THIRTY-SEVEN
No Rest for the Weary

"Thank you, Your Honor." Vinny turned to Boydetto and gave him a thumbs up. "Good luck, Aidan...or is it Lindsay?" he asked with a smirk. "Take care."

"I can't thank you enough, Mr. Gambini," Boydetto said, then lamented, "No one understands what I go through. I owe you, big time. Thanks." He turned and moved off.

"Nice work," Doucette said, relieved to have dispensed with the nuisance case. He checked his watch. "We've got exactly two minutes to get downstairs before Judge Brick Balls finds us both in contempt."

"Judge Brick Balls?"

"Sure," Doucette said as he packed his briefcase. "Ex-marine—tough as nails. Some years back he declared a vendetta against the Chinese triads and they sent two hit men to his house to kill him. Wound up he disarmed one guy and broke three of his ribs before calling the police. Put the other guy in traction."

"He does look pretty intimidating up there on the bench."

"Believe me, you don't want to piss him off." Doucette snapped the lock on his briefcase. "Ready?"

Lisa took Vinny's picture as he and Doucette raced from the courtroom. Triumphant, Vinny had a huge grin plastered across his face. "I'll see you downstairs," he hollered to her and continued forward under a full head of steam. "Thanks for saving my ass, Lisa."

Lisa blushed before gathering her things.

A gray-haired woman in the next aisle said, "That attorney was pretty darn good wasn't he?"

"Pretty good? He kicked that prosecutor's ass. He's my fiancé."

"What a lucky girl you are to have such a successful boyfriend."

Lisa smiled but kept her mouth shut, knowing she hardly had enough money in her purse for gas.

The two attorneys took the stairs two at a time, scrambled across the lobby in haste, and burst through the courtroom doors before Judge Whorhatz entered the courtroom. Doucette checked his watch: 9:29 a.m. "Thank God. We made it with just seconds to spare."

Vinny glanced at Theresa as she was led to the defendant's table. "You okay, kid?" he asked.

She nodded, doing her utmost to present a brave face.

"Okay, listen. There's no way this case ain't goin' to trial, so don't get rattled. The ADA is gonna state his argument and call some witnesses, which we know are all gonna be bullshit. But that don't matter because there's nothing I can say or do that's gonna prevent the inevitable. Try your best not to get down on yourself. Okay?"

She nodded again, this time far less convincingly.

Vinny glanced at Doucette and noticed he was seated in the second-chair position. The man in the first chair had dark, closely shorn hair and wore a black yarmulke. "Who's that?" Vinny mouthed to Doucette.

Doucette raised his eyebrows. His reply came in the same noiseless manner as he mouthed, "The boss."

CHAPTER THIRTY-EIGHT
Outstanding

"So *that's* the DA," Vinny said in a hushed tone.

"What?" Theresa asked.

"The DA is trying the case himself."

"That sounds like bad news."

"It only means it's an important case, which we already knew, and the DA wants to make sure nothing gets screwed up. It don't matter what his title is because you're innocent. It wouldn't matter to me if Robert Morgenthau himself was standing over there."

"Who's that?"

"Morgenthau? He was one of the longest-serving district attorneys in United States history. They talk about him in all the law schools. He's practically a legend—especially here in New York where he served."

"So you're feeling pretty confident. That's good, right?"

"Just let me do my thing." He heard a man clearing his throat, turned, and saw the DA next to him. He extended his hand. "Vincent LaGuardia Gambini. Pleased to meet you."

"Mr. Gambini, Morton Gold, District Attorney for Kings County. Please call me Morty."

"Thanks, Morty. You can call me Gambini if you want to." A moment of uncomfortable silence passed. "So, we've got one hell of a high-profile case here, Morty. I guess that's why you're here."

"I'm here because the schlemiel mayor said I had to be

here. I was supposed to be on vacation in Miami Beach instead of here in this frozen wasteland."

"Maybe we can get this thing over quickly and you can get back to your trip," Vinny said.

The quiet of the courtroom was disturbed by the sound of a creaking door, followed by the clerk's announcement. "All rise…"

"I doubt it," Gold said, a grave expression on his face as he turned away.

The clerk continued. "The Honorable Larsen Whorhatz presiding." He read the docket number and case.

"Be seated." Whorhatz got comfortable in his chair. "Mr. Gold, an honor to see you in my courtroom, sir. I take it you'll be first chair?"

"A pleasure to stand before you again, Your Honor. ADA Doucette will be second chair for the prosecution.

"Outstanding." Whorhatz grinned at the ADA. "Mr. Doucette…as always." He then turned to Vinny. "Mr. Gambini, are you prepared for preliminary arguments?"

Vinny's hands were clenched nervously in front of him. "I am, Your Honor…yes."

Whorhatz repeated, "Outstanding," but this time with a lackluster ring to it. "Mr. Gold…If you'd be so kind."

Vinny looked around, smiled at Lisa, and studied the other faces in the public section of the courtroom, which was at full capacity. The veins on his temples began to throb.

The DA stood and buttoned his suit jacket. He scanned his notes one last time before beginning his argument. "Your Honor, Ms. Cototi, the defendant is accused of murder in the first degree. The people will prove that Ms. Cototi ruthlessly killed her boyfriend, one Samuel Cipriani, in an act of premeditated murder by pushing him off the roof of the apartment house in which Ms. Cototi currently resides."

"I presume that you have witnesses to call?" Whorhatz asked.

"Yes, Your Honor."

"Well then, let's get them up here, Mr. Gold. I'm not getting any younger."

CHAPTER THIRTY-NINE
Taking out the Trash

The doors at the back of the courtroom closed with a thud, announcing the arrival of Deputy Mayor Anthony Cipriani. He was dressed in a somber black business suit.

The courtroom became hushed, acknowledging the arrival of the victim's very important brother.

Both the judge and the DA acknowledged Cipriani by nodding as he took a seat behind the prosecutor's table. As was the case for a preliminary hearing, the judge alone decided whether a case was strong enough to go to trial. The juror's box was empty.

Theresa tried desperately to make eye contact with Cipriani, but he focused straight ahead and would not meet her gaze.

Greta Träsch was on the stand. She had broken off her reply in mid-sentence when Cipriani arrived and the proceedings temporarily halted. She crossed her long legs, left over right before glancing up at the judge for the signal to proceed.

"Please continue," Whorhatz said.

She spoke with a German accent. Her English was interpretable but not without serious concentration. "Can you please repeat the question?" She fanned herself in a dramatic manner. "All this commotion, it's overwhelming, *ja?*"

"Happy to oblige," Gold said. "Can you tell us where you were on the night of February twenty-sixth?"

"Oh *ja*." She tossed her long blonde hair over her shoulder. Her makeup was applied so thickly it looked as if it she had gotten the ninety-nine dollar special at Earl Scheib. "I was out for the evening with a friend and got home about three in the morning. We went to dinner and then back to his place for drinks."

"I see," Gold said. "And can you tell us what happened next?"

"I was getting comfortable. I was sitting on the edge of the bed when I noticed someone across the street on the roof. Naturally, I thought it was a peeping Tom," she said as she combed her fingers through her hair. "I was going to ignore him but then I heard a thud and the screeching of automobile tires."

"Did you go to the window to get a better look?"

"Objection," Vinny shouted, rising from his chair. "Your Honor, Morty is leading the witnesses."

"Morty?" the judge asked. "Getting a tad informal, aren't we, Counselor?"

"Not really, Judge. He *told me* to call him Morty not fifteen minutes ago."

The judge turned to Gold who shrugged before confirming with a nod.

"Mr. Gambini, in the future, you will address the DA as Mr. Gold, or the DA, or the District Attorney. You can call him Morty after we recess," the judge said with a grin. "He is right with his objection though. Sustained, Mr. Gold."

"I'll rephrase," Gold said. "Ms. Träsch, what did you do next?"

"Why I went to the window, of course."

"Can you please tell us what you saw?"

She pointed at Theresa. "I saw that woman standing alone on the roof and she had blood on her shirt."

"Anything else?"

"*Ja.* Down below, a bloody man on the street and a car racing away."

"By any chance did you happen to see the license plate number of that car?"

She shook her head. "*Nein.*"

"Thank you. No further questions, Your Honor," Gold said wrapping up.

The judge grinned at Vinny with the same pretentious grin he'd used before. "Cross, Mr. Gambini?"

"You bet your ass," Vinny mumbled.

"*What?*"

"Uh, yes, Your Honor," Vinny said quickly. "Thank you."

The judge turned from him, scowling.

"Ms. Trash," he began as he approached the witness stand. "Hello, dear. How are you today?"

"It's *Träsch* (Tresch), not Trash," she said. "Can't you hear the difference?"

"Um...no. Not really. I thought that was just your accent."

"What accent?"

"The one you speak with."

"What are you talking about?"

"With all due respect—you don't think you got an accent?"

"Very slight," she conceded. "Most people tell me they hardly hear it at all."

"I find that amazing. *Most* people? Is that most *deaf* people? Because from over here it's pretty clear that English ain't your first language. Just for the record, you are German, right?"

"My God, you must be omniscient," she replied sarcastically. "You know what that means?"

"Yeah. I know what that means. It means I know stuff. Like right now I know that you're being a wiseass."

"Language, Mr. Gambini," the judge warned.

"Sorry, Your Honor." He thought for a moment before continuing. "So I guess you speak German most of the time."

"*Nein.* I speak English practically all the time"

169

"Except just then."

She grinned at Vinny antagonistically.

"So, Ms. *Träsch*, you said that you went out for dinner, then drinks. Is that right?"

"That's what I said, isn't it?"

He mocked her, parroting her response with a German accent, "Yes I know 'that's what' you said."

She turned to the judge waiting for him to reprimand Vinny, but he ignored her and looked away.

"What kind of food did you go out for?"

"Mr. Gambini," the judge interrupted. "Where are you going with this?"

"Just laying some groundwork, Judge..."

"You'd better get to your point, and fast."

"I will, Your Honor. So, what kind of food did you get... German?"

"You think I get a figure like this from eating deep-fried schnitzel?"

"I don't know...you look like the kind of woman who enjoys a good schnitzel."

"Last warning, Mr. Gambini!"

"Sorry, Your Honor."

"I'm a vegetarian," she said.

"Vegetables are kind of bland. They usually add lots of salt and seasonings to make them tasty, don't they?"

"*Ja.* I suppose."

"Did you get thirsty?"

"Yes. Okay? I got thirsty."

"So how did you hydrate, dear?"

"What does it mean, hydrate?"

"It means, what did you drink?"

"Oh. Riesling."

"That's wine, right?"

"*Ja.*"

"So you had wine, then you went to your friend's house

for drinks. I'm assuming that when you said 'drinks' you didn't mean Kool-Aid. Is that right?"

She shrugged.

"Alcohol. Did you drink alcohol?"

"Ja."

"The average street width in that section of Brooklyn is approximately seventy-five feet, not counting setbacks for sidewalks on both sides of the street. Let's call it a hundred feet. Yet after drinking wine at dinner and more alcoholic beverages with your 'friend' until four a.m., you were able to positively identify my client in the pitch black of night?"

Träsch seemed taken aback, at a loss for words.

Lisa lowered head, covered her mouth, and shouted, "She's full of it!"

The judge searched the public section but was unable to find the culprit.

Vinny quickly closed. "No more questions, Your Honor."

CHAPTER FORTY
Sizing Up the Opposition

"That was great, Vinny—really great. I liked the way you handled that phony *fräulein* on the witness stand." Lisa locked arms with him as they walked side by side from the courthouse.

The DA was a step behind them, struggling to catch up.

"Morty?" Vinny said as they came to a stop. "This is my fiancée and legal assistant, Ms. Vito."

"She *is*? Generally, I think it's a bad idea to mix business with pleasure. But in Ms. Vito's case...I can see the need for a precedent."

Lisa blushed. "Nice to meet you, Mr. District Attorney."

He checked the time. "Ninety-minute recess—you out to lunch?"

Vinny thought for a moment. "Literally or figuratively?"

He laughed. "Literally. Of course. Why don't you let me take the two of you to lunch since we're on opposite sides of the aisle and I don't know you from Adam."

"Yeah. Okay. You good with that, Lisa?"

"Actually, I'm gonna bow out. I think it's better if the two of you go to lunch by yourselves. You know, just the boys."

"I wouldn't hear of it," Gold said. "Please."

"I think you should come," Vinny whispered aside to her. "You don't want to insult the guy, do you?"

"I'm not being impolite. I broke a nail," she said at full volume. "There's a nail shop next door to the parking lot. I think I'll get some French tips." She smiled politely. "You'll give me a rain check, won't you, Mr. DA?"

"Of course, Ms. Vito. I'm sorry you won't be joining us."

"Next time." She grabbed Vinny and yanked him aside. "Excuse us for a minute," she said and whispered in Vinny's ear. "Beware of Greeks bearing gifts."

"What the hell are you talking about, Lisa? He ain't Greek."

"I know he ain't Greek. The Trojan Horse, Vinny. He's gonna try to work you," she said. "Don't let this guy get into your head."

He winked at her and whispered, "Got it...see you after lunch," he boomed so loudly that his remark sounded like an obvious cover up. He watched her move off.

"Your fiancée is lovely," Gold said. "A real beauty."

"Thanks. She is kind of all right. Where do you wanna go for lunch?"

"Are you in the mood for anything in particular?"

"Yeah," he said. "Anything but German."

"Do you like pastrami?"

"Absolutely."

"I know a place where they make a pastrami sandwich thick enough to choke a horse and I could use a hearty meal. I have to begin a fast, starting tonight."

"How come? Jewish holiday?"

"No. Scheduled colonoscopy."

The restaurant décor was nothing special and the waitress looked like a barfly who'd seen far better days. But the sandwiches were every bit as enormous as Gold had promised, and the meat was melt-in-your-mouth tender.

Vinny noticed the odd-looking meal a man was eating at the next table. He was layering a pita with a lumpy tan spread. "What the hell is that guy eating?"

Gold glanced over, made eye contact, and waved. "That's Elon. He's one of the best personal injury attorneys in the area. Looks like he's layering a pita with hummus and topping it with sliced olives."

"Strange concoction, ain't it?"

He laughed. "Not for an Israeli. For him it's the equivalent of you or I making s'mores. Anyway, I think my eyes were bigger than my stomach," Gold said.

"I think the *sandwich* was bigger than your stomach. I'm gonna take the other half to go." He pushed his plate toward the center of the table and leaned back in his chair.

"So, Gambini, you said you just won a murder trial? Can you share some of the details with me?"

"I guess you want to *voir dire* me to see what kind of experience I got." He folded his arms and waited for Gold's reply.

"Just talking shop, Gambini."

Right. Sure you are. "That's okay." Vinny regaled him with the details of the Alabama case, careful not to mention his three contempt charges or that it was his first-ever courtroom victory. "The trial ended about two weeks ago."

"You did one hell of a job for those boys. It's wonderful when you're rewarded like that, isn't it?"

"Not really. I did that case pro bono being it was my cousin Billy who was on trial for his life."

"That's not what I meant. I mean the sense of fulfillment you received for a job well done—seeing those two wrongly accused boys set free."

"Oh yeah. Of course."

"Frankly, I don't know how you figured it out. You must have *some* incredible problem-solving skills. I can't imagine what your IQ score must be."

Vinny shrugged.

"Being modest again?"

"Not really."

"It must be *off* the charts."

174

He placed his hand behind the chair and crossed his fingers. "You could say that."

"Well then I guess lightning struck or something."

"Not that I remember. I mean there were a couple of heavy downpours during the trial but it was winter, so...no electrical storms."

Gold smirked. "No. I mean you must've had a grand revelation—that moment when you see something clear as day for the very first time. You know what I mean...seeing it in a way you never saw it before."

"Yeah, it was a real eye-opener."

"I still think you're being modest. Either that or you're being cagey."

Vinny's shoulders swayed back and forth while he decided where to take the conversation. "I got back about two weeks ago, like I said, and been busy as hell ever since."

"And yet Mr. Doucette said you opposed him in a case as an assigned lawyer. I'm impressed. Where do you find the time to help the indigent? I mean, it's hardly lucrative work."

Vinny sensed that Gold was prying. "Oh. The bad check thing?" He waved his hand dismissively. "I did that case as a favor for someone."

"But Doucette said he's never opposed you in court before, nor had he ever met you before last week."

"Yeah. Well, Brooklyn was a change of venue for me," he said, thinking on his feet. "I used to practice in the Bronx, but I got this classic red Cadillac convertible you see, a gorgeous 1960, Model 62—I mean it's really something to see. It was a gift to me from my *dear* friend Judge Molloy. Maybe you heard of him."

"Judge Henry Molloy?" he asked both impressed and circumspect at the same time. "Who hasn't heard of the great Henry Molloy? He's a legend in Kings County."

"Yeah. That's him. Anyway, it—I mean *the Caddy*—kept gettin' vandalized, so I decided it would be better to shift my practice here to Brooklyn where there's a secure parking lot near the courthouse. It's also much closer to home so my commute is shorter. I figured that was good for the environment."

"You couldn't have just started taking the subway? You decided instead to move your entire practice?" He leaned forward. "You're an interesting man, Vincent Gambini. A very interesting man." He placed his coffee cup on the saucer. "Do you have any questions for me?"

Vinny had been taught in law school that a strong offense was often the best defense and felt this was his opportunity. "Yeah. We got us one hell of a high-profile case, being it was the deputy mayor's brother who got killed. Does that put any undue pressure on you or the judge?"

The question seemed to weigh heavily on Gold's mind. "As long as we're being blunt, yes, absolutely it does. Judge Whorhatz and I are both up for reelection at the end of the year and the support of the mayor's office is critical to both of us. Does that mean either of us would do anything inappropriate?" He challenged Vinny with an accusatory gaze. "I think you know better than that, Mr. Gambini."

"No offense, Morty. It's just that Whorhatz went from the arraignment to hearing preliminary arguments in the blink of an eye. I barely had time to prepare."

"You think that was fast? Wait until you see how fast this goes to trial. Is Whorhatz showing favoritism to the deputy mayor? Yes. But pushing a trial to the front of the line doesn't constitute misconduct—not as long as the accused isn't being denied due process. And frankly, Gambini, I doubt Judge Whorhatz gives a damn."

CHAPTER FORTY-ONE
The Man of Steel

Judge Whorhatz came back from lunch in a foul mood, snapping at the prosecutor and the defense attorney, glaring at them defiantly from up high atop his bench. "Come on, Mr. Gold. Let's go. Let's go. We don't have all day."

Gold glanced at Whorhatz, surprised by the hostility. "The people would like to call Dr. Clark Kent, director of the Charles S. Hirsch Center for Forensic Sciences."

Vinny blurted, "Clark Kent? For real? Has he leaped any tall buildings lately?"

"Act like an adult," Whorhatz groused.

"Sorry, Your Honor. Guess I just had to get it out of my system."

Gold waited until the doctor was sworn in. "Dr. Kent, we understand that the forensics team found a set of shoe prints on the rooftop of eighteen-fifty-nine Cropsey Avenue, the location from which the victim was allegedly pushed. Is that correct?"

"Yes."

"Can you please expand upon that for us?"

"Surely." He pointed to a diagram of a grooved shoeprint. The toe portion of the shoe was highlighted in red. "The red portion of the shoeprint indicates the area we found on the rooftop, where someone stepped in blood. It allowed us to reconstruct the balance of the sole pattern. We have thousands of branded shoe profiles in our database. This particular tread pattern is specific to a ladies' Nike brand Air Max 95, size 7, standard width."

"And what size shoe does the defendant wear?"

"Why size seven."

"Excellent. No further questions."

Whorhatz turned to Vinny. "Care to cross examine the witness, Mr. Gambini?"

Vinny was distracted, taking notes. "Eh. No thanks," he said without looking up. He realized after a long moment that the courtroom was silent. He glanced at the bench and saw that Whorhatz was looking at him as if he were going to explode, his chest heaving, his face purple. "Uh...you okay, Judge?"

"Do I look okay, Mr. Gambini?"

"No," he replied. "You look like you're about to have a stroke or something. You should take a couple of deep breaths."

Whorhatz continued to glare.

"Try it, Judge. In and out. In and out—it'll do wonders for your blood pressure. "

"Are you screwing with me, Mr. Gambini?"

"No, Judge. I ain't screwing with you. You look like you're about to explode. I'm trying to prevent you from having some kind of a catastrophic event."

"Please read back Mr. Gambini's response to the court."

The court reporter read, "'Eh. No thanks.'"

"How does that sound to you, Mr. Gambini?"

"It *sounds* like I don't want to cross examine the witness, Judge."

"In my chambers," Whorhatz hollered. He slammed the gavel. "Fifteen minutes recess."

Vinny turned to Lisa, his hands open as if to catch an oversized beach ball as he shrugged, then mouthed, "What did I do?"

She shook her head disbelievingly.

Whorhatz yanked off his robe the moment he entered his office, walked over to a photograph on the wall, and pointed. "What do you see here, Mr. Gambini?"

Vinny took a close look. "I see a bunch of soldiers belly down in the mud."

"Wrong!"

"Wrong?"

"Wrong. What you see is unwavering courage. This is fortitude. This is bravery. This is everything you're not when you address the court with your head down, speaking like a vagrant."

"Your Honor," he said, desperate to have the judge understand. "I didn't mean no disrespect. It's just the way I talk."

"Mr. Gambini, you're an attorney. You passed the bar. Are you trying to tell me you haven't mastered the rudiments of the English language?"

"I'm sorry, Your Honor. I'll try to be more *awares* of the way I speak."

"*Awares*? All right," he said as a prelude to action. "Have a seat."

"Thank you, Judge." Vinny did as instructed.

"Judge Molloy and I had a chat right after the arraignment and he told me that you were his protégé of sorts. He told me that you were more resourceful than any litigator he'd ever met. He also said that you were a damn clever lawyer."

Vinny sensed there was more to come.

"None of that matters to me. I'm a decorated marine. I served in Viet Nam, carried wounded soldiers out of the swamp, and stood up straight and tall for roll call. Personally, I think everyone should spend some time in the military, but in your case..."

"In my case what, Your Honor?"

"Stand up," Whorhatz ordered. He got right in Vinny's

face and pummeled him like a drill sergeant. "Gambini, you're soft and you're undisciplined and all the alleged smarts you have in your head won't get you through this hearing if you don't learn to walk the walk. You're a lawyer, aren't you? Well, talk like one for God's sake. And you snap to attention when I address you or you address me. Are you feeling me, Gambini?"

"Yes. Your—"

"*Acta non verba*," he blurted, dismissing a verbal response before it could be uttered. "That's an expression we use in the military. It means deeds not words. Now get back out there and prove to me that I didn't just waste fifteen minutes of everyone's time."

The DA stood. "Your Honor, the people call Detective Nirmal Parikh to the stand."

Parikh was spry. He reached the witness box so quickly that he had to wait several moments for the slow-moving court officer to swear him in.

"Now, Detective," Gold said. "You've been assigned to the investigation of Samuel Cipriani's death, have you not?"

"Yes, I have," Parikh said.

"And you've ruled the death a homicide?"

"That's correct."

"Please tell the court what led you to arrest Theresa Cototi."

"Mr. Cipriani suffered a gruesome death and we were unable to locate a suicide note."

"And is that uncommon?"

"Oh yes."

"Two face," Vinny muttered.

"So this was a clue to you that the victim's death might not be a suicide?" Gold asked.

"Yes, one of them."

"What happened next?"

"A call came into the station."

"An unsolicited call?"

"Yes. A witness had spotted the defendant on the roof moments after the victim fell. That's when we interviewed Ms. Träsch."

"And she identified Ms. Cototi?"

"Yes. We then obtained a warrant and searched the defendant's apartment."

"And you found evidence there?"

"Yes, the same model of Nike sneaker that made the impression on the rooftop that the crime lab had discovered."

"And then you made your arrest?"

"Yes, but not before we discovered the presence of blood on the roof."

"Shouldn't the crime scene investigators have discovered the blood long before that, Detective?"

"No. We originally thought the death was a suicide and didn't expect to find blood evidence. It appears that great effort had been taken to clean it up."

"The blood?"

"Yes."

"But you found it anyway."

"Yes. With the use of Luminol."

"I see. Anything else?"

"Yes. When the blood was revealed, we saw that something had been written on the rooftop near the ledge."

"In blood?"

"Yes."

"The victim's blood?"

"Yes."

"Please tell the judge what the message said."

Parikh turned and made eye contact with Theresa. "The letters 'TMC' were written out. It looked to me as if the victim wrote those letters in an attempt to identify his murderer."

Vinny objected. "Calls for speculation."

"Sustained. Strike the witness's response," Whorhatz said.

Gold directed a comment to the judge. "Your Honor, let the record show that the defendant's initials are also TMC— Theresa Mary Cototi."

CHAPTER FORTY-TWO
A Good Ass-Kicking

Vinny paced back and forth in front of the bench, never looking up at the judge. "And when you found the Nike sneaker in Ms. Cototi's apartment, did it have blood on it?"

"No.

Vinny repeated Parikh's answer with emphasis for the judge's benefit, "No!" He racked his brain, searching for another damaging question but the well had run dry. "No further questions, Your Honor."

"Mr. Gold?" Whorhatz asked.

"No additional witnesses, Your Honor."

"Fine," Whorhatz said, deliberating mere seconds. "I find sufficient evidence to send this case to trial." He set a date for jury selection that gave the attorneys a meager three weeks to prepare.

Vinny watched Anthony Cipriani skulk from the courtroom like a hoodless version of the grim reaper.

Lisa hurried to his side. "It's all right, Vinny. You did all you could. We already knew the case was going to trial. You said so yourself."

"I know I did," he said, his head hanging down. "It's just that—"

"Hey, listen, *Mr. Attorney*, this is what you signed up for—the reason you worked and sweated for ten long years. Did you really think the judge was gonna throw out the case just because Vincent LaGuardia Gambini was on the job?

Stop feeling sorry for yourself. This is the way it's done."

"Yeah. I thought we had a shot until they found Theresa's initials written on the roof in the victim's blood. Stuff like that's pretty hard for the judge to ignore."

"So *what*?" she said. "This is legal procedure. It's what you learned in Haller's courtroom. You can't skip all the steps and go straight to acquittal. I'll tell you right now, if this is what you're gonna go through every time you have a hard day in court, you can forget about marrying me," she said jesting. "You think I want to look at that sad face night after night?" She opened her bag and pulled out her compact, forcing it into his hand. "Take a look at yourself. You look like death warmed over. *No way* I'm gonna spend my life with a miserable son of a bitch that looks like that. So would you please pull yourself together and show me what you're made of?"

"Yeah. Yeah. What's eatin' you anyway?"

"I'll tell you what's eatin' me. I just spent two months wondering if Billy was gonna get the electric chair and I ain't going through that again. Leave your work at the office."

"Lisa, look around. I *am* at the office. It's just that you're here with me, watching me go through a tough moment."

"All right. Look, we got three weeks. We'll figure it out. I looked this girl in the eye and I know she didn't do it. She's a victim in all this. All you got to do is figure out what really happened like you did for Billy."

He saw Judge Molloy at the back of the courtroom signaling to him. "There's Judge Molloy. I think he wants to talk to us."

Lisa turned around and waved.

"Come on," he said.

"Vinny, look at his expression. He don't want to talk to us. He wants to talk to *you*. Go over there and talk to the man."

"Vincent!" Judge Molloy called out.

Vinny approached with the demeanor of a whipped puppy.

"Uh oh, I always know you're pissed when you call me Vincent."

"I stopped in before," Molloy said.

"Before when?"

"When Judge Whorhatz called you into his chambers. Now if I'm right, and I'm sure I am, my colleague, the ex-marine, probably dragged you into his office, bent you over, and broke his shoe off in your hind parts."

"Yeah, I know. The guy is kind of a ball break—"

"I would've done exactly the same thing. Vinny, you can't come into a senior judge's courtroom throwing around *dese*, *dem*, and *dose* like you're one of the Eastside Kids. I'm angry with you. I went out on a limb for you and told Judge Whorhatz that you were a tough young attorney with a sharp mind and a tenacious spirit. How am I ever going to be able to look him in the eye again?"

"I'm sorry, Judge Molloy. I'm really sorry. It's just that, well you know—old habits die hard."

"Oh yes? Well unskilled attorneys die pretty damn easily. I don't ever want to see another show of disrespect in this courtroom or any other. Are you clear?"

"Yes, Judge Molloy. I'm clear."

"You'd goddamn better be. I entrusted you with the crucial task of defending a dear friend in a fight for her liberty. Don't you dare make me regret having made that decision." His eyes flashed angrily and he left.

CHAPTER FORTY-THREE
Poor Defenseless Forest Creatures

Vinny spotted Lisa coming down the stairs the next morning. She was ready and put together, her hair and makeup flawless. Her clothes fit as if they had been custom tailored.

He was still in his nightclothes, his hair tousled, scratching his head, and yawning. "It ain't hardly nine o'clock. Where are you going so early in the morning?"

"I got a call from Gloria at the salon. She asked me if I could fill in today. She said a couple of her girls called out sick and she's got a lot of appointments booked. I figure we could use the money." She sat down next to him on the couch. "You bent out of shape over the judge's decision or from gettin' reamed by Molloy?"

"Both, I think. Judge Molloy is really mad at me. I didn't hardly sleep at all last night."

"You look exhausted. Maybe you ought a go back to bed for a while."

He looked at her haplessly. "You think he'll get over it?"

"Who, Molloy? Of course he will. Listen, Vinny, he knew who you were from the day he first listened to you fighting that traffic ticket. He knows you didn't graduate from Cambridge. The man likes you for who you are."

"He implied that I sounded like a moron."

"No, he didn't. Do you sound like one of those other polished ass-kissers? No. But that's what makes you special. You don't try to put on airs because that's not who you are."

She thought for a moment. "It's kind of like this...picture you're in an elegant restaurant and you're being served the greatest meal of your entire life. The décor is beautiful. The lighting is just right, you're being waited on like you're royalty, and the food is just out of this world. Now, I ask you, would you complain about a meal like that just because the table wobbled a little?"

"No. Of course not."

"Of course not," she repeated. "Because it's form over substance. You got the mind of a brilliant attorney. It just don't come out of your mouth sounding that way. So, do you think anyone would complain about an attorney who won case after case just because he was a little rough around the edges?"

"I guess not."

"Right. Trust me—Judge Molloy probably said a couple of things he didn't mean because he was so upset. But I'll bet what really ticked him off is you not doing the things you know you're supposed to do."

"Like what?"

"Like standing up straight and tall and addressing the court with respect, that's what. Didn't you learn nothin' from the last murder trial? Molloy is harping over the same exact things that Judge Haller complained about. It's not about how you sound, Vinny. It's your attitude. These judges have worked their butts off to get where they are and you're crapping all over them like they're bums or something."

"Ya think so?"

"I know so. The question is, do you know so?" She patted him on the leg. "I'll make you a pot of coffee and then I gotta go to work. Gloria won't be happy if I'm late. What are you gonna do today? I mean *after* you get your head out of your ass?"

"Very funny, Lisa. I figured I'd call the DA's office and get my hands on their files."

She smiled and kissed him on the cheek. "You see—you did learn something from the last trial."

"You mean discovery?"

"*Yeah*, discovery. And when you get dressed you won't have to worry about the pants you're gonna wear because you don't have to finesse the DA by hunting some poor little defenseless doe-eyed deer. Don't that make you feel good?"

"I guess," he said with uncertainty. "Besides, Gold don't exactly strike me as an outdoorsy type of guy. I doubt he goes hunting anyway."

"And what makes you think that?"

"Because, Lisa, the man is kosher. He needs a rabbi to supervise the slaughter."

Lisa grimaced. "I'm so glad you got my point."

CHAPTER FORTY-FOUR
The Guy

Joe looked as big as a house as he walked through the door of Barone's Deli. He was wearing a quilted vest over a bulky fisherman's sweater, his arms hanging at his sides like King Kong. "Hey, Barone," he said. "Give me a large coffee, will ya?"

"The usual?"

"Yeah. Half coffee, half cream, five sugars."

"You know the cream and sugar cost more than the coffee. I should charge you extra."

"Oh yeah?" Joe said. "And I ought to buy my coffee at the place down the block where they don't use the same coffee grinds to brew the coffee all day long."

Barone snapped a lid on the paper cup and handed it across the counter. "You're lucky I like you so much or I'd piss in the cup."

Joe eyed his coffee suspiciously. "Seriously? You done that before?"

Barone nodded. "You bet your ass. I mean only a few times over the years, but a couple of real miserable pricks got a free urine sample."

"But not me, right?"

"No, Joe. *Moron,* would I tell you if you were one of the guys I did it to? You like to break my shoes but you're not a prick. There's a difference." He planted his hands on the counter. "Anything else?"

"Yeah. Cut me a chunk of crumb cake outta that tray you got back there and don't be cheap. Cut me a nice size chunk." When Barone turned to cut a square from the baking sheet Joe removed the lid and cautiously sniffed his coffee.

"What are you all bundled up like that for? It's cold outside, but it ain't that cold."

Joe sipped his coffee. "I been out all day."

"How come?"

"I'm looking for a guy."

"A guy?"

"Yeah."

"What guy?" Barone asked.

"A guy. A guy. What difference does it make? A guy."

"Which guy?"

"Someone Vinny's looking for."

"Why's Vinny looking for this guy?"

"It's for one of his cases. He don't tell me all the particulars. He says, look for the guy, I look for the guy."

"Yeah? How is Vinny-Bag O' Donuts?"

"Vinny? He's great. He just got back from Alabama. Won his first big murder case."

"Murder, huh? *Marone.* Don't get me wrong, *Joe,* but, uh, I never saw your brother practicing that kind of law. I figured him more for an ambulance chaser."

"Oh yeah? He's doing really good. He's got cases coming out his ass. Gonna be a big-time lawyer, my baby brother." Joe chomped into his crumb cake. "Hey, this is fuckin' great," he said with a mouthful of food, crumbs falling everywhere. "You do something different?"

"Yeah. I started adding extra butter to the cake batter. Everyone focuses on the crumbs and don't pay nearly enough attention to the cake part. Big difference, right?"

"Fuckin-a. This is delicious."

"Your brother used to eat a ton of my coffee cake. All those years he was studying for the bar exam, he'd come in here with his books, buy a big coffee and a hunk of cake, just like you're doing right now." Barone grabbed a towel and wiped away the pile of crumbs Joe had deposited on the counter. "You gonna tell me about this guy or what?"

"It's just a guy. What do you care?"

"Maybe I know this guy."

Joe pushed out his lips. "Oh yeah? You think you might know this guy?"

"Maybe. I don't know. What's his name? I see a lot a guys in here."

"Bald Louie."

"Bald Louie?"

"Yeah."

"Really? Bald Louie?"

"Yeah. You know him?"

"Of course I know Bald Louie. I know everyone in this neighborhood."

"No shit?"

"No shit."

"So where can I find this guy?"

"How the fuck do I know? Do I look like the fuckin' mailman to you or something? You want to find this guy? Pack yourself up in a refrigerator crate and mail yourself to his house."

"Ah. Fuck you," Joe snapped, showing him the back of his hand.

"No, fuck you. Bald-fuckin'-Louie don't come in here no more."

"How come?"

"Because, Bald Louie is not only a crazy bastard, he's an ornery-fuckin'-prick. I served the jerkoff a steaming hot cup of Barone one day. Believe me. He don't come around here no more."

CHAPTER FORTY-FIVE
The Dreaded Tribunal

Gloria's was a small shop that catered mostly to neighborhood women. Lisa had gotten laid off at the end of the year because business was slow, but now with business on the upswing and some of the girls calling out sick...

Gloria left Lisa to close up.

She was exhausted and eager to leave, but she needed a few minutes to rest and sprawled out on a stylist's chair, rolling her head from side to side with her eyes closed. She opened her eyes when she heard a tap on the window, looked up, and smiled. Her friend Mimi was waving furiously and dancing in place because of the cold. Lisa slid out of the chair, walked to the door, and unlocked it. "Where the hell have you been?" Lisa said scolding her as she wrapped her arms around her friend and gave her a kiss on the cheek. "I ain't seen you in a dog's age."

Of all Lisa's friends, Mimi was the least inhibited. Her skirt was beyond short, her heels were stilts, and when she unzipped her jacket, she flaunted a staggering amount of cleavage. "You look freakin' great, Lisa. I guess you and Vinny had a ball down there in Alabama."

"A ball?" she answered cynically. "You got no idea. That place is the sticks. I got woken up at all hours of the night by giant whistles and squealing pigs at the stockyard next door to the hotel. And Chinese food, please, don't even get me started."

"A real dump, huh? But you look good." They kissed again.

"Do you mind if we sit down?" Lisa asked. "I'm friggin' exhausted. I was working on Mrs. Terazini's hair so long that everyone else went home."

"How come?" Mimi said as she dropped her purse and took off her jacket.

"You know how she's got that bald spot on the back of her head?"

"No."

"Maybe you never noticed it *but* her hair has gotten really thin in the back and you can see clear down to her scalp."

"I hope nothing like that ever happens to me, old woman problems like that." She whispered, "I heard that when some women get really old they stop self-lubricating." Mimi pretended to retch. "Could you imagine anything worse than a dried-out coochie?"

"Don't worry—with all the traffic your coochie gets, you'll wear out your internal parts long before anything dries up down there. Why are you whispering anyway? You think Gloria's got some state-of-the-art surveillance system?"

Mimi blinked but offered no response.

"But anyway, I'm teasing and teasing and spraying and spraying, but no matter how hard I work at it, she complains every time I hold up the mirror to show her the back of her head. I swear I must've used up three big cans of hairspray on her. I teased her hair so high and so thick that a plummeting meteor couldn't penetrate it." She sighed and fell backwards into an empty chair.

"I'm so glad to see you, Lisa. I got news," she said.

Lisa's eyes lit up. "Gettin' engaged to Mickey?"

"No. Something even more wonderful." She had an impish smile on her face.

"Like what?"

She rubbed her belly in a circular motion.

Lisa flew out of her chair. "Are you friggin' kidding?" That's wonderful," she screeched as she hugged her friend again. "When are you due?"

"September."

"I just can't believe it, you and Mickey having a baby. Jesus, you're not even showing. I guess you're planning to get engaged," Lisa rambled. "I'm gonna throw you the best baby shower of all times. Who's gonna be the godmother?"

Mimi cleared her throat interrupting her and turned away casting her gaze at the ceiling. "Um...it's not Mickey's," she said.

" *What*?"

"Yeah. He's not the father."

"No? Well who the fuck is?"

"Ralph."

"Ralph? Ralph who? I don't know nobody named Ralph."

"Oh, Lisa, he's a dreamboat," she blustered. "And a lover...*Marone a mia*. He makes me scream like I'm flying down the rollercoaster at Six Flags." Her eyes rolled up. "He grabs me by the thighs and just slams the ever loving..."

Lisa raised her hand. "Whoa. Whoa. Whoa. That's way too much information. Why don't you just show me a porno while you're at it?" She shook her head in disbelief. "Okay. You know what? I get it. I really do. You met some hunk and got swept away in the moment. But what about using birth control? You never heard of the pill?"

"Yeah, I tried them a couple of times but they make me kind of crazy. I gained weight and had headaches...they weren't too good for my complexion neither. I got zits bigger than Rudolph's red nose."

"Oh yeah? Those headaches any worse than the one coming down the road?"

Mimi gazed at her blankly.

"How about a condom? Those make you crazy too?"

She stared at Lisa with a sheepish expression. "I guess he didn't have any."

"What'd you use?"

"Rhythm?"

"*Rhythm?*" Lisa was aghast.

"So you let a guy you hardly know have sex with you without using protection? What's wrong with you? You were so in the moment you just figured, 'Hmmm. Let him stick it in and I'll worry about it later?' Why didn't you use the morning-after pill?"

"I never understood how you could take something after you did it." She scrunched her brow. "That's a real thing?"

"Yeah, that's a real thing. It's been around for years."

Silence.

"What about Mickey? Does he know?"

"Uh-uh."

"What? You didn't tell him?"

"No fuckin' way."

"You're gonna dump him after all the time you've been together? Just like that?"

"Lisa, you know how sometimes you buy a pair of shoes because you just gotta have 'em but they hurt like hell and it gets to the point where you just can't look at them no more?"

"Yeah?"

"Well, Mickey was kind of like that, only he didn't come with a ten-day money-back return policy."

Lisa put her hands against her cheeks. "You know what? I need a strong drink."

"Yeah. Now that you mention it, I could go for a cocktail myself."

"*What?*"

"What's the matter?"

"Moron, you're pregnant. You can't have no alcohol. It'll mess up the baby."

"That's a thing, too?"

"Mimi, what are you doing? Just how bad do you want to screw up your life? How well do you know this guy, Ralph? Does he have a good job? Is he gonna take care of you and the baby?"

She sniffled. "I don't know. He don't call me back no more. Don't judge me, Lisa. I'm not like you. I don't have a guy who adores me. I ain't got a Vinny."

"Adores me?" Lisa snorted. "If he adores me, he sure don't show it. Don't get me wrong—I know he loves me but does he ever show it? Not *ever*. I don't ever get cards or flowers. He don't even tell me he loves me. Adore me? Yeah. Don't get me started on that either."

"So why don't you dump him? You're still super hot, Lisa. You're pretty as hell and your legs and ass are like a teenager's. So why don't you..."

"*Because*, lamebrain, I *love* him. We've been together more than ten years and I ain't nearly ready to throw all that away, only..."

"Only what?"

"Only the man doesn't have one romantic bone in his body. He don't know how to express his feelings."

"Maybe you got to seduce him. You know, turn up the hem of your skirt a little. Stop wearing panties. Maybe even have sex with him in a public restroom."

"You're some piece of work. It ain't about making love. Vinny's got plenty of sex drive, only...well I just told you. I don't know what else to say about it. Sometimes he makes me want to scream."

"So what *are* you going to do about it, Lisa?"

"I don't know, *Mimi*. I ain't thought past having a double bourbon. And as for you, I'd do some heavy soul searching if I were you."

"But I want to have this baby."

"Are you ready to raise a kid on your own? Have you told Rebecca?"

"No."

"What about Carmen?"

"Your sister? No fucking way. She frightens me to death. No, just you."

"Let's get them on the phone right now. I'm gonna convene a tribunal.

Mimi's jaw dropped. "Lisa, please," she begged. "Not the tribunal."

"Yes, the tribunal. You're out of control. If you won't listen to me, maybe you'll listen to them."

CHAPTER FORTY-SIX
Tough Love

Vinny had his head in the pantry scrounging around for something to eat when he heard the deadbolt turn on the front door. "That you, Lisa?" he called as he walked out of the kitchen. "There ain't a thing to eat in here. Not so much as a morsel."

Lisa shuddered as she walked through the door. "Holy shit. It's freakin' cold out there." She wrinkled her forehead. "And what do you mean there's nothing to eat? Ma just did a huge shopping for us."

"That's all fresh stuff that needs to be cooked."

"You're forty years old. You couldn't cook something for yourself? You're capable, right? Or were you just planning on going on a hunger strike?"

"Funny, Lisa. Real funny. Where you been anyway?" he asked holding the door open for her. "I'm starving." He attempted to close the door but a hand reached out and stopped it from closing. He seemed confused to see Lisa's friend Rebecca entering. "Oh...hi," he said greeting her.

"Hi, yourself," Rebecca said uncoiling her scarf.

He once again attempted to close the door.

"Uh-uh, Vin. Don't close the door," Rebecca said. "Mimi and Carmen are right behind me."

"You gotta be kidding me," he said. "A fuckin' tribunal?"

"Yeah. A fuckin' tribunal. The girls have the room. You gotta go."

"I gotta go?" he complained. "It's freezing out. I thought we'd stay in and you'd cook dinner."

"I guess you thought wrong."

"Okay, you ain't gotta cook. I'll just have some coffee and a thick buttered slice of that gain-a-ton bread."

"Gain-a-ton?"

"Yeah. Ain't that what you call it?"

"You mean panettone bread?"

"Yeah, the sweet bread with the dried fruit in it. Can't I stay?"

"No way. How are we gonna talk openly with you snooping around?" She pulled his jacket off the coatrack and stuffed into his arms. "Now get the hell out of here. It's an emergency meeting."

Mimi walked in, puckered up, and blew him a provocative kiss. "How you doing, Svengali?"

He turned to Lisa in puzzlement.

She shrugged, sidestepping his inquiry.

"So I got news for you," he said.

"I ain't got time. Can't you tell me later?"

"But this is good news."

"Oh yeah. What's the good news, Vinny—twenty words or less."

"The insurance company settled on Angie's case."

"Really? That was fast."

"I guess they figured they was outgunned."

"Yeah, of course. That's like the United States being outgunned by Luxembourg."

"They offered ten grand and Angie accepted. We get thirty percent."

"Three grand? Vinny, that's really great." She gave him a kiss. "Now get your butt out of here. We got important work to do."

"Jesus. What kind of emergency is this anyway? Did something of earth-shattering proportions take place? Has some revolutionary new shade of lipstick just been released?"

Lisa playfully flipped him off.

"All right," he moaned. "I guess I'll go over to Luigi's and grab a slice."

"Grab *two*. You just made three grand. You can afford it. And don't come back before ten." She shoved him out the door and flung it closed behind him. "Quick," she said as she turned toward the girls. "Someone get on the phone with Ping's and order takeout. I'm friggin' starving."

Rebecca had a bottle of wine in her grasp and was struggling with the corkscrew. "Here," she said as she handed the bottle and corkscrew to Lisa. "I'm all thumbs. You're the one who's good with tools and shit."

Carmen hung up the telephone and sat down next to Lisa. "The Chinese food will be twenty minutes and they're throwing in free cheese wontons. What are we doing here anyway?"

Lisa turned toward Mimi. "You wanna tell them or should I?"

Mimi cracked her gum. "No *way*. You tell them. I don't want to be here in the first place."

"Well, is someone going to tell us?" Rebecca barked. "I'm missing my favorite TV shows for this."

"All right. I'll do it," Lisa said turning to the others. "Mimi's got a bun in the oven and it ain't from the Pillsbury Dough Boy."

"Oh my God," Rebecca said. "You and Mickey—that's so great. You set a date to get married?"

"No," Lisa snapped.

"No what?" Rebecca asked. "No date?"

"No. Not no date," Lisa said. "No Mickey."

"What the hell are you talking about?" Carmen asked.

"She's saying Mimi got knocked up by someone else," Rebecca said as she stood up. "Lisa, you got anything stronger than wine? I figured we were here to discuss someone's bad dental hygiene or something. I wasn't prepared for all this. I need a real drink, not just some prissy bottle of wine."

"Yeah," Lisa said as she pointed toward the dining room. "I think we got some booze in the bottom cabinet. Bring three glasses. We're all gonna need it...except for Mimi that is."

Rebecca had already pounded down a couple of shots of tequila by the time the food arrived. She over-tipped the delivery boy because she thought he was cute, but the other girls said it was just the hooch talking and that he looked like a skinny version of Kim Jong-un with a big square face and a rice bowl haircut. She returned from the front door on wobbly legs and set the food on the coffee table.

Mimi reached into the bag and pulled out a bag of spring rolls. "Look how tiny these egg rolls are," she whined. "They're not big enough to fill—"

Carmen snorted. "Your vagina?"

"No, a cavity. A fuckin' cavity," she said. "Ain't that how the saying goes?"

"What's the matter?" Carmen asked. "They ain't big enough to be keepers?"

"What do you mean, keepers?" Mimi asked.

Lisa answered, "Like in fishing, you dope—when you gotta throw back the small ones. Anyway, they're not egg rolls. They're spring rolls and they're supposed to be that size."

"So what's that got to do with fish?" Mimi asked, still confused. "I hate fish. They're all slimy and shit."

"It's a metaphor," Lisa said. "Don't you get it?"

Mimi shrugged. "What's a metaphor?"

Lisa rolled her eyes. "It's a comparison. Carmen is comparing the size of a spring roll to the size of a man's penis."

"I ain't like that," Mimi huffed. "I ain't never kicked no one out of bed for having a small dick."

"Believe me, we know," Lisa said. "That's why we're here. And now you got pregnant with a guy you hardly know. Couldn't you have made him use a condom, Meems?"

"I ran out," she said sheepishly.

"Jesus," Carmen said. "I know you go through a lot of them but it ain't like they're being rationed by the government or something. You can get all you want at any corner drugstore."

"Ain't it the man's responsibility?" Mimi asked.

"Yeah, *right*," Lisa said. "You know what the man's responsibility is? It's getting all the tail he possibly can. You think this Ralph character was worried about gettin' you pregnant? The only thing he was worried about was how fast he could have sex with you."

"What makes you such an expert, Lisa?" Mimi said. "It ain't like you and Vinny got the perfect relationship."

Rebecca and Carmen's mouths dropped.

Lisa jumped to her feet, staring down at Mimi, her finger pointed accusatorily. "How dare you bring that up. I told you that in confidence because you were jealous that you didn't have what Vinny and me had and I wanted to make you feel better about yourself. We're here to help you, you little empty-headed jerk. Why, I ought to go into the garage, get a roll of duct tape, and tape your knees together. That would fix your problem once and for all."

"Sorry, Lisa," Mimi said. "It's just that everyone was getting on me and…"

"Just forget it," Lisa snapped with a flick of her wrist. "So what are you gonna do about the baby, Mimi? You got any idea what it's like to bring up a kid on your own?"

"No, I gotta think."

"Well you better think fast," Lisa said, "Before it's too late to do something about it." When she turned to sit down she saw Rebecca and Carmen staring at her. "Okay. *What?*"

"What's with you and Vinny?" Rebecca asked. "There trouble in paradise?"

"No...well, yeah. A little bit," she said. "Vinny ain't romantic. He's got no idea how to treat a woman, and he thinks he's doing just fine. He just don't get it."

"I told her she ought to wear her skirts shorter," Mimi said.

They rolled their eyes in unison, ignored her, and went back to their conversation.

Carmen grabbed Lisa's hands. "What's he doing wrong, sweetie?"

"We don't have no tender moments. He don't bring me flowers or send me cards. Forget about a romantic, candle-lit dinner. He don't even tell me he loves me."

"He's just who he is," Rebecca said. "It's like he was born with the romance portion of his brain damaged, or maybe it got banged around too much from all the years he spent in the boxing ring. Maybe he took too many jabs to the head."

"Yeah. Maybe someone pounded the passion right out of his head," Carmen said. "I hear that's a thing now, like all those high school and college football players who got their brains banged in so badly on the football field—now they're quadriplegics. Some of those poor guys can't even feed themselves. So I guess you didn't make out too bad, Lisa."

"It ain't the same thing. You're either romantic or you ain't. Vinny *ain't* and I got no idea how to make him understand that something is wrong."

"Have you told him?" Carmen asked.

"Yeah. I told him. I tell him all the time." Lisa frowned. "It just don't sink in and I don't know if I can marry someone like that and spend the rest of my life with him."

"But you've been together so long," Rebecca said. "You need to make it work."

"I keep *telling* her," Mimi said. "She needs to start wearing shorter skirts!"

CHAPTER FORTY-SEVEN
Just Whisper It in My Ear

"Yo!" Joe hollered after spotting the postman pushing his cart down the street the next morning. He rumbled down the block to catch up with him. "Thanks for waiting up for me, Dan." Dan Collier had been delivering mail in the neighborhood for decades. He'd been the postman for as far back as Joe could remember. Barone had only been screwing with him when he suggested he mail himself to Bald Louie, but Joe didn't have anything else to go on and figured it was worth the shot.

The street looked bleak under a gray sky. Branches on barren trees looked like old gnarled fingers and the small gardens in front of the row houses seemed desolate.

Dan was wearing his heavy winter uniform and thick-soled shoes. "Joe, right?" the mailman asked. "I remember you. You're Nunzio's kid, right?"

"Nah, you're thinking about my cousin, Pasquale."

"Pasquale?"

"Yeah, Pasquale. He's my second cousin on my mother's side. We kinda look alike."

Dan rubbed his chin. "My memory isn't as good as it used to be but I don't remember a guy named Pasquale. Who were his parents?"

"He's Freddy's and Vera's kid. They lived over on Nineteenth Avenue, by the high school."

"Yeah, I remember Freddy, but who was Vera? I can't

picture her. I thought Freddy was married to Phyllis."

"That was his first wife. Remember he had that hot little number renting out the basement apartment?"

"I don't think so."

"Trust me, you'd remember Vera—redhead, beehive hairdo, big set a cans. She used to wear go-go boots like Judy Carne from *Laugh-In*."

"Judy Carne? The 'Sock it to me!' girl?"

"Yeah. Looked a little like her too."

"Ah, now I remember her. She had an ass that moved up and down like shifting sacks of mail. That was this Pasquale's mother?"

"Yeah. Freddy worked days and Phyllis worked nights at the phone company. He used to sneak down to see Vera when Phyllis was at work. Next thing you know...Vera's got a bun in the oven and Phyllis is yesterday's news."

"Huh? I always wondered what happened to Phyllis. So Pasquale was that hot little number's kid?"

"Yeah."

"And he looks like you?" Dan's expression saying, *The poor fucker—what the hell happened to him?* "So who are *your* folks?"

"I'm Rocco and Mary's kid. Mom and Dad are in Florida now. I'm Vinny's older brother."

His expression brightened. "Vinny Bag O' Donuts?"

Joe nodded. "Yeah, everyone knows Vin."

"He used to keep me in stitches, your brother. Always clowning around."

"Yeah, that's Vinny."

"I remember he was good in the boxing ring. How come he never pursued that?"

"He fucked up his wrist and that was that. The docs told him he couldn't box no more." He wiped his nose with the back of his hand. "Say, you wouldn't happen to know a guy by the name of Bald Louie, would you?"

"Bald Louie what? I'm in the family name business. In case you haven't figured it out yet I don't have Madonna, Prince, or Beyoncé on my route."

Joe gritted his teeth. "I don't know his last name, Dan. All I got to go by is Bald Louie."

"Joe, my boy, do you have any idea how many people named Louis I have on my route? Is there a distinctive way he spells his name, like L-E-W-I-S? Because I've only got one of those."

"I don't know how he spells his goddamn name. All I know is that he got out of the slammer about six months ago." He saw that the wheels had begun to turn in Dan's head. "What? You know something?"

He averted his eyes.

"Come on, Dan, this is important."

"I'm not sure I can help you."

"Why not?"

"It's a federal offense. It could cost me my job and I'm almost ready to retire. I just can't throw away thirty-five years of shoe leather."

"Who's gonna know, Dan? Just whisper it in my ear. No one will know, and I'll take it with me to my grave."

He shook his head. "I can't." He grabbed the handle of his cart and began pushing it away. "I'm sorry. I wish I could—"

Joe called after him. "Are you sure? It's for Vinny."

Dan slowed and came to a stop.

Joe saw an opening and went straight for the jugular. "It could mean the difference between an innocent kid getting life in prison, and not."

"Shit!"

Joe sensed that Dan was conflicted. He'd sold used cars at one time and knew the power of the presumptive close. He leaned in close and tapped his earlobe. "Whisper it in here," he said. "That's all you gotta do."

* * *

Joe followed Dan from a distance of half a block back until he turned onto the avenue and entered the lobby of an apartment building on his route. He waited a few minutes and followed him in.

Dan had a bundled stack of letters in his hand. He held it so that the name and apartment number on the top envelope was exposed and visible. The letter was addressed to Louis Rolfe from the New York State Department of Corrections.

Joe had cased the building's interior on his way in—no security cameras. Aside from Joe and Dan, the lobby was empty. Despite this, he winked at Dan inconspicuously and continued up the stairs in silence.

Three flights. Four flights. Five. The six-flight climb had winded him and he needed a moment to catch his breath. Leaning against the wall he could see the apartment he was looking for and pushed on.

His fist was the size of a catcher's mitt. He pounded on the door like a sledgehammer, the vibrations causing dry plaster from around the doorframe to fracture and fall. He could sense he was being watched through peepholes from behind closed doors but no one dared to step out into the hallway. He pounded away at the door until he decided Bald Louie was either not at home or had no intention of answering. His shoulders settled in a heap. In a last-ditch effort, he reached down and twisted the doorknob. His eyes grew wide and his spirit rallied. "Well, look at that."

CHAPTER FORTY-EIGHT
Suck Wind

Lisa awoke late morning to find Vinny sitting in a chair next to the bed, reading, or trying to. She yawned and stretched until her long fingernails clicked lightly against the headboard. "Whatcha readin'?" She rubbed her eyes and yawned again.

"I'm trying to read this book about jury selection strategy but the print—it looks like the whole page is swirling around."

"Your dyslexia, huh? Did you ever have that particular symptom before?"

"Sometimes," he said. "When there's a lot of small print on a big page, like in this book."

"Let me just go to the bathroom. I'll help you with it."

"No, that's okay. I wanna try to do it myself."

"By *yourself?* You're trying to do it by yourself right now. How's that working out for you? The words are spinning round and round like they're caught in a twister and your forehead is wrinkled up like a sun-dried prune. There's no shame in being dyslexic, Vinny. It's not like you're a child molester or something. Just how long you gonna have that chip on your shoulder?" She hopped out of bed and hurried into the bathroom. "The friggin' floor is ice cold in here," she called out. "We gotta get a floor mat for the bathroom...So what about it? Can I help you with your reading or not?"

The phone rang before he could answer her. He picked it up. "Yeah?"

"Mr. Gambini?"

"Yeah. Who's this?"

"It's Anita Relise with the Sixty-Ninth Precinct."

"*Seriously?*"

"Yes. Can you hear me? This is Anita Relise with the Six-nine."

He covered the receiver. "Hey, Lisa," he said. "We got another one. It's *I. Need. A. Release* from the Sixty-Ninth Precinct," he laughed. "Watch this."

"Ain't you learned your lesson? Don't make the same mistake you made with Detective Parikh, sticking your foot in your mouth the way you did."

"Yeah, yeah, all right," he complained before uncovering the receiver. "How can I help you?"

"Joseph Gambini is on his way to central booking and he asked us to advise you of same."

"Joe's on his way to central booking? Seriously?"

"Yes. Seriously. Do you know the address?"

"Yeah, I've been there before." He heard an odd poof-poof sound. "What's going on over there, dear? You all right?'

"COPD," she groaned. The poof-poof sound returned followed by a slight gasp. "I'm using my Formoterol pump."

Vinny covered the receiver again, *A Ford motor oil pump?* "Hey, Lisa, I really think this is a prank call. You ever hear of a Ford motor oil pump helping someone breathe?"

"Vinny, what the hell are you talking about?" she asked. "That ain't a thing."

"Ah. Never mind." He uncovered the receiver. "This Ford motor oil pump got anything to do with Joe getting arrested? He get nabbed for parting out cars or something?"

"No," she laughed. "I didn't say a Ford motor oil pump. I said a *Formoterol* pump. It's an inhaler. It helps me breathe, Mr. Gambini."

"So this is for real then? Joe really got arrested?"

"Yes, Mr. Gambini. That's what I told you in the first place."

CHAPTER FORTY-NINE
At the Crack of...

Vinny thought about racing down to the court in his sweats, but the browbeating he'd taken from Judge Molloy was still fresh in his mind. His suit needed to be pressed but it was the best he could do on short notice. He yanked it off the hanger and began to get dressed.

Lisa entered the bathroom and reemerged twenty minutes later looking immaculately groomed—as neat as a pin. "What happened to your suit? You didn't throw it in the washer, did you?"

"Of course not. I guess it needs to be cleaned."

"You think?" She sighed and held out her hand. "Give it to me. You can't go into court looking like a homeless person—I'll press the fuckin' thing."

Joe had already been processed by central booking and was awaiting his arraignment when Vinny and Lisa arrived. Vinny spotted his brother and hurried over without taking the time to open the case file.

"What did you do this time, Joe?" Lisa said. "Ya flash a nun this time? Walk into a church with your fly open?"

"Easy, Lisa. Give him a chance to speak," Vinny said as he eyed the familiar face of Judge Temperance Finch processing a case from up on the bench. "You're kind of making a habit of this, Joe. What's going on?"

"I was looking for a guy."

"What guy?"

"Your guy. Bald Louie."

"You found him?" Vinny asked.

"No. But I found where he lives. The place was empty."

"*Shit.* When you say 'empty' do you mean completely empty or just partially empty?"

"What do you mean?" Joe asked.

"Did it look like someone was living there?"

"Yeah, I guess."

"But you got no idea where Bald Louie went?"

"None, Vinny.

"Could it be that he just wasn't there when you paid him a visit?"

Joe shrugged. "I guess so."

"I see...so, before the case is called...how'd you get pinched?"

"One of the neighbors must've seen me pounding on Bald Louie's door. I guess they called the cops."

Vinny opened the file and located the charge. "Joe, exactly how'd you get into Bald Louie's apartment?"

"I walked in. The door was open."

"Was it opened or just unlocked?"

"Before or after I turned the doorknob?"

Vinny rolled his eyes. "*Before,* Joe. *Before.*"

"Closed."

"It says here that the arresting officer found you in the apartment rented by someone named Louis Rolfe—I guess that's Bald Louie. You're charged with criminal trespass, a Class B misdemeanor."

"What's that mean, Vin?"

"It's—" Vinny's mouth was wide open and about to answer when Joe's case was called.

"What are you gonna do?" Joe asked.

"I don't know. I'll think of something."

Judge Finch studied the complaint while the court officer read the summary charge. She looked up and shook her head. "Always a pleasure to have the Gambini boys in my court."

"Thank you, Your Honor."

"I was being facetious, Mr. Gambini. This is turning into a regular Laurel and Hardy routine. Mr. Gambini. How does your client plead?"

The tough love lesson from the other day was still fresh in Vinny's mind. He stood up straight and tall. "Not guilty, Your Honor."

"Mr. Doucette, do the people request remand?"

"Yes, Your Honor," he replied. "This is the second time in mere weeks that the accused has been brought before the court." He turned to Vinny and mouthed, "Sorry."

"Anything to add before I rule on bail, Mr. Gambini?"

"Yes, Your Honor. The accused was merely trying to locate Mr. Rolfe. He was carrying no burglar's tools, nor was he carrying any lethal weapons and entered the premises without criminal intent. The door was unlocked and he entered just *to make sure* that Mr. Rolfe wasn't dead or nothin'. He was merely carrying out the duties of a concerned citizen. I'm standing before you, his brother, so you know he has ties to the community. We *respectfully* request that the accused be released on his own recognizance, Your Honor."

"You've become quite a refined orator, but I'm not sure which Mr. Gambini I prefer."

Vinny seemed puzzled. "Um...what do you mean, Your Honor?"

"I'm not sure whether I prefer the lawyer I met last week or the one who has evolved into such a polished ass kisser he takes my breath away."

Vinny struggled for a comeback but couldn't think of one.

DA Gold had just entered the courtroom and was whispering in Doucette's ear.

"Your Honor," Doucette said. "May we approach?"

"Okay," she replied, seeming puzzled by the request.

"What's this all about?" Vinny asked as he stood before the bench.

"Your Honor, this is a nuisance case—likely a misunderstanding," Doucette said. "The people would like to dismiss the complaint, if that's all right with you."

Vinny blurted, "No shit! Um...I mean really?"

Judge Finch grinned. "There's the guy I know and like so much. Are you sure you want to dismiss, Mr. Doucette?"

"If it's okay with you, Your Honor."

"Hell yes, it is—one less case for me to preside over? Are you kidding?" She made a notation on the file before turning to Vinny. "Mr. Gambini, you're starting to grow on me, *but* the next time you appear before me, it better not be to defend any siblings, relatives of any kind, friends, or acquaintances. Is that clear?"

"Absolutely, Your Honor."

"Not even someone you bumped into in the elevator. You know what they say about three strikes, don't you?"

"Yes, Your Honor."

"Good. Because the next time I see your brother Joe in here, I'm going to throw the book at him. I don't care if he was arrested for failure to share a square of toilet paper in a public restroom." She leaned forward, her eyes blazing into his. "You hear me, Counselor?"

"Yes, Your Honor. Thanks. Is that it?"

"That's it." She was still smiling as she waved goodbye. "See you around, Mr. Gambini."

Vinny turned to Joe and made a ta-da gesture, his arms out from the elbows, his palms face up. "How'd you like them apples?"

"Thanks, Vin," Joe said, giving him a celebratory hug.

"No problem." Vinny grabbed his briefcase. When he turned around, he saw Joe trudging away just as his pants fell to the floor.

As he stared at his brother's butt crack he heard Judge Finch's derisive comment, "Perfect. That's *absolutely* perfect."

Lisa pulled out her camera and snapped a picture before turning to Vinny. "Hall of fame collection?"

He was still shaking his head in disbelief. "Oh yeah... without a fuckin' doubt!"

CHAPTER FIFTY
Favor of the Month

Lisa covered her eyes out of sheer embarrassment as Joe bent over to yank up his pants. "The hell is wrong with you, Joe?" she asked the moment they were out of the courtroom.

"It wasn't my fault. They took my belt away when I was in lockup and lost it. I guess my pants are a little loose."

"Imagine that," she said and gave her head a disbelieving shake. "And what's with those eyesore boxers you're wearing? Half of your ass was uncovered."

"I guess the waistband is a little worn out."

Vinny caught up with them and smacked Joe on the butt. "Nice cheeks, big boy. I think the judge wants to ask you out on a date."

"For real?"

"No, Joe. *Not* for real. Do you have any idea how embarrassing that was for me? Now every time I'm in that courtroom, the judge will be looking at me but she'll be thinking about *your* big, hairy ass. I'll be the laughing stock of the Brooklyn court system."

"Sorry, Vin, but like I told Lisa, they took my belt."

"And *my* dignity," Vinny said.

"Ease up," Lisa said. "It's not as if you're Clarence-fuckin'-Darrow. So Joe dropped trou, so what? You think the judge doesn't see a hundred wackos every day? She'll get over it."

"Yeah. *Whatever.*" He saw DA Gold leaving court. "Don't

go nowhere. I'll be right back." He hurried to catch up with Gold who was galloping down the steps to the main floor. "Morty," he called. "Hey, wait up."

"What's with your brother, Gambini?" Gold asked. "For some reason the two of you seemed to have arrived on the legal scene at exactly the same time."

"Thanks for what you did back there, Morty. I know it was you who told Doucette to cut Joe a break. You know, he's really pretty harmless. He was just in the wrong place at the wrong time."

"That won't keep him out of jail the next time he drops his pants or gets caught breaking and entering."

"I got it, and...thanks. I'll make sure it don't happen again."

"I can only do so many favors for you, Gambini. I trust you won't need another one in the near future."

"Absolutely not. Thanks again."

Gold checked his watch. "I'm running late, but call my office. I think the discovery documents you requested are ready—waiting for an address to deliver them to."

"Great, I'll send somebody to pick them up right away."

"In a hurry, are you?"

"Yeah, you could say that."

"See you in court, Gambini. Tell your brother to keep his nose clean...and his pants up around his waist where they belong." He rushed off.

Vinny turned around and was about to walk back up the stairs when he saw that Lisa and Joe were already on their way down. "Why do you think he did that?" Vinny asked. "I mean doing it the first time was one thing but...that was a really nice thing for him to do a second time."

"Ain't it obvious," Lisa responded. "He wants you to think twice before challenging him in court. Don't you know nothing? I told you not to let that man into your head. You think he took you to lunch and kicked Joe's case because he's in the running for the Nobel Peace Prize?"

"Trotter didn't do nothing like that. He was an honorable guy."

"Gold ain't Trotter. Trotter was the DA of a miniscule Alabama parish. All he had to do to get reelected was invite everyone over to his place for a hoedown, grill some corn-dogs, and pour moonshine. This is New York, Vinny. You're up against a DA who wants to get reelected at the end of the year. He'll do anything to make that happen, and convicting the woman who killed the deputy mayor's brother is just the ticket he's looking for. It don't matter that she's not guilty. He's got to put someone away."

"Jesus," Joe said. "Lisa is friggin' smart, Vin."

"Yeah, I know," Vinny said. "Sometimes I think I really don't deserve her."

"What now?" Lisa asked, ignoring his self-deprecating comment.

"I'm thinking we split a couple of those ginormous pas-trami sandwiches. Then I'm gonna get my ass back to work."

CHAPTER FIFTY-ONE
Emergency Service

Three Weeks Later

All was quiet in Vinny and Lisa's home. The digital clock on the nightstand read 3:00 a.m. They were in bed, sound asleep, the muffled flutter of Vinny's snoring filled the bedroom with a hypnotic hum. They'd gone to bed early so that he'd be well rested and sharp for the first day of jury selection.

That was their plan, anyway.

When 3:00 clicked over to 3:01, the night exploded. Their eyes shot open in unison. Dazzling lights breached the gaps in the window shades, turning their bedroom into a strobe-lit dance floor. The house shook as if succumbing to the seismic shocks generated by an earthquake, but the riveting thunder of a jackhammer said otherwise. They were literally vibrating in bed.

"You got to be fuckin' kidding me," Vinny said in a strained voice. "A construction crew? Here? At this hour?"

Lisa made a face, then yanked the pillow out from under her head and covered her face with it. "Maybe they followed us home from Alabama."

"That's not funny."

"Just make it stop."

He rubbed his eyes, pushed back the covers, and shivered as his feet hit the cold wooden floor. He pushed the window shade aside, making the room as bright as if it were high noon. "Son of a bitch!" he swore as he took in the turbulent scene taking place on the street in front of their driveway. Three gas company trucks and a half-dozen hardhats were hustling about while a jackhammer ate huge chunks of asphalt, creating a six-inch deep trench in front of of their driveway. He'd been sleeping in his sweats and needed only to step into his boots before leaving the bedroom. He clumsily navigated down the staircase and out the front door.

"Hey!" he yelled above the roar of the jackhammer to get the attention of one of the hardhats. "You got any idea what time it is?"

The worker turned to him. "What?"

He formed a megaphone with his hands and yelled, "I asked if you got any idea what time it is?"

"Emergency gas leak," the hardhat replied, his shout barely discernable above the roar of the pneumatic jack-hammer.

"Emergency gas leak," Vinny muttered in defeat. "How long you gonna be here?"

"What?"

Vinny once again pulled out the megaphone. "I said, how long you gonna be here?"

"As long as it takes, Mack."

Vinny glanced down at the broad channel being cut in front of his driveway. "How am I gonna get my car out? I gotta go to work in a few hours."

"What?"

He repeated his question with his arms folded across his chest, shivering, his teeth chattering. "How am I gonna get my car out?"

"You'd better pull it out now," the hardhat yelled, "before it's too deep. I've got no idea what we'll find when we get down there."

"'Pull it out now,'" Vinny repeated in a muffled voice before trudging back into the house to fetch his car keys.

He yawned long and loud from within the passenger compartment while he waited for the massive V-8 to warm up. He rubbed his eyes to clear them, but they were glassy and the glare of the bright mobile lights were blinding. He threw the gearshift into reverse and barreled down the driveway faster than he should have, lack of sleep and overconfidence overriding good common sense. The workers scattered as the red gargantuan convertible came straight for them. The jackhammer operator dropped his large power tool and ran for cover.

Vinny cut the wheel sharply but not in time to avoid the jagged rift in the street. He popped the left rear tire, deflating it completely. He knew what had happened the second he heard the loud pop and the *whoosh* of escaping pressurized air. He stopped the car and covered his eyes with his hand as the irate construction crew rushed toward the car. "I can't fuckin' believe it," he said. When he looked up again, Lisa was at the window, once again shaking her head in disbelief.

CHAPTER FIFTY-TWO
Almost 10:16

"Four thousand eight hundred and fifty pounds, *plus* your own *very svelte* body weight, puts the weight of the Caddy at over five thousand pounds," Lisa preached much to Vinny's chagrin.

He glared at her from behind the wheel on their way to court as snow fell and the Caddy slid on icy sludge.

"*Now*, given the fact that the Caddy rides on fifteen-inch, tubeless, bias-ply tires, coupled with the frigid ambient air, which must've shrunken the steel rim just a fraction of an inch, when you plowed into the pothole at excessive speed, there was no way the seal wasn't going to rupture. Why the hell were you backing down the driveway so fast?"

"Lisa, *please*. I don't need to hear your expert lecture on the dynamics of automobile tire failure under adverse road conditions. I've been up since three o'clock in the morning. I had a confrontation with half a dozen men in hardhats. I changed a flat tire in the freezing cold. I've got a hard-ass judge who just loves to tell me what I'm doing wrong, a two-and-a-half-ton sled that's sliding back and forth over the road like a puck on an ice hockey rink—not to mention that today is the first day of jury selection for the murder trial of an innocent woman. I got plenty on my mind already."

"Bad timing?"

"Ya *think*?"

* * *

The snow was two inches deep by the time Vinny and Lisa marched up the courthouse steps. They stomped their feet to get the snow off their shoes and proceeded through security. "You feel prepared?" Lisa asked as she smoothed the shoulders on his suit. "You look prepared. I think you're ready."

"Yeah, I guess I am," he said halfheartedly.

"Listen, Vinny, I know you're tired but you gotta shake out the cobwebs. This is no time to start doubting yourself. You got to go in there and show the jurors who you are or they won't have no respect for you. You think you can do that?"

"I can. I mean...*yes.*"

"Great," she said, supplying all the enthusiasm he seemed to be lacking. "Now get up there and do your thing."

"Thanks, Lisa."

"I gotta run," she said. "I can't sit there for jury selection anyway, and Gloria wants me in the shop by eleven."

"You sure you're okay taking the train?"

"Yeah. What's the big deal? Besides with the snow sticking like it is and every asshole with a driver's license out on the road, I'm safer on the subway than I am behind the wheel. Pick me up at the shop tonight, okay?" She kissed him and hurried off.

Gold was first to *voir dire* Rose Donnelly, an elderly woman clinging onto the handle of her cane in the jury box. He read from the juror questionnaire she'd completed in advance before looking up and greeting her with a smile. "Good morning, Mrs. Donnelly. You're looking fine this morning."

She grinned absently and checked her watch before answering in a thick Irish brogue. "Ten-fifteen."

Gold's forehead wrinkled as he inched closer to the jury

box. "Mrs. Donnelly, can you hear me all right? I didn't ask the time. I said, you're looking fine."

She checked her watch again and clarified her response, "Almost ten-sixteen."

Gold glanced at the judge, who said, "Thank you for your service, ma'am. You're dismissed."

"I'll be missed?" she asked.

"Yes, very much." Whorhatz motioned for the court officer to escort her from the room.

All the jurors moved over one position until Mrs. Donnelly's seat had been filled. An alternate juror moved to the jury box to bring the total number back to twelve.

Gold tried again. The next juror was also elderly, a balding man who exposed gaps between his teeth when he smiled in anticipation of being spoken to. Gold smiled. "Good morning, Mr. Goldberg. How are you today, sir?"

"Me? I'm wonderful," he said in a heavy Yiddish accent. "We got a Gold and a Goldberg, two Hamish boys in a court of law. What could be bad? I started the day with a cup of sweet tea and a nice thick slice of chocolate babka. I was out of the shower by five a.m., dressed and ready to do my civic duty."

"And we appreciate your enthusiasm. Thank you." Gold seemed pleased as he checked the questionnaire. "I see that you've served as a juror in the State of New York before. Can you tell me about that experience?"

"Why sure. I'd be delighted to. Some big shot *gonif* attorney embezzled—"

Gold's hand shot up.

The judge grinned and dismissed the juror.

It was after three and only six jurors had been selected. Vinny seemed worn as he questioned a prospective juror, a woman who appeared to be in her late thirties. She was on the plain side but wore lots of makeup,

"How are you, Ms. Matthews?"

"Fine. Thank you."

"And are you looking forward to performing your service as a juror?"

Again her answer was curt. "Yes."

"Yes. And do you feel that you could participate fairly in a murder trial?"

"I do."

"Good. You don't have a lot to say, do you?"

"No."

"Can you expand on that?"

She grimaced. "What?"

"Never mind, dear. I was just trying to lighten the mood."

Her poker face didn't budge.

"Do you have any reason for not wanting to sit on this trial?"

"Yes."

"Yes. And for the record, would you please explain why?"

"With pleasure. My filthy rotten son of a bitch husband left me to be with his twenty-three-year-old secretary when I was pregnant with our first child."

The sudden outpouring of emotion stunned Vinny. "I'm very sorry to hear that. Truly I am, but why would that prevent you from being an impartial juror?"

"Because."

"Because why?"

"Because my son of a bitch husband was a lawyer," she said. "And I can't stand the sight of any of you philandering pieces of shit!"

It was late in the day, later than Whorhatz would've cared to continue, but they'd made progress and had selected eleven of the twelve jurors. The next prospective juror stood up, prominently displaying a book entitled *The Best Defense* by Alan Dershowitz. Gold asked Whorhatz to dismiss him with-out asking a solitary question.

CHAPTER FIFTY-THREE
Big Sal

Lack of sleep and the long, difficult day of selecting a jury had really done Vinny in. Five inches of snow had accumulated on the roadway contributing several accidents on the BQE. The thirty-minute drive took almost two hours, making him too late to pick up Lisa and necessitating her getting a ride home with one of the other girls from the shop. She was dropped off at her parent's house where they were both supposed to have dinner with Ma and Augie.

Just ahead of him, a street plow cleared the snow all the way to the curb right in front of Barone's Deli. Nature abhors a vacuum—likewise Vinny felt compelled to pull into the newly cleared space. He did so on impulse—it was as if he'd made it that far, had run out of steam, and could continue no further. Ma and Augie lived only ten minutes away but he just didn't have the energy to go on. He sorely needed a little peace and quiet and knew he wouldn't get any from Lisa and his future in-laws.

"Barone," he boomed as he walked into the store stomping snow from his shoes.

"Vinny? Vinny Bag O' Donuts? You son of a bitch." He closed his phone book, walked around the counter with it still in his hand, and gave Vinny a man hug. "I can't believe it."

"You can't believe what?" Vinny asked.

He held up his personal phone book. "See this? I was just looking for your phone number."

"*My* phone number? You were looking for *my* phone number? How come? You feeling lonely or something? You feel an overwhelming need to reminisce?"

"Yeah, right? I haven't been ranked out in ages and I figured my self-esteem could use a good kick in the balls. Who better to break my shoes than you?"

"Barone, I just drove two hours on the BQE in bumper-to-bumper traffic. I'm physically and mentally exhausted after a really long day in court. My legs are numb, my neck is stiff, and I'm just dying for a hot cup of coffee. Maybe you could just tell me what you're talking about in plain English."

"Sure. Sure," Barone said as he nudged Vinny into a corner. "I can't believe you came in here when you did," he whispered. "Your brother Joe told me you were looking for that guy, Bald Louie, and—"

Vinny perked up. "You know where he is?"

"No, but something almost as good." He pointed to a man alone at a table in the back of the store chomping down a monster sub. "You know who that is?"

"Uh-uh."

"That's Sal Sauseech wolfing down about two pounds of cold cuts back there. I ain't seen him around here in ages but he's here now and so are you. It's like fate chose to bring the two of you together at the same time."

"Sal Sausage?"

"Yeah…Sauseech actually."

"Ain't it the same thing?"

"Yeah."

"So? He's got a big appetite. So what? I ain't with Ripley's Believe It Or Not. I don't care if he swallows an entire roast beef and washes it down with a Virginia ham."

"Vinny, Vinny," he said. "Who do you think Bald Louie was working for when he got pinched and went away?"

"Don't tell me it was *this* guy?"

"Yeah. Louie was one of Sal's guys."

229

"No kidding."

"Maybe if you chat him up he'll tell you something that might help you find him."

"Really? You think so?"

"Couldn't hurt to ask. What's the worst he could do, pull his piece and shoot you in the ass?"

"Very funny, Barone. Why do you say that? Is this guy mobbed up or something?"

"Does a chicken have lips?"

Vinny scowled. "Why do people ask that? Everyone knows they don't."

Barone became pensive. "You know that's a good question." I've been saying that my whole life and I never thought about it before. I guess you're right."

"About what?"

"Chickens."

"Any chance we could get past the chicken anatomy lesson?"

Barone peered at Sal Sauseech. "That hero sandwich is whizzing past his teeth like a kindling through a wood chipper. You'd better hurry up before he finishes."

"Right. Give me a—"

"Don't worry. I got it." Barone wrapped up a hunk of coffee cake, poured coffee, and pushed them into Vinny's hands before he could take out his wallet.

"But I didn't pay."

"Just hurry up. Catch me on the way out."

"Okay, thanks."

Sal was a large man wearing a wool coat with a fur collar that hid his neck. He extended his teeth to bite into the foot-long hero like a shark would to engulf prey in its powerful jaws.

Vinny sat down at the next table. As he took a sip of coffee, he noticed that Sal was eying him. "That's a hell of a good-looking sandwich you got there. What's in it? On second thought, it might be easier to ask what's not in it."

"You talking to me?" he asked with his mouth full, his voice gravelly. It sounded as if he had begun smoking while still in the womb.

"Yeah. I'm talking to you. I bought this here coffee cake but you got me thinking maybe I should've ordered something more substantial. You got any mortadella in there? I love that stuff."

Sal put down the sandwich and pinned him with an icy cold stare. "You a cop?"

"Me? No, I ain't a cop. I'm a lawyer."

"You a DA or something?" he asked cautiously.

"No, I'm a defense attorney." He reached over and offered his hand. "Vincent Gambini. Nice to meet you."

He wiped the crumbs from his mouth before accepting Vinny's hand. "Sal Sauseech."

"Huh. That's an interesting moniker you got there, Sal. You named for your favorite meal or something? I like sausage myself, especially with peppers and onions on a roll like at the Feast of San Gennaro in Little Italy."

"Not this kind of sausage you don't...at least I hope not."

"What do you mean?"

"My name ain't about street vendor food. They call me Sal Sauseech because I'm hung like Seabiscuit."

Vinny's eyes grew wide. "I guess I spoke too soon."

"Glad to hear it."

"So you're well endowed, huh?"

"Damn thing hangs down near my calf. It's so long I ain't been able to cross my legs since I was eight years old."

"No kidding?" Vinny laughed. "You must be very popular with the ladies."

"Let's put it this way—I ain't hurting for female companionship. Me and the anaconda..." He laughed heartily. "We do pretty fuckin' good for ourselves."

"I guess that expression *size don't matter* is a crock."

"A steamin' crock. Although...there have been a couple of dames who took off running after they saw it. One babe got so bent out of shape, she went through the screen door on my patio."

"Huh, who ever thought that having a big *shlong* would be such a problem? Can't the doctors do nothin'?"

"You mean like shorten it or something?"

Vinny shrugged. "I don't know. I guess."

He grimaced. "Would you?" He took out a switchblade and placed it on the table in front of Vinny. "Let me see you lop off part of *your* manhood."

Sal picked up his sandwich and took another bite. "Maybe I can throw you some work being you're on the right side of the law. You got a business card?"

He produced a card and placed it on Sal's table.

"What kind of cases you work?"

"Right now I'm defending someone on murder charges."

"Really? You think you'll get them off?"

"I hope to...yeah. Actually, I'm in here looking for a guy right now—someone to help me make my case against the prosecution."

"A guy?"

"Yeah, I hear he lives around here. You think maybe you might know him?"

"Nah, I don't know nobody," he said. He leaned toward Vinny and beckoned for him to get closer. "You didn't sit down over here to chat me up with the specific intention of finding out about this *guy, did you?*"

"No, of course not. We were getting friendly and I figured I'd ask because I really need to talk to this guy about the case I'm on and I've been asking everyone around here."

"Maybe you ought to finish up your cake and leave. It's coming down pretty hard out there. A guy could get buried in all that snow." He looked at Vinny pointedly and placed his hand over the switchblade. "Know what I mean?"

"I *think* I *do*. I guess I'll go look for this guy somewhere else."

The Swiss bell over the front door rang as a heavyset man entered. He ignored Barone and walked straight to the back of the store where he pulled out a chair and sat down at Sal's table.

"It done?" Sal asked as he slipped the switchblade back into his pocket.

"Yeah, it's done," he said.

"Good. You hungry?" Sal asked as he pushed his sandwich across the table. "I've had enough capicola to choke a horse."

The Swiss bell rang again. The door swung wide as two uniformed cops raced in, guns drawn.

"You fucking idiot," Sal swore. "They followed you." His hands went up. "Don't shoot," he yelled. "I'm just eating a sandwich."

"Cuff 'em," one of the officers said. "All three of them."

It was after 1:00 a.m. when Vinny was taken for arraignment. He'd called Joe and asked him to take the subway down to the courthouse and to call Lisa to tell her that the other rear tire went flat on the way home. With no spare in the trunk, they'd have to pull the bad tire and find a gas station that was open late. They'd have to ferry the bad tire back and forth and didn't know when they'd get home. He'd get around to telling her the truth in the morning but didn't want to scare her to death in the middle of the night with the details about mobsters and his arrest.

Judge Finch was fatigued. As a courtesy, she'd switched sessions with a colleague and wasn't used to working the graveyard shift. She read the complaint quickly and in her mind confused Vincent Gambini with her frequent visitor Joe Gambini. She looked up expecting to see Joe alongside his brother the attorney, but instead it was Vinny that stood accused and Joe in the front row of the audience section behind him. She appeared aghast, shook her head, and said, "Mr. Gambini, I don't *even* want to know."

CHAPTER FIFTY-FOUR
That Feels So Much Better

"You're lucky the judge likes you," Joe said from the passenger seat.

"It could have been much worse. She thought you were being brought in for the third time and was ready to throw the book at you like she said she was going to. I think she was so tired that she was giddy. So, when I explained that I had nothing to do with those two thugs...I think she was so exhausted she just didn't care. Anyway, the whole thing got expunged."

"What do you mean the whole thing got sponged?"

"Expunged, knucklehead. It means all records of the arrest were deleted from the system, the arrest, the booking, and the arraignment. It was like it never even happened."

"What are you gonna tell Lisa?"

"I ain't gonna tell her nothing until she's had a good night's sleep. You want me to wake her up in the middle of the night to tell her that I got pinched along with two wise guys at the neighborhood deli? She'll think I'm running book again like back in the old days before I went to law school."

"Oh yeah. I get it."

Vinny spied an all-night diner as they drove home from court. "I ain't eaten all day and I'm so hungry my stomach thinks my throat's been cut. I didn't even get a chance to eat Barone's coffee cake." He pulled into the diner parking lot. "I gotta have a sandwich or something. You hungry?"

"Does a chicken have lips?"

Again with that stupid expression? Can't anyone think of something more clever to say? He glared at Joe. "I don't know. *Does* it?"

Joe was still mulling over the question as Vinny closed the car door and walked into the diner.

"No."

"No, *what?*" Vinny asked looking up from the menu.

"No, a chicken don't have no lips."

"Oh yeah? I guess you learn something new every day." His focus returned to the menu. "I think I'm gonna get some eggs. What are you gonna get?"

Joe picked up the menu and quickly looked through it. "Maybe the rigatoni with meatballs, broccoli rabe, sausage, and cannellini beans."

"At this hour? Joe, it's almost three o'clock in the morning."

"So? I'm hungry too."

"You don't think that's a tad too heavy for this time of night?"

"No. You're eating eggs. What's the difference?"

"The difference is that eggs are eggs and what you're gettin' sounds like something that gets fed to hogs."

"I don't know what you're talking about." Joe took a small prescription bottle out of his pocket. He withdrew the dropper and put two drops on the tip of his tongue.

"What the hell is that? You taking liquid vitamins like when we was kids?"

"I got a terrible earache. The doctor gave me these drops and told me to use them four times a day."

Vinny furrowed his brow. "Let me see that." He reached across the table, snatched the bottle, and read the label. "Joe, how long you been taking these?"

"Almost a month."

"Helping any?"

"Not so much and they taste fuckin' awful."

"You ever read the label?"

"Uh-uh."

"So then, *no*...you ever wonder why the drops ain't working?"

"Maybe they ain't fresh no more."

Vinny smacked the bottle down on the table. "Well maybe if you put them in your fuckin' ears like you're supposed to... Jesus, Joe, there's a reason they call them eardrops."

"Oh shit. Really?" He laughed. "Huh, imagine that."

Vinny closed the menu. "You know you got your head up your ass most all the time. You're a smart guy but you don't apply yourself. It's like me with my dyslexia. I can't read nothing unless I really put my mind to it and you're the same way."

"I don't know. I kind of found Bald Louie, didn't I?"

"You only found out where he lives. I mean that's a good start and all, but..."

"I told you I'd keep looking for him."

"Yeah. I really need to locate the guy. It's a key part of my defense strategy. I thought I was gonna get lucky unexpectedly meeting Sal Sauseech. But now..."

"You think that Sauseech guy will get sprung?"

"I got no idea what he was brought in for but when they questioned me at the police station I told them that I was just enjoying a piece of cake and coffee and that I had no idea who the guy was."

"That was probably smart. You don't want to get on that goon's bad side. Well, I'll keep trying to find Bald Louie for you." He tilted his head to one side then the other, putting a drop into each ear. "That feels really weird."

The waitress seemed worn. She came over, took their

order, and vanished into the kitchen without making any polite chitchat.

"So I been thinking, Vin. Maybe I should sell the house."

Vinny frowned. "Our house? Mom and Dad's house?"

"Yeah. You know they hardly come up from Florida anymore and I'm in debt up to my eyeballs. I ain't paid the taxes in over two years and this morning they shut off the electric."

"Jesus Christ. Are you for real? You'll freeze in there without power. The pipes will burst."

"I know, I know. But if I sell the house I can pay off what I owe, and you and me can split the profits. I don't need a whole house for myself. All I need is a small apartment somewhere. I know you ain't exactly flush neither."

"You talk to Mom and Dad about selling the place?"

"Not yet. I figure the few times they come to visit, I could put them up at one of them extended stay places."

"How much you figure we can get for the house?"

"Some realtor knocked on the door and told me she could get between six and seven. She said Brooklyn is really hot right now."

Vinny's jaw dropped. "Six or seven hundred thousand? Holy shit. That would solve both our problems."

"You think I should call Mom and Dad?"

"Are you kidding? I'd call them the minute the sun comes up."

Joe's eyelid twitched. "Jesus. My right ear feels weird." He shuddered and a thick chunk of wax fell on the table. "*Whoa.* That feels so much better."

"Yeah." Vinny grumbled. "Imagine that."

CHAPTER FIFTY-FIVE
Relax!

Vinny ran three red lights at Joe's insistence, the tires of the big red Caddy screeching to a stop as they pulled up in front of Joe's home. The heavy meal he'd devoured at three a.m. was not sitting well with him and he was in urgent need of relief. He scrambled up the steps to his house and disappeared within, presumably to grope around in the dark desperately searching for the john. He had in his pocket every last dollar Vinny was able to withdraw from the ATM, enough to have the electricity turned back on in the morning.

Vinny smiled as he watched Joe scramble into his house. He jumped when the passenger door opened and saw a gun pointed at his nose.

A gruff voice demanded, "Don't move, Gambini!" Sal Sauseech slid into the passenger seat and yanked the door closed. "Drive," he ordered.

"Drive? Drive where? This here Caddy look like an Uber to you?"

"You're pretty tough for a guy with a gun in his face."

"Yeah. Like you're gonna shoot me over a coffee cake." He threw the gearshift into Park and took his foot off the brake. "It's almost five a.m. At best, I'm gonna get two hours sleep before I got to get up and go to court. So if you want to shoot me, do it now and put me out of my misery. You'd be doing me a favor."

"Relax! If I wanted to shoot you there'd be a hole in the

center of your forehead already." Sauseech lowered the gun. "Just an old habit I have trouble shaking."

"Oh, *now* you want to talk? First you put a gun in my face, then you want me to drive you around like I'm your personal chauffeur. Would you make up your friggin' mind already?"

"My lawyer says you didn't tell the cops nothing and being you was an officer of the court yourself, I'm thinking it must've gone a long way towards my arrest getting kicked. I figure I owe you a favor, and if I were you, I'd take advantage of my generosity while the offer is on the table. Who's this guy you're looking for, the one you interrupted my dinner to ask about?"

"I'm looking for a guy goes by the name of Bald Louie."

"Bald Louie, huh?" He stuffed the gun back into his holster. "Sure, I knew him. Back in the day when he still had hair we used to call him Louie the Louse. Why do you need that guy anyway? He's nothing but a miserable prick—skimmed from his collections. Why do you think he went away? He knew I was gonna whack him and turned himself in. You find him—tell him he owes me twenty large."

"So you ain't seen him?" Vinny shifted in his seat to face the mobster. "Like I said, I got a client on trial for murder and I thought Bald Louie might know if anyone hated the victim enough to murder him."

"Trying to create doubt in the minds of the jurors, huh? You must be one hell of a goddamn clever lawyer."

"Actually...no, that wasn't my intention. I figured if I find the guy who really did it..."

"All you got to do is confuse one juror out of twelve and you're home free. The guy who really did it?" He gave Vinny a distant look. "What are you, a lawyer or a private eye?"

"A little of both I guess. I got his address and all but he wasn't there. I don't think he's living there no more."

"I see." Sauseech mulled over Vinny's dilemma. "There

was a dame I remember, a real Clydesdale named Big Donna that he was sweet on. Maybe she'll know where he is."

"Big Donna, huh? Any idea where I might find this... equine?"

"Ha! Yeah sure. She used to tend bar over at The Cotillion."

"The catering hall?"

"Yeah. You stop by the place and you'll find her for sure. She's a goddamn fixture over there—been there forever."

"Gee thanks, Sal. That's a big help. I'll check it out right away."

He reached for the door handle. "Don't mention it, kid. Now we're square."

"Before you go I got to ask you, was you telling the truth about the—"

"The beast?"

"Yeah."

"It's the stuff of legends, kid."

"You mean like a unicorn."

"Not exactly, kid...more like a Cyclops."

CHAPTER FIFTY-SIX
They Got Nothing

Vinny was operating on just an hour of sleep as he looked for a place to sit down before the trial began so that he could practice his opening statement. He spotted a space just wide enough for him to squeeze in between two men on a public bench. "Excuse me," he said as he wiggled into the small space, opened his briefcase, and pulled out his file.

The man on his left began to fret, "Jesus, what a mess this is."

Vinny noticed that the gent's briefcase was also open on his lap and concluded he too was an attorney. "Hey, you okay?"

The man shook his head.

"Whatsamatta?"

He drew a deep, troubled breath. "I'm defending Martin Shrekatelli."

Vinny thought for a moment trying to place the name. "Oh! You mean the guy who jacked up the price of a necessary life-saving medication like five thousand percent? The guy who is perhaps the most hated man in America?"

The attorney nodded.

"You poor bastard." Vinny rolled his eyes. "Good luck with that one. You might as well be defending Hitler. You don't need a defense. You need a fuckin' miracle. If I were you I'd dump that case faster than yesterday's rotting garbage."

"I really don't know how I'm going to defend him."

"That's exactly right. Maybe you ought to say that your client is so despised that he can't get a fair trial."

The man smiled after a moment. "That's brilliant."

"It is? I mean you really think so?"

"Are you kidding? Thanks, fella. I'm going to call my partners and begin building a defense around your suggestion." He handed Vinny his business card, closed his briefcase, and stood. "Stan Serica. What's your name?"

"Gambini. Vincent Gambini."

"Well, Vincent Gambini. Thanks. I won't forget your name. You call me if you ever need a job. You're *terrific.*"

"Thanks. I will." He handed him a card of his own and went back to his reading. After a few minutes, the elderly man on his right tapped him on the arm. "Are you a lawyer, sir? I heard you talking to that other gentleman."

As always, Vinny was struggling with his reading and was trying very hard to commit his opening statement to memory. He wasn't happy about being disturbed and responded in kind. "Yeah, I am. But as you can see, I'm kind of busy."

"Can I ask you a quick question?"

"I just told you I'm—" He turned to face the elderly man who had jagged bangs, enormous buckteeth, and the ears of a bat. *Holy shit. Look at this guy. The poor guy really got smacked with the homely stick.* "If you can make it fast—I got a trial starting in a few minutes."

"I want to know if I can sue my wife's surgeon."

"Malpractice?"

"I think so."

Vinny reached into his pocket for a business card. "So what went wrong with the operation? Was she left with a horrifying permanent disfigurement? Is she in chronic pain? Is she unable to work as a result of the botched surgery?"

"No, none of that. My wife lost all interest in sex right after the surgery."

"What kind of surgery?" He pointed to his groin. "Did they take out some of her vital working parts?"

"No, he removed her damn cataracts. Gave her twenty-twenty vision."

Vinny bit his lip and slid his business card back into his pocket. "You know, I'd leave that one alone if I was you. It sounds like a tough one to win." He spotted Lisa returning from the ladies room. "Oh thank God."

"Excuse me?" the man asked.

"I just meant, thank God the old girl is still in good health." He jumped up and made good his escape.

"What did that guy want?" Lisa asked.

"He wanted to know if he could sue his plastic surgeon."

She took a hard look at the man and literally recoiled. "Son of a *bitch*. I'd take *that* fuckin' case if I were you." She fussed with his tie. "You got your opening statement memorized? I think it's really, really good."

"I think so. I've been reading it over and over. I just hope it sunk in."

"I think you're gonna be great. Like I been saying, you learned a lot from Billy's murder case in Alabama. You're much more experienced now."

"You really think so?"

"*I* know so. Judge Molloy obviously thinks so as well or he wouldn't have told Theresa to hire you. Just don't go getting your ass thrown in jail again. We can't afford it."

He checked his watch. "Time to go in. Wish me luck."

She kissed him on the cheek and with a smile said, "Break the other fuckin' leg."

Gold stood, buttoned his suit jacket, and strode toward the jury. "Your Honor. Ladies and gentlemen of the jury. Theresa Cototi is a killer! And the evidence in this case will show you that the person she pretends to be is not who she really is at all.

"On February twenty-sixth of this year, on a frigid evening at approximately four o'clock in the morning, Ms. Cototi willfully murdered Samuel Cipriani by maliciously and pre-meditatedly pushing him off the roof of eighteen-fifty-nine Cropsey Avenue, the eight-story apartment building in which she maintained a permanent domicile. You will also learn that the victim was a rehabilitated prior offender recently released from prison after paying his debt to society over a period of seven *long* years."

"Yeah," Vinny snickered. "*Or* you could just say he was an ex-con."

Whorhatz narrowed his eyes at Vinny but didn't challenge him.

Gold scanned the jury to determine their individual reactions before approaching the jury box and resting his hand on the railing. "You will hear the testimony of an eyewitness who positively identified Ms. Cototi and placed her on the roof of eighteen-fifty-nine Cropsey Avenue with bloodstains on her clothing, mere seconds after the victim was pushed from the roof. You will also hear that the victim fell to his death and landed on the avenue where an unidentified driver hit Samuel Cipriani and ran away in a most heinous fashion after causing him further physical injury. You will also hear testimony from forensic experts positively proving that Ms. Cototi indeed murdered Samuel Cipriani. We'll establish her motive for carrying out this monstrous and selfish act of wanton violence. Lastly, you'll be shown a photograph of the victim's ghastly last message in which the victim undeniably named his killer.

"Now, the defendant's counsel will very skillfully attempt to cast an illusion, an illusion showing that the evidence is nothing more than circumstantial. He'll attempt to discredit our eyewitness, and he'll try to convince you that the killer's motive is just not true. *But* in all this there is one thing that cannot be denied and on this you must remain focused—and that's the sad fact that Samuel Cipriani lost his life at the young age of twenty-eight—a man who had learned the error of his ways, who wanted nothing more than to reestablish his place in the community and carve out a small slice of happiness for himself. *And now he's dead.* Why is he dead?" He pointed a finger at Theresa. "Because that woman killed him! Thank you."

"Mr. Gambini...if you please," Whorhatz said.

Vinny turned to Lisa and saw that she looked worried. He rubbed his throbbing temple, patted Theresa's hand, and stood. "Your Honor and ladies and gentlemen of the jury." He filled his lungs. "This here is nothing more than a case of mistaken identity. In other words, they got the wrong guy. Um...woman." He was encouraged that most of the jurors laughed at his premeditated quip. He approached and faced them squarely, shoulders even, eyes focused, looking for the one juror he could most easily sway. "The experts will tell you that *the most* common and yet *least reliable* evidence in a criminal murder case is the testimony of an eyewitness. The experts will also tell you that the appeal of determining who the guilty party is, is really, really strong. And *because of that* really, really strong appeal, the experts will tell you that a person who looks like the culprit, is likely not to be the actual culprit at all. Now the DA and his team of *seriously accomplished attorneys* has no doubt labored *long and hard* to come up with a motive, a made-up story explaining why my client did it, but that ain't nothing more than fiction, dear. Sorry. Um...I meant ladies and gentlemen of the jury." He got another laugh out of them and it bolstered his confidence. "It's what we guys from Brooklyn call *baloney.*"

The jurors laughed yet again.

Gold objected but wasn't quite sure of the reason to give. "Your Honor..."

Whorhatz grinned. "Overruled. Mr. Gold. Mr. Gambini, at the risk of disappointing the jury, please try to be a little less...*colorful* in your attempt to discredit the prosecution."

"Absolutely, Your Honor."

"Good. Proceed."

"Now the DA has spared no expense in preparing for this trial and will march a long list of 'experts' in front of you. And the reason he's gonna go to such great lengths is because he ain't got nothing. So he's gotta parade all these academic types in front of you hoping you'll be impressed with their credentials." He stopped and rubbed his chin, presumably in thought. "Let me ask you a question. You know how you get a little cold symptom, so you do tons and tons of research to figure out what it is, right? And at the end of doing all that investigation, you start thinking that you've got some terrible disease, and you start worrying and worrying? *Or* you're perfectly healthy but you read this long article on a debilitating disease and when you finish reading it you're one hundred percent sure that you've got it too?" The jurors began to murmur in agreement. "The DA is gonna attempt to do just that. He's got no case so he's gotta make one up and try to sell it to you as the truth."

He felt confident that he'd found the one compassionate juror he could connect with, Mrs. Faraday, a black woman with a kind face and a warm smile. He continued on, addressing them all but actually speaking to her and her alone.

"In summation, their witness didn't see what she thought she saw, *no motive exists*, all the expert opinions you'll hear will only corroborate *circumstantial* evidence, *and*...these *mysterious* last words from the victim are nothing more than random letters and don't prove nothin'. The only thing Theresa Cototi is guilty of is that she loved her boyfriend so deeply that she remained faithful to him while he did his time. Thank you."

Vinny felt confident that he had planted the seeds of doubt

in every juror's mind and made a solid first impression with his plain talk and humor. He couldn't suppress his smile as he walked back to the defense table, but it disappeared when he saw tears streaming down Theresa's face.

CHAPTER FIFTY-SEVEN
You Checking up on Me?

"Good work today, Counselor. I'm feeling much more at ease about entrusting you with the responsibility of defending my dear departed friend's only child."

Vinny recognized his mentor's voice and spun around, smiling. "Judge Molloy, I'm surprised to see you here again. You checking up on me?"

A barely perceptible nod of the head indicated that he was. "And I liked what I saw today. You were prepared and to the extent of your ability you were eloquent as well. That was as fine an opening statement as I've heard in my thirty years on the bench. You touched the jurors and they responded to you." He patted Vinny on the shoulder. "But as trials go, you're at the very beginning and I don't foresee a sprint to the finish line. I hope you're prepared for a marathon, Mr. Gambini." He raised a questioning eyebrow.

"I am, Judge Molloy. I learned a lot from my first murder trial."

Lisa stood behind the judge just off to the side, basking in the praise he lavished on her fiancé. When he finished speaking, she approached him and kissed him on the cheek. "There's my favorite judge."

"Ah, the lovely Ms. Vito, a pleasure as always."

Lisa blushed before resting her head on Vinny's shoulder. "He did good today, didn't he?"

"He certainly held his own against a very formidable

opponent. DA Gold is as sharp as they come but I have the feeling Vinny is going to give him a run for his money." He checked the time. "I have to be seated in a few minutes." He doffed an imaginary cap. "If you'll excuse me."

Vinny watched him disappear through the doors at the back of the courtroom. "What a great guy."

"You owe him a lot, Vinny. I hope you won't never forget it." She flicked his earlobe affectionately. "You were really great out there today. You kicked the DA's ass." She grabbed him and pressed her lips to his cheek. "Let's go celebrate. I've got money from the beauty parlor. Let's go someplace special for dinner."

He'd told her about his chance encounter with Sal Sauseech as well as all the subsequent developments that had unfolded the evening before. "Yeah, okay, but I wanna talk to Joe first. It could really strengthen the case if we can track down this Big Donna that Sal told me about. If we find out something useful, maybe Joe can do some legwork for me when I'm in court tomorrow."

"Sure. We can stop by Joe's place right after we hit the Cotillion. Maybe he'll want to come out with us. I'm proud of you for giving him the money to turn the electricity back on." She kissed his cheek again. "It shows you ain't selfish. You think he's gonna sell the house?"

"I think so. Only he's gotta talk to my folks first. He said he was gonna talk to this realtor again today to get a better handle on what she thought we could get for the place."

Across the aisle, Gold and Doucette packed up their things. The normally affable DA bounded from the courtroom without saying goodbye.

Reporters on the courthouse steps mobbed Vinny and Lisa as they left, each jockeying for position. Vinny was a bit overwhelmed by the onslaught of reporters stalking him.

The most determined reporter pushed through the crowd, the foam-covered tip of her microphone mere millimeters from Vinny's face. "Mr. Gambini," she said. "Lena Kyle with ABC News. What was the atmosphere in the courtroom on the first day of trial?"

Ordinary women had no effect on Vinny but Lena Kyle exuded a powerful sexuality he found impossible to ignore. Taken off guard he blabbed, "About eighty degrees. They got the heat turned up way too high."

The inadvertent quip took the reporters by surprise causing them to laugh. Lisa elbowed him and pointed at the news camera. "Vinny, you're gonna be on TV," she whispered. "Don't fuck it up."

"Seriously, Mr. Gambini," Kyle said. "What was the mood?"

"Um...tense. I think. Yeah. It was tense. After all, an innocent young woman is on trial for murder. So naturally everyone's all worked up."

Kyle pursued him, drawing so near he could practically feel her body against his. "Are you intimidated by the deputy mayor and the fact that you're defending the woman accused of his brother's murder?"

"Intimidated? No, I'm not intimidated. I might be if I had the slightest suspicion that my client was guilty, but she ain't."

"You seem very sure of yourself," Kyle said, putting her hand on Vinny's arm.

Lisa watched the exchange with the trained eye of a woman watching another woman making a move on her man.

"You know I can't discuss the case with you but I'm sure the facts will speak for themselves, and there ain't no way the DA, as smart as he is, is gonna be able to deceive all twelve jurors into believing my client is guilty."

Lisa had the instincts of a professional campaign manager.

She yanked Vinny by the arm and hollered, "Thank you. No more questions."

"Hey? Why'd you do that?" Vinny said. "I had a lot more to say."

"I know," Lisa replied as she hustled him away. "You can thank me later."

CHAPTER FIFTY-EIGHT
Big Donna

Vinny looked around examining the catering hall décor. The Cotillion's marble floors had yellowed and the gold leaf on the figures in the circular fountain had long ago corroded—as a result, water spouted from the mouths of angels that looked as if they had leprosy. Life forms yet undiscovered by modern science were evolving out of the primordial ooze at the bottom of the fountain.

"What do you think of this place?" he asked as he admired the chandelier.

"For *what?*" Lisa asked, her nose wrinkled.

"For our wedding."

"In *this* dive? Vinny, you've got to be kidding. I wouldn't be caught dead in here. It looks like Europe after they bombed the crap out of it."

"I don't know—I don't think it looks so bad."

"You got about as much chance of marrying me in here as Quasimodo does of getting to first base with Taylor Swift."

"All right. I get it. The place ain't good enough for you. I'm sorry I brought it up. Maybe I'll phone the queen and see if Buckingham Palace is available."

She was sneering at him when someone called out. "You here to book a wedding date?"

They looked up to see an amazon of a woman in barman's attire drying a wine glass with a dishtowel.

Lisa snorted. "*My* wedding? *Here*? I don't think so."

"Stop it," he said out the side of his mouth. "I think that's her." He called out, "You wouldn't by any chance go by the name of Big Donna, would you?"

"Yeah, I would. How can I help you?"

Donna noticed her shirt was wet and her bra was grinning through the cloth, which drew attention to her oversized chest. She used the dishtowel to dry the wet spot.

Lisa whispered aside to Vinny, "I bet she didn't buy *that* bra off the rack."

They approached but were held at bay by Donna's enormous bosom, which was about level with Lisa's nose.

"Everything's custom, babe."

Lisa turned red. "I guess you heard me. I'm really sorry."

"*Ha.* Don't give it a second thought. I've been lugging these things around with me since I was fourteen—believe me, I've heard every wisecrack in the book." She dabbed at the wet spot one last time. "I used to think I was hot shit when I was developing as a teenager and all the guys were following me around with their tongues hanging to the ground. Look at me now—I can barely squeeze these things through the air-port metal detector. Forget about using the onboard lavatory. Thank God for cell phones—If I had a buck for every time I had to be rescued from a phone booth..."

"I'm sorry to hear about your...logistical dilemma," Vinny said. "I'm sure it ain't easy being as amply endowed as you are." He offered his hand. "My name is Vincent Gambini. I'm a lawyer, and this is my assistant, Ms. Vito. You mind if I ask you a few questions?"

"What's this about?" she asked suspiciously.

"I'm a defense attorney and I'm looking for a guy who might be able to help me win a murder case."

"A murder case? Who got whacked?"

"That ain't real important. What is important is that my client is innocent and the information this guy might have could help set her free."

"What's this guy's name?"

"Someone you were allegedly involved with years ago...someone called Bald Louie."

"That two-timing twerp? We didn't exactly end on the best terms."

"So you ain't seen him since he was released from prison? We understand he's been out of the joint about six months."

"Oh, I've seen him. The leech knocked on my door the same day he got sprung, crying about how he had nowhere to go and how much he loved me."

"How'd you handle that?" Lisa asked.

"One night," she said, holding up her pointer finger. "Him on the couch and me locked in my bedroom with a Louisville Slugger. He figured I'd be happy to see him and throw him a welcome-home booty call, but I didn't want any part of him. Who knows what he could've picked up in the joint? I wouldn't go near him if he was wearing a radiation suit."

Lisa nodded. "Smart move, Donna. They got bugs now that can't be killed with an atomic bomb."

"So you got no idea where he might be?" he asked.

"No. But the jerk gave my phone number to his parole officer as his contact. I've been getting calls twice a week all month long. I don't think Louie's been keeping any of his appointments."

"You wouldn't happen to know the parole officer's name, would you?"

"Jay something I think." She mulled it over. "Or maybe it's Ray? I can't remember. Here..." She pulled her cell phone out of her pocket. "I added the phone number into my contacts under: Don't Answer. That way I know enough to ignore the call when I get it."

Vinny wrote down the number. "Thanks a lot."

"I hope it helps."

Lisa smiled at her as they headed off. "Thanks, Donna... and good luck with your future air travel."

CHAPTER FIFTY-NINE
I Hope He Ain't Making a Monkey out of Himself

They stopped home to change before going out to dinner. Lisa looked especially radiant and Vinny more relaxed than he'd seemed in a great while.

"Look at that," Lisa said pointing at a car parked in front of Joe's house. The license plate on a white Audi read: SEL-UR-HSE. "Joe must be talking to the real estate agent inside. It would be a good thing for you to hear what she has to say, Vin—it being half yours and all."

"Yeah, that's a smart idea," he said as he parked the Caddy. "I hope this works out. Joe's up to his ass in debt, and our share would give us enough for a down payment on a place of our own."

"You know what I think? I know that we've been together ten years but I think this is just the start for us—you a successful lawyer and me..." She thought for a moment. "I can be your PI. I'll find 'em and you'll fry 'em."

"Whoa, whoa, whoa." Vinny took a long look at her. "I'm happy you got such grandiose plans for the two of us but maybe we should concentrate on one case at a time before we go turning into a *Law & Order* spinoff. We got weeks of trial ahead of us and the DA's got lots of ammunition."

"Sounds like you're worried about the case. Is that it?"

"Yeah, of course. I'm seriously worried. It ain't gonna be easy." He pulled the lever, opening the door. "But we'd better get inside so we don't miss nothin'."

"You think we ought to ring the bell?" Lisa asked as they walked up the steps.

"Nah, it's busted, remember? Besides, Joe never locks the front door."

"Well that ain't the safest thing to do."

"Believe me, Lisa, every second-story man in a five-mile radius knows that Joe's got nothing but lint in his pockets. Trust me, he's plenty safe."

"I guess. I just hope he ain't making a monkey out of himself in front of this realtor."

Vinny shrugged and pushed the door open. They walked in on Joe, his bare, naked butt crack once again staring them in the face. The realtor was on the couch looking up at Joe with her skirt hiked up around her waist and her legs straddling his shoulders.

CHAPTER SIXTY
Hey! Who Asked You?

Lisa kept her eyes covered while the realtor tugged down her skirt and stepped into her pumps. She grabbed her coat and raced toward the door, her face bright red.

"Don't forget these, dear," Vinny said as he scooped her panties off the carpet. "Victoria's Secret. Very nice. Hey, Lisa, you think you'd like a pair of these?"

Lisa had her eyes covered. She split them just wide enough to see what he was holding. "Vinny! For God's sake, would you just hand her the damn thing. I'm mortified over here."

She snatched her panties from Vinny and disappeared out the door.

Vinny walked to the door to shut it behind her but not before the sound of screeching tires filled the air. "Way to go, Joe. I didn't think it was possible for you to be a bigger embarrassment than you already are but you just took the damn thing to a whole new level. Look at Lisa for crying out loud. She's horrified over there. She may have to go into therapy."

"Does he have his pants on yet? I'm afraid to look."

Joe had tugged up his jeans and was slowly cinching his belt. "Who's embarrassing who? You ever think about knocking before you come into someone's house?"

"Eh...it's my house too, Joe."

"Eh...but you don't live here, do you, Vin? You've been cock-blocking me my whole life."

Lisa lowered her hand. "You ever think you might lock the

door when you're in here knocking boots with the local realtor? Put a necktie around the doorknob or something? For Christ's sake, that's the second time in a month I've seen your johnson. I swear to God—I'm gonna go blind."

"The two of yous relax." Joe pointed to the couch. "Sit down and let me explain."

Lisa recoiled. "No way! I ain't ever sitting on *that* couch again."

"Suit yourself," Joe said plopping down in the exact spot in which the realtor's butt had made a deep indentation. "It's not like I planned it or nothing."

"So, Svengali, just how did this tender moment come about?" Vinny asked.

"Like I said, it wasn't planned. I asked her over to get a better idea of how much we could get for the place before I called Mom and Dad. That was your suggestion, Vinny. Remember?"

"Okay. Yeah. So?"

"So she wanted me to sign a realtor's agreement at six percent and I told her that she had to sweeten the deal. How was I supposed to know how'd she react? I just wanted her to lower her commission rate. I mean what would you do if all of a sudden you had bare naked beaver staring you in the face?"

Lisa cringed. "That's very couth, Joe. Why don't you just call it a muskrat?"

"Exactly what words did you use when you told her, 'sweeten the deal?'" Vinny asked.

It took Joe a moment to recall. "Oh yeah. I said, 'You want this deal, sweetness? You'd better drop your pants.'"

Vinny shook his head. "Joe, you're un-fuckin'-believable."

Lisa snorted. "I guess she's one hell of an accommodating salesperson."

"Well, Lisa, he *did* tempt her with his John Han-*cock*."

Joe gave Vinny the finger, paused a moment, then shared one with Lisa as well.

"What'd she say about the house anyway?" Vinny asked.

"Six seventy-five."

"Wow," Vinny said. "That's pretty good. What do you think, Lisa?"

"That's sound like a lot of money. But are you sure your parents want you to sell their home? I mean they lived here almost forty years."

"Lisa, they gave it to us," Vinny said.

"Yeah? Well that don't mean they expected you to sell the fuckin' thing. I wouldn't get too excited about this big transaction until you get it straightened out with them first."

Vinny wandered over to a chair and carefully checked it before sitting down. He exhaled a deep sigh. "She's got a point, Joe."

"But like *you* said, Vin, they gave it to us."

"Yeah. I know, but thinking about it, I ain't sure that means anything."

Joe's shoulders drooped. "And here I thought all my problems were solved."

"You sure this is okay?" Joe asked as he squeezed into the Caddy's backseat.

"Yeah," Vinny said. "I need to bring you up to date about the lead we got on Bald Louie."

"I know but I don't wanna get in the way if yous was planning a romantic evening."

Lisa laughed. "Yeah. Good one," she said with deep sarcasm.

Vinny took offense at her comment. "Um...what's so funny about you and me having a romantic evening?"

"Give me a break," she said. "Joe, Vinny's idea of a romantic evening is eating pizza and watching the ball game in his boxers."

"Come on. Don't say that," Vinny said.

"Tell me it's not true."

"It's not true. There's been plenty of times I been romantic."

"Oh yeah? Name *one.*"

"There was the time I…"

"Name one time you brought me flowers."

"Lisa, what's this all about?"

She pursued him like a heavyweight boxer who had his opponent on the ropes. "How about a card or chocolates? How about perfume?"

"Come on. I brought you those things."

"Oh yeah? When? Give me a date, or an occasion."

Joe cleared his throat loudly. "Maybe you two ought to go out by yourselves. I got a can of tuna and some chips in the pantry and I'm just aching for a homemade tuna noodle casserole."

"Sit right there," Lisa said. "You're not going anywhere. I want you to hear this. Well, Vinny, you got any of those dates for me? How about one?"

"Um…I ain't so good with dates. You know that."

"Then name an occasion, a birthday or an anniversary perhaps."

"Vinny, you don't do none of those things?" Joe asked seemingly stunned by the news.

"Hey! Who asked you?"

"I did," Lisa said.

"You know I ain't so good at that kind of stuff. It's just not me."

"Oh no? Well it's me, Vinny. Don't that count for nothin'?"

Joe tried to reach for the door button but Lisa slapped his hand.

"No. You stay. *I'll* go," she said. "The two of you can talk about Bald Louie and Big-fuckin'-Donna with her immense knockers, and I'll eat the stinking tuna noodle casserole." She grew still angrier. "And what the fuck was that with the news reporter the other day, that Lena Kyle? You was practically dry humping her on the courthouse steps."

"Me? I didn't do nothin'."

She kicked the door open and got out.

"*Lisa*," Vinny said, "Don't be like that."

But her hand was up in front of her ear, showing that she didn't want to hear him.

Vinny turned to Joe with a scowl on his face. "'I don't wanna get in the way if yous was planning a romantic evening,'" he repeated, mocking his brother. "When are you going to learn to keep your fuckin' mouth shut!"

CHAPTER SIXTY-ONE
That Means Nothing to Me

"I can't believe you and Joe went to dinner last night and left me to eat a can of tuna in your brother's house."

"You made me do that," Vinny said as he piloted the car through traffic. "You got out of the car and ran into Joe's house."

"So what, was there some kind of invisible force field around the property that prevented you from coming in after me? No. You just took off and left me for dead."

They'd been going at it from the moment they opened their eyes and were now behind schedule. "What the hell are you talking about?"

"I sat there fifteen minutes waiting for you to come in and get me. But did you do that? No. You and Joe went out, ate like kings, and left me in a house with an empty pantry and no ride home."

"Joe's car was there."

"But not the car keys, genius. Was I supposed to hotwire your brother's car?"

"Look, Lisa. I'm sorry but I thought that's what you wanted. I figured you needed time to cool off."

"Does it look like I'm cooled off? You're completely clueless, Vinny. That was a test and you failed miserably."

"I don't need no tests right now. I gotta be in court to defend Theresa in an hour and I gotta be focused. You think I could take your pop quiz tonight, after we get home from court?"

"Are you coming home after court or are you gonna body slam Lena Kyle again? She got so close to you during that interview I thought she was gonna slip her microphone in your pants."

"Lisa, what are you talking about? All I did was answer a few questions—that's it!"

Lisa became silent and stayed silent, which disturbed him all the more, distracting him while he wrestled with rush hour traffic.

Whorhatz was already on the bench when Vinny dashed into the courtroom.

"Nice of you to join us, Mr. Gambini. Do you know what time it is?" Whorhatz asked.

Vinny checked his watch. "Yeah. It's exactly nine-thirty."

"And what time was court scheduled to begin today?"

"Nine-thirty, Judge. I'm right on time."

"Not in my book."

"What book is that, Judge? Because when I learned to tell time, nine-thirty was nine-thirty. You judges learn something different?"

"That's right, Mr. Gambini. As a marine I was taught that if you're not fifteen minutes early, you're late. On time is late, and late is unacceptable. So what do you think? Are you on time or are you late?"

"I think one of us needs a new watch."

The jury members and the audience laughed but Whorhatz was not amused. He turned to the DA. "Call your first witness, Mr. Gold."

Gold called Detective Parikh, who once again explained the sequence of events that led to Theresa Cototi's arrest, relating the details for the jury as he had for the judge three weeks earlier at the preliminary hearing.

"So the victim died on February twenty-sixth, is that right?" Vinny asked as he began his cross-examination.

"Yes," Parikh said. "At approximately four in the morning."

"You were there at the crime scene?"

"Yes, I was the detective assigned to the case."

"So you investigated the scene and then I guess you called the forensics team?"

"Yes."

"And they did their stuff. And then what?"

"One of the onlookers thought he recognized the victim."

"How could that be, Detective, being that the victim's head was pulverized by a hit and run driver?"

"He recognized the victim's basketball jacket."

"Really? This bystander must've been especially astute to have remembered that jacket so well."

"Not really. It was very distinctive, a royal blue and orange Knicks basketball jacket. You don't see too many of those anymore."

"You mean on account they stink and can't hardly win any games?"

"Yes." He laughed. "With a big orange thirty-three on the back."

"Patrick Ewing's number?"

"Yes."

"He's retired now. Didn't he get traded from the Knicks more than a decade ago?"

"Well it makes sense, doesn't it? The victim had been in and out of jail for the last ten years."

"You mean that he'd own an older jacket, one he purchased before he began to make prison his home address?"

"Yes."

"I guess it does. Okay. What happened next?"

"This gent, he owns the grocery store down the block and

remembered that the victim had been in to buy some groceries the other day and that he was with Ms. Cototi. She's a regular customer. He was able to provide her name and address from deliveries he had made to her apartment."

"I see. So at that point you paid a call on Ms. Cototi?"

"Yes."

"And how did that go?"

"It appeared that I had woken her up. She seemed groggy."

"Groggy like she had just gotten out of bed?"

"I already said that."

"*Right*...and she knew absolutely nothing about the victim's fall from the roof?"

"No, nothing."

"And I guess at that point she became hysterical from hearing such terrible news."

"Yes, that's correct."

"At that time did you have any suspicion at all that Ms. Cototi might've been involved in the victim's death?"

"No, not at all."

"How come?"

"It was just my first impression, I guess."

"They say that first impressions are usually pretty good. Actually, they say that first impressions are best. Maybe you should tell us about that."

"She seemed to be in a genuine state of shock, and...well it was her appearance I guess."

"What do you mean?"

"She way sleepy, terribly groggy. She was rubbing her eyes and yawning when she opened the door. And her stature, she kind of looked like a kid."

"'Like a kid,'" he repeated. "Almost childlike?"

Parikh thought before answering. "I guess so, yes."

"She's kind of tiny, ain't she?"

"Yes, she is petite."

Vinny returned to the defense table and checked his notes. "The victim was weighed in at the morgue at a solid one hundred and seventy-two pounds. It make any sense to you that this childlike person, a mere five-foot nothing, who's maybe ninety pounds after eating a large tray of lasagna, could maneuver a fully grown man up the stairs to the roof, and then force him over the ledge? That strike you as kind of improbable?"

"It did," Parikh said. "I mean, yes."

"You know, I think I would draw the same conclusion as you. You think almost any detective would?"

"Objection," Gold said. "Calls for conjecture."

"Sustained."

Vinny continued. "And at that time you considered the death a suicide, is that correct?"

"Yes."

"I see. So what made you change your mind?"

"Well for one thing, there was no suicide note."

"That's right," Vinny said. "You said in your testimony that you couldn't find a suicide note and that it's pretty rare that the victim doesn't leave one behind. Is that right?"

"Yes."

"Um..." Vinny bit his nail. "Any idea what the national statistic is for finding a note when a suicide is committed?"

"I'm not quite sure."

"Well don't you think that you should be sure?"

Gold objected. "Badgering the witness."

"Your Honor," Vinny began. "The witness stated that the incidence of not finding a suicide note was, in his words, 'pretty rare.' I'm just trying to determine what 'pretty rare' means."

"The prosecution's objection is overruled," Whorhatz said.

Vinny continued. "Detective Parikh, would it surprise you to know that the national statistic for the frequency of suicide victims leaving notes is somewhere between fifteen and thirty-eight percent?"

Parikh seemed startled. "Yes."

"On average, a suicide note is left a mere twenty-six percent of the time. What do you think now, Detective? Is not finding a suicide note rare or is it a pretty common occurrence?"

"I guess it's pretty common," he admitted.

"I guess the next time you find a body you won't jump to the conclusion that it's a homicide just because there ain't no note. That sound like a fair assumption?"

"Yes. I suppose."

Vinny grinned at Whorhatz. "No more questions, Your Honor."

"So, Ms. Trash," Vinny began.

She scolded him. "That's Träsch."

"That's what I said."

"No, you said Trash."

"Whatever," he said. "Anyway, you testified that you had wine with dinner and then even more drinks at 'a friend's house.' In total, how many drinks would you say you had during the course of the evening?"

"Maybe three or four."

"Let's call it four. Two glasses of wine and two cocktails, if I remember correctly, because you said you had cocktails at your friend's house. Over how long a period of time did you consume those four alcoholic drinks?"

"Five...maybe six hours. I'm very careful with my drinking. I pace myself."

"And how much do you weigh, Ms. Trash?"

"Träsch!"

"Okay, Träsch. How much, dear?"

"I'm a very svelte one hundred and fifteen pounds."

"That's quite a bit of alcohol for a woman of your meager weight to process. Do you know what the legal blood alcohol limit is in New York State?"

"Oh I was fine. I can hold my liquor."

"Really? Exactly where do you hold it?"

"What do you mean?"

"Well on this planet, alcohol stays in the blood. Unless you're from somewhere out in the solar system..." The jury laughed. Vinny reviewed a printed table before continuing. "Would it surprise you to know that a one-hundred-and-fifteen-pound woman who has consumed two glasses of wine and two cocktails over a period of six hours has a blood-alcohol level of zero point one-five-six."

"That means nothing to me."

"Well maybe it means nothing in the motherland but here in New York it means that you were legally impaired. Your blood-alcohol level was nearly twice the legal limit. Yet, you maintain that you positively identified my client while legally impaired from a distance of roughly one hundred feet."

"*Ja.* That's right," she insisted. "I saw her clear as day."

"Except that it wasn't day, was it? It was four a.m. in the morning, a full two hours before sunrise."

"So?"

"So, it was pitch black, and you were one hundred feet away, drunk as a skunk. Are you still sure it was my client that you saw on the roof and not someone else?" Before she could respond Vinny added, "No more questions, Your Honor."

CHAPTER SIXTY-TWO
I Said I Want a Proper Wedding

"How do you feel about the way things went today?" Lisa asked as soon as court adjourned.

"Oh, so you're talking to me now."

"Yeah, I *am*."

"In the future, it would be nice if you started out the day talking to me so that I don't have to walk into courtroom half out of my mind thinking that you hate me. Do you think maybe you could do that tomorrow?"

"Yeah, I'll do that if you don't leave me in Joe's house to eat cat food."

"Lisa, can we please put this behind us? I asked you to marry me and you said no. First you wanna go to dinner and then you don't. You're driving me out of my mind."

"Think about it, Vinny, did I say, 'No, I don't want to marry you?'"

"Yeah, you said 'No.'"

"I never said that. I said that I wanted a proper wedding."

He scrutinized her face. "So you do wanna marry me?"

"Yeah, I wanna marry you, but not until you're prepared to do it the right way."

"You mean you want a church wedding."

"Yeah, a church wedding and all the bells and whistles that go along with it."

"Tell you what. As soon as this murder case is over, why don't we sit down and plan the wedding you want?"

"You mean it?"

"Yeah, of course I mean it. We'll have the wedding of your dreams. That make you happy?"

"Yeah," she said halfheartedly.

"You don't sound too excited."

"Seeing is believing, Vinny. We haven't even set a date."

"Right after this trial, Lisa. I really mean it."

"You'd better. Anyway, not to change the subject but how do you think it went today?"

"All things considered, I think it went pretty well. I discredited Gold's first two witnesses and I didn't get thrown in jail. That's a big improvement over the way things went during Billy's trial. But Gold's gonna call his forensics witness tomorrow so I gotta prepare."

"Let's go home and I'll fix some dinner."

"Why? Is it broke?"

She rolled her eyes. "Maybe I'll cook some fish."

"Why fish? It'll smell up the house."

"Don't ya know nothing? Fish is brain food."

"You think eating a piece a swordfish is gonna make me some kind of legal genius?"

"It couldn't hurt. Scientists believe the reason civilization began in Mesopotamia was because the people there had a virtually unlimited supply of fish from the Tigris and Euphrates Rivers."

"You're saying that without the fish we'd still be living in mud huts and crapping in the woods because our brains wouldn't have evolved?"

"Precisely."

"So if primitive man lived in a completely landlocked area like say, Arkansas or West Virginia, we wouldn't be driving in cars or flying in planes?"

Lisa teased him with her expression. "And I'm making kale also."

"Kale? That's a healthy thing?"

"It's jam-packed with antioxidants, vitamins, and minerals."

"I still don't think it's a good idea."

"Why not?"

"I don't digest it so good. One large dish of kale and I could singlehandedly solve the planet's dependency on fossil fuels."

CHAPTER SIXTY-THREE
What's with the Glasses?

Vinny made sure that he got to court early the next day to avoid another reprimand from Judge Whorhatz. The room was empty as he prepared for trial, arranging his notes and legal pad so that he'd easily be able to find anything he needed.

Clark Kent was scheduled to be Gold's next witness and was the next one to arrive in court. He did his best to avoid eye contact with Vinny, but Vinny wasn't having it. "Hey, Dr. Kent, can I ask you a question?"

"We really shouldn't be talking, Mr. Gambini."

"That's all right. It ain't about the case."

"Is it another Superman question? Because people have been asking me those annoying questions my entire life."

"Yeah, you really took it between the eyes on that one. The hell were your parents thinking?"

"I wish I knew. So, you said that you have a question?"

"It ain't about Superman neither. It's about Clark Kent."

"Clark Kent the forensic scientist or Clark Kent, Superman's alter ego?"

"The second one."

"*What?*"

"What's with the glasses?"

"Excuse me?"

"The glasses, the ones Clark Kent wears. I been watching Superman since I was a kid and I can't never figure it out. He puts them on and he's Clark Kent. He takes off the glasses and he's Superman, only he's the same guy with the same face, with or without the glasses. How come no one can tell it's the same guy? Are they some kind of magic glasses that hypnotize everyone, or is it just one of them things like people are whispering behind his back, 'There's Clark Kent over there. We all know he's Superman but we're not gonna say nothing?'"

"It's fiction. You have to suspend disbelief."

"Um...what do you mean?"

"It means you go along with it for the sake of the story."

"Really? Even though you know it's just plain dumb? I mean he's Superman. He can do anything he wants but the best disguise he can come up with is a pair of Buddy Holly glasses? That shows a serious lack of imagination. At least Batman has a mask."

"I don't know, Mr. Gambini. I'm a forensic scientist. I'm not a comic book superhero." The court began to fill. "I think you better take your seat. Looks like we're about to get underway."

"Good talking to you," Vinny said as he wandered back to the defendant's table.

The door to the judge's chamber opened and Whorhatz took the bench. "I see you're early today, Mr. Gambini. *Fifteen* minutes early I trust?"

"Thirty," Vinny said. "I figured I'd make up for yesterday."

Whorhatz grinned but muttered something under his breath. He turned to the prosecutor's table. "Call your next witness, Mr. Gold."

Dr. Clark Kent was called to the witness stand. The infamous shoe print was displayed on a presentation board as it had been during the preliminary hearing. Kent again explained how his team found a partial bloody shoe print on the roof and from there reconstructed the sole pattern for a size 7 sneaker.

"Thank you," Gold said. "I'd now like to discuss with you the blood evidence found on the rooftop. Can you tell us about that, please."

"Yes, of course," Kent said. "There were no visible signs of blood on the roof but blood was subsequently revealed by the use of the chemical agent Luminol."

"On the rooftop?"

"Yes."

"Would you be good enough to tell us whose blood you found?"

"The blood belonged to the victim, Samuel Cipriani. We achieved a thirteen core loci point match to the victim's DNA, which was on file with NDIS, the National DNA Index System."

The jurors seemed to be listening intently.

"Why was the victim's DNA catalogued with NDIS?" Gold asked.

"Because of his past criminal record."

"Is the DNA of all convicted felons on file with NDIS?"

"No. But the victim's DNA was established and catalogued during the course of a previous incarceration."

"So in your expert opinion, is there any possibility that the blood found on the roof did not belong to the victim, Samuel Cipriani?"

"None whatsoever."

"Thank you, Dr. Kent. No more questions."

Whorhatz turned to Vinny. "Mr. Gambini, would you like to cross examine Dr. Kent?"

"Yes, I would, Your Honor." Vinny rose and approached the witness stand. "So, Dr. Kent, you testified that the sole pattern found on the roof was that of a ladies Nike Air Max ninety-five athletic shoe. Is that right?"

"Yes."

"And for the record, can you please tell us which athletic shoes are most commonly found at crime scenes here in the Unites States and in Europe as well?"

"It's the Nike Air Max ninety-five."

"The same shoe, right?"

"Yes."

"That's a women's running shoe, ain't it?"

"I believe so, yes."

"And what is the number one selling size for the Nike Air Max ninety-five ladies running shoe?"

"Why it's size seven."

"So, the shoeprint you found came from the athletic shoe most commonly found at crime scenes practically everywhere in the civilized world, and was also Nike's best-selling size of women's shoes. Is *that* correct?"

"Yes."

"And did you examine the defendant's own personal pair of Nike Air Max ninety-five athletic shoes?"

"Yes."

"And were you able to detect any traces of blood on the defendant's shoes?"

"No."

"None?"

"That's correct."

"Not even the teensiest little bit?"

"No."

Vinny walked back to the defense table. He picked up a running shoe with Nike logos on each side and held it high in the air. "Dr. Kent, can you tell me what I'm holding in my hand?" He walked toward the witness stand and presented Kent with the solitary shoe.

"It looks like the Nike Air Max ninety-five."

"Exactly like the shoe found in the defendant's apartment? The same kind that deposited a bloody print on the rooftop?"

"I can't be one hundred percent sure."

"But it appears to be?"

"Yes."

"Your Honor, for the purposes of demonstration, the defense has purchased this Nike Air Max ninety-five running shoe which is identical in every way to the shoe that made the bloody imprint on the rooftop." He held the shoe with the sole facing Kent. "Dr. Kent, do you have any idea just how many deep grooves there are in the sole of this shoe?"

"Quite a few."

"Right—quite a few. You know I tried counting all the grooves but it made me dizzy. My best count was somewhere over three hundred intricate little grooves." He retrieved a second shoe from the table. "I placed this shoe in a pan of blood I got from the local butcher, let it dry, and then tried to scrub away all the blood to see if I could completely remove every last trace from the grooves. I used bleach and detergent, and soaked it for a period of two hours." He showed the sole to the judge and then to Kent. "What do you think, Dr. Kent? Can you still see blood stuck in the grooves of this shoe?"

Kent studied the shoe. "Yes."

Vinny then walked to the jury box with the shoe in hand and allowed the jurors to examine it. "Dr. Kent, in your opinion is there any way that the defendant could've made a bloody imprint on the roof wearing this model of shoe, then scrubbed away every last bit of blood?"

Clark was hesitant but finally said, "It seems unlikely."

"*No.* That's what I thought too. In your opinion, is it possible that someone else wearing ladies Nike Air Max ninety-five athletic shoes left the bloody shoeprint on the roof and not my client?"

Kent removed his glasses and rubbed his eyes. He replied in a meek voice. "Yes."

"I'm sorry. I'm all the way over here by the jury box. I didn't hear your answer. Would you mind repeating your answer in a loud and clear voice?"

He replied in a shrill tone. " *Yes.* "

Before speaking, Vinny looked at Mrs. Faraday and noticed she was grinning. "I'm through with the Man of Steel. No more questions, Your Honor."

CHAPTER SIXTY-FOUR
Soul Symphony

Gold rose and handed the clerk a photograph. "Your Honor, the people would like to introduce Exhibit number one into evidence."

The clerk logged in the photograph Gold handed him before transferring it to the judge. Whorhatz examined it for a moment and handed it back to Gold.

Gold approached the jury box and gave the photo to the foreman. "As you can see, ladies and gentlemen of the jury, Samuel Cipriani attempted to name his killer. You can see in this photograph that the initials TMC are clearly spelled out on the rooftop in his own blood. If it please the court, I'd like to remind everyone that the defendant's initials are TMC as well: Theresa Mary Cototi." He returned to his seat while the jury members passed around the photo.

Vinny stood. "Ladies and gentlemen of the jury, the photograph you just examined don't mean nothin'. There's no proof the victim actually wrote those three letters on the roof and we have no idea what they mean. For all we know those letters could stand for The Movie Channel, or nothin' at all. As a matter of fact, the more I look at it, I ain't sure these are letters at all—they kind of looks like ancient hieroglyphics...thank you."

Whorhatz turned to Gold. "Are you prepared to call your next witness, Mr. Gold?"

Anthony Cipriani sat in the first row of the public section

behind the prosecutor's table, his face contorted with anger.

Gold glanced at him before answering. "We are, Your Honor."

"We'll break for lunch and your witness can take the stand when we return."

Vinny met with Theresa over the lunch break. She looked glum, her head hanging down, staring at the table. Her meal remained uneaten on a tray before her. "They slammed us this morning, didn't they?" she asked.

"No, I wouldn't say that, dear. I mean, yeah, they had an expert witness and physical evidence but it's nothing I didn't expect." He laid his hand on hers. "Remember, they need a unanimous vote of all twelve jurors to convict you and there's *no way* that's gonna happen."

"How can you be so sure?"

"Like I told you before, Theresa, all their evidence is circumstantial. There's nothing tying you to Sammy's death except that Träsch broad's testimony. And I think we demonstrated that she just ain't a credible witness." Theresa absorbed the information without comment. Seeing that she still looked worried, Vinny tried a different tact. "It's like that street art you see everywhere in the city."

"You mean graffiti?"

"Well, yes and no. But I'm sure you've seen it. From a distance you'd swear that there was a huge jagged rift in the street, with raging waterfalls, and giant beasts clawing their way to the top. *But* when you get closer, it's just some fancy artwork. Understand what I'm saying?"

Her response was unconvincing. "I think so."

"Don't worry about that stuff—it's an illusion. What I am afraid of is Sammy's brother. You got any idea what he's gonna say when he gets up on the stand?"

She shook her head. "I told you, Mr. Gambini, I don't

know what's wrong with him." She sniffled. "We used to be so close. I mean he was always there for me when Sammy was in prison, and now he's acting as if he hates me."

"*He thinks* you pushed his brother off the roof. I don't think he's acting."

"But he knows I would never do that. He knows how much I loved Sammy. I just can't see him going from hot to cold like that. I mean without even hearing my side of things."

"He's probably still in shock."

"Well how long will it take for him to come around?"

"I ain't got no idea. Look, he'll be on the stand right after lunch. That should tell us a lot. Just try to remain calm, especially in front of the jury. Remember, you're grieving, so it's all right to look sad. But it's not okay to look like you're running for your life because you ain't."

"I'll try to remember that."

"Good and I'll try to kick some ass this afternoon." Vinny gave her a reassuring hug and left.

"The people call New York City Deputy Mayor Anthony Cipriani to the stand," Gold said as he watched Cipriani rise to his full six-foot-four inches of stature. He walked in an odd way, drawing his knees high to the chest like a stork or a crane.

He was sworn in and Gold went to work with a deliberate eagerness that Vinny found troubling. "For the record, would you please state your full name?"

"Anthony Michael Cipriani."

"And you're the brother of Samuel Cipriani, the deceased?"

Cipriani grew visibly stricken. It was as if he collapsed in on himself at the mention of his brother's name. "Yes, that's correct."

"Are you okay to go on?"

Cipriani took a long moment but finally nodded.

"Mr. Cipriani, how would you describe your relationship with your brother?"

"We were very close. We always were. In fact..." His throat tightened and he swallowed with difficulty. "I prob-ably...I probably wouldn't be alive today if it weren't for Sam."

"How's that?" Gold asked, trying to sound unrehearsed.

"I had childhood leukemia. The doctors tried every therapy in the book but none of them worked. My folks were sure that I was going to die, but then Sam gave me some of his bone marrow. It literally saved my life."

"So you loved your brother very much."

"Yes." He wiped a tear from his eye. "I'd do anything for Sam. *Anything.* Unfortunately, we didn't have a lot of time together."

"Can you please elaborate, sir?"

"Sammy was a good-hearted man but he got mixed up with the wrong group of guys, and well...what can I say? He spent almost all of his adult life in prison. But I didn't love him any less because of it."

"Of course not." Gold flipped the page on his legal pad. "Sam was very fortunate. He had a big brother who stuck with him through thick and thin and a doting girlfriend as well, didn't he?"

For the first time since the legal proceedings began, Cipriani made eye contact with Theresa without showing any hostility—only for a second and then he looked away. "Yes, he and Theresa were deeply in love. She visited him in prison even more than I did. In a way, she did as much to save Sam as he did to save me. She was always there for him."

"So with so much support..." Gold paused. "I'm at a loss, sir. Why is Sam Cipriani dead today?"

Vinny jumped up. "Objection, Your Honor, calls for speculation."

"Objection sustained." Whorhatz turned to Gold. "Please rephrase."

"Of course, Your Honor." Gold thought for a moment. "Do you possess any knowledge that might assist the court in understanding what happened to your brother?"

Cipriani glanced at Theresa again, this time guilt was unmistakable in his expression. "Seven years is a long time, a long time to be without your brother, and a long time to be without the one you love. Theresa and I..." He closed his eyes for a moment. "We helped each other through it."

The jurors looked from one to another as a murmur rose among them.

Gold waited until the courtroom was once again silent. "Are you saying that the two of you were intimate?"

"Emotionally, yes. Not physically. We spent more and more time together." He looked at her again and saw that she was crying. "It helped to ease our pain."

Vinny had a sense of doom, a sense that something terrible was about to happen.

And then it did.

Cipriani was still looking at her when he spoke again. "All that time together...we fell in love."

Gold played it out, waiting for just the right moment to hit a crescendo. Like a maestro directing a rehearsed symphony orchestra, he knew just when to transition from a whisper to a roar. "But you never acted on it, did you? That's to say, you never made love."

"No. Never. But we wanted to. We ached to. She once told me..." He broke down and sobbed. "I'm just as guilty as she is. She told me that we could never be together as long as Sammy was alive. I...I just never realized how far she would go."

The murmur grew into rolling thunder, juror talking to

juror and stranger talking to stranger in the audience. Vinny was able to pick out Lisa's familiar voice above the others as she said, "Holy fuckin' shit!"

Theresa cried hysterically. Vinny did his best to calm her down but Cipriani's testimony had destroyed her. She erupted like a volcano.

"Silence!" Whorhatz yelled. He banged his gavel repeatedly. "We'll have silence in this court."

It took a long time for the commotion to subside—one by one the voices went quiet until the courtroom was silent again.

"Resume," Whorhatz said.

"Please forgive me, Mr. Deputy Mayor. I had no intention of tearing open such a large and painful wound." Gold turned to Whorhatz. "No more questions, Your Honor." He struggled to suppress the gleam in his eye as he returned to the prosecutor's table.

"I think we've had enough excitement for now," Whorhatz said and with a rap of his gavel. "One hour adjournment. I'm sure the Deputy Mayor would appreciate a little time to himself."

CHAPTER SIXTY-FIVE
God Smacked

"What's with Gloomy Gus," Ma said as Vinny dragged himself through the front door of Lisa's parent's home at the end of the day.

"Lay off him, Ma," Lisa said. "He got blindsided in court today. The deputy mayor testified that Vinny's client had a motive for killing his brother. Vinny put her on the stand after the recess and she denied everything he said, but the damage was already done. He don't need none of your crap tonight."

"So sorry, Vinny my boy," Ma said as she pinched his cheek. "Give me your briefcase and coat. Augie's inside watching the news. Go keep him company until dinner is ready."

Vinny seemed powerless and deflated. He put down his briefcase and allowed his coat to slide off his shoulders into her arms before trudging into the den, lifeless, hanging on by a thread.

"What the hell happened to him, Lisa?" Ma whispered. "Your fiancé looks like someone died. Was it that bad?"

Lisa took her by the arm and dragged her into the kitchen. "I just told you. An important witness gave some very damaging testimony today. Up until now the DA couldn't prove motive, but now he's got motive up the ass."

"Goddamn lawyers," she swore as she held her fingertips together. "I'd like to kill every last one of them."

"Yeah? How about Vinny? You want to kill him too?"

"Of course not. But are you sure you want to stay for dinner? Maybe you ought to take him home and put a smile on his face."

"You mean take him home and screw his brains out? Is that what my dear mother is telling her youngest daughter to do?"

"Come on will ya. Who are you, Jane the Virgin? The poor guy doesn't look like he's gonna make it through the night. Least you could do is let him die with a smile on his face.

"Enough already. I suppose *you* never had a bad day?"

"I never looked like that even on my worst day. Vinny looks like a five-year-old whose puppy got run over by the milk truck *twice*. What kind of lawyer is he gonna be if he comes home looking like who-did-it-and-ran every time he gets slammed around in court. Maybe he ought to open a pet store. You can't get agita like that from a tank of goldfish."

Lisa noticed a peculiar look on Ma's face. "What? What are you holding back?"

"Nothing."

"Nothing my ass, Ma. What's going on?"

"All right already." She went to the door and peeked out to make sure she wouldn't be heard. "I was gonna tell you but when Vinny came through the door looking like death warmed over…"

Lisa fell into a chair. "Oh God. What? Is it Dad?"

Ma nodded, her brave face melting like butter over a flame, her lips clenched, her eyes becoming glassy. "The doctor called with his test results."

Lisa braced. "And?"

Ma dragged a chair next hers and sat down. "He's got early onset Alzheimer's, Lisa."

"They're sure?"

Her chin quivered as the words came out. "Yes. They did some cognitive tests and he had issues with like five out of ten of them."

"That don't sound conclusive. That's only half."

"I know but the doctor wanted to be cautious so he did some additional tests and it turns out that it's hereditary. Augie's got some kind of genetic mutation. The two of us always used to joke about his Uncle Terry losing his marbles. We didn't know enough at the time but thinking back, well, he probably had the same thing."

A tear trickled down her cheek. "What's gonna happen to him, Ma?"

"Now don't go thinking the worst. The doctor said there's no proof that early Alzheimer's progresses any faster than when it happens later in life. We just gotta keep an eye on him is all. They got some medications for this and your brother Dino is gonna have to be more of an adult. He's gonna have to be less of a playboy and spend more time in the garage with Dad to make sure he don't get into any trouble."

"I can spend more time there too."

"No, Lisa, you and Vinny are just getting started. He's finally got his career on track and God knows it looks like he's gonna need all the help you can give him. *No.* I love your brother to death, but Dino's got his car and his women and he don't seem to care about nothing else. He's gonna have to step up...for the family. Your father will be all right," she said sounding as if she were trying to convince herself. "Now give me a hand and let's get some dinner on the table for those men."

Vinny barely had the strength to greet Lisa's father. "Hi, Augie," he said and collapsed into a thickly padded chair. Augie seemed wrapped up in the news and was quiet while Vinny pried off his boots and closed his eyes.

"Look at this son of a bitch," Augie complained as he pointed at the TV screen.

Vinny had begun to doze, but his eyes snapped open when

he heard Augie's comment. "What? What happened?"

"Nick 'The Knife' Galatino's kid, Matteo. He got busted on racketeering charges."

"The mobster's son?"

"Yeah."

"The one who was supposed to be a legitimate business-man?"

"Yeah."

"The one who's always on TV talking about how the mafia does more good than harm?"

"Yeah. Turns out he's a no good wise guy just like his father. They can't help themselves these wise guy's kids. It's in their blood."

"Being a mobster is in their blood?" Vinny asked with skepticism.

"Like automobile repair is in Lisa's and Dino's blood. It's hereditary."

"You saying there's a gene that made this kid a thug?"

"That's right. It's passed down from generation to generation. I'll bet the very first Galatino was a piece of shit and every Galatino down the line since."

"That's impressive, Augie. I had no idea you knew so much about that kind of stuff. You ought to give up the garage and start one of those look-up-your-family-tree com-panies."

Augie gave him the finger without turning around. "Vinny, I love you but sit on this a while, will ya? I'm trying to watch the news." After a moment, he turned with a huge grin on his face that dropped the second he saw Vinny's face. "Holy shit, Vinny. What the hell happened to you?"

"What?" Vinny asked.

"What's with the puss? You look like you ate some stale corned beef. *Marone*. Vinny. You okay?"

"Yeah. Yeah. I'm okay. I just had a bad day in court."

"Maybe you ought call out sick tomorrow. You know, play hooky."

"You can't do that with a trial going on, Augie."

"Why not?"

"You just can't. It ain't done."

"Who says?"

"Me. I says."

"Then you'd better get your shit together before court tomorrow morning because the way you look right now your client's going to the fuckin' chair."

"Gee. Thanks for the words of encouragement."

Lisa was standing in the doorway tapping her foot impatiently.

Ma shouted from the kitchen. "He needs, like a vitamin B shot or something. I told Lisa to take him home and throw him some ass."

Lisa frowned. "Are we finished discussing the therapeutic value of my vagina yet? Because if we are, dinner is on the fuckin' table."

A meatball fell from the ladle with a thud that almost cracked the dish. "A good Italian dinner will fix you right up, Vinny. How many meatballs you want?" Ma asked.

"One."

"*Bullshit,*" she said, dropping another bocce ball into his dish and dumping a trough of sauce on top of it.

Augie picked up the remote and turned on the small TV in the kitchen.

"Augie, we're eatin'," Ma complained. "Shut the friggin' thing off."

"I want to hear more about the Galatino kid's arrest. I knew that kid would go bad. Like I told Vinny, it's in the blood."

Vinny had been resting his head on his hand, despondent

and exhausted, but suddenly came alive. "What was that?"

"What was what?" Augie asked while staring at the TV.

"What you said—about the blood."

"I said it's in the kid's blood, Vinny. You're really out of it, aren't you?"

"In the blood? That's what you said, right?"

"Yeah. So?"

Vinny reached for his briefcase and frantically tore through it.

"Whatcha looking for?" Lisa asked.

"A business card."

"A business card?"

"Yeah."

"Whose?"

"Hercules."

"Hercules the pimp?" she asked with uncertainty.

"Yes, Lisa. Hercules the pimp."

Ma rolled her eyes. "Call Creedmoor, Augie. They've both gone off the deep end."

CHAPTER SIXTY-SIX
Special Delivery

Soft bossa nova music whispered from Anthony Cipriani's audiophile-quality hi-fi while he slipped his dinner dishes into the dishwasher and sipped the last of a 2005 estate bottle of pinot noir. There's a marked difference between being lonely and feeling alone. At the moment, Cipriani felt both tugging at him. He switched off the lights in the kitchen and wandered over to the panoramic windows in his high-rise apartment, uncertain of how to fill the empty evening hours. The sky was clear with bold stars as he looked out on the city, lights twinkling on and off in the apartments and office suites before him. He wasn't expecting anyone and was surprised when his doorbell chimed. He set down his wine glass and hurried to the door, somewhat confused because he hadn't gotten an advance call from the doorman.

"That you, William?" he called out expecting a reply from the building concierge. He opened the door and was stunned. Standing before him was the most visually alluring young woman he'd ever seen. Her hair was done up like Rosie the Riveter with a red and white polka dot bandana. She was wearing skin-tight spandex coveralls and red six-inch patent leather platform pumps. She was hanging onto a leather tool bag. He looked her up and down. "Okay. Is this some kind of gag? Who sent you?"

"I'm here to fix your plumbing." She reached down and grabbed his package. "You got a bad clog here." She laid her hand on his chest and drove him back into the apartment. "Looks like a tough job," she said in a seductive voice. "Good thing I've got a mouth like a Hoover."

His eyes snapped open like overwound window shades. Despite knowing he shouldn't, he yielded to her advance. "Okay, who sent you? Was it Wallace?" he asked with a huge grin on his face. "My birthday isn't for another week."

She slowly unzipped her coverall, her ample breasts emerging inch by inch until they were almost fully exposed. She stepped forward, teased him with her mouth against his, then bit his bottom lip.

"Ouch!" Cipriani touched his lips and found a drop of blood on his fingertip.

"Sorry." She dried his bloody lip with a tissue and stuffed it in her pocket. "If you don't like it rough I can be really submissive." She turned around presenting her sumptuous rear end. "Smack my ass, *papi*. Show me you're the boss. Give that big fat *culo* a good swat. Come on. You know you want to." She twerked, pressing her butt against him until he was on the verge of exploding.

"I've got a feeling you're trouble."

"How's this feel?" She took his hands and pulled them around her until they were on her large soft breasts. "That's more like it, *papi*." She then grabbed his necktie and dragged him toward the bedroom like a conquest in tow. She undid his tie before pushing him onto the bed and bit off his shirt buttons with her teeth one by one.

"I'm not going to regret this, am I?"

"Of course not, *papi*. No worries," she whispered in his ear, her breath warm and intoxicating. "No regrets—nothing except right here and now." She licked his earlobe. "And what happens in Shangri La stays in Shangri La." She undid his belt and slid off his slacks. "You with me on this?"

He moaned defenselessly.

"I'll take that as a yes," she said and spoke no more.

CHAPTER SIXTY-SEVEN
Baby Food

Lisa tried without success to buoy Vinny's spirit. She gave him encouragement and tried to support him as best she could but was dead on her feet by the time they got home. It was almost midnight. She was ready to crawl into bed and ritualistically walked to the front door to make sure it was locked before turning in for the night. As she tested the deadbolt, a large black SUV swung into the driveway, its tires screeching, the blast of the stereo loud enough to dislodge brick and mortar. She squinted to make out the faces of the pair in the front seat but didn't recognize them. Their images grew clearer as they got out and approached the front door. "Hey, Vinny," she called out. "You expecting anyone?"

"No, why?" he replied from the upper landing.

"Because we got what looks like a prostitute and her pimp coming up the front steps," she said in an offhand manner. "There something you want to tell me?"

Vinny hustled down the steps in his sweats, rubbing his eyes. "Yeah, you're always complaining how I'm not so exciting to be with. I figured I'd spice things up a little." He peeked out through the window. "It's Hercules."

"Yeah? Who's that wearin' the coochie-length micro-skirt? His virgin sister escaped from the fuckin' convent?"

"That, my dear Ms. Vito, is what's known as a gold package, delivered in under an hour, and guaranteed to please."

"Yeah? Please who?"

He ignored her and unlocked the door. The woman shuffled in first. "Mr. Gambini?" she asked as she extended her hand. "I'm Giselda. We spoke on the phone. It's so nice to meet you, *papi*."

"Giselda...of course."

"Hercules told me all about you." She pressed her frozen cheek to his before moving on toward Lisa. "You must be Lisa, right? My God, you're really beautiful." She kissed her on the cheek as well before rubbing her hands together. "I ain't wearing too much under my jacket. You got a hot cocoa or something? I feel like I got icicles between my legs."

"I'll bet that's different," Lisa quipped as she looked her over. "I love your jacket. Real fox?"

She grinned. "I sure am."

Lisa snickered and led her to the kitchen.

Hercules entered a moment later.

"Come in. Come in," Vinny said in a hurry to shut the door to prevent the bitterly cold air from entering the house. "You got it?"

Hercules handed him a brown paper bag, then blew into his cupped hands to warm them. "Everything you wanted, Mr. Gambini."

"That's great. Have a seat."

Hercules settled into an armchair.

Vinny opened the bag and removed a baby food jar without the label. Within it was a tissue stained with a drop of blood. Vinny smiled. "You did real good, Hercules, but what's with the baby food jar?"

"Giselda's kid goes through like a million of those a week. She sterilized it and figured it was a good way to transport the evidence."

"Smart girl. How much do I owe you for your very special package?"

"Nothing, Mr. Gambini. We're in business together.

294

Besides, Giselda said Cipriani was a piece of cake. She was in and out of his place in no time."

"I see. You'd think a big important guy like that would have more staying power." He noticed another jar in the bag. "What's this?"

"Backup."

"Backup?" Vinny asked. He removed the second baby food jar that contained a milky translucent substance. He grimaced. "Tell me this ain't what I think it is."

"Yeah, Mr. Gambini, Giselda does everything one hundred and ten percent. She saw how small the bloodstain was and was worried it wasn't enough to be analyzed. After she bit his lip she went down on him and drained him like a dollar store battery." He smiled so wide that Vinny could see every one of his teeth. "She did good, huh?"

CHAPTER SIXTY-EIGHT
Subterfuge

It was 9:00 a.m. sharp. Joe barged into the Brooklyn Area Community Supervision Office and marched up to the reception counter. "I'm here for a meeting with my parole office—only I forgot his name."

The elderly woman peeked at Joe over the top of her glasses. "Are you serious, young man?

"Yeah. I'm serious. I don't wanna be marked down that I missed my appointment. So do me a favor and look it up for me. I think his name is Ray or Jay but I ain't sure."

She shook her head in disbelief and tapped on the computer keyboard. "Name?"

"Bald Louie."

She looked up at him, squinting, examining his thick head of hair. "Did you say, 'Bald?'"

Oh shit! He gulped. "Medical-fucking-science—what a blessing."

"Lucky you. Name?"

"Eh. Sorry. Rolfe, Louis Rolfe." He waited patiently while her fingernails clattered away on the keyboard.

"Your parole officer is Ray Stanz, but he's out of the office. Are you sure your appointment was for today?"

"I thought it was. Where's his office? I'll wait for him."

"You'll have to sit in the waiting area until he gets back. But are you sure you want to do that? He may be out for the day."

"Yeah, okay. Maybe waiting around ain't the best idea. You got his business card? I'll call him and check on my appointment."

"Wait here."

Joe watched her walk down the corridor noting the office she'd entered. He pretended he wasn't watching when she returned with the business card.

"Here you are, Mr. Rolfe."

"Yeah. Thank you. You'll let him know I was here?"

"Yes, I will."

"Um...thanks. Can I use the can before I go?"

"You mean the restroom?"

Joe nodded.

She handed him a key that was attached to a foot-long wooden ruler and pointed to the restroom.

"Thanks. Be right back."

Joe sauntered off in the direction of the men's room but never made it there, instead taking a detour to Ray Stanz's office. He quietly closed the door and switched on the lights.

CHAPTER SIXTY-NINE
This Is Gonna Make Your Fuckin' Day

Vinny had spent the wee morning hours doing research and arrived at the courthouse early for the 11:00 a.m. scheduled start time, his arms weighted down with heavy reference books too cumbersome to fit into his briefcase. He was amazed to see that his brother Joe was already there waiting for him.

"You kicking ass in here, Vin?"

"Doing my best to hold my own," he said. "You got anything for me on Bald Louie?"

"I just went through his parole officer's filing cabinet. Came straight here when I was finished."

"You're kidding. How'd you manage that?"

"I got my ways, Vin. I'm not completely useless."

"Joe, no one ever said you were useless. Anyway, I only got a few minutes before court begins. What did you find out?"

"Bald Louie ain't kept a one of his scheduled appointments in over a month. There's a warrant out for his arrest. I really wanted to find him for you but that's the best I could do. I know you're kind of running out of time."

"That's all right. You did really good, Joe. Anyway, I think I got this under control." His face was mired in thought.

"What is it?" Joe asked excitedly. "You figured something out?"

"Yeah. Well...maybe. Before you go, you got the name of

298

Bald Louie's parole officer? Just in case."

"Yeah, of course I got it." He reached into his pocket and handed him Ray Stanz's business card.

He gave Joe a love tap on the jaw. "That's perfect, Joe. I got this. Thanks."

He pulled out his phone and dialed the number on the card as Joe headed off. "Mr. Stanz?"

"Yes. Who's this?"

"My name is Vincent Gambini. I'm an attorney."

"How can I help you?"

"I've been looking for a guy who goes by the name Bald Louie. You probably know him as Louis Rolfe. I think he's a rehabilitated former offender under your supervision. Is that right?"

"I'm looking for him too, Mr. Gambini. He's been AWOL for weeks."

"Yeah, I thought so and I kind of got an idea of where you might be able to find him. Got a minute?"

"Sure. I'm listening."

"Well then this is what you're gonna have to do."

Lisa had dropped Vinny off in front of the building and driven off to park the Caddy. She entered several minutes later and headed straight for the ladies room. She reemerged afterward and was taking off her coat when she heard a distinctive voice coming from down a side corridor. She pressed her back against the wall and peeked around the corner so she wouldn't be seen. She covered her mouth to suppress her own voice, "Holy shit!" She reached into her purse for her trusty pink camera. "Wait until Vinny sees this," she whispered in astonishment and she snapped off a succession of shots.

* * *

Vinny's phone rang just as Whorhatz entered the courtroom. He pulled it out of his pocket and saw that the caller was Aidan Boydetto, the client he'd helped weeks earlier. He turned away from the bench and buried the phone between his jacket and his chin trying to hide it from the judge. "Yeah," he answered impatiently. "Mr. Boydetto, I'm in court. Can I call you back?"

"Okay, sure, Mr. Gambini, but it's important. I've been following your trial on the news and I've got something you're going to want to see."

"Okay." He could feel Whorhatz's eyes burning right through him. "I'll call you right after court." He hung up and stashed his phone.

"Important call?" Whorhatz asked with a scowl.

"Yes, Your Honor…sorry."

"You know they have a new app for people who use their cell phones at inappropriate times."

"I ain't heard about it. What's that called, Your Honor?"

"It's called *Respect*." He huffed and turned to the court officer. "I believe Mr. Cipriani was on the stand when we adjourned."

Cipriani took the stand once again and was reminded that he was still under oath.

"Mr. Gambini, you may cross-examine the witness."

"Mr. Cipriani, let me first offer my condolences on your brother's untimely passing. It sounded as if the two of yous were close."

"Very close," he clarified.

"Very. Right. I got that…If I remember correctly you said that he actually saved your life."

"Objection," Gold said. "Asked and answered, Your Honor."

"Objection sustained," Whorhatz said. "Let's try to avoid repetition, Mr. Gambini."

"Your Honor, a little leeway, please. I'm pursuing a line of questioning."

"Very well, Counselor, but make your point and move on."

"You said that he donated his bone marrow to you and that it saved your life because you had leukemia."

"Yes, I already said that," he snapped.

"Just to refresh everyone's memory would you mind saying it again?"

Cipriani glared at Vinny defiantly, then from memory rattled off what he'd said the previous day, almost verbatim, "I had childhood leukemia. The doctors tried everything but nothing worked. I thought I was going to die. Sam gave me some of his bone marrow and it saved my life."

"Thank you. No further questions at this time. Your Honor, I'd like to recall Dr. Clark Kent."

Gold furrowed his brow. He turned and scoured the court-room. "Your Honor, Dr. Kent is not in the courtroom."

Whorhatz sighed and banged the gavel. "Then we're adjourned. Round him up, Mr. DA. Time is money."

"Thanks, I'll be waiting for you."

"Who was that?" Lisa asked after waiting for Vinny to get off the phone.

"You know that guy I represented, the one who passed the bum check?"

"You mean the guy who thinks he's Lindsay Lohan?"

"Yeah. Well he says he's been following the trial on TV and he's got something he thinks could really help the case."

"But he didn't say what it was?"

"No, not exactly—a picture of some sort. He said I got to see it."

"They reach Superman yet?"

"Yeah. Unfortunately he's not gonna be able to get here

until tomorrow morning so we're gonna adjourn for the day."

"Is that gonna mess up your cross examination?"

"No, I'm hoping for some stuff to fall into place anyways, so the delay might work to our benefit."

She swept the hair off his forehead. "A night's sleep did you a world of good. You got that gleam back in your eye and I can tell that you've got something up your sleeve, don't you?" she asked with an impish grin. "Whatcha got, Vinny?"

"I ain't one hundred percent sure yet but I'll know the minute I get The Man of Steel back on the witness stand."

"It's something big though, ain't it?"

"Maybe, Lisa, I got all my fingers crossed."

"Well I got something too."

"*You* got something?"

"Yeah. Yeah I do."

"More tire marks?" he asked with a sly grin.

"Better. Come with me." She grabbed him by the arm and led him down the corridor. "You know how you're always busting my chops because I take too many pictures? Wait until you see the pictures I got now."

They were on their way when Vinny spotted Parikh. "Lisa, give me two seconds. I got to ask the detective something." He reached into his briefcase for the baby food jar he'd gotten from Lopez and hurried after the detective.

"Hurry up," she said. "Because this is gonna make your *fuckin'* day."

CHAPTER SEVENTY
The Quintessential Vinny

The lighting hadn't been upgraded nor was the sun shining with greater intensity than the day before. Yet for some reason Vinny felt as if the courtroom was somehow brighter when he entered the next morning. Whorhatz was on the bench scowling, Cipriani was glowering, and Theresa was once again dabbing at tears. And yet he felt as if he had it all under control. He approached Dr. Kent with a renewed sense of confidence. "What am I wearing?" he asked with a smile.

"A suit?"

"No," Vinny said. "I mean under the suit. Am I wearing boxers or briefs?"

Whorhatz cast a sneer, threatening like an impending storm.

"Sorry, Judge. Just trying to lighten things up. Dr. Kent, the last person to sit in that seat, Anthony Cipriani, stated that his brother, the now deceased Samuel Cipriani, literally saved his life by donating his bone marrow. Did you hear him say that?"

"Yes, when he testified the other day."

"So what I said was an accurate account of what he said, is that right?"

"I believe so. Yes."

"Good. Well I ain't no expert in the field of genetics or the forensic sciences like you are, but I just spent the last twenty-four hours studying my butt off and—"

"Is there a question in this, Counselor?" Whorhatz asked.

"There is, Your Honor. If you'll just give me a minute."

"Continue."

"Like I said, I've been studying and it seems to me that if Samuel Cipriani donated his bone marrow to his brother Anthony, then *even to this day*, Sam's DNA would still be floating around in Anthony's blood. Would you or would you not say that's correct?"

"Yes. That is correct."

A low murmur went through the courtroom.

"It is? I mean yes, it is." He paused while he made eye contact with the members of the jury. When he continued, he spoke in the tone of a seasoned orator. "And isn't it possible that in performing a standard DNA analysis that the crime lab may have mistakenly confused Sam's blood with Anthony's because his blood contains Sam's DNA as well as his own, even though they're not identical twins and were not conceived from the same fertilized egg?"

Kent labored a while before responding. "In an unequivocal match of one hundred percent of the loci, *no*. But the standard law enforcement testing only matches thirteen loci."

"And in matching *only* thirteen loci could the police lab have mistaken the blood of one brother for the other? I mean *in this case* where one brother received the other brother's bone marrow?"

"But, Mr. Gambini, the standard thirteen-point match gives one in one hundred and thirteen billion odds of a false–"

Vinny wagged his finger admonishing the esteemed doctor. "Uh. Uh. Uh. That ain't what I asked. A simple yes or no will do."

Kent sighed. "Regretfully...yes."

Vinny echoed Kent's response with a resounding, "*Yes*," as the court filled with oohs and ahs.

Vinny noticed Cipriani place his huge hand on Gold's shoulder. "The hell is going on here, Mr. Gold?" Cipriani asked. "You have this under control or not?"

Whorhatz banged his gavel. "Are you conducting your own trial, Mr. Cipriani?"

"No, Your Honor."

"Mr. Cipriani, this is a court of law and your position in the mayor's office affords you no special treatment in this trial." He pointed the gavel at him. "You will remain silent during these proceedings unless you are called upon as a witness and are addressed by me or one of the attorneys. Is that clear?"

"Yes, Your Honor. It won't happen again."

"Good."

"Your Honor," Gold said. "Mr. Gambini is attempting to confuse the jury with his thinly veiled aspersion that Deputy Mayor Cipriani may have played a hand in his own brother's death. I ask that his entire cross-examination be stricken from the record, and the jury be instructed to disregard what they've heard."

"Mr. Gold, whether your opponent is trying to confuse or elucidate is a matter for the jury to decide." He turned his head askew, staring at Gold with a far-off look. "Was that an objection? A challenge? I'm not even sure what that was. Are you feeling all right, Mr. Gold?"

"Yes, Your Honor."

"I'm almost sorry to hear that. At least a raging fever would explain that amateurish outburst." He shook his head. "Mr. Gambini, you may continue."

"No further questions for Dr. Kent, Your Honor. I recall Greta Träsch."

Vinny saw Cipriani slam the back of Gold's chair with his hand.

Gold stood. "May we request a recess, Your Honor?"

"*Now?* Just when things are getting interesting?" the judge asked.

"If you please, Your Honor."

He rapped the gavel. "Thirty minutes."

Theresa jumped up and hugged Vinny while tears streamed down her cheeks.

He patted her on the back. "See, dear. It ain't over until the fat lady...well, you know."

CHAPTER SEVENTY-ONE
Not Bad, Right?

As Vinny stepped away from Theresa he caught a glimpse of Mrs. Faraday in the jury box. She was whispering in another juror's ear. She caught Vinny's glance and winked at him as he left the courtroom.

Aidan Boydetto was waiting for him in the lobby. Vinny whisked him down the corridor where they could talk alone. "So you got something to show me?"

Boydetto slid a photo out of an envelope and handed it to him.

Vinny's mouth dropped. "Holy shit! I can't believe it. Why didn't you come to me with this sooner?"

"I didn't know the picture existed."

"You didn't know? How could you not know?"

"I didn't take the picture, Mr. Gambini."

"Well who—" Vinny's nostrils flared and then revelation struck. "Don't tell me."

"Yes," Boydetto said. "Lindsay took it. I didn't see it until yesterday when I was deleting pictures to create more space on my phone's memory card."

"It's got a date, time stamp, and everything. Jesus, Aidan, I could kiss you...but I think I'll wait to thank Ms. Lohan instead." He laughed.

"I figured it was the least I could do to pay you back for the great job you did representing me. I've been following the murder trial closely—I mean I live right around the corner from where it happened."

"What? You're kiddin', right? I mean I saw your address at least five times when I was working on your file and I never realized...around the corner, huh? Small world. Anyway, don't mention it." Vinny slid the photo back into the envelope. "I was glad to help you but I gotta run now, Aidan. Let's get in touch after the trial." He laughed again. "I'll take you and Lindsay out for drinks."

He saw Lisa standing close by and hustled over to her.

"Vinny, you were great in there," she said as she threw her arms around him, lavishing him with kisses. "You were holding out on me, weren't you?"

"Not bad, right? I think we got a fighting chance."

"I'm impressed. How'd you figure that out?"

"It was what Augie said."

Lisa seemed confused. "My dad? What did he say?"

"He was watching the news in the kitchen and he said, 'It's in their blood.' I don't know why but it came to me right then and there."

"Uh-oh." Lisa tapped Vinny on the shoulder and pointed. "The grim reaper wants to talk to you, Vinny."

Gold and Doucette were standing twenty feet away, waiting to be acknowledged.

"Wonder what they want," Vinny said. He shot his cuffs and stepped forward with determination. "I'll be right back."

CHAPTER SEVENTY-TWO
Can You Identify the Man in this Photograph

Vinny studied Gold's and Doucette's faces trying to figure out what they were up to. "What can I do for you two gentlemen?"

"We had a short meeting with Deputy Mayor Cipriani and as you know he has always had a warm spot in his heart for the defendant. I mean all those years pining away for his brother has to count for something, doesn't it?" Gold asked with a shit-eating grin.

"I don't know. Does it? It didn't seem to mean shit up until now."

"Gambini, this is just business. You know I've always tried to help you out when I could. Like your brother Joe's two appearances before the bench—we took care of those two minor inconveniences for you, didn't we? I think we've more than demonstrated that we take care of our own."

"How are you planning to take care of your own now?"

"We'll reduce the charge to involuntary manslaughter. That carries a minimum three-year sentence."

"Yeah, and a maximum of fifteen. Let me ask you something. Why the hell would we take a plea now when I'm on the verge of pulling down your pants and spanking you right in front of the judge and jury? Where the hell is your leverage?"

"I can be a powerful ally," Gold said. "That's nothing to sneeze at."

"Yeah? Well in case you ain't noticed, I ain't got a cold, not so much as a sniffle."

"You're required to take our offer to your client," Doucette advised.

"I'll do that. But just until she turns you down officially feel free to take your offer and stick it."

Vinny entered the courtroom relishing the challenge of once again crossing paths with the Teutonic Greta Träsch. He was ready with his opening salvo of questions as Whorhatz entered the courtroom and took his place on the bench. While he waited for the court officer to call Träsch to the stand, Gold struck preemptively.

"Your Honor," he said, "before Ms. Träsch takes the stand we'd like the opportunity to recall Mr. Cipriani."

Whorhatz exhaled through his nostrils. "Very well."

Vinny grimaced as Anthony Cipriani sat down on the witness stand.

"Mr. Cipriani," Gold began. "Can you please tell the court where you were on the night of February twenty-sixth of this year?"

"I was in Los Angeles."

"So you were not even in the state of New York on the night your brother died?"

Cipriani shook his head. "No, and I'll have to live with that guilt for the rest of my life."

"Can you tell the court which airline you used to travel back and forth to Los Angeles?"

"American Airlines."

"So, you were three thousand miles away when your brother died?"

"Yes."

"No further questions," Gold said.

"Mr. Gambini?" the judge asked.

"No questions at this time," Vinny said with a slight note of defeat in his voice. "We recall Greta Träsch, Your Honor." Träsch was reminded that she was still under oath and again took the stand.

"Ms. Trash."

"Träsch," she shouted.

Vinny ignored her. "You testified that on the night Samuel Cipriani died you were out with a friend. For the record, please tell the court the name of this 'friend' you spent the evening with."

"I don't see what that has to do with my testimony."

"Please answer the question," Vinny said.

She remained silent, her eyes darting back and forth between Vinny, Gold, and the judge.

"Please answer the question," the judge said.

She lowered her gaze and wrung her hands but remained silent.

Vinny retrieved the photo that Lisa had been so excited to show him the other day. "Your Honor, we submit into testimony Exhibit A for the defense." He handed it to the court officer, who delivered it to the judge.

Whorhatz scrutinized it before handing it back to Vinny with a disturbed look on his face. "Continue, Mr. Gambini."

Vinny handed Träsch the photo. "Can you please tell the court the names of the people in this photograph?"

She stared at the picture in her hands, before scowling at Vinny like an angry bear.

"I didn't hear you." He gave her another moment to comply before snatching the photograph out of her hands and delivering it to the jury foreman. "Let the record reflect that the witness, Greta Träsch, and Deputy Mayor Anthony Cipriani are pictured in this photograph, canoodling right here in the courthouse. Just so we all know, is the deputy mayor a good kisser?"

A rumble of oohs and ahs went through the courtroom

along with whispers and accusations.

Vinny glared at Gold before turning to Lisa and giving her a thumbs up.

Cipriani seemed unsteady as he stood and hurried toward the back of the courtroom.

"Uh. Uh. Uh. Not so fast, Mr. Deputy Mayor. The defense ain't through with you yet."

"Have a seat, Mr. Cipriani," the judge ordered. "Do you wish to recall Mr. Cipriani at this time, Mr. Gambini?"

"Ye—" Vinny noticed Parikh entering the courtroom and that he was smiling at him as he took a seat in the audience. "Your Honor, the defense reserves the right to recall Mr. Cipriani, and I'm through with Ms. Träsch. At this time, we'd like to recall Detective Nirmal Parikh."

Parikh popped out of the seat he'd just taken and approached the witness stand with zip in his step.

"Now, Detective," Vinny began. "It has been argued by the DA that Mr. Cipriani was not in New York at the time of his brother's death. What do you got to say about that?"

"I was quite uncomfortable with some of the testimony I heard in the courtroom this morning," Parikh began in his thick accent. "I checked with the local airlines to confirm the dates that Mr. Cipriani left and returned to New York."

"And what did you find out?"

"I found that Mr. Cipriani did indeed purchase a round trip-ticket from New York JFK to LAX, leaving on February twenty-fifth and returning on February twenty-eighth."

The audience murmured in response to Parikh's testimony. Cipriani grinned.

"Anything else?" Vinny asked.

"Yes. I pulled the flight manifest for the American Airlines flight Mr. Cipriani was scheduled to take out of New York. "

"*And?*" Vinny asked with piqued interest.

"There is no record of Mr. Cipriani boarding that flight or any other." There were gasps from the jury.

"So what you're saying is that he paid for a ticket but never left New York?"

"That is correct."

"Thank you. Anything else?" he asked. He caught Mrs. Faraday's eye and could see her smiling.

"Yes. A DNA match is so conclusive that we rarely bother to type blood these days. When I heard Dr. Kent confirm the possibility that we might've mistaken the victim's blood for the blood of Anthony Cipriani, his brother, I asked the lab to type the blood samples we found on the roof, which is a simple ten-minute procedure."

"*And?*"

"The blood evidence we collected didn't come from Samuel Cipriani."

The audience began to rumble once again.

"Can you explain?"

"Prison records indicate that Samuel Cipriani had Type O negative blood, but the samples we collected at the crime scene were AB positive."

"And isn't type O negative blood the universal donor type, and AB positive the universal recipient?"

"That's right."

"I *see*," Vinny said. "So for the record, did you find any traces of Samuel Cipriani's blood on the rooftop?"

"No."

"No! Not even a drop?"

Parikh played into Vinny's hands, "Not even a drop."

"Thank you, Detective. No more questions."

Vinny scrambled back to the table and delighted in Theresa's emerging smile while he retrieved another photograph. "Your Honor," he said, while waving an eight-by-ten photograph high in the air. "We would like to submit this photograph into evidence as Exhibit B." The photo was logged into the official record, traveling from the clerk to the judge.

Whorhatz's eyes grew wide.

"I object, Your Honor," Gold said. "Why wasn't the prosecution made aware of these photographs? I move that they be disallowed from evidence."

"Your Honor," Vinny said. "This photograph only became available during our last recess. There was no time to provide it to the prosecution until now."

"How did you come by the photograph I now hold in my hand?" Whorhatz asked.

"Your Honor, that photograph was hand delivered to me not thirty minutes ago by a private citizen."

"Does this private citizen have a name?" Whorhatz asked.

"Yes, Your Honor, the photograph was taken by Ms. Lindsay Lohan."

Startled, Whorhatz asked, "The film star?"

"Well, yes and no, Your Honor."

"Explain."

"You see, the photographer's actual legal name is Aidan Boydetto, a former client of mine. However, Mr. Boydetto suffers from a psychological affliction. Maybe you've heard of it…dissociative personality disorder, formerly referred to as multiple personality disorder."

"You can substantiate this?" Whorhatz asked.

"Yes, Your Honor. As a matter of fact, Mr. Doucette was opposing counsel when I defended Mr. Boydetto on an unrelated matter and can personally attest to his long struggle with this condition."

Whorhatz turned to Doucette. "Is that correct, Counselor?"

Doucette reluctantly nodded.

"But how does that explain why the witness just chose to come forward at this late hour?" the judge asked.

"Because, Your Honor, the photo was taken by Ms. Lohan and Mr. Boydetto was *unawares* that the photo existed until just recently when he was deleting photos off his phone to clear space on the memory card."

Gold challenged him. "Are we to believe this preposterous story, Your Honor? Is a man who thinks he's another person a credible witness in a murder trial?"

"Although I agree that the story is bizarre...I've heard stranger. Pending authentication of the photograph and the photographer's medical history, I will allow it," Whorhatz ruled. "You're on a roll, Mr. Gambini. *Please* continue."

Vinny hand delivered the photograph to the foreman. "It just so happens that the photographer lives just around the corner from where the victim fell to his death. As you can clearly see from the angle at which this photograph was taken, a car is about to strike a body. The timestamp and date indicate that the picture was taken at four-oh-three a.m. on the morning February twenty-sixth of this year, and the cross street signs are of those where Samuel Cipriani fell to his death." Parikh was still on the stand. Having made the rounds in front of the jury box, Vinny handed the photo to Parikh. "Detective Parikh, for the record, can you clearly identify the man behind the wheel of this car?"

Parikh's jaw dropped. He scrutinized it carefully before answering, "The man behind the wheel is New York City Deputy Mayor Anthony Cipriani."

CHAPTER SEVENTY-THREE
Rub a Little Dirt on it, Mr. DA

"Your Honor," Vinny said, his voice barely audible above the clamor coming from those in the courtroom. "No further questions for Detective Parikh."

"Silence," Whorhatz yelled with a slam of his gavel. "Silence in the courtroom."

Gold was so busy slapping Cipriani's hands off him that he almost missed his opportunity to address the judge. "Your Honor, look at the lateness of the hour. I'm sure the members of the jury are fatigued. Wouldn't it make sense to adjourn for the day and continue in the morning when everyone's fresh?"

"That sounds like an awfully desperate attempt at postponing the inevitable, Mr. Gold." He addressed the foreman. "Too tired to go on, sir?"

"Not a chance," the foreman said. "The sooner I get home to my family the better."

Whorhatz addressed Mrs. Faraday. "How about you, ma'am?"

"I wouldn't miss this for the world."

"Anyone in the jury too tired to go on?"

Their responses were universal.

Whorhatz turned to Gold. "We have an expression in the marines—rub a little dirt on it, Mr. DA. The jury is good to go. Mr. Gambini, you have the floor."

"Yes!" Lisa blurted from the audience.

Vinny turned to see her pump her fist, but wasted no time.

"The defense recalls Dr. Clark Kent." He was now on autopilot and no longer needed to check his notes. "Dr. Kent, the victim, Samuel Cipriani was pronounced dead at the scene. Is that correct?"

"Yes."

"And the victim died from lethal head trauma. Is that also correct?"

"Yes. It is."

"Are you familiar with the coroner's findings?"

"Completely."

"From your considerable knowledge of forensics, and the coroner's report, was any determination made as to whether the victim died as a result of the fall or from the automobile injury?"

Kent thought long and hard before answering. "Actually, no. The two head traumas occurred within mere seconds. Forensically speaking, there was no way to tell them apart."

"So is it possible that Samuel Cipriani was alive when he was struck by that hit-and-run driver?"

"Yes."

"Thank you. No more questions."

"Cross? Mr. Gold?" the judge asked.

The DA struggled with his decision. "Not at this time."

"Then you may continue, Mr. Gambini."

Vinny jumped at the opportunity. "Your Honor, the defense recalls Deputy Mayor Anthony Cipriani."

Gold was again on his feet. "Your Honor, the deputy mayor has urgent business to attend to at City Hall. Surely you can be sensitive to the importance of his position and his integral role in running the city. I insist that we adjourn so that Mr. Cipriani can attend to these urgent matters."

"You *insist*?" Whorhatz asked with a look of disdain on his face.

"Yes, Your Honor, I do."

"You know, I admire a man with a take-charge attitude,

Mr. Gold. However, it just so happens that I'm up here and you're down there." He pointed his gavel at Cipriani and roared, "Sir, you've been called. Please take a seat on the witness stand."

Cipriani seared Gold and Doucette with his gaze as he reluctantly stood. He moved to the witness stand and was reminded that he was still under oath.

Vinny bit his fingernail. "Mr. Cipriani, got anything to say?"

"Not unless you've got a question."

"For the record, what is your blood type, Mr. Cipriani?"

"I don't remember."

"You don't remember?"

"That's what I said, isn't it?"

Vinny walked to his table and produced a document. "Your Honor, I hold in my hand a lab report, which is only being produced to jog the witnesses' memory and is not being submitted into evidence. I hold in my hand a lab report dated this week. The specimen belongs to Anthony Cipriani and states his blood type is AB positive, the same blood type as the specimens collected at the crime scene."

"How the hell did you get that?" Cipriani asked. "I didn't give a blood samples to anyone."

Whorhatz banged his gavel. "You're out of order, Mr. Cipriani. If there's a question to be asked, the DA will ask it." He glanced at Gold. "Do you have a question, Mr. Gold?"

"What's the source of the specimen?" Gold asked.

"The blood sample was collected within the last few days," Vinny said.

"Your Honor," Gold said. "It appears that Mr. Cipriani has no knowledge of a blood sample being drawn in recent memory."

"Let me refresh the deputy mayor's memory," Vinny said. "Don't you remember? The lab didn't want to inconvenience you so they sent a young lady over to your apartment the other night and she collected blood along with other semi-nal...excuse me. That's embarrassing. I meant to say other *samples*, not *seminal* fluids." He gave Cipriani an obvious wink. "Does that ring any bells?"

Cipriani's eyes flashed and he turned red with embarrassment.

"Are we okay to proceed, Mr. Gold?"

Gold read the expression on Cipriani's face and said, "I believe so, Your Honor."

"Proceed, Mr. Gambini."

"Mr. Cipriani, at any time over the last seven years did the defendant, Ms. Cototi ever give you a key to her apartment?"

"Yes."

"You see where this is going, don't you?" he asked.

"Objection, Your Honor. The defense is leading the witness," Gold said.

"Actually he's not leading him at all, Mr. Gold. Overruled. Please answer the question, Mr. Cipriani."

"No, I don't see where this is going," he said with irritation.

"Okay, let's see what we now know," Vinny said. "First of all, the victim's blood was not found on the rooftop *and* the only eyewitness to the *alleged* homicide has a romantic connection to the individual whose blood *was* actually found at the crime scene *and* who was photographed in a hit and run accident believed to involve the deceased. You also had a key to the defendant's apartment, which afforded you the opportunity to drug the defendant so that she wouldn't know that you were taking Samuel Cipriani up to the roof."

Vinny strutted around the courtroom for a moment before going back on the attack. "Now, under these circumstances, it would seem to me that you'd have plenty to say." Vinny smiled at the jurors before propping himself up on the defense table. "Take your time," he said. 'We'll wait."

Cipriani's face turned still redder and the veins in his neck stood out and pulsed. "Why you little worm," he spat. "Do you know who I am? I'll destroy you!"

"Really? You'll destroy me? That's your response? Just so we know, how are you planning to destroy me, literally or figuratively? Because I could handle a good browbeating mind you, but I'm not too hot on being destroyed in the literal sense. Are you planning to blow me to kingdom come or just run me over with a car like you did to your brother in the wee hours of February twenty-sixth?"

"Goddamn it! I didn't run over my brother!"

Vinny held up the photo of Cipriani behind the wheel of the hit and run vehicle. "It certainly looks like you did."

Cipriani sighed and his head fell into his hands. "I *didn't* kill Sammy."

Vinny egged him on. "I'm sorry. Did you say you didn't do it? Because from this photograph it certainly looks like you were just about to turn someone's head into a falafel."

"I told you," Cipriani screamed. "I didn't kill Sam." He lifted his head, his eyes red and veiny. "He's—"

Everyone turned as the heavy wooden doors at the back of the courtroom burst open. A man entered the courtroom holding a legal folder in his hand, hollering, "Samuel Cipriani is not dead!"

CHAPTER SEVENTY-FOUR
"Broccoli? On his butt?"

The courtroom burst into an uproar. Whorhatz slammed his gavel repeatedly while he yelled, "*Order.* There will be order in this court!" It took several moments for the clamor to subside. He pointed at the intruder and demanded, "Identify yourself, sir."

"Raymond Stanz, Your Honor. I'm a parole officer for the State of New York."

"And what is your business with this court?"

"Your Honor, please pardon this intrusion, but I possess information vital to the outcome of this trial."

Vinny took a few steps toward the bench. "Your Honor, the defense calls Ray Stanz."

Gold protested. "Your Honor, I vehemently object. It's not yet the defense attorney's turn to call the new witness."

"Well, Mr. Gold, are you prepared to put the new witness on the stand?"

Gold gritted his teeth and shook his head.

Whorhatz motioned for Gold to approach the bench.

"Yes, Your Honor?" Gold asked.

The judge whispered, "Blow it out your ass," and dismissed him with a wave of his hand. He pointed to the court officer. "Escort Mr. Stanz to the witness stand and swear him in."

Vinny waited for Cipriani to sit down and for Stanz to be

sworn in. "Mr. Stanz, would you please state your full name and profession for the record."

"My name is Raymond Stanz and I'm a parole officer for the State of New York."

"Now, you said that you have vital information for the court?"

"I do. Yes."

"And what might that be?" Vinny asked.

"I'm the parole officer for a rehabilitated former offender, specifically one Louis Rolfe."

Vinny hammed it up. "Of what significance could this *possibly* be to these proceedings?"

"Louis Rolfe was released from prison approximately six months ago. He found gainful employment, a permanent residence, and up until about a month ago, had made every one of his check-in appointments with me as scheduled."

"I'm glad that Mr. Rolfe was a model parolee, but I still fail to see the significance of his post prison release record to this trial," Vinny said, playing the devil's advocate.

"As I said, Mr. Rolfe fell off the radar about a month ago. He last reported in on February twenty-fourth of this year. At this point, there's an open warrant for his arrest for violating the terms of his parole. In the course of searching for him and interviewing other paroled offenders we thought Rolfe might have come into contact with, it came to light that Rolfe was extorting money from former prisoners, threatening to go to the police with damaging information he'd acquired on the inside if they didn't pay up."

"Not a great guy, is he?"

"No."

"Anything else?"

"His body was just found."

A large collective *ah* rose from the audience.

Vinny asked, "And where was Louis Rolfe's body found?"

"A body with unrecognizable facial features was just exhumed from the grave of the deceased."

"Excuse me?"

"The deceased in this trial," Stanz said. "The grave of Samuel Cipriani."

Everyone gasped.

"Quiet! Quiet in the court," Whorhatz barked.

Vinny waited for the turmoil to subside. "I fail to see how you could possibly identify this body as belonging to one Louis Rolfe if his facial features were unrecognizable."

"Mr. Rolfe had a very distinctive birthmark not affected by the head injury. It was shaped like a head of broccoli you see, completely unique—photographed and memorialized in his prison records."

"And why was it this very unique birthmark wasn't found before?" Vinny asked. "I mean when the coroner was studying the body thought to belong to Samuel Cipriani?"

"The birthmark was in a place where it wasn't readily noticeable."

"Oh really? So where was it?"

"It was between the cheeks of his butt."

"Broccoli? On his *butt*?"

"Yes, that's correct."

Vinny had to wait for the courtroom to once again grow quiet before speaking. "Thank you, very, very much for your very important and timely testimony. No further questions. Your Honor, the defense recalls—"

Whorhatz held up his hand. "Thanks for doing all the heavy lifting but this one's on me, Mr. Gambini." He pointed at Cipriani, his expression screaming outrage. "Get your ass back on the witness stand."

CHAPTER SEVENTY-FIVE
I Beg to Differ

Theresa collapsed when she heard that Sam Cipriani, the love of her life was still alive, delaying the proceedings until the EMTs could revive her.

"My brother's alive," Anthony Cipriani admitted. "Alive and well, and someplace where you'll never get your hands on him.

"Why?" Vinny asked. "Why'd you go through all this?"

"Because Samuel Cipriani the three-time loser didn't stand a chance in hell of making it in this world." He looked up at the ceiling and shook his head cursing all that had gone wrong. "But with a new name and a clean slate..." His confession was punctuated with a deep and troubled sigh. "This guy, Bald Louie. He was a real piece of shit. He cozied up to Sam when they were in prison together and found out things he shouldn't have known, things that could've put Sam back behind bars for a very long time. He tried to shake Sammy down as soon as he got out of prison, threatening to blab secrets to the authorities. If Rolfe ever made good on those threats...We figured we'd kill two birds with one stone."

"In other words, old Sam had to die so that new Sam could live."

He spoke through gritted teeth. "*Yes.*"

"So the defendant, Theresa Cototi, never had a thing for you, did she?"

"No."

"Let me see if I got this straight. You framed a poor innocent girl for your brother's death, planted false evidence, perjured yourself, plotted with your lover to provide false witness, and all the while your brother was living it up somewhere under an assumed identity. Is that about it?"

Cipriani scowled at Vinny but was too infuriated to answer.

"Answer the question," Whorhatz ordered.

"Yes," he answered, his lips twisted and gnarled. "I bought Greta the same kind of sneakers I knew Theresa wore. She tracked my blood on the roof a couple of days before we planned to get even with Bald Louie. I'm familiar with police protocol and standards. I knew my DNA would pass for Sammy's in a standard NYPD forensics analysis."

"I don't understand—why didn't you just use your brother's blood to leave the bloody footprint on the roof?"

"Because," he ranted, "Theresa couldn't keep her goddamn hands off Sam for a minute. So, I had to plant the evidence in advance."

"Your Honor," Vinny said, "it's our contention that Samuel Cipriani pushed Louis Rolfe, his former cellmate off the roof of eighteen-fifty-nine Cropsey Avenue, and then Anthony Cipriani intentionally ran over the victim, with the specific intention of rendering Mr. Rolfe unrecognizable."

"Your Honor, I object," Gold said. "This is pure conjecture and outside the scope of this trial."

"Yes. Possibly," Whorhatz ruled, taunting the floundering DA. "*Overruled.* Mr. Gambini, you may proceed."

"And so, Your Honor and ladies and gentlemen of the jury, I propose that the bloody initials TMC don't stand for Theresa Mary Cototi at all. They stand for Sammy AKA "Tool Man" Cipriani, the name he was given in prison because of his mastery with burglar's tools. That's who Louis Rolfe was attempting to identify with his last breath." He focused on Cipriani. "So, I guess Sam lured Bald Louie to

Theresa's rooftop where he'd been told he'd receive his payoff. Only…I guess we can figure out the rest. Isn't that right, Mr. Deputy Mayor?"

He seared Vinny with his gaze and flipped him the bird.

"Whoa! The F bomb right here in court? I'm astonished. Not that it's gonna matter where you're going. That's one hell of a reversal of fortune, ain't it? Sam's on the way up and you're on the way…"

"I damn well know what it means," Cipriani screamed.

"I've heard enough," Whorhatz said. "Officer, place Mr. Cipriani and Ms. Trash under arrest."

"That's Träsch," she barked as the cuffs were ratcheted down on her wrists.

"I beg to differ," the judge said in a haughty tone. "Take the two of them away."

CHAPTER SEVENTY-SIX
No One Pulls the Wool Over the Eyes of a Gambini

Judge Molloy stood at the back of the courtroom applauding the performance of his protégé long after the case against Theresa Cototi was dismissed and the courtroom cleared. His confidence in the novice attorney had not been misplaced. Seeing the earnest smile on Vinny's face was payment in full for all the time and effort he'd invested in the young attorney's career. Vinny had rewarded him with a shrewd legal defense that had spared an innocent woman an extensive and unjust jail term.

Lisa was glowing and anointing her fiancé with kisses and praise when she heard Molloy clapping, and saw him standing just beyond the last aisle of the audience section.

"Judge Molloy," she said. "Look, Vinny! Look who's here." She dashed over, meeting him halfway down the aisle as he approached. "Did you see him, Judge? Wasn't Vinny great?"

"*Did* I? Why at this very moment DA Gold is probably meeting with a career counselor, and Doucette is likely on the phone trying to nail down an associates position at an obscure out-of-town law firm. There isn't a DA between here and Sheboygan who'll sleep soundly tonight knowing that Vincent Gambini is on the job."

"Ah. Thanks, Judge Molloy," Vinny said. "I was just doing the best I could. And that kid, Theresa, she was as innocent as innocent could be. Lisa knew she didn't do it the first time they met. It just took a little while for me to figure out what was really going on."

"Vinny, my boy, you sparkled out there today. You took on a political powerhouse and kicked his goddamn teeth in. Most small practitioners would've gone running for the hills the moment they realized they had to go up against a New York City deputy mayor, but not you. You hunkered down and stuck it out." He turned to Lisa. "Are you proud of our boy?"

"You know *I* am."

"How the hell did you figure out that the Cipriani boys switched this Louis Rolfe fellow for Sam Cipriani?"

"That was just a hunch, Judge. But when Cipriani lost his cool and blurted out that he didn't kill his brother...the whole thing just fell into place. I mean this Rolfe guy disappeared just a couple of days before Sam allegedly died. What can I say; I don't believe in coincidences."

"No one pulls the wool over the eyes of a Gambini," she said.

"No, they certainly don't," he said. "Vinny, this is a happy and proud day for me. You rescued a dear friend of mine from unjust incarceration and you showed me just how right I was to place my faith in you. But..." He turned to Lisa, grinning. "What about you?"

"What about me?" Lisa asked.

"I haven't received a wedding invitation in the mail as yet, and he said he'd marry you after he won his first case. That was the deal, wasn't it, Gambini?"

"Yes, Judge. Yes, it was."

"Well it's only March and you've already won two murder trials this year."

"So?" Vinny asked.

"You're not getting any younger. How long do you expect this ravishing young woman to wait for you?"

"Yeah! What about the wedding?" Lisa chimed in. "You think I'm gonna wait around forever? I got a niece—the daughter of my sister who's getting married and—"

"Lisa," Vinny said with a sly grin as he stomped his foot on the wooden floor twice. "I know, your biological clock is ticking."

"*I'll* take a run at her if you don't marry her soon," Molloy teased. "How do you feel about older men, Lisa?"

She blushed an intense shade of red.

He slapped Vinny on the shoulder. "You know there's a long standing tradition of buying the victorious attorney a drink. You and Lisa up for a couple of cocktails?"

"Yeah, sure, Judge Molloy, only I got to pay. It's the least I can do."

"You flush, Vinny? I'm asking because I've been known to throw back quite a few when I celebrate."

"I think I got it covered. I rang up a lot of billable hours putting together Theresa's defense. By the way, I didn't ask for no retainer. She's good for the money, ain't she?"

"Don't worry, Vinny. She'll pay. As a private practitioner, you've got to be a lawyer as well as an accountant. It's not like when I grew up—nothing's cheap these days."

"No, Judge. Definitely not."

"Why when I was a young boy, my mother would send me to the corner store with a buck and I'd come back with two loaves of bread, a sack of potatoes, milk, cheese, and a dozen eggs."

"*Really?* All that for a buck, Judge Molloy?" Vinny asked skeptically. "I know you're getting up there in years so it was a long time ago, but I mean that's a hell of a lot of stuff for just one dollar."

"Yes, Vinny. It's true. But you can't get value like that these days."

"Why? Inflation?"

"No. Security cameras."

CHAPTER SEVENTY-SEVEN
The Quintessential Lisa

The dining room table in Vinny and Lisa's home was lined with aluminum trays over lit Sterno cans, a makeshift steam table filled with eggplant parmigiana, baked ziti, chicken Marsala, stuffed mushrooms, and fried calamari. Lisa and Ma had cooked for two days straight and invited all their friends, neighbors, and relatives.

"I still don't see why we got to have another party," Vinny said as he groomed his hair in the bathroom mirror. "We just had one before this trial started. We gonna celebrate like this every time I win a case?"

"So you win case after case and we celebrate each one with your friends and family. I'm so sorry to put you through such an ordeal," Lisa said. "I mean *what a fuckin' nightmare.*"

"I don't mean that I don't like parties. It's just that you don't need to go to so much trouble. Between helping me with my cases, the beauty parlor, and Augie's repair shop..."

She put her arms around him. "This is your first big New York victory. I wanted to do something special." She kissed him passionately. "And then when the house is empty..." She winked seductively. "Maybe we can do a little celebrating of our own."

"And maybe we should skip party number one and proceed straight to party number two." He leaned in for a kiss just as someone knocked on the door.

"Hey, Vinny, people are starting to show," Joe shouted

through the closed bedroom door. "You knocking off a piece in there, or what?"

Lisa yanked the door open, her hands at her sides, hollering, "He ain't knocking off no piece. We'll be right down."

"Eh, sorry, Lisa. I mean it's your house. You and Vinny want to go at it, you go right ahead." He turned and trudged down the stairs, his paper plate heavy with food.

"I just told you, we weren't doing nothing," she reiterated with fire.

Over Joe's shoulder, she could see Mimi breeze through the door holding a small gift bag. She shook the bag. "Get your ass down here, Vito. I got you a gift."

Lisa turned back toward Vinny. "I'll meet you downstairs, Vinny." She scrambled down the stairs to greet her friend. They hugged, and Mimi handed her the gift bag. "What's this for? It ain't my birthday or nothin'."

"It's just a little thank you gift. You know, for being such a good friend to me."

"Thanks but you didn't have to do that."

"I wanted to."

"You make any decisions? About having the baby I mean?"

"Not yet, Lisa, but you really made me think. By the way, you look super hot in them boots."

She looked down at them. "You really think so?"

"They make your long legs look even longer than they actually are. You look like one of those Victoria's Secret runway models."

"Ya think?"

"Shit, I'd fuck you."

Lisa snickered. "Meems, that ain't no compliment."

"Why not?" she said sounding a bit insulted.

"Because, everyone knows you'd fuck anything."

Mimi shrugged.

Lisa moved the tissue paper aside and peeked into the bag.

It contained a white rubber ducky with a ball gag, wearing a spiked dog collar and a hot pink studded corset. "What the hell is this?"

Mimi whispered in her ear. "Isn't it adorable? It's an I Rub My Duckie massager," she boasted. "I got one in every bathroom in the house. I love 'em. You know, for those long lonely nights when Vinny's acting like a dope. You like it?"

Sure. Because nothing says friendship like the gift of a vibrator. Racking her brain for a compliment, "That's a very thoughtful gift."

Lisa's brother Dino walked through the door wearing a jean jacket over a wife beater. "So Vinny won another big case," he said as he hugged his sister. "Who would've thunk it?"

"Hey, lay off Vinny," Lisa said. "He did really good."

"Hi, Dino," Mimi said, sidling up to him. "Long time no see."

"Yeah, hi. How you been?" he asked as he stripped off his jacket revealing his brawny muscles and olive skin.

"I'm good *now*," she said taking his arm. "Let's get you a plate of food, you big muscley man."

Lisa yanked him back. "I need to talk to Dino for a minute, Meems. He'll catch up with you. Why don't you go say hello to my folks."

Mimi walked off, looking disappointed.

"Stay away from her," Lisa warned. "She's easier to get into than a safe with a Chinese padlock."

"What else is new?"

"I'm just warning you, Dino. I know you're not exactly one to put up a fight and that girl..."

"All right. All right. Don't be such a nag, Lisa. I won't touch your friend."

"Good."

He smirked. "I suppose a BJ is out of the question?"

Lisa slapped his arm. "Go get some food," she said as she

spotted Joe once again filling his plate. "Joe's already going back for seconds and we've only got one tray of calamari. If he scarfs down any more of that squid he'll sprout a fuckin' set of tentacles."

"What's in the bag?" he asked.

"Mimi brought me a vibrator."

"Wow, she really is a fun girl, isn't she?"

"Yeah, you could say that. I'm gonna hide this upstairs before it causes me any more embarrassment."

Vinny was still in the bedroom ready to leave when Lisa walked past him. "Why'd you come back upstairs?" he asked.

"Mimi brought me something. I'm gonna leave it up here."

"Penicillin?" he asked with a laugh.

"You ain't far off." She dropped it on the bed just as the phone rang. "Hello...Oh, hi, Mom...Yeah. We're having a little celebration party for your son, the big shot lawyer... Thank you...Yeah. He's right here. Hold on." She covered the receiver. "It's your mother. She's calling from Florida."

"Yeah. I get that, Lisa. Thanks."

She passed him the phone and left the room.

"Hi, Mom," Vinny said. "What's new in Florida? It just about time for the early bird special, ain't it?" he asked with a laugh.

"Vincent, it's only one o'clock in the afternoon."

"So what? You ate already?"

"Don't bust balls, son of mine. The weather is balmy down here. Eat your heart out in that frozen wasteland you call New York."

"I was just kidding. How's Pops?"

"He's playing cards with some of the men at the club-house. He won two dollars last night."

"*Marone*, Mom, two whole dollars? Maybe you can make a down payment on a yacht—maybe sail around the world two or three times."

"All right, wise guy. Congratulations on winning your big

New York case. Joe told us all about it."

"He did?"

"Yeah. Sounds like our youngest son is turning into a big successful lawyer. Thank God for Judge Molloy. He made you see that you had it in you to make something of yourself."

"Yeah, he's a good friend. I really owe him a lot."

"So your brother told us you want to sell the house. Is that right?"

"Yeah, Joe really needs the money. It wouldn't hurt Lisa and me neither. How do yous guys feel about that? I mean being you lived there so long and all?"

"We gave the house to the two of you but we never thought you'd want to unload it so soon. We figured it would be there for us when we came up to visit."

"So. Um...no?"

"I didn't say that, Vinny. We're coming up for Easter and we'll talk about it then. But that's not the real reason I called."

"It's not?"

"No, it's not. How are things with you and Lisa?"

"Good. I mean okay I guess. *Why*?"

"Because Joe told us you had a gigantic fight."

"That dope."

"You treating your woman the way you're supposed to?" she asked.

"I think so."

"You'd better know so. All the business success in the world doesn't mean anything unless you've got someone you love to share it with. You hear what I'm telling you?"

"Hey, Mom, we've been together more than ten years. I *think* we're okay."

"Oh yeah? So when are you getting married already? When is that lovely girl gonna give us grandchildren? You said you were going to marry her after you won your first case. Are you a liar, Vincent? You gonna break a promise to the woman you love?

"No, Mom, I ain't breaking no promise to her."

"Well you won two cases already. What the hell is going on? Is there trouble in paradise?"

"I don't know. Sometimes she gets on me about not saying or doing the right things."

"So why aren't you doing the right things? You want to lose her?"

"*No.*"

"Well then why don't you do something about it?"

"I *will.*"

"All right, I don't want to beat a dead horse. We love you. Enjoy your party. You earned it."

"Love you too, Mom."

The main level of the house was abuzz with friends and family having a good time and reconnecting after not having seen one another over the long and brutal winter.

His Cousin Billy noticed him coming down the stairs and began to chant at the top of his voice. "*Vinny. Vinny. Vinny.*" Everyone soon joined in. The noise level grew and grew until Vinny put a smile on his face and assumed the role of being the life of the party—the role he was born to play.

"You have fun?" Lisa asked after everyone had gone.

Vinny was sprawled out on the bed, a little drunk with a silly grin plastered on his face. "Yeah, thank you, Lisa. That was really nice. Like I said, you didn't have to go to all that trouble."

"But you're happy that I did, right?"

"Of course I am. That was a seriously great party. And well..."

"And well what?"

"Well you know."

"*No.* I *don't* know. There something you want to tell me?"

"Yeah." He got choked up. "You're the best thing that ever happened to me."

She egged him on. "*And?*"

"And I intend to keep the promise I made to you. First thing tomorrow let's sit down and plan the wedding. That make you happy?"

"Happy? I'm fuckin' ecstatic." She threw her arms around him and overpowered him with kisses. "Vincent LaGuardia Gambini, I think there may be hope for you yet."

They continued to kiss until Vinny accidentally rolled over onto the gift bag. "What the hell is this?"

She answered offhandedly, "I told you before. It's the present Mimi gave me."

"What the hell kind of present is this?" he asked after removing it from the gift bag. "It looks like some kind of S&M rubber ducky. What do you do with something like this?"

"It's a tub toy."

He examined it more carefully. "Seriously?"

"No, Vinny. Not seriously. It's a vibrator. It vibrates. What do you think it is?"

"Why'd she get you one of these?"

"How should I know what makes her tick? You know how Mimi is. What can I tell you?"

Vinny became pensive. "Is this because of me?"

"Vinny, it don't mean nothin'. Mimi's a dear friend but she's got the IQ of a turnip."

"Are you *sure* this ain't about me?" he said giving her a sly glance.

"Yeah. I'm *pos-i-tive.*"

"Then why are you always complaining about me being such a dope and all?"

She was growing emotional. "*Vinny,* I call you a dope but

I don't think you're a dope in any way, shape, or form. Don't you understand?"

"Not exactly."

"I call you a dope because you're not romantic." She shook her head and sat down on the bed next to him. "Look, this is *your* day. We've got issues to work through just like any other couple but we don't have to do it right this minute. I mean Rome wasn't built in one fuckin' day, was it? Why don't I slip into something sexy and you can show me just how much of a man you really are."

"I don't know."

"You don't know what?"

"Maybe I ain't in the mood no more."

She knew that he was teasing her. "*Please*, a man who's not in the mood…that ain't even a real thing. Come on, it'll been a perfect ending to a perfect day." She nuzzled his neck and kissed his earlobe softly but he didn't respond. "*What already?*"

"You should know."

"Oh, *I* should know?" She gave him a distant look. "Giving me a taste of my own medicine, is that it?"

It was that old cat and mouse game starting all over again. "*Yeah.* That's it."

"Don't be like that. Don't go and muck up a really nice day."

"I don't know. My feelings are a little hurt."

"Oh really?"

"Yeah. Really"

"Vinny, I just cooked for two straight day's and invited everyone we know just to make you feel good about yourself." She jumped off the bed and struck a provocative pose with her hands positioned on her hips. "Are you really gonna turn down *this?*"

"What if I am?"

"Still being cute, huh? You know it's possible for a man to overplay his hand."

"How so?"

"You never heard of blue balls?"

He seemed skeptical. "You wouldn't."

"Oh no?" she said with a smile. "Go ahead…test me."

"What makes you think I ain't got just as much leverage over you?"

She burst into laughter. "You lost your mind or something? How much did you have to drink anyway?"

"*Hey*. That's insulting."

"Is it? I tell you what," she said teasing him with a naughty smile as she picked up the rubber ducky and rested it in her open palm. What's it gonna be, *Romeo*? Are we gonna do it, or am I off to take a bath?"

ACKNOWLEDGMENTS

My heartfelt thanks to Dale Launer for creating the two most endearing and memorable comic characters in modern motion picture history, and for entrusting me with their futures.

It takes tons of work to generate a quality novel, and I would be remiss if I didn't acknowledge all the help I receive from my wife, Isabella, the unsung hero of my work, who quietly reads late into the night to make sure that each and every one of my books is the absolute best it can be.

I didn't know it at the time but when my wife gave birth to our children in 1984 and 1987, she was giving life to the two toughest literary critics to ever walk the face of the earth. To Dawn and Chris with all my love, for keeping me on the straight and narrow.

I was so very fortunate to find a publisher who was so much more than I could have ever hoped for. My sincere thanks to Eric Campbell and Lance Wright at Down & Out Books for their support and encouragement on this project, and to Rebecca T. Bush at RTC Publicity.

This book would not have been possible without my publishing attorney, Jessica Kaye, who deftly navigated the tumultuous waters of lawyers and legalese to deliver the many and varied contracts which were party to this deal.

Lawrence Kelter never expected to be a writer. In fact, he was voted the student least likely to step foot in a library. Well, times change, and he has now authored several novels including the internationally bestselling Stephanie Chalice and Chloe Mather Thriller Series. Early in his writing career, he received support from literary icon Nelson DeMille, who was gracious enough to put pencil to paper to assist in the editing of the first book, and felt strongly enough about the finished product to say, "Lawrence Kelter is an exciting new novelist, who reminds me of an early Robert Ludlum."

He's lived in the Metro New York area most of his life and relies primarily on familiar locales for story settings. He does his best to make each novel quickly paced and crammed full of twists, turns, and laughs.

LawrenceKelter.com

OTHER TITLES FROM DOWN AND OUT BOOKS

See www.DownAndOutBooks.com for complete list

By Jerry Kennealy
Screen Test
Polo's Long Shot (*)

By Dana King
Worst Enemies
Grind Joint
Resurrection Mall (*)

By Ross Klavan, Tim O'Mara
and Charles Salzberg
Triple Shot

By S.W. Lauden
Crosswise
Crossed Bones (*)

By Paul D. Marks and
Andrew McAleer (editor)
Coast to Coast vol. 1
Coast to Coast vol. 2

By Gerald O'Connor
The Origins of Benjamin Hackett

By Gary Phillips
The Perpetrators
Scoundrels (Editor)
Treacherous
3 the Hard Way

By Thomas Pluck
Bad Boy Boogie (*)

By Tom Pitts
Hustle
American Static (*)

By Robert J. Randisi
Upon My Soul
Souls of the Dead
Envy the Dead

By Charles Salzberg
Devil in the Hole
Swann's Last Song
Swann Dives In
Swann's Way Out

By Scott Loring Sanders
Shooting Creek and Other Stories

By Ryan Sayles
The Subtle Art of Brutality
Warpath
Let Me Put My Stories In You (*)

By John Shepphird
The Shill
Kill the Shill
Beware the Shill

By James R. Tuck (editor)
Mama Tried vol. 1
Mama Tried vol. 2 (*)

By Lono Waiwaiole
Wiley's Lament
Wiley's Shuffle
Wiley's Refrain
Dark Paradise
Leon's Legacy (*)

By Nathan Walpow
The Logan Triad

(*)—Coming Soon